Angels of Detroit

Angels of Detroit

A Novel

Christopher Hebert

BLOOMSBURY

NEW YORK · LONDON · OXFORD · NEW DELHI · SYDNEY

Bloomsbury USA
An imprint of Bloomsbury Publishing Plc

1385 Broadway   50 Bedford Square
New York   London
NY 10018   WC1B 3DP
USA   UK

www.bloomsbury.com

BLOOMSBURY and the Diana logo are trademarks of Bloomsbury
Publishing Plc

First published 2016

ISBN: HB: 978-1-63286-363-8
       ePub: 978-1-63286-364-5

LIBRARY OF CONGRESS CATALOGING-IN-PUBLICATION DATA IS AVAILABLE.

British Library Cataloguing-in-Publication Data
A catalogue record for this book is available from the British Library.

2 4 6 8 10 9 7 5 3 1

Typeset by RefineCatch Limited, Bungay, Suffolk
Printed and bound in the U.S.A. by Berryville Graphics Inc., Berryville, Virginia

To find out more about our authors and books visit www.bloomsbury.com. Here
you will find extracts, author interviews, details of forthcoming events and the
option to sign up for our newsletters.

Bloomsbury books may be purchased for business or promotional use. For
information on bulk purchases please contact Macmillan Corporate and Premium
Sales Department at specialmarkets@macmillan.com.

For Margaret

Speramus meliora; resurget cineribus
(We hope for better things; it shall arise from the ashes)
Motto, official seal of the city of Detroit, adopted 1827

Spring

One

THE CAR WAS a late-model Oldsmobile, the interior dank and musty, and the driver bore the distinctly sweet, rotting smell of overripe bananas. Lucius was his name. Thick dark hair sprouted from his knuckles in wild tufts. They were in southeastern Kansas, heading east as Patsy Cline quavered through a pair of broken speakers.

Dobbs hadn't slept in days. He couldn't put a firm number to it. The days whipped by like telephone poles. He feared he was losing the ability to see anything head-on. It was as if he and everything around him existed on separate planes, veering toward one another but never quite touching.

The noise of the highway made it sound as though Patsy were singing in the heart of a tornado.

After a couple of hours, they reached Lucius's southbound exit, and Dobbs got out, shouldering his bag, moving on by foot.

★ ★ ★

At a truck stop in Topeka, he ordered coffee. Perched atop a pearlescent stool, he watched the pot empty its brown dregs into his cup. He imagined the coarse grit in the grooves of his teeth, the caffeine percolating through his veins.

There were only two other customers, each in his own remote booth. It was the hour for solitary travelers. The griddle was at rest, reflecting shimmery streaks of carbonized grease. A waitress hobbled from table to table with a magazine of straws clutched under her elbow.

"Your hair," she said when she got to him. "Is it really that red?"

Dobbs caught his reflection in the mirror behind the counter. The color did seem unusually bright, the curls loose and wild. But his skin had the pallor of egg white. He was like a diseased tree, directing every last nutrient to its remaining leaves.

Every few minutes a thin, aproned boy came by and dropped a stack of dishes in the bus tub beside the counter. The dishes landed with an explosive charge buried at the base of Dobbs's skull. Through the wall of hazy windows, he watched for trucks pulling in. He waited.

Other rides came and went. The drivers began to slip Dobbs's mind the instant they pulled over, the moment they ducked to meet his eye through the open passenger window.

One night he found himself shivering, curled in the back of a pickup truck, sheltered within some sort of camper. Beneath the blankets lay a bed of cold steel. His eyes fluttered closed. He couldn't seem to stop them.

In his dream, Dobbs was underwater. From somewhere up above, the light trickled down, like something solid falling. His lungs were strong. Rather than surface, he swam deeper and deeper. There was someone following him he couldn't seem to shake.

And then the water was gone. Dobbs was sitting at a table in a cavern carpeted with sand. Exhausted from his swim, the man who'd been chasing him lowered himself heavily into the opposite chair. He smiled. They were like old friends meeting for a beer. But the man's face bore only the faintest outline of something vaguely familiar. He spoke of women he'd known. His tone was nostalgic. He gestured lazily with his hands.

In his own hand, Dobbs held a wooden pepper mill, tall and slender, the curves perfectly contoured to his fist. The man winked, as if to beg Dobbs's indulgence. Dobbs winked back. And then he raised the pepper mill. And then with a lunge, he smashed it back down, cracking the grinder against the man's temple. Under the blow, the man swayed backward, but it was as though he were merely stretching. He sighed.

Dobbs struck him a second time, a third, a fourth. The blows left not a drop of blood, not a scratch, not a bruise. The man displayed no hard feelings, no discomfort, no indication of thinking things should be any different than they were.

Dobbs awoke with a shudder. The truck was slowing. They came to a stop on something loose and gravelly. Shards of light knifed through the door. Dobbs felt as though he were back underwater. But this time his lungs were spent.

He groped for a knob, a handle. There seemed to be no way out. Kicking aside the nest of blankets, he used his shoulder as a ram, but the wooden door of the camper absorbed him with indifference. Dobbs edged back and tried with his foot. But it was as if the light were pushing back.

Someone on the other side was yelling at him, but the cars slashing by warped the words. The lights formed blue and white and red spots on his eyelids.

Dobbs sat in the back of the cruiser as the cop fiddled with his computer, putting the finishing touches on the speeding ticket.

Up ahead, the truck and its makeshift camper pulled away from the shoulder of the highway, leaving him behind. Dobbs thought he felt something inside himself pull away with it.

On the other side of the partition, the cop cleared his throat.

Why don't you have an ID? he wanted to know.

I don't drive, Dobbs said.

Where are you coming from?

Phoenix.

What were you doing there?

A job.

Doing what?

It was temporary.

What was your address there?

I was only passing through.

A motel?

A house.

What was the address?

No one sent me any mail.

The cop had been looking down at the computer screen, occasionally keying something in as he talked. Now, for the first time, he lifted his face to look in the rearview mirror. His disembodied eyes hung there a moment, and Dobbs saw in them a weariness not unlike his own.

"Don't you know hitchhiking is illegal?" the eyes said, raising one brow.

"I wasn't hitching," Dobbs said. "I was riding."

"And you think it's legal to be riding in the back of a pickup?"

"It is in Kansas."

Which was true. And the cop knew it, too. Which was why he sighed.

These were the kinds of things a person had to keep track of. Walking the line required knowing exactly where the line was.

And so they rode in silence until they reached the border, Missouri on the other side.

"You're someone else's problem now," the cop said, pulling over at the bank of the Kansas River.

For the next hour or so, Dobbs loitered through a light rain at a gas station just outside Kansas City.

"I'm trying to get to Detroit," he said, as each new car pulled up to the pump.

No one would admit to being headed in his direction.

Of the next several days, Dobbs remembered only a gray-eyed man in a camouflage hat, gnawing on a pipe stem, saying, "Why don't you get some sleep? You look like you could use some sleep."

And Dobbs saying, "I'm fine, fine."

Then minutes or maybe hours later, Dobbs was aware of the driver emerging from a fog of smoke to lean across the passenger seat and open the door. In Dobbs's mind, there was a sudden clearing, like a flock of crows exploding from a treetop. He got out of the idling car, slowly testing the ground, one foot at a time. The car skipped away from the curb.

Dobbs was standing in front of the bus terminal. The sign at the gate said WELCOME TO DETROIT! The exclamation point was twice the size of the letters, as if whoever put it there were anticipating skepticism.

Dobbs didn't remember having asked to be dropped off here. It was a strange choice. Had the driver thought the first thing he'd want to do as soon as he arrived was turn around and leave?

It was morning, early. The sky bleary. Dobbs was standing on a one-way street, but he turned to look in both directions. There were no other cars, no buses in the parking lot. There was no one out here but him. Down an embankment to his left ran the highway, but even it was mostly quiet.

He started walking, following the one-way arrows, heading south. He wasn't far from downtown, but he was far enough that there was little to see—just a few sparse industrial buildings and a lot of fenced-off parking lots. He passed through a wide, nearly empty intersection, then another.

In a few minutes, he reached the river. The land along the shore was closed off from the road by a fence that appeared to stretch for miles, ending nearby at a cluster of high-rise apartment towers. Dobbs tossed his duffel bag over, then climbed the fence and dropped down on the other side.

Across the dense green water of the Detroit River was the dingy backlit skyline of Windsor, Ontario, the buildings all aglow. It was April, and every waitress in every diner across the plains had talked of little else but the arrival of spring. So far Dobbs wasn't impressed. A chill had followed him all the way from the desert, never breaking. Now, standing on the windy shoreline, he fastened the button at the throat of his peacoat.

He'd spent the last week studying maps of the city. He knew the names of the streets, knew where they went. But the sights were unfamiliar, and the first ones he saw surprised him with their grandeur. Heading east, approaching downtown, he passed an old Gothic church with a towering green spire and limestone bricks that looked to have been chiseled by hand. Across the street, from a whole different century, rose a massive art deco building, all sharp lines and smooth stone block, arched windows trimmed in bands of bas-relief.

The city grew rapidly from there. Parking garages, towers, and offices of brick and glass. He reached a roundabout, circling a park. It was a peaceful, quiet place, ringed with birch and elm, paved in granite. The fountain hadn't yet been switched on for the season, and at this hour, the shops and restaurants were still closed. But he could imagine people here, crowds.

He was in the heart of the city now. In the distance he caught a glimpse of the baseball stadium and the football field. Up the avenue to the north were the museums, the theaters, the opera house. Around the corner, the casino and restaurants. This was where the tourists came. This was where they stayed.

From his pocket, he removed a small square of paper.

Cross over the freeway.

The freeway marked the dividing line. Walking across the bridge, he could already feel the landmarks, the attractions, slipping away behind him. In the distance he saw a wall of graffiti bordering a compound of barren factory buildings clad in corrugated siding. The other part of the city, waiting to greet him. He kept walking, passing a cluster of crumbling brick industrial facades, vandalized, wrapped in rusted barbed wire. Then came a strip of storefronts, boarded up, tagged sill to sill in spray paint.

The note in his pocket said *Go straight, quarter of a mile.*

The avenue widened. On the opposite side was a group of warehouses, razor-wired parking lots stuffed with idling trucks. Faded block letters on cinderblock walls spelled out IMPORTS and EXPORTS, PRODUCE and POULTRY and MEAT.

The directions said *Cross.*

The sun was fully up now, but Dobbs was still chilled. At last he saw people: three men on a loading dock, gathered around cigarettes and steaming Styrofoam cups. A forklift beeped its way in the belly of the dark garage. They saw Dobbs, too, several sets of eyes following him as he went around the bend. Their expressions seemed to say *where are you going?* As if they knew something he didn't.

But Dobbs already knew what lay ahead. Even so, he wasn't quite ready for it, the moment the landscape changed again. It happened in an instant, as though a slide had been triggered before his eyes: a quick flash, and the warehouses vanished. The pavement gave way to weeds. The parking lots gave way to prairie. He'd simply turned a corner, and suddenly he found himself standing among barren fields framed by sidewalks. The city grid intact, but the city itself had disappeared. Empty. Whatever had once filled the emptiness was gone. Burned down, torn down, who knew?

Along with the maps, he'd gathered a few facts, a couple of which had stuck: a city of one hundred forty square miles, a third of it abandoned, the emptiness combined larger than the entire city of San Francisco. Boston. Manhattan. Almost two million inhabitants at the city's height. Two-thirds of them now departed.

The directions said *Keep going*, but he couldn't be sure where he was. The street signs had disappeared, too. There was the occasional house down one or another side street. Some of them had cars parked out front. Here and there among the weeds were the outlines of foundations. This must have been a residential neighborhood once. He tried to imagine what was missing: flower beds and latticed porches and picture windows framed in lace.

The directions stopped. He was supposed to have turned. But where? He went back, retracing his steps. What finally caught his eye was something just beyond a streetlight, tucked around a pair of crooked maples. From the side, as he approached, the place looked enormous, a dilapidated farmhouse shedding weathered gray clapboard. But as he got closer, he realized it was long but narrow, an old row house.

The place was all crazy angles. The front looked like a gingerbread castle, with a rounded tower honeycombed in hexagonal shingles. Every window on the front of the house was shaded by frilled, blue-and-white-striped aluminum canopies, which looked as though they'd been stolen from a boardwalk ice cream parlor. A rusty chain-link fence leaned in toward the house like a tightly cinched belt. Juniper shrubs that must once have been decorative now reached as high as the second floor, shielding the house completely from the empty corner lot next door. Between this house and the nearest neighbors were a couple of football fields' worth of chest-high weeds.

There was no number on the house. None on the directions, either. But this was the place. It was exactly what they would choose.

The porch floorboards bent beneath him. The door was locked. Not so much as a wiggle in the knob. Reinforced and jimmy proof. There was not one dead bolt but two. The door was the only solid part of the entire house.

Downspout, the directions said. And so it was. They'd driven a nail through the gutter a few inches from the bottom. He slid off the key.

The inside of the house smelled of earth, of darkness. The windows had been papered over. The switches on the wall were dead. Once his eyes adjusted, he saw the place had been stripped bare. The hardware was gone from the doors and cabinets. Where before there'd been fixtures, there were now only holes.

Aside from securing the door and covering the windows, they'd done nothing else. The floor was crunchy with the shards of acorn shells. A couple of overturned soup cans had tumbled together into the corner. There wasn't a single piece of furniture. There was no broom either, but he went outside and with his knife cut a needly branch from one of the overgrown shrubs. He swept the filth out the back door. Little by little fresh air trickled in.

In his dream, Dobbs was somewhere familiar, but he wasn't sure where. He knew only that he'd been here before. The people were familiar too, but their features were vague. It was as if their heads had been carved in stone that had washed away over time. There was something Dobbs was trying to tell them, something important he needed them to understand. They stood in a circle around him, as if awaiting instructions, but they seemed to be ignoring his every word. And so Dobbs went around the circle, one at a time, knocking them to the floor, beating them with his fists. Each patiently awaited his turn.

He woke up, leaning against the wall, his spine feeling as though it had been scraped with a dull blade. His watch said it was three o'clock in the morning. The only light in the house was a slight trickle coming from under the front door. In that trickle Dobbs noticed something that hadn't been there before, a torn envelope folded over once. On the inside was that same familiar handwriting.

Three weeks. Be ready. Don't fuck it up this time.

★　★　★

In the morning light, the paper-covered windows glowed like Chinese lanterns. Dobbs drank what little was left in his canteen. The house had no pipes, let alone a faucet.

It would be like camping, he told himself. Like being back again at the lake as a child, roughing it in the middle of nowhere. The scenery outside right now didn't even look that different from what he remembered of the view from his grandfather's cabin. Dobbs could recall the long drive north from St. Paul, past weedy logging roads and the sagging gates of ancient sawmills. Northern Minnesota. By the time Dobbs was a child, the forests all around his grandfather's place had been reduced to pincushions. The quarries looked like meteor strikes. Along the backcountry highway, all that had remained were cinderblock shacks with rusted tin roofs and hand-painted signs offering diesel and bait.

His grandfather's cabin had been off the grid, but Dobbs had loved every bit of it: lying on a cotton-stuffed sleeping bag on a slab of peeling plywood; peeing on trees and eating everything out of the same dented tin bowl; washing off in the turbid lake and fishing for dinner and building fires out of twigs and branches. Maybe nothing else lasted—not veins of iron or swaying pines—but the cabin itself had seemed as if nothing could touch it. After a week there, Dobbs had felt he could survive anything.

The guys who'd readied the house hadn't bothered to paper the upstairs windows. From the second floor, Dobbs could see for miles. To the south were the warehouses, the importers and exporters. Beyond them, the neat and tidy downtown, the slim pocket of tourist attractions. In every other direction stretched the emptiness, interrupted only occasionally by a house or a distant smokestack.

What stood out most to him, though, were the trees. Some, he could tell, had been anchored there for decades, old and barnacled, scraped away by tire swings. But it was the new trees that surprised him, saplings springing up even from cracks in the sidewalk.

For several minutes he'd been standing there, studying it all, when suddenly he was startled by a rustling in a thicket of undergrowth at the corner. At first there was nothing to see but a ghostly shaking in the web of branches. But then a white beak poked out, set upon a green head half-hidden behind a red eye mask. The neck that followed ended in a thick white ring. The body was a gradient of golden russet brown, stippled with white and black spots. The bird stepped cautiously out into the dew, and Dobbs watched it stroll, almost skipping, to the curb, dragging a tail almost as long as its body. A grouse? A pheasant?

What else was out there?

He ate the last of his food, half a granola bar and two-thirds of a spoonful of peanut butter. He ran his finger inside the jar.

And he waited. It was spring, and the days kept getting longer. Nightfall seemed to take forever to come.

§

He started with a mattress, a small table, a chair. An abandoned city was an easy place to find cast-offs. Dobbs carried things back one at a time, going out only at night. It wasn't hard to avoid getting spotlit by streetlights. Most of them didn't work. There was the occasional shadow crossing a distant intersection, tinted cars shaken by their stereos. But mostly it was dogs he saw roving the empty streets, many of them too hungry even to bark.

Late one night, several miles from the house, Dobbs came across a whitewashed brick building. Out front there was a display window, still intact, behind a grille of steel bars. Books. They'd been sitting there so long in the sunlight, he had to squint to read the bleached titles: gardening manuals, Beat poets, a thick, unjacketed tome by Marx. The placard in the window said CLOSED, but Dobbs could see a faint light burning somewhere deep inside.

A black van was parked at the curb, a hi-top conversion job with chrome rims and a fresh coat of wax. Everything on it shone, except for a small, peeling bumper sticker pasted in the rear window. BRICOLEUR, it said in a typewriter-like script set beside a crude sketch of an ordinary office stapler. No particular interest in being understood.

Dobbs was standing up on his toes, attempting to peer into the van's rear window, when the door to the bookstore opened. He ducked, slinking across the dark street just in time.

They emerged from the bookstore with the glazed disorientation of an audience strolling out into the falling dusk after a long matinee. There were three of them at first, an odd mix. There was a tall, thin blonde who looked pale and fragile, except for the thick, black strokes she'd painted on her lips, as if she had something to prove. The brunette stood two heads shorter. Stepping onto the sidewalk, she raised the hood on her sweatshirt, framing a face worthy of Japanese anime: tiny, doll-like nose and mouth little more than smudges under the huge reflecting pools she had for eyes.

The black man between them was big but unimposing, a softness to his movements and gestures. The way he matched his strides to theirs, he and the girls were friends but nothing more.

Two more men appeared in the doorway half a minute later. There was a second black guy—black from his sneakers to his stocking cap, too. A revolutionary look suited to Beats and Marx. The white guy behind him looked like a reader of neither. He was tall and blond and prep-school handsome, his hair artfully mussed. His torn, faded jeans looked like the kind that cost three hundred dollars a pair.

The revolutionary flipped through a key ring, looking for the one that would lock the steel accordion security gate.

They seemed too old to be college students. Too aimless to be working. To quiet to be looking for trouble.

The five of them lingered for a moment beside their van, the Scooby-Doo gang gone underground. Dobbs could hear them talking, saying their goodbyes. Then three of them climbed into the van and drove away. But the anime girl and the revolutionary were walking.

Dobbs was too far away to hear much of what they were saying. The woman repeated the name Myles. Every sentence she spoke either began or ended with his name. She used it exhaustedly, sighing. She kept stabbing her finger back in the direction of the bookstore, even once it was well behind them. She seemed to be complaining that Myles had said or done something back there to upset her. Myles in turn called her McGee, speaking the name as though it belonged to a sullen child.

"There's nothing to worry about," Myles kept repeating. "Nothing to worry about."

They walked for at least a mile. When they finally stopped, they stood in front of a brick building with a loading dock overlooking a gravel lot. They approached the overhead door, and Myles unlocked it. A few seconds later two cloudy second-story windows lit up.

Not homey, Dobbs decided, but it seemed it was there they'd spend the night.

He was back at the house just before dawn. He'd been walking all night, and he couldn't walk anymore. He sat down on the mattress, head against the wall, eyes as wide as he could make them. He'd gone two days without sleep. He thought he had it in him to manage two more.

He reached into his bag, hoping there might be something in there he could eat, something he'd forgotten. But the bag was empty, except for a square of brown paper that hadn't been there before.

Stop fucking around, it said. *Get to work.*

I know what I'm doing, he said aloud to the empty house. Everything's under control.

He wished he could talk to Sergio directly, reassure him. I still have what it takes.

§

The door to the bookstore was propped open with a fat hardcover, the spine separated, the dust jacket mottled with rain: *The Encyclopedia of Urban Architectural Design.*

The place was a front for something, he'd figured, waiting at the house for night to return. A bookstore with nothing else around for miles? But a front for what?

Once inside, he was surprised to discover the place really was a bookstore after all. Along the baseboard, vertical stacks of faded books at staggered heights created a miniature skyline sprinkled evenly with dust. The case just inside the door was jammed floor to ceiling with history books. The light was poor and oddly brownish, as if it were rising up from the dirty floor. After a few steps, another tall, unsteady bookcase appeared on his right, and he had to inhale to squeeze through the narrow passage.

At the other end of the passage, the shop opened up slightly. Somewhere across the store Dobbs heard voices. Men's voices. Neither one seemed to fit the group from the night before.

Soon several more long bookcases appeared on Dobbs's right, leading off into the shadows. It was as if they'd been set up to make it impossible to see more than a few yards ahead. He turned left for no other reason than that the aisle was the most passable. But the window turned out to be another dead end.

The voices had grown more audible, but Dobbs still wasn't even sure where they were coming from. Above his head ran a length of pipe wearing a furry coat of cobwebs and dust. A security camera peered down at him from the corner. Cameras, for used books?

He'd just come to another dead end when he located the voices somewhere around the corner.

"Risky." The man seemed to be straining to keep his voice down.

"What'd you expect?" the second man said.

"I don't know," said the first. "I just—"

The second man sighed. "We've talked about this a million times."

Dobbs was sure now that neither man had been among the ones he'd seen the night before. They sounded older, too eager not to be overheard.

He started off in the other direction. Around the bend he came upon a wooden desk and chair. And there was a side table supporting a primitive cash register. Beside it, a tiny flower-patterned teacup in a matching saucer let off a steadily climbing twist of steam. He thought of the blonde and the girl with anime eyes, and he wondered which of them the cup belonged to. The china was delicate, like the blonde. But there was no trace of her dark lipstick on the rim.

The desk was cluttered with books and paper, a stack of blotchy flyers dangling over one edge: *Bricoleur @ The Woodshed. No cover. All ages. Video premiere. Music + Revolution.* And the same odd line drawing of a stapler that he'd seen on the van's bumper sticker, no less obscure here.

Dobbs folded a copy of the flyer into his pocket. Then he turned to go. But that was the moment the two men appeared in front of him, each carrying an armful of books. They were both middle-aged. The black man wore some sort of uniform: dark blue pants and a matching shirt. The photo badge clipped to his pocket said his name was Darius. The Hispanic man was stocky, with long hair pulled back into a ponytail. His clothes were spotted with paint and stain, and his dry, coarse hands were nicked and scraped.

"You surprised me," Dobbs said. "I didn't hear you come in."

The Hispanic man looked around. "Do you work here?"

Dobbs lowered himself into the chair behind the desk. "Find everything you were looking for?"

The two men set their books down on top of the posters. As if he'd been doing it all his life, Dobbs folded back the covers. The prices were penciled in the top corner of the first page, as always. The two men watched in silence as he tried to add up the numbers.

Wiring. Farming. Home electronics. "You must be pretty handy," Dobbs said.

17

Darius had a look on his face like he'd been caught with a stack of porn.

"How much?" the Hispanic guy said.

At the bottom of the pile, unrelated to any of the rest, was a guidebook to Mexico, ten years out of date. "Beautiful country," Dobbs said.

The Hispanic man's face grew taut.

"For you two," Dobbs said, "an even twenty."

Each man fished ten bucks from his pocket.

The Hispanic guy picked up the books and turned away in silence, taking a step in the direction of what Dobbs hoped was the exit. The black man started to do the same, but at the last moment he paused, catching a glimpse of something over his shoulder. "Do you play?"

Following Darius's finger, Dobbs saw an old Fender propped up on a chair, its red finish crosshatched with scratches.

"I'm learning."

"I played once," the black man said. "I was pretty good."

"Darius!" the other yelled.

Darius might have gone on, but he saw his partner's jaw rocking in its socket. "I'll see you," he said.

Dobbs gave a broken wave. "Come again."

As soon as they were out of sight, Dobbs put one of the tens on top of the register. The other, his commission, he put in his pocket.

In his dream that morning, the two men from the bookstore came to him dressed as generals, donning pointed hats and sabers. Even without a weapon of his own, Dobbs knocked them off their horses, before single-handedly taking on their armies. But then why, when he woke up in the middle of the afternoon, did he feel so afraid?

Two

EVERYTHING ON THE monitors was gray: the blacks were a dark charcoal gray; the whites were like newspaper pages. The walls of bookcases appeared as undifferentiated smudges of darkness. Because of its size, the china cup was only a blur against the dark desktop, but Myles knew it was there. He'd dropped the tea bag in just moments before the meeting started, and then he'd forgotten it. All the way up the stairs and across the store—there was no way for him to get it now. And anyway the tea would be too bitter. He liked two minutes of steeping, no more, no less, with water just shy of boiling.

"Myles," McGee said. "Is there anything you want to add?"

Myles turned his head at the sound of her voice, finding himself once again in the world of color. Everyone at the table was staring at him, McGee straddling her ladder-backed school chair. To see her there, surrounded by pads of yellow paper and three eager friends, made Myles happy and hopeful. They'd been meeting almost every night this week to go over plans for the demonstration. Finally they were down to the last details.

"It all sounds great," he said.

McGee frowned. "I said I'm worried no one's going to show up. Again."

"It's going to be fine," Myles said.

"You always say it's going to be fine," McGee said. "And then no one shows up."

Across the table, Holmes and April watched the volleys in silence.

"It'll be fine," Myles said. "It'll all work out."

Myles could see by her expression that she wasn't convinced, but when was she ever? She was too hard on herself. Lately she couldn't see the good in anything they did. More than anything else, he wished he could show her.

He returned his gaze to the monitors, to his forgotten cup of tea. But something in that brief time had changed upstairs. Myles detected movement on one of the cameras. Two customers, men—one dark, the other a medium shade of gray—stood inside the doorway of the bookstore. The black man had pulled a book off the shelf and was leafing slowly through the pages. Arms folded across his chest, the other looked furtively up and down the aisle.

The cameras were a recent addition, installed with Holmes's help. Now Myles could take part in meetings while also keeping an eye on the store. If customers needed him, he would know. And then, of course, there was security. Things being the way they were these days, you couldn't be too careful.

The two men came in and out of view, the black man leading. The other man kept looking over his shoulder. He was stocky, with long dark hair tied into a ponytail.

What were they looking for?

Feeling a hand on his shoulder, Myles turned around, eyes reluctantly following his head. McGee was holding a piece of paper. She was waiting for him to take it.

"This is a draft of the press release," she said.

Holmes grabbed a copy, barely glancing at it. "It's just more of the same," he said, letting the sheet float back down to the table.

"I think it's good," April said, eyes still gliding down the page.

"This environmental stuff," Holmes said. "No one cares. The city's such a fucking mess."

"It's not the same," McGee said. "I'm trying to make it clear these are global issues that affect us locally—" All at once she stopped, her lips still parted.

Myles felt her gaze narrowing in on him.

"Seriously?" she said.

In the corner of his eye, Myles could see something happening on the monitors, but McGee continued to hold him there with her binocular stare. "What?" he said.

But she wasn't looking at Myles. It was Fitch this time, slumped in the chair behind him, unshaven chin bobbing against his chest. Holmes and April had noticed, too, and they seemed to be waiting to see what McGee would do, what she'd say.

The only sound across the entire basement was something burbling in Fitch's throat. In his sleep, his knee shot up, thumping into the table. One of McGee's red markers rolled to the edge and onto the floor. It was that dull clatter of plastic on cement that finally caused Fitch's eyes to pop open.

"What's going on?" he said.

McGee's nostrils flared, the way they always did when she was angry. "Why do you even bother?" she said. "What's the point in showing up at all?"

Fitch yawned into his elbow.

"We were up late rehearsing," Holmes said.

Fitch laid his head down on his arms. "There's just something about people talking."

"He always used to fall asleep in school," April said.

McGee looked from one to the next. "Why are you defending him?"

21

"We've been talking about the same stuff for weeks," Holmes said. "What are you afraid he missed?"

The stubble had been on Fitch's face for three days. His clothes had been on him even longer. And yet somehow he looked the same as always, like one of those guys paid to glower in his underwear next to strips of scratch and sniff cologne. And April could have been the pouty, negligéed beauty draped over his neck. First cousins, and even perfect strangers couldn't miss the family resemblance. Was there something in the country club water, Myles sometimes wondered, that bred people like these?

"Moving on," McGee said, making no effort to hide her anger. "We need to get the banners finished. We're running out of time."

At the front of the store, where the two men had entered only a few minutes before, Myles now saw another guy, newspaper white, wearing a winter coat. All last week they'd gone without a single customer. Now they suddenly had three at once? As Myles debated whether to go upstairs, he watched the man in the winter coat move from monitor to monitor, coming closer with each step to the other two men.

Myles was hunched over the desk, squinting at the screen, when McGee called his name again.

"What?" he said quickly. "What?"

"I asked if you think those friends of yours are still coming."

"What friends?" he said.

McGee gave him a pained smile. "You said you knew some people who'd help us out."

"Yeah," Myles said, already turning back toward the monitors. "Sure."

But McGee had another question for him, and another, and then another, and he wanted to tell her what was happening upstairs with the three suspicious guys, but the way she was looking at him made it impossible for him to tell her to wait a second, just one second, just long enough for him to get another look. Her eyes wouldn't let him go. Five minutes passed, then ten. He waited for the bell at the cash register to ring for his assistance, but the ring never came.

And then the meeting was over, but by then it was too late.

As McGee straightened her papers and markers, Myles glanced from one monitor to the next. The men upstairs had vanished without him having any idea why they'd come. And now the meeting had ended, and he had no idea what had been decided.

The walk home began in silence, except for the scraping of McGee's boot heels on the cement.

"It went well," Myles said. "Didn't it?"

McGee didn't speak or slow down or turn her head.

"It's going to be great," Myles said. "People are going to be excited."

"Please stop talking," she said. "It was better before, when you weren't paying attention."

She was surprisingly fast for someone with such short legs.

When they reached the building, she waited for him to open the door, the one bit of chivalry he was allowed. The overhead door was heavy, but she was like an ant, a thousand times stronger than anyone would think. Sometimes he wondered if she stepped aside out of pity, just to make him feel useful.

The building had once been a factory of some kind. Ball bearings, according to one story, but it was hard to imagine something so small leaving such a mess. The lower half of the building was still full of metal drums spray-painted with skulls and crossbones. Myles had pointed them out to McGee on the day she'd brought him here for the first time, eager to show the place off.

"Well, they're sealed, aren't they?" she'd said.

Even though this was exactly the sort of stuff she was constantly getting agitated about. Brownfields and poisoned groundwater and toxic sludge. But for some reason she found it more compelling when these things happened to people other than them.

He and McGee were the only ones living in the building. The rest of the second floor had been converted to artists' studios. Maybe the light blasting through all those vast, uninsulated windows was flattering to canvases. On sunny days, Myles found the dirty glass had a way of making his life feel sepia-toned.

Before the sun went down, though, the artists fled. Myles didn't know where they went, but he liked to imagine little cottages in the suburbs with herb gardens and roaring fireplaces. He almost never talked to his neighbors. One was a mailman, or maybe he worked at the DMV. Something awful. His paintings were dark and blobby, like album covers for heavy metal tribute bands. And there was the middle-aged woman who rolled clay into thin gray turds that she assembled into something she called jewelry boxes but in fact looked like colanders made of Lincoln Logs. The third was a batty old hippie who taught art at the community college. Myles had never seen her stuff. She was always finding reasons for shutting her door whenever he came near.

McGee didn't mind the exposed ceilings or the wall of windows looking out over an old railway bed. Or the floorboards slathered in gray industrial paint. She didn't notice that their futon, lying in the corner beneath a mound of blankets, looked like a jumble of newspapers swirled together in a dirty alley. She didn't care that the bathroom had been an afterthought. There hadn't been one at all when McGee found the place. But there were some things, thank God, even she was unwilling to live without.

McGee had put Holmes in charge of building the bathroom. But Holmes didn't know anything more about plumbing than the rest of them. His main qualification was that he owned tools and had at least a vague idea what to do with them. Holmes had stuck the bathroom where he could, in the middle of the sidewall, where it was easy to access the pipes crisscrossing nakedly overhead. A shower stall and toilet, side by side. Around them Holmes built a Sheetrock cubicle with a curtain for a door.

On the other side of the bathroom was the kitchen. A single sheet of drywall was all that separated the toilet from the two-burner stove. The plastic, paint-splattered utility sink was the only fixture the place had come with.

The day she'd given him that first tour, Myles had willed a convincing grin, saying, "It's perfect." And she'd taken him by the arm then, smiling her pixie smile, making his lie worthwhile.

But that had been more than five years ago. Tonight, as soon as they came inside, McGee began to pace, walking back and forth in front of the windows. She didn't take off her jacket, didn't even turn on the lights.

If Myles tried to talk to her when she felt like this, he'd only piss her off more. He'd say the wrong thing or in the wrong way. When she was upset, the best thing was to let her be, to pretend he didn't notice anything was wrong.

He sat down in front of the computer. But before he could switch it on, McGee was standing behind him.

"Are you going to work on that *now*?"

He was silent for a moment, trying to decide what was the right answer. "Not if you don't want me to."

"I thought you were done."

"I'm going to finish tonight," he said. "There's just a few small things—"

She turned back toward the windows. At this hour, the only thing to see outside was the electrical substation on the other side of the old railway bed. At night, lit up from below, it looked like an enormous loom.

"Do whatever you want."

He pressed a button on the keyboard, and the computer awoke with a click and a hum.

For the last two months, in his spare time, Myles had been working on a project of his own, assembling a video from footage of the protests they'd organized over the years. The idea had come to him one night in the basement of the bookstore. They'd been having a meeting, but really they'd just been arguing, and it had struck him that they'd all forgotten why they were there. They'd started out wanting to fix the world. Now they were just bickering and trying to keep each other from falling asleep.

Myles had tried to explain his idea to McGee. "It's about inspiring people," he'd said. "Reminding them why we do this."

Reminding ourselves, he'd nearly added.

"We don't need nostalgia," she'd said. "We need to move forward." And ever since then she'd been rolling her eyes every time he tried to work on it.

But he knew once the video was done, once she saw it, she'd understand.

He didn't know what time she went to bed that night. At some point he looked over, and she was no longer in front of the windows. There was a new lump on the futon.

When he crawled into bed, hours later, his video footage at last burned onto a disk, daylight was creeping around the corner.

"It's done," he whispered into McGee's ear. He traced a finger around her shoulder, hoping she might wake.

§

The cinderblock walls bore patches of blue and green and brown, some of which looked suspiciously like mold. The floors were sealed with a shellac of beer and sweat and the gunk that traveled in the treads of shoes. Myles had never been to the club during daylight hours. He'd only ever seen the place in the dark. And now he thought he maybe understood why they usually kept it that way.

He'd spent the walk over from the loft trying to remember when he'd been here last. Years, but how many? Back when Fitch and Holmes had started playing together, Myles and McGee had come here all the time. April, too. She'd just started seeing Inez. Holmes had just come out. It felt like forever ago.

Walking past the bar now, Myles could tell a lot had changed. But what, exactly, he wasn't sure. It was just a feeling, an unsettling sense of things being out of place.

Fitch and Holmes were setting up onstage.

"Is it done?" Holmes said when he saw Myles coming.

Myles handed over the disk. "I was up all night."

Holmes tossed the plastic case onto the floor behind him and resumed rooting through a jumble of cables and equipment.

"Have you seen McGee?" Myles said.

Holmes tugged on a knotted cord. "It's early."

"I told her seven," Myles said.

"It's ten of."

"I know," Myles said. "It's just—"

Holmes looked up impatiently, an effects pedal dangling from his fist like a rat trap. "I'll let you know when we're ready."

When Myles woke up that afternoon, McGee had been gone. She was at the bookstore, he'd assumed, but he hadn't wanted to call. He didn't want to bother her, didn't want to give her reason to remember she was mad at him.

The place wasn't open yet. The bartender was talking on his cell phone. The sound guy was playing Pac-Man in the alcove by the bathrooms. Fitch sat with his legs dangling over the edge of the stage, tuning his guitar. And then there was April. At the last minute, Fitch and Holmes had asked her to fill in for Chad, their usual drummer. Last week, without any warning, Chad had decided to move to L.A., leaving town in such a hurry he'd left his whole kit behind. When they'd told Myles, three days before, he'd thought they were joking. April had never played drums in her life. Or anything else. But here she was, hunched on her stool, looking tense and shivery, as if she were perched above a dunk tank. They could've found an actual musician, but Myles could tell Fitch liked the novelty of it. Sweet, pretty April, flailing away with a pair of sticks.

When the bartender finally got off the phone, Myles went over and asked for a glass of water.

"What?" the kid said.

"Water."

The kid had a shaved head and a scepter tattooed on his neck. "We don't have water."

"Tap," Myles said. "Just tap water in a glass."

The kid slid the water across the bar, sloshing all the way to the end. The glass arrived half empty.

"Was that really necessary?" Myles said.

The kid had already turned away, punching a button and bringing the phone back up to his ear.

Myles wondered what had happened to the old bartender. He'd played bass in a band of his own, and he'd known them all by name, even though Fitch was the only one among them who drank.

In a few minutes, the overhead lights dimmed. The bouncer went over to unlock the door, propping it open with a hubcap and then sitting down on a folding chair, leaning his head against the wall. Nobody came in.

Myles took out his notes. He'd written down some ideas, things he should say. The video would speak for itself. But not everyone understood the history, the context. All their old friends would know, people who'd been involved. But there'd also be kids here tonight too young to have seen any of it for themselves. High school kids. College kids. They'd need to be told what it all meant.

Up on stage, the gear was set up. Amps, mics, guitars, drums. Fitch and Holmes and April must have gone backstage to wait. Myles thought about joining them, but he kept watching the door, wondering why the place was still so empty.

Over in the corner, two guys and a girl were playing pool. The girl was learning. She was pretty, with long dark hair that got in her way every time she leaned over the table. One of the guys—her boyfriend, presumably—took every chance he could to help her, guiding her hands and arms, positioning her legs and hips. The other boy watched and waited, forced smiles on his face. He was in love with her, too.

Two bored-looking guys leaned backward against the bar, staring into their beers. The bartender sat on a case of whiskey, half hidden, sending texts.

The girl at the pool table shrieked. Myles looked over in time to see the cue ball go over the edge. All three of the players jumped back when the ball hit the floor, laughing harder than seemed necessary, managing to hold themselves erect only with the help of their sticks. The one who wasn't the boyfriend retrieved the ball, setting it back upon the table as if it were a pearl on a velvet pillow.

It was the same pool table, or at least the same spot, where he'd tried to teach McGee to play. She'd been in college then, just a little older than these kids were now. Myles himself must have been twenty-four. McGee had been in town for the summer. They'd met at a party. Even now Myles didn't really understand how their circles managed to cross, friends of friends of friends. She'd been with a group of college kids, white kids from the suburbs with rings in their faces. She had a summer job counseling women, victims of domestic abuse. All her friends had jobs like that. April was teaching autistic kids to use computers. Others were feeding old people or rescuing dogs or chaining themselves to trees. They weren't even jobs. They were volunteers. Nobody was getting paid, but still they had apartments and bought beer and cigarettes and managed to eat. McGee and April were sharing a place in Ferndale, even though they could have stayed at home with their parents for free.

Some of Myles's friends had been to school, too. He'd done two years of community college himself. But by the time he met McGee, he and Holmes had normal lives and normal jobs. Myles had been working in a video store, clueless that the place—that the entire idea of the place—was about to go extinct. Holmes had been doing odd jobs for his uncle, patching up houses and apartments on the cheap. He still was.

Myles still remembered being perplexed when McGee explained the work she was doing then, helping abused women.

"What do you say to them?" he'd asked her that first night at the party. "What do you say to these women?"

"I help them," she'd said. "I show them resources."

"But what do you actually *say*?"

He couldn't seem to explain what he meant. What could a girl twenty years old, a girl with no experience of the world, a girl who'd never been married, what could *she* possibly say that a grown woman—an adult who'd gone through genuine horror—would bother listening to? He wasn't trying to be mean. He'd just wanted to understand. He couldn't imagine ever saying anything that would be of any use to anyone.

A few nights after the party, they'd come here to a show, and Myles had shown McGee how to hold a stick. It was a test, partly, to see how close she was willing to let him get. It had been years since he'd heard her laugh like she did that night, miscuing balls all around the table.

The brown-haired girl was ready for another try. She bent over the table and sighted along her stick. This time there was a solid clatter, and something sunk in one of the pockets. All three of the kids threw up their arms and cheered.

The rest of the club remained quiet. The floor in front of the stage was still empty, but a couple of kids had gathered along the back wall, smoking and talking. Myles didn't recognize any of them. They seemed so young, children with cigarettes dangling from their mouths. Where was everyone else? Where were all the people they'd known, the ones they'd always run into at shows, the ones who'd come to hear Fitch and Holmes play?

And where was McGee? She was supposed to close the store and come straight here. There were still no messages on his phone. No texts.

He started to type "where are you?" with the tiny keys, but then he stopped himself. It wouldn't do any good to sound impatient, to make it seem he was checking up on her.

"Come on," Fitch said, appearing behind him. "We're on."

April was back on stage, tapping out an unsteady beat.

"Shouldn't we wait?" Myles said.

Fitch squinted at him. "For what?"

Myles checked his phone once more. "We should've asked for a later slot. We should've gone last."

"Are you nuts?" Fitch said. "We're lucky we even got this."

"Maybe we can switch with someone else," Myles said.

"The only reason we're here at all," Fitch said, "is because I called in a favor. *For you.*"

"The video," Myles said. "No one's here."

"What were you expecting?"

"It's important," Myles said. "People have to see it."

Fitch put his hand on Myles's shoulder. "I say this as a friend: I'm pretty sure no one here gives a shit."

Myles's phone said quarter after seven. "McGee—"

"She can see it at home."

"I made it for this," Myles said. "The big screen. So people would remember it."

"They come to hear music," Fitch said.

"I passed out flyers."

Fitch shook his head. "We're openers for the openers."

"Don't make me do this." April thrust herself between Fitch and Myles, teeth tearing at the nail of her pinkie finger.

Fitch took her other hand. "Let's get this over with."

The club fell into darkness, only the dimmest glow bleeding onto the stage and dance floor from the bar.

Holmes was a blur in the darkness at the front of the stage, pointing a remote control at the ceiling. Behind him, an enormous square of blue light flashed on a white bedsheet suspended above the band. Then the blue light flashed to black, a sign the video was about to begin. But before the images came the sound, the speakers crackling to life with the roar of a crowd. The silent kids all around Myles looked at one another, as if they feared a mob were just outside, ready to storm the room.

Within moments, the roar in the speakers began to ebb just slightly, the voices coalescing, changing to a chant. At least it was supposed to be a chant, but the words were so amplified, so heavy with bass, they sounded more like the grunt of industrial machines.

After a few seconds, the black projection gave way, and at last an image appeared: a crush of bodies, protesters, mouths only slightly off sync with the chant. The camera pulled back, taking in more of the surroundings—the street, a skyscraper. Then the camera slowly panned over the front of the crowd, pressed up against a police barricade, fists in the air, shouting and pointing. On the other side, next to a dented gas canister, four riot cops stood shoulder to shoulder, rifles at the ready.

At the lower edge of the screen, the crowd continued to swell. Against the pressure of all those people, the police barricade rocked, about to fall. One of the cops lowered his head, speaking into the radio strapped to his shoulder. The movement of his lips was firm and explosive.

The chants intensified, thumping like drums. Now there were twice as many protesters in the crowd as before, picket signs bobbing. On the other side of the barricade, the riot cops were multiplying, too. And just when it seemed—even to Myles—that the tension on the screen was about to reach its breaking point, the girl appeared.

The girl was maybe sixteen, and she seemed to come out of nowhere, materializing at the side of the cop with the radio. Between the cop and the girl there was just that teetering board, the flimsy barricade. The girl was skinny, bony, in jeans and a faded turquoise T-shirt. The cop threw up his palm, ordering her to stop. In response, the girl opened her arms, revealing a white daisy painted across the front of the shirt. I'm harmless, she was saying. Look.

Again the cop gestured for her to stop. Turn around, his fingers said. Go back.

But the girl kept coming. And when she couldn't go any farther, she reached out over the barricade, and with a smile for all the crowd to see, she wrapped her arms around his waist. The camera zoomed in, and the screen filled with arms and badge and weapon. The cop lowered his head, as if in order to speak into the girl's ear. They looked as though they were dancing. The speakers moaned with applause.

Myles looked around the club. Sticks in hand, the three billiard players stood in a row facing the stage. So did the bartender. He'd even put his phone away. The two guys at the bar had raised their eyes from their beers.

But there was still no sign of McGee.

Up on the screen, the cop put his free hand on the girl's shoulder, trying to pry her off.

The girl hung on, cheek against his stomach, smile straining.

And then the moment came: desperate and out of ideas, the cop placed his gloved hand against the girl's chest, square on the yellow disk of the daisy. Leaning into it, with all his strength, he shoved her backward onto the pavement. The instant the girl hit the ground, the barricade fell, and before they had a chance to flee, the riot cops themselves tumbled under a wave of bodies.

Just then a few of the stage lights flashed on, and the screaming voices of the crowd in the video were replaced with an even louder rush of music, as Fitch, Holmes, and April started to play.

The music came fast, Fitch and Holmes bent over their guitar and bass, grimacing. In the back corner of the stage, just below the sheet, eyes wide in terror, April hammered an unsteady beat. Fitch's voice thundered over the speakers. The kids had moved away from the wall, watching with open mouths.

On the screen flashed a fractured collage of images: crowds and banners and dancing protesters. The images flickered as fast as Holmes's bass, returning once every twenty seconds to the continued unfolding of the opening scene.

Some of the kids around Myles were shouting at the screen, their faces flush and alive. This was the passion Myles had been talking about. This was what he'd been trying to explain to McGee. They needed to recapture the pleasure, the joy. He looked around again. She still wasn't here.

He had to remember this scene, every detail; he would have to describe it to her in a way she'd understand. He'd have to tell her everything she'd missed.

The kids around him were raising their fists. He saw clenched teeth, sharpened lines across their brows.

And that was when he realized he'd been wrong. This wasn't joy at all. The kids' mouths were twisted and angry. Myles glanced at the screen. They were delighted by the trampling of the police, thrilled.

"No," Myles said out loud, but nobody heard him. No one could. "No," he said again. They'd gotten it all wrong.

By now Myles had seen the video at least a hundred times. But even so, watching the events unfold on the screen was like reliving them all over again. He felt himself clutching the camera. He felt himself running.

Then the screen went black.

The video cut off so suddenly, so unexpectedly, that it was as though the ground had given way beneath him. Myles thought he might fall. The room had changed, become just a room. He could see the kids around him felt it too. But then they began to move to the music. The band played on.

Myles was the only one left standing against the wall. He raised his arms and waved. He needed to tell them—Holmes, Fitch, April. Anyone. They had to do something to fix the video. But Holmes stared vacantly out at the audience. Fitch was gazing at his shoes. April's eyes looked as though they were closed.

Still waving, Myles made his way across the floor, bumping into the scattered crowd. He was halfway to the stage when he felt someone touch him—a tap on his shoulder.

"They can't see you." There was a guy standing beside him with wild, curly red hair, dressed in a winter coat. The guy was older than the kids, but Myles wasn't sure if he was supposed to know him, if he was one of those people from back in the day.

The guy pointed toward the ceiling. "The lights," he said.

Myles kept going. He waved until he'd nearly crawled up onto the stage, and then it was Fitch, not Holmes, who saw him first. Fitch followed Myles's finger. He saw the blue screen. He nodded. But he showed no sign of having understood. There were too many wires on the stage, too many plugs. Myles looked for the remote control, but it was too dark.

Between songs, Holmes got the video running again, but by then the pool players had returned to their game, the bartender to the bar, the others to their tables and their drinks. The narrative had been broken. Myles was afraid only he remembered how it all began, the original embrace, the innocent expression of hope. The kids had missed all the beauty—what might have been. They'd missed the whole point.

Myles reached into his pocket and took out his notes. He'd have to explain to them all the things they'd misunderstood.

Three

THE MOMENT HE opened the door, Darius heard the garbled sound. It was five A.M. At that hour, no one should have been awake. He stood very still, and the sound returned, muffled and distant. It was dark inside the apartment, but Darius could have walked the rooms blindfolded. He slipped his shoes off silently, holding back the handle as he shut the front door. He eased the dead bolt through, making sure it didn't scrape. He knew the loosest floorboards, knew where the kids liked to drop their shoes and bags. He'd come to appreciate this one bit of sloppiness their mother allowed. When he went days without seeing them, he had only the kids' clutter to remember them by.

Down at the end of the hall, a pale, bluish light flickered in the weave of the carpet under Shawn's door. One hand on the knob for balance, Darius put his head to the hollow wood. There was laughter, a smattering of applause.

Shawn lay in basketball shorts and an undershirt, warmed by the glow of the TV. The rest of the bed was blanketed in video game cases and plastic cups. As Darius pushed the door open further, Shawn rolled over, wrapping his arms more tightly around the pillow. He was twelve, and soon he would be bigger than his father.

Darius turned off the set, and he stood there for a moment, waiting. But Shawn didn't awaken.

Outside his daughter's room, Darius paused, but here there was only silence. Nina was sixteen now, her door gummy with the white papery residue of stickers, the faces peeled. She was erasing every trace she could of childish things.

In the bedroom at the other end of the hall, Sylvia lay on her stomach, one arm outstretched onto his side of the bed. He closed the door behind him, and the heavy curtains blocked out every last bit of light. Darius forgot himself for a moment as he undid his pants, allowing his buckle to swing into the side of the dresser with a clatter.

Sylvia didn't stir.

He lifted her arm to make room for himself. She let him reposition it without protest. When he kissed her between the shoulder blades, she remained perfectly still.

When he awoke, she would be gone.

§

Darius accepted her body as he would a blanket, as another component of a dream. Not knowing what he felt, he felt her slide in next to him, hot against the cool sheets. Eyes fluttering back to sleep, he was vaguely aware of fingers folding around his shoulder and breath upon his neck. He might have slept through that too, were it not for her perfume, which smelled of gasoline and dried flowers and made him gasp for air.

"Isn't it about time for you to get up?" a voice said. He couldn't be sure the voice wasn't his own. The words repeated in his head. *Isn't it? Isn't it? Time?* they insisted. The twitching lids of his eyes shot open. There were red lines on the clock, and at first he had no idea what they meant. As he watched the lines change, assembling themselves in a different order, he failed to make note of the body next to him. Finally the lines settled themselves into something he knew as numbers.

It was only 12:46 in the afternoon. Not yet time to get up. Fourteen minutes. Fourteen precious minutes remained. Darius rolled onto his back with a sigh. Then he saw Violet lying next to him, perched on one elbow. She was silent and smiling. He sprang up against the headboard, dragging the blanket with him.

Violet ran her fingers over the strip of his bare chest not covered by the blanket.

"You're not happy to see me?" She'd learned to pout even while smiling. Her nails flickered with a fresh coat of polish, her favorite ruby red.

"How'd you get in here?" He pulled the blanket up the rest of the way.

Violet removed all but her index finger from a swirl of chest hair and looked at him sideways. "What's your problem?"

He cupped her shoulder in his palm. The softness of her skin invited touching. His fingers slid down her fleshy arm, lower, up the incline of her hip, and around the curve of her behind. She was entirely naked and larger, fuller than he was.

"It's too early for surprises . . ." he began. And then again, "How'd you get in here?" He spoke slowly, the better to control the anger he felt rising in his throat.

She rolled over onto her back, fluttered her eyelashes. The sheet had slid down below her breasts. They were smaller than Sylvia's but firmer, and they made it impossible for him to forget how young she was. Violet's skin was a deeper, richer brown than his wife's, and soft—the softest living thing he'd ever touched.

"Sylvia let me in to borrow an egg—" Violet paused, adding a moment later, "As she was leaving." Then she sighed, dramatically, her chest rising and falling. "Looks like I forgot to lock the door when I left."

He saw her arm move, and then he felt her hand between his legs.

"I remembered there was something else I needed to borrow." Her fingers fumbled in the fly of his boxers. She gripped his shorts by the elastic and gave them a tug.

Darius held on to the side of the bed, and she let the elastic snap back against his hip.

"What's your problem?" she said, turning away.

From behind he could see the outer swell and lift of her breast, and he felt regret. He reached out and put an arm around her waist. She allowed herself to be pulled toward him, even helped. Their bodies came together, stopping only when they both felt the length of his erection between her buttocks.

"So you are happy to see me," she said.

He was, in part, and it was that part that ruled the moment.

They finished just seconds before the alarm went off. Darius was glad when its wail gave him an excuse to let Violet go.

He was a stupid, stupid man. As they lay silently, several inches of sheet between them, Darius swore to himself that it would never happen again. But then again, not only could he remember each of the reasons he'd already thought of for breaking off the affair—finally and completely—he could recall himself on this bed, in exactly this position, making the exact same pledge.

Violet stood naked before him, her body strong and confident and intimidating.

"Shouldn't you be at work?" he said.

She slipped on her panties, a faint sliver of fabric that somehow seemed to make her even more naked than before. "I switched." She pulled on her sweatpants and a T-shirt that had been washed almost to transparency.

"Otherwise I never get to see you." She reached out and touched his toe, and the sweetness of the gesture only increased his misery.

When she bent down to pull up her socks, Darius ducked under the blankets. He allowed a minute to pass, pretending to search for his underwear. When he resurfaced, Violet was gone.

He leaped out of bed, still undressed, and sprinted to the living room. As he locked the front door behind her, Darius felt again the loss of those fourteen minutes. There'd be no getting them back, not when every minute of the next five hours was accounted for in advance. He'd already promised Sylvia he'd do the shopping. They'd talked about it the night before. He always called her during his break, just as she was getting into bed. He'd been careful to set aside just enough time to get to the store, but that was before Violet.

He walked over to the window and lowered himself into the recliner with a sigh. Now, on top of everything else, he'd have to wash the sheets, too.

The vinyl cushion squeaked against his naked skin as he reached out to raise the blinds. The afternoon sun washed through the glass, pouring over his body. He didn't bother to cover himself. There was nobody outside to see him. The street below was empty. The building across the street was empty, too. There'd been a fire a couple years ago. But if it hadn't been a fire, it would've been something else. The emptiness was everywhere. All across the city it was the same, a landscape full of monuments to loss and oblivion.

He stood in the shower just long enough to rinse off the smell of Violet's perfume. He passed a razor over his cheeks and chin. And then he was running down the stairs with the laundry basket. It was a three-and-a-half-block sprint to the Laundromat, and he made it there in record time, only to find that the few washers not out of order were already in use.

The TV in the corner was playing a telenovela, but the Guatemalan lady who ran the drop-off service was nowhere in sight. Darius collapsed against the wall, letting the basket fall to his feet.

A woman sitting in one of the slick plastic chairs by the windows nodded at the TV. "He doesn't know she's his sister. *Hermana*," she said. "It means sister."

Darius glanced at the screen, an airbrushed young couple smashing their mouths together.

The woman in the plastic chair wore fuchsia stretch pants with matching toenail polish. "I dated a Spanish guy once."

Darius slid into the seat beside her. A zipper ticked in one of the dryers, round and round with every rotation. It was impossible not to feel the time slipping away. "I have a hard enough time following these things in English."

"You get the hang of it," the woman said. "Everyone's diddling everyone. The ball to keep your eye on is who's got the loaded gun."

Darius turned back to the drop-off counter. "Do you know where she went?"

The woman shrugged.

He hadn't seen one of these shows in years, but nothing seemed to have changed. "They're too beautiful," he said.

"You want to watch ugly people going at it?"

"It just doesn't feel real," Darius said.

"That's kind of the point."

It was hard to see how that made anything better. Was that what he needed to feel less guilty about his own bad choices—better lighting and a personal stylist?

The telenovela broke for commercials, a white woman lathering her head in the shower.

"You like to live dangerously?" the woman beside him said.

"I'm just waiting for a machine."

She nodded toward the window at his back. All he saw outside was a paper cup blowing down the sidewalk.

"There." She reached out, pointing.

It was something in the glass itself, a small hole just level with his

41

chin. Darius touched it with his finger, feeling the smooth, sharp edge. A bullet hole.

"Why would anyone shoot at a Laundromat?"

The woman turned back to the TV. The show had come back on. "I want to shoot it up every time I'm here."

There was no point trying to make sense of it. Three days ago the super's kid had gotten shot buying pop at the gas station. Four o'clock in the afternoon, and he never even saw who did it. A couple of weeks before, it had been one of Shawn's friends, standing on a street corner, mistaken for someone else. Or so Shawn said, but who knew? In the end, what did it even matter?

Where was the future in this? That was what Michael Boni had said, that day two weeks ago when he and Darius had first met. The words had been echoing in Darius's head ever since, demanding an answer. Michael Boni had been talking about the city, but Darius had come to see it was a conversation about his entire life, about all the mistakes he'd made, that he continued making. Where was the future in this?

The day he'd met Michael Boni had started out a lot like this one: a visit from Violet, a pile of errands. The landlord accepted only postal money orders. The ones from the check-cashing places weren't good enough. So there Darius was at the post office, like every month. But that day the wait was even worse than usual. For five minutes already, his sneakers had been glued to the same grimy square of vinyl tile. Before him in line stood a stocky Hispanic guy with a ponytail carrying a package wrapped in a diaper box.

Ten people in line, and no one saying a word. Darius hated that, people all stuck together, pretending they were alone.

"Whatever happened to the wanted posters?" Darius had said.

The Hispanic guy in front of him moved his package from one arm to the other.

"Remember those?" Darius said. "Every post office had them."

The Hispanic guy gave him a quick glance.

"When was the last time you saw one?"

"It's been a while."

"Now it's just pictures of stamps," Darius said. "Warnings not to mail explosives." He pointed at a bright orange sign on the wall. "Is there anyone that doesn't know that?" he said. "Are there people walking into post offices, saying, 'Yeah, I'd like to mail this hand grenade'?"

The guy shifted the package again, his arms sinking lower under the weight.

"I miss the posters," Darius said. "I liked to look at the faces. You wonder about their stories—why people do the things they do."

The guy seemed to nod. Or maybe he was just stretching his neck.

It was hot in there, the boiler swamping the windows along the street, turning April into August. There was nothing to see outside but the boarded-up courthouse across the street.

"I remember when mine were that small." Darius nodded at the diaper box, the little white baby blindfolded by a strip of brown packing tape.

The Hispanic guy was already turning back toward the front of the line.

"How old's yours?" Darius said.

"My what?" the guy said sideways.

"Your baby."

"I don't have a baby."

"The box," Darius said. "I thought—"

"It's just a box."

The line still hadn't moved. Everyone ahead of them, it was like they'd never been in a post office before, had no idea what one was for. The two clerks looked as though they'd been startled awake from some deep, traumatic dream.

Through the condensation on the glass, the old courthouse across the street was a glistening ruin. Darius and Sylvia had gotten their marriage license there. By the looks of the place, that must have been a century ago. Really sixteen years, Sylvia just pregnant with Nina. But in that time there'd been what the city called a "streamlining of services," by which they seemed to mean injecting an atmosphere of punishment into every department of the government, the post office included. The old courthouse was beautiful but too expensive to maintain. Or so they said. A vine had climbed halfway up the flagpole.

"I was listening to the radio the other day," Darius said, drifting a bit closer to the Hispanic guy. "I heard them talking about turning it all into farmland."

One of the post office clerks had wandered off, leaving a confused old woman at the counter clutching what looked like a sock full of coins. The Hispanic guy dropped his heavy package to the floor.

"All of it," Darius said. "The whole city. Tear it all down."

Every couple of months it was something new, some grand plan to bring the city back from the brink. Artists were going to save it, filling empty warehouses with ceramics and easels. Or urban hipsters would come, spawning microbreweries and coffee shops. Or all the empty factories would be converted to make solar panels. Or engines that ran on cow manure. Or the entire city would become a post-apocalyptic film set, permanently on loan to Hollywood. Or maybe a Saudi prince would turn the place into his personal amusement park.

But a farm! Steam-shovel up the courthouse, till the lawn around the flagpole. And plant what, exactly? Acres of corn just off the interstate?

The line shuffled forward. The Hispanic guy toed the diaper box a few inches ahead. "Fuck it," he said, gesturing toward the courthouse. He'd seen where Darius was looking after all. "Why not?"

From up front came the shriek of a tape gun.

"Are you going to become a farmer?" Darius said.

"It's just going to waste."

So what, put the city in a time machine and pretend the whole last century never happened? Even the people on the radio hadn't been entirely serious, pointing out all of kinds of obstacles. "For one thing," Darius said, "they'd have to tear everything down first."

The Hispanic guy raised his paint-splattered boot and rested it on top of the diaper box, using the baby's head as a footstool. "They tear stuff down every day."

"Most of what's left," Darius said, remembering another piece of what he'd heard, "they don't know who owns it. They can't tear down what's not theirs."

"People are always burning shit down. They do it for fun."

He wasn't wrong. Kids did it, drunks did it. For a gallon of gas, it was cheap entertainment. Scavengers did it, too, trying to get to valuable scrap hidden in walls. The burned-out shells stayed there forever, until the rain and the snow brought them down. But that was criminals. The city couldn't go around setting things on fire.

"And it's expensive," Darius said. They'd mentioned a number on the radio, the price tag a crazy fortune.

At the front of the line, an old man was flipping through the plastic pages of a binder—slowly, as if the stamps between the sheaths were pictures of old friends.

"It doesn't have to be." The guy mimed pressing down on a dynamite detonator like Wile E. Coyote.

Darius tried to chuckle. Look, he wanted to say, we're only joking. But no one else in line was paying attention.

"If they want a farm," Darius said, "they'd have to get rid of us, too." And he pressed down on his own imaginary detonator to make his point. "I don't know about you," he said, "I'm not going anywhere."

"You have a family?" the guy said.

Darius nodded.

The guy pointed back to the abandoned courthouse. "Where's the future in that?"

The old man had finally picked out his stamps. The line edged forward. But the Hispanic guy remained where he was, the diaper box at rest between his feet. He extended his hand.

"Michael Boni." The man's fingers were discolored with what looked like cherry stain.

"Darius."

"The farm," Michael Boni said. "It's a pipe dream."

"I was just talking," Darius said.

"That's all anyone ever does." Michael Boni lifted his diaper box. "But you're right."

For a long moment, Darius stared at him, wanting to agree but unsure what he'd be agreeing to.

"A clean slate," Michael Boni said. "How else are you going to start over?"

Was that what Darius had said? They didn't sound like his words. But the way Michael Boni spoke them, no hint of doubt, no uncertainty, made Darius proud to claim them as his own.

Darius had to wait another twenty minutes before a washer freed up at the Laundromat. And then, of course, the bus was running late. With all the stops, it took three-quarters of an hour to get across town; the only decent grocery store was miles away. Darius knew he was gambling with the sheets. The woman in the fuchsia stretch pants had said she'd watch them, but who knew if they'd still be in the dryer when he got back? He had only enough time to race from aisle to aisle, filling the cart almost without looking. He grabbed whatever seemed familiar, whatever he remembered having gotten last time.

Half an hour later Darius was stumbling down the narrow aisle of the bus, hoisting the plastic shopping bags as high as he could. But they were heavy, and he couldn't seem to keep them from banging against the backs of the seats. *Sorry*, he said, *sorry. Sorry sorry.* The passengers sitting by the aisle bent toward the windows as he passed.

He flopped down, groaning like an old man, into the second-to-last seat. Around himself he built a fortress of groceries, which he spent the next forty-five minutes struggling to keep from falling to the floor.

"You're late," Michael Boni said.

Darius slumped down beside him on the marble bench. It was twenty minutes after six, and he felt as if he'd been sitting all day, somehow without a single moment's rest. He tossed back his head, taking in the columns of mirrored windows hovering above him.

"And you look like a tourist," Michael Boni said.

They sat in the evening shadow of the HSI Building, the sun setting at their backs. No matter how many times Darius looked at the tower, he couldn't understand how anything could be so big and yet stand so effortlessly.

"It's what a city should look like," he said. The *whole* city, not just a few square blocks, what passed here for a business district. The plaza was immaculate. In the flower bed beside the bench, even the dirt was tidy, the soil so deeply and evenly black, it appeared to have been painted. The chrysanthemums were all the exact same height. From down here it was impossible to tell that nearly a third of the building's floors were vacant.

At this hour, everything was shutting down. The parking ramps and streets were choked with cars waiting to get on the interstate, out toward the suburbs.

"They can't get out of here fast enough," Michael Boni said.

Darius reached out to pick up a straw wrapper from the flower bed.

"What are we?" Michael Boni said. "The ladies' auxiliary?"

The sawdust in Michael Boni's hair seemed to sparkle in the day's remaining light. He leaned in closer to Darius. "We can't meet here any more."

Since that day at the post office two weeks ago, Darius and Michael

Boni had met here five times, always just before the start of Darius's shift.

Michael Boni pointed at three men in suits who'd just pushed through the revolving door. "We're like foxes in a henhouse."

"What are you talking about?"

"I've been looking through those books," Michael Boni said. "I've made a list of what we need. But we can't talk about it here."

"Why?"

"It's too dangerous."

Michael Boni gestured over Darius's shoulder. Over there was a second tower, with a second plaza, virtually identical to their own. An old man was rising from one of the benches.

"Watch," Michael Boni said.

As the old man moved toward them, Darius saw he was wearing dark glasses and a brown straw hat, carrying a blind person's cane. At the crosswalk, the old man stopped, standing with four others, men and women in business suits. The old man was saying something, talking into the air. A businessman in a gray flannel suit reached out and let the old man take his arm. The light changed, and the five of them started across.

"Watch carefully," Michael Boni said.

Darius felt he must be missing something. It took just a minute for the men to reach the other side. When they did, the old blind guy offered thanks, bowing and waving goodbye. On his own again, the blind guy navigated his way to a bench not far from where Michael Boni and Darius were sitting.

"Did you see it?" Michael Boni said.

"See what?"

"The way he pocketed the guy's wallet. The blind guy."

Darius glanced at Michael Boni, expecting to see he was joking.

"I watched him do the same thing twenty minutes ago," Michael Boni said. "I was the only one who noticed it."

Darius saw no point in arguing over something he hadn't seen.

"That's what I'm talking about." Michael Boni leaned in, lowering his voice. "There might be someone here saying the same thing about us, watching us every day."

"But we haven't done anything," Darius said. And he was sure no one had ever noticed them. Darius was hardly the only black man in a uniform. And Michael Boni wasn't the only Hispanic guy in stained jeans.

"What do you think we're doing?" Michael Boni said. "Just shooting the shit?"

"I'm just saying, we haven't done anything. Not yet."

"Don't think I'm not keeping an eye on you, too," Michael Boni said.

Darius pushed the straw wrapper deeper down into his pocket. "Fine," he said. "We'll be more careful."

Michael Boni turned away, his eyes falling once again upon the old man with the cane. He seemed serious about the dangers the blind man represented. But more than that, Michael Boni seemed pleased by what the blind man had done.

§

In the five months since he'd been assigned the night shift at HSI, Darius had never faced a security breach more serious than a drunk setting up camp in the doorway. After six o'clock, there was never more than a handful of people left. Every night, from the booth in the lobby, he watched the stragglers trickle out, a few each hour until, by eight or nine—ten at the latest—the last of them had gone. It was always the same people.

That night, like almost every night, the last to leave was Mrs. Freeman, from the third floor. Even before he knew her title, Darius could tell she was someone important. She was in her late sixties, and she had a leisurely way of crossing the lobby from the bank of elevators, as if she had nothing to prove, no reason to hurry. Maybe no one was waiting for her at home. It made him sad to think so.

"It's all yours, Darius," she said, pausing at the booth, tossing him an imaginary set of keys.

He caught them midair, as always. "We'll get it spic 'n' span," he said. "A fresh coat of wax."

She raised her eyes toward the high ceiling. "I don't know how you can stand all this quiet."

"The girls get here," Darius said, "and I drive them crazy, talking their ears off."

"You're a bad influence."

He smiled.

"Well," Mrs. Freeman said, giving him a wave. "Goodnight."

Outside in the plaza, she opened her umbrella. Darius hadn't realized it had started to rain.

At eight, his partner, Carl, arrived, toting sixty-four ounces of radioactive pop. Darius poured himself a cup of lukewarm coffee. Carl flipped through a magazine, page after glossy page of sports cars, posed like centerfolds.

"Did I ever tell you my uncle used to build Vettes?" Carl said, holding up the magazine for Darius to see.

The thing in the photo looked more like a flying saucer than a car.

"Ever drive one?" Darius said.

"So fast, bugs vaporize on the windshield."

"Is that something you need?"

"What's need got to do with it?" Carl turned the page and did a double take at a little red convertible. "Get your boy one of these," he said. "Zero to pussy in three point one seconds."

Darius's coffee had grown cold. "Carjacked in three point two."

At nine, Darius had his first break. He walked to the far side of the lobby, where he could have some privacy. He called Sylvia. She was already in bed.

"Thanks for doing the shopping," she said. "Did you wash the sheets, too?"

"I spilled coffee," he said. "Sorry."

"They feel nice."

Darius asked about the kids, about her day at work, about everything that crossed his mind, but none of it helped to distract him from what he'd done that morning, what he'd promised himself he'd never do again.

His voice nearly failed him when it was time to say goodbye. "I love you."

She said, "I love you, too."

Why wasn't that enough?

By the time his break was over, the cleaning women had settled in on their floors and commenced their work. Darius began his rounds. It was exercise of sorts, and talking to the women while they cleaned made the time go a little faster. But then at midnight, when it was time for Carl's break, Darius had to return to the booth and the quiet tedium of the security monitors.

By midnight, Darius knew, Sylvia was long asleep. Shawn and Nina, too. And then there was Michael Boni. What would he be doing? He probably never slept. Darius didn't know where he lived, but he imagined him in a narrow room, on a bare mattress, a pile of books on an unsteady side table. There'd be no carpet or rugs. The paint would be yellowed and peeling. Windows? Maybe a small one. Michael Boni would be sitting on the bed with his back to the wall. No television. No radio. He'd be smoking. Did he smoke? Darius had never seen him smoke, but it seemed likely. Michael Boni would be staring at the peeling walls and plotting.

Some of the facts of Michael Boni's life might still have been hazy, but what Darius knew for sure was that his new partner was a man of absolutes. Their chance meeting in the post office, their rendezvous downtown, their trip to the bookstore to see what they could learn—all of it confirmed his first impression, that once Michael Boni made up his mind, there was no going back. For Darius, there was something irresistible in Michael Boni's clarity, and it pleased him that it had been his own idea that Michael Boni had latched on to. A clean slate. They could start over, fresh.

It was midnight, and Violet would be getting into bed. She slept in the nude, he imagined. Darius had no way of knowing for sure. They'd never spent a night together. Was there a good reason for sleeping with a girl just three years older than his daughter? There was not, though there were plenty of bad ones. Did Sylvia deserve better? She did. So who was he to be sitting here supervising the cleaning women, dusting and vacuuming and polishing, making sure they didn't try to sneak home with a roll of stolen toilet paper?

He'd made a mess of things. With Sylvia, with Violet. He'd known this for months, since the first time he'd let Violet into his bed. And yet still the affair continued, because he'd been too weak to make it stop. But now he had Michael Boni to show him how to follow through.

No more weakness.

A clean slate.

Start over.

Four

IN HIS DREAM, gray slippery smoke in the shape of a lamprey slid under the door of the bookstore. There were five people in the basement. The smoke asphyxiated them in their sleep. After its work was done, the smoke came home and curled up at Dobbs's feet.

He awoke on the floor, bathed in sweat. He got up and went outside. The street was a well of darkness. To the north and east, there was more of the same. But to the west and south, the trees wore faint halos of light. He buttoned up his coat and bolted the door behind him.

After a couple of blocks, Dobbs had left the residential streets behind. The road led to a small bridge crossing over a grassy canal. Down the center of the canal ran parallel depressions that must once have held train tracks. On the other side of the bridge loomed a pair of water towers dipped in rust, held up by spider legs. The factory underneath looked as though it were being consumed from within by some sort of cancer.

He reached an intersection. There was no traffic, but across the street he saw a faintly illuminated shadow, tinted as the signal flashed from green to yellow to red. An elderly woman, slightly stooped. In her arms she held a small wooden crate she seemed to be struggling to keep from tipping over. In a moment, she reached the curb, stepping down into the crosswalk.

From somewhere up the street thundered a low, steady rumble. A boxy sedan emerged from the dark, trailing a bloom of incandescent smoke. As the car sped closer, the rumble doubled down, saturating the pavement with sound. The vibrations quivered their way up Dobbs's legs and into his intestines, clenching hold of his chest. There was no way the old woman could have missed the noise herself, and yet she kept coming. As she crossed the double yellow line, Dobbs could see her and the car converging. He meant to yell, but there was no time. He got only as far as filling his lungs with air.

The tires squealed. Dobbs's entire body flinched.

He opened his eyes just in time to see the car swerve into the other lane. The old woman looked up briefly, as if she thought she'd heard someone call her name.

"Are you okay?" Dobbs said when she reached the sidewalk. She looked startled by the sound of his voice.

"Fine," she said. "How are you?" The old woman wore a purple floral housedress with nothing over it, but she seemed not to feel the cold. She was dark-skinned and even older than he'd thought, well into her seventies. There was a mole on her right lobe that looked like an earring, a black pearl. She was so calm, it seemed pointless to mention what had almost happened.

The crate in her arms was filled with what looked like tools, garden implements. Trowels, pruners, weeders, claws—the metal corroded with dirt and rust. "What are those for?" he said.

"What do you think?"

In their condition, they could have passed for weapons, slow death by tetanus. "Are you a gardener?"

"You shouldn't be here," she said. "It's late."

"I'm looking for a place to eat."

The old woman looked up and down the street. "You find it," she said, "you let me know."

She resumed walking, heading north, disappearing into the shadows of an old stone church.

Dobbs kept going, farther than he'd been before. Every once in a while there was a house, but more often there wasn't anything at all. The streetlights worked in unpredictable patterns. Entire blocks might be completely dark, followed by blocks that hummed and glowed.

Without meaning to, he found himself circling back to the bookstore. Like everything else at this hour, it was closed.

He was getting nowhere, and he was wasting too much time.

He needed a car.

He remembered loading docks, fleets of paneled delivery trucks. Back where he'd started, the wholesalers and produce distributors.

But when he got there, he realized he'd forgotten the fortifications, the trucks corralled within razor-wire fences.

It took him two more nights to find what he needed.

It was a low, nondescript building of earth-colored block. Peering through one of the small, dirty windows around back, he saw the enormous garage inside.

The building belonged to the department of water and sewerage. Administrative offices, by the look of it. At least it had been. But now it seemed to be the dumping ground for their unneeded junk. No one appeared to have been inside in ages.

In the garage he found four trucks: a tanker, a dump truck, and two utility vans. The keys to all of them hung in a flimsily padlocked cabinet in a wood-paneled office.

One of the vans wouldn't start at all. The other took a few moments to consider what it would do before grudgingly coughing itself to life.

What pleased Dobbs maybe even more than the van was the locker room. They were the water department, after all, and they hadn't bothered to shut off their own supply. The water was brown and cold, and there was no soap, but it had been at least a week since he'd taken a shower.

He stayed in the spray until his feet went numb, then dried himself off with a new blue jumpsuit, fresh from the plastic package, a water and sewerage department patch stitched to the chest.

He spent the next couple of days working on the van. He changed the oil and the plugs. He drained the old gas and bought a new battery and filled the tires. There was rust on the rotors but not enough to make him worry. At a dead stop, the van vibrated like a washing machine. Dobbs guessed the timing belt had jumped a notch. Maybe two. So he cleared away the other belts and pulleys and removed the covers and tried to remember where to go from there. It had been years since he'd done anything like this. And he'd only ever been barely competent in the first place.

He'd been in high school when he'd decided to learn about engines. At the time, he didn't have a car of his own. He had to borrow his parents' when he needed to. Jess was away at college then, out east. At least he didn't have to share with her, too.

Both his parents' cars were leases. Every couple of years they got something new, swapping out before anything needed to be fixed. They were smart people, both of them professors. His father's specialty was nineteenth-century German literature. His mother taught political science. They didn't know the first thing about machines.

During the summer months, his parents rarely left their offices. They each had one at the house, a personal cocoon of monographs and scholarly journals. They had articles and book proposals to keep them distracted. Dobbs liked that about them, the way they threw themselves into projects, little worlds of their own.

But one afternoon Dobbs's father emerged into the sunlight to run an errand of some kind. He was in his new Volvo, stopped at a traffic light. At the opposite corner of the intersection was a gas station with a repair shop. He happened to look over, and there was his son, bent over a Chevy in an open garage bay, smeared with grease.

That night when he got home from work, his parents called him into the living room. They sat him down on the sofa, while they settled stiffly into armchairs on either side of the fireplace. The scene felt like an inquisition.

"Why didn't you tell us?" Even though it was July, his father was wearing a sweater. He liked to use the air-conditioning to regulate the seasons at a steady seventy degrees.

"Are you interested in *cars*?" His mother smiled as if the word hurt her teeth.

"Not really."

"Then why?" his father said.

It was as if they'd caught him with a bag of weed. Although he couldn't help suspecting they'd be more laid back about drugs—at least the suburban, recreational kind.

"Curiosity, I guess."

The lines softened across his father's brow. Turning to Dobbs's mother, placing a reassuring hand on her knee, he said, "We'd talked about how maybe engineering might be a good—"

Dobbs shot up from his chair. "Not this again."

"What?" his father said.

During a science lesson one day when Dobbs was seven, in second grade, he'd learned about the ozone layer, about the hole leaking UV rays, about Freon and aerosols and cataracts and carcinoma. That evening, over pork chops, he'd been sullen and silent. His mother spent an hour trying to get him to explain what was wrong.

"Everyone's going to die!" he'd finally shouted, smashing his fork into a mound of cold mashed potatoes.

"It's going to be okay," his mother had said, guiding him into her lap, humming the same aimless tune she had when he was little.

"I'm not a baby," he said, wriggling loose, stomping off to his room.

Later that night she'd come upstairs, knocking softly, sitting down at the foot of his bed.

"You could become a climatologist," she'd said. "Maybe you'll find a solution."

He buried his head under the pillow until she left.

When he was nine, Dobbs heard about the destruction of rain forests and the disappearance of the Panamanian golden frog. At school he'd demanded an assembly. Against a backdrop of graphs Magic Markered onto poster board, he'd lectured on the perils of global warming and the extinction of species.

The principal told him afterward he was destined to become a professor, just like his parents.

At twelve, Dobbs took to washing and reusing Ziploc bags rather than throwing them away, forbidding his father from fertilizing the lawn, putting rocks in the toilet tanks. To Jess's disgust, he posted rules for flushing.

On his fourteenth birthday, he renounced pork chops and fish caught with anything other than a pole.

Ecology, his parents had agreed.

It was as if they believed the world couldn't be extinguished as long as there was graduate school.

That summer evening three years later, facing his parents in front of the fireplace, Dobbs said, "I thought it would be cool to know how to fix a car."

His father removed his glasses and squinted almost blindly. "As a hobby?"

"To be prepared."

His mother looked like a startled bird. "For what?"

"What if your car breaks?" Dobbs said.

His father folded the temples of his glasses in a display of calm and reason. "You take it to a mechanic."

"What if there are no mechanics?"

His mother went stiff in her chair. "Why wouldn't there be mechanics?"

"Or what if we ran out of gas?" Dobbs said.

His mother offered a patient smile. "We'd get more."

"I mean, what if there wasn't any more?" Dobbs said. "What if you needed to fix the engine so it would run on something else?"

"Why would you need to do that?" his father said.

He couldn't seem to make them understand. These were potential questions of life and death. Who knew what the future held?

The final fix for the van was the city seal, making it disappear. A can of spray paint, and Dobbs was done.

He took to the highway first. Not knowing where he was going, he circled around and around, ramp after ramp, swooping and rising, as if the road were a roller coaster. There was the city, laid out before him, mile after mile of emptiness. The place seemed simpler speeding by, its vastness shrunk.

But the most promising places were ones that couldn't be seen in passing, the dark spots on the grid where nothing seemed to be. He headed north, and on a whim he pulled off the highway near an old assembly plant. The place was huge. The miles of streets surrounding it still contained a couple of small houses. Old blue-collar neighborhoods, by the look of them. But there were no cars, no lights.

Dobbs turned east and found main street, the old commercial drag. Everything was long out of business. What made the street different was that everything here was still standing. The buildings were packed in together: a pizzeria, a grocer, a tailor, a cocktail bar, a dry cleaner with an airy upstairs apartment. And there was a nightclub of some sort done up in tar shingles, its marquee pointing the way inside. The strip went on for blocks, and at each intersection there was a traffic light, still cycling through the colors, as if they mattered. A ghost town within a ghost city.

Behind the storefronts on the northeast side of the street ran an alley. And back there, utterly hidden unless one was looking for it, was a warehouse, cut off from the surrounding streets by shade trees. Even without knowing what was inside, Dobbs knew it would be perfect.

Five

THEY STOOD IN the wind and intermittent rain, waving the signs McGee and April had spent the night painting. The words were already washing away. Except for the ten demonstrators, the plaza was empty. It seemed the only other people in the entire downtown were the ones perched up there in the tower, unaware that anything at all was going on down below.

The cold had come out of nowhere, blowing into town early that morning while they were still asleep. The air felt ominous, full of bad intentions. And being tucked away in the van, McGee had discovered, was no better than being out on the sidewalk. Outside they could at least move around when they needed to keep warm.

She breathed on her fist, turning away from the window. She hadn't thought to bring mittens. The newspaper had put her on hold almost ten minutes ago. Since then she'd been taking turns shifting the phone from hand to hand so at least one of them would be warm at a time. The synthesizer solo in her ear was beginning its fourth loop.

They couldn't afford to run the engine just for heat. Fitch and his parents were fighting again; they'd taken his credit card away. For almost a week the van had been running on fumes.

McGee didn't usually mind the cold. She was used to making do. It just felt odd to be suffering here, in Fitch's playhouse on wheels. His parents had sprung for every amenity: a full-size flat-screen TV, surround sound, gaming system, massaging captain's chairs, a mobile table with charging ports. It was a vehicle that could have been built only by people unaware of the existence of human suffering.

The music stopped. A voice cut in at the other end.

"Yes." McGee straightened her legs, her knees creaking like ice cubes. "Hello, yes, I've been holding." She'd been waiting so long it took a moment to remember what was going on, who had called whom.

The man at the news desk sounded as if he were shuffling cards. "Something about a demonstration?"

"Downtown." Her brain seemed to have slowed in the cold. "HSI."

"Didn't we just do this—like two weeks ago?"

"This is different."

"I'll let them know." His voice sounded far away, as if his handset were already descending back toward the cradle.

"The press release," McGee said quickly. "Did you get it?"

"Hundreds of times."

"The one I sent yesterday," McGee said. "The accident." She finally felt the pieces jarring loose. "Last week a drone built by HSI misfired, destroying a rural school and a nearby clinic—"

"Right," he said.

"You got it?"

"The kids were away, weren't they? Some kind of holiday?"

"There were known flaws," McGee said. "Poorly trained outsourced labor, substandard facilities, little oversight, no accountability."

She heard tapping at the other end, as if he were actually typing this down.

"How many protesters?" he said.

McGee looked out the window. So few that in a glance she could see someone had gone missing. She'd have to count herself just to stay in double digits.

"Thirty."

"Including pigeons?"

"Just send someone," McGee said. "It's important."

The line clicked dead.

She'd always hated the telephone, ever since she was old enough to use one. In junior high, the other girls had blathered endlessly from the moment they got home from school to the moment they went to sleep, the phone like an iron lung. Her best friend then was Jennifer Stern, who had long blond hair and a phone in her bedroom shaped like a stiletto heel. It was impossible to say anything that mattered to someone with a shoe in her ear. When McGee's parents weren't there to make her answer it, McGee let her own phone ring and ring until finally Jennifer stopped trying. McGee hadn't realized at the time how that decision would mark her, how lasting the effects would be. Eventually, though, she came to enjoy the pleasures of solitude.

McGee would've loved to hand off this job to someone else. But April was too easily flustered. Fitch could flirt and charm, but he didn't care about the facts. Holmes was better with his hands. Myles could talk to anyone, but he worried too much about being liked, telling people only what they wanted to hear, afraid to push back when they said *no thank you.*

She took a deep breath and pulled her hand out of her pocket. With stiff fingers, she dialed the next number on her list.

"Hello," she said, turning away from the foggy window. "I'm calling about a demonstration downtown . . . HSI, yes. To protest . . . Yes, there are forty of us so far. Yes, we're expecting a lot more. You should come and . . ."

The next number rang and rang until she gave up.

She needed a cigarette.

Across the street, a woman in a long tan raincoat climbed the three steps from the sidewalk to the plaza. As the woman made her way toward the revolving door, April raised her sign: MERCHANTS OF DEATH. Because of the rain, the words looked almost as if they were bleeding. Through the plush, carpeted walls of the van, McGee could just barely hear the faint rhythm of their chant. *They're making a killing, making a killing, making a killing.* Myles stepped into the woman's path, smiling, holding out a flyer, and the woman let the paper brush against her sleeve, not even glancing as she pushed through the door.

Myles had said he'd enlisted some high school students to paper the city with flyers. So far McGee hadn't seen any trace of the kids *or* the flyers. It happened every time. Myles wanted to win the kids over, so he made all of this sound like a party. But as soon as they realized there was work involved, they moved on to other things.

Not a single reporter had shown up. No one at all had come whom she didn't know personally.

Beneath the canopy at the side entrance of the building, a security guard pinched a cigarette to his lips. McGee watched the glow and burn, feeling her mouth run dry.

Maybe she could just roll down a window. Fuck Fitch's upholstery.

She dreaded the thought of making another call. So many times she'd dialed these numbers, and almost nothing ever came of it. A couple of sound bites on the lowest-rated local news. Or a blog where the comments got hijacked by raving lunatics. She wondered sometimes if this was how actors felt—they spoke a line so many times, they no longer had any heart for the role. But an actor could always move on to playing a different part. If McGee tried that, there'd be no one to take her place.

She patted her pockets, searching for her lighter. Through the hazy windshield, she spotted a man hovering beside a light post only a few yards from the van. He wore a ratty peacoat with an upturned collar, curly red hair flattened by the rain. Above his head he held a newspaper.

The guy looked over as McGee stepped out of the van. Had she not known they were strangers, she might have thought he looked happy to see her. She handed him one of the flyers.

"This'll explain why we're here."

Across the street, in the otherwise empty plaza, the group had formed a semicircle around Myles, who was shouting into the wind and rain, shrouded in a gray mist, fist pumping the air. When he chose to be, he could be as passionate as anyone.

She wished just then she were at his side, her fingers laced with his.

The guy in the peacoat tipped his newspaper umbrella, letting the rain dribble down. "Looks like he's waiting for someone to capture his likeness in bronze."

There it was, tucked away in the inside pocket of her jacket. Despite the rain, the lighter came to life with a single flick. The end of her cigarette burned.

McGee had stayed up all night, finishing the now illegible signs, making last-minute preparations. She'd been planning this day for weeks.

"Fuck you," she said.

They were the most gratifying words she'd spoken all day.

§

"I don't think it went that bad," Myles said.

It was late. The demonstration had been over for hours. On the way home they'd stopped for mushy bean soup and soggy french fries. Now he and McGee were lying in bed together, too tired even to remove their coats. The lights of the electrical substation outside the window pulsed along the ceiling.

"It was pretty bad."

Myles's fingers walked across the blanket until they found McGee's hand. "It was just small."

She rolled onto her side, and her hand disappeared from under his. "They're always small."

"I know what'll make you feel better." Myles pulled himself upright.

McGee flopped facedown onto her pillow. "Not that video again."

"Just once," he said. "I made it for you."

McGee rolled over and pulled the covers up to her chin. "Would you turn out the light?"

"It'll just take a minute," he said. "It'll make you feel better."

"I don't want to feel better."

He crossed the floor as slowly as he could. But it was pointless to wait for her to change her mind. And anyway, looking around the room now, he couldn't seem to find the disk he'd made. He could've sworn he'd left it on the desk, but it seemed to have disappeared.

In the dark, the substation lights above their heads shuddered like empty frames through a movie projector.

She moved over as he settled down on the mattress.

"What *do* you want?" he said.

"Your video," she said. "It would just make me cry."

He could feel her shivering, and he wanted to wrap his arms around her. "It's hopeful," he said, "not sad."

In the dark, McGee inched closer. It had been so long since they'd allowed themselves to have a quiet moment like this, just the two of them, like they'd used to have, back in the beginning. Myles wanted to tell her how much warmer it would be without all these layers between them.

"Just once," she said, "I want to win."

"Who says we're not?"

He wished he could see her face; he wished she could see his. There were simple ways to communicate understanding. The distance between them lately—it was all unnecessary.

"We've been aiming too low," she said. "Picket signs—what's the point?"

Myles propped himself up on his elbow, letting his hand come to a rest on her hip.

A strand of hair was caught on a link of the silver chain draped across her throat.

He reached around and found the thick, cold zipper of her coat. He gave it a tentative tug.

She didn't resist.

He said, "Just tell me what you want to do."

Six

THE HOUSE HAD been his grandmother's. When she died, he didn't know what else to do with it. There were already dozens of empty houses in the neighborhood that nobody wanted. Her place was small, a stuffy bungalow with a cracked foundation and paint peeling off the sides in spotted-cow-like patches. But it was free, so Michael Boni moved in. He loaded his tools into his truck, his table saw and miter saw and router table. Everything in his workshop. The few other things he owned fit into the gaps left over. Priscilla rode beside him in the passenger's seat.

The best thing about the house was the garage. It was big and airy, with plenty of space for working. The only thing in it was his grand-mother's dead Mercury, which Michael Boni rolled into the yard, mowing a path through the weeds.

He left the rest of the house almost exactly as it was. His grand-mother's furniture, her drapes, her cups and plates and tasseled lamps. He cleared the bottom drawer in the dresser for his pants and socks and underwear. He pushed her dresses in the closet a few inches to the side to make room for his shirts.

His grandmother's stuff was nicer than his anyway. She had an old walnut bedroom set and a dining room table of solid maple. The buffet was beautifully lathed. Looking at the neighborhood now, it was hard to believe people had once lived here who could afford pieces like these.

Michael Boni had never bothered to make anything decent for himself. It was all thrift-store crap—particleboard pasted with half-assed laminate, grains not found anywhere in nature. Priscilla couldn't tell the difference, and there was no one else Michael Boni felt any need to impress.

For the move to his grandmother's, he left all the junk behind for his landlord. George was an asshole anyway. He had no appreciation for Priscilla, claimed he could hear her squawking from two floors down. Two floors of brick and cement. Not to mention Priscilla was a caique, not a macaw. She'd never squawked in her life. The only time she made any noise at all was when the cops raced by. She answered their sirens with one of her own, an uncanny impression. Laced, Michael Boni liked to think, with more than a touch of mockery. But George was too dumb to appreciate the subtlety of birds. He had one of those shitty little dogs whose bark was like a finger in the eye. All night, all morning, all day, his yaps sounding to Michael Boni like a challenge. *Break break break my neck break break break break my neck.*

Let that asshole throw the shitty furniture away.

Michael Boni got by on his grandmother's food, too. Her pantry looked like a munitions depot. There were stockpiles of beans and tomatoes and corn and everything and anything that could be found *en escabeche.* But most of all there was *pozole.* Case after case after case of the stuff. Until he found her supply, he'd had no idea pozole even came by the can. He was no purist, but he couldn't picture his *abuela* pouring anything into a bowl and calling it dinner, the gurgle and suck and greasy splash. His grandfather had brought her here from

Michoacán. Michoacán to Michigan. Maybe the name had persuaded her it wouldn't be so different from home. Grandpa had heard there was good money to be made up north assembling chassis and stamping fenders. He was right about the money, but he'd underestimated the cold. Abuela never forgave him for that. Shortly before Michael Boni's mother died, she admitted Grandma had been a bitter old lady by the time she was twenty. His grandmother had spent the long Michigan winters stirring endless pots of hominy and pork shoulder, keeping warm by the stove. But eventually she must have modernized, like the factories. It made no difference to Michael Boni. The stuff in the can tasted almost exactly like what he remembered from when he was a kid. It seemed all Abuela had added was a garnish of cilantro and a squeeze of lime.

By the time she died, she couldn't have made pozole from scratch even if she'd wanted to. The Mercury's tires had been flat for years, and the neighborhood had become a wasteland. The only available food hung in cellophane wrappers from gas station pegboards. The neighborhood was biding its time until the wrecking ball came.

Only now that it was too late did Michael Boni realize he'd done nothing to help her. He'd been a horrible grandson. But then again, she'd never seemed to care much for being a grandmother. The cold had ruined her. When he was a kid, there'd been a dairy less than a block away, and she'd often sent him there for milk and butter, always with exact change. She believed ice cream caused nightmares, or at least that's what she said. She was the kind of person no one grew overly attached to. Everyone else in the family but Michael Boni had moved away, many of them following their parents' old jobs south. But even the ones who'd gone only as far as Dearborn never thought to come back for a visit.

Michael Boni had barely known his grandfather, who'd bought this house when he'd started working at Dodge Main, just before the war. He'd timed it perfectly. He'd joined at the boom, and he'd left just before the bust. The year after he retired, pension in hand, the auto plant was razed. The year after that, when Michael Boni was eight, his grandfather died of a heart attack. Or as his father put it once, Grandpa retired once and for all from Grandma.

Grandma had outlived them all. His parents, his sister. She'd outlived the neighborhood, too. The dairy was now an empty cube of cinderblock. The barbershop she'd been too cheap to send Michael Boni to had burned down to the crossbeams. What remained looked like the exoskeleton of a giant insect.

Her house was on the corner. There was an overgrown hedge and bars on the windows. The garage was around back. Michael Boni built a new workbench below the only window, which looked out over the pair of empty lots across the street. He spent a lot of time staring out that window, waiting for glue to dry and joints to set. The empty lots made for an awkward view. What he saw when he looked outside were the naked backs of a pair of houses a block over. After a while, he began to feel indecent, as if he were accidentally seeing up a woman's skirt.

Mr. Childs had lived in one of those lots when Michael Boni was a kid. Mr. Childs had been a spot welder, and Michael Boni remembered him spending his Saturdays tuning up an old Triumph in the driveway, rattling the glass in his grandmother's china cabinet. She'd had a special hatred for Mr. Childs. What little Spanish Michael Boni knew he'd learned while she stood with her arms crossed, scowling over the hedge. The motorcycle didn't need half the work Mr. Childs put into it, but even as a boy Michael Boni could appreciate the lengths certain people went to just to piss his grandmother off.

The only immediate neighbor now was Constance, who was seventy-something and lived alone in a Craftsman with a roof felted in mold. Constance's son had moved her to the neighborhood the year before, wanting her to be close to her great-grandchildren. Michael Boni had never heard his grandmother mention Constance. It wasn't until he moved in that he realized how odd that was, two old ladies living side by side with nothing else to do but meddle in each other's business.

71

Several days after the funeral, Michael Boni had come to look at his grandmother's house. He hadn't spent much time there since he was a child. Once both his parents were dead, he'd lost touch not just with Abuela but also with his cousins and aunts and uncles, all of whom claimed they couldn't afford to make it to town for the services. That day he saw Constance sitting on the porch next door and went over to introduce himself.

"I'm thinking about moving in," he'd said.

Constance had rocked back in her chair and scratched her armpit. "I'm not going to try to stop you."

And that was the moment Michael Boni began to wonder if maybe the block hadn't been big enough for Constance and his grandmother to share.

Constance hadn't gone to the funeral. But her son Clifford had, a black man dressed like a WASP accountant in khakis and a button-up. For two hours, he and Michael Boni were the only living bodies in that cold, curtained parlor, and as they left the funeral home afterward, Clifford took Michael Boni aside and shook his hand with a double clasp, as if he were greeting a foreign dignitary.

"Your grandmother was a wonderful lady," Clifford said. "We went shopping together almost every week."

There was something about the man that made Michael Boni want to behave badly.

"You kept her in pozole," he said.

Clifford's grip grew firmer. "Someone had to."

It was a mystery to Michael Boni why Clifford remained in the neighborhood instead of joining the genuine WASP accountants in Bloomfield Hills. And why he was willing to move Constance to such a wretched place. Except it turned out that Clifford wasn't an accountant at all. He made his actual living selling discount cell phones, and this neighborhood was all he could afford, having to support not just himself and his wife but also his mother, his daughter, and her two children. The daughter and her two girls lived with him, too, in his tiny three-bedroom rowhouse with a neat bed of flowers. All that was missing was the white picket fence.

One damp morning in late April, after Michael Boni had been living in his grandmother's house for about a month, he was standing at his workbench, planing away at a piece of oak, and he happened to look up. Through the foggy window he saw Constance in the empty lot across the street, wearing a purple floral housedress beneath a gray cardigan sweater, black rain boots reaching past her hem. The boots were so bulky, they made it look as if she didn't have legs, as if the muddy earth were in the process of swallowing her whole. A cloudy plastic milk jug hung heavily from her fingers. Constance was staring at the ground, turning in a slow, halting circle, as if looking for something she'd lost.

She seemed so old and so confused that Michael Boni decided to go out and help her. But just as he was brushing the wood shavings from his sleeves, Constance started back to her house. That was the last he saw of her that day.

But the next morning, at almost exactly the same time, she was back, standing in the same spot in the empty lot. Wearing the same dress, same sweater, same rain boots, even though the ground had dried overnight. And with the same milk jug in hand, Constance turned in the same slow circle. But this time Michael Boni noticed something spilling from the jug, splashing from the earth, onto her boots. She looked like a homeless shaman performing some kind of mystic ceremony for ancient ghosts. Michael Boni's first thought was of Mr. Childs and his departed Triumph. His second thought was dementia. Constance was losing her marbles, and Michael Boni's thoughts wandered to the conversation in which he got to break the news to Clifford.

"Your mother's a wonderful lady," he'd say, clutching the man's hand with two of his own. "I've been keeping an eye on her when you're not around. I'm sorry to have to be the one to tell you she's batshit crazy."

Constance repeated her ritual every day that week: purple dress, rain boots, milk jug, circle.

Finally on Friday morning, as he watched her return for yet another round, Michael Boni decided he'd seen enough. From the window in the garage, he followed her through all her usual gestures. And when she was done and turned to go, he raced for the door.

"Morning," he said, reaching the front walkway just as she was clopping by in her rubber boots. But he'd forgotten to take off his dust mask, and his greeting had seeped out like a demented moan.

Constance froze like a squirrel. The milk jug slipped from her fingers, the plastic folding in on itself as it hit the sidewalk, liquid glugging out into the street.

Constance clutched her cardigan. "Jesus Christ."

Michael Boni stooped to pick up the jug, sliding the mask down to his chin. "I don't think it's broken."

"It's not exactly an heirloom."

He handed it back to her. "I thought it might be important."

She turned the jug upside down, and one last trickle dribbled out.

"It doesn't matter," she said. "Nothing will grow."

Michael Boni studied the crust of dried mud on her boots. "It's a garden," he said, trying not to sound surprised.

She poked her finger in the dented plastic. "What did you think?"

He was already on his way across the street. "Can I see?"

The lot looked no better from up close than it had from the garage. Plastic wrappers and aluminum cans stood out among the weeds and dirt like baubles on a dead Christmas tree. Constance pointed to a dark spot in the soil. A stick poked out of the ground, propping up nothing.

Constance's eyes sifted through the features of his face. "Think you can do better?"

He wouldn't even have known where to begin. Even Priscilla knew better than to count on him. When she was hungry, she stabbed his knuckles with her beak. When the cage needed cleaning, she kicked her droppings onto the carpet.

"What is it?" he said.

"Lettuce."

"I don't think it likes it here."

Michael Boni squatted down, as if getting closer would make things clearer. Not knowing what else to do, he grabbed a pinch of wet soil, rubbing it between his fingers the way farmers in movies did. When the grit was gone, he discovered in his palm a piece of smooth green glass in the shape of Brazil.

"Maybe it's the dirt," he said. From his haunches, Michael Boni surveyed the rest of the lot, imagining Mr. Childs with his solvents and oilcans.

Constance let the milk jug plunk down at her feet.

Michael Boni pressed his hands to his thighs and pushed himself up. The gesture made him feel wise. "Maybe your son could help."

Constance responded with something between a snort and a sigh, and then she walked away, leaving the milk jug where it lay in the dirt.

Three days later, the milk jug was still there. It hadn't rained, and when Michael Boni walked over to check on things, the ground was hard and dry, like baked pottery. He still wasn't sure what he was looking for. He wouldn't know a lettuce from a sycamore tree. But it was easy to see nothing, and nothing was the only thing there.

He went back across the street to his workshop. The woodpile was full of scraps, but none of them were more than a foot or two long. Among his few full-length boards was nothing he wasn't saving. There were a pair of yellow pine two-by-sixes he'd bought to replace some bowed rafters in the garage. And in the corner, stacked securely by themselves, were a half-dozen one-by-sixes of quarter-sawn oak, the grain marbled like filet mignon. The stuff had cost a fortune, and he'd been saving it for something special.

It took only a minute to cut the pine to size. He made a rectangular frame, six feet by four. He joined the corners by mortise and tenon. It was overkill, but he could be sure it would hold. When he was done, he hiked the frame onto his shoulder and carried it to the lot, centering it over Constance's stick as if it were a piece of art.

There was a gnarled old hickory in the corner of his grandmother's yard. Within the span of its limbs, the grass didn't grow. The spot was too shady, and a dozen years' worth of unraked leaves and rot ringed the trunk. But under the leaves the earth was black and loose and moist. Michael Boni didn't have a wheelbarrow, so he carried the dirt across the street a bucket at a time. It took him six hours to fill the frame. By the time he was done, it looked as though he'd dug a burial plot.

In the morning, Priscilla shuffled on the counter while Michael Boni made coffee. She seemed anxious, moving back and forth, back and forth.

"What is it?"

She allowed him to scratch her head, but without her usual bliss. She made it seem as if she were doing him a favor, her deep black eyes locked on him in cold judgment. He couldn't hide anything from her. The favor he'd done Constance had cost him. Priscilla knew he'd fallen behind. By now, the table he was making was supposed to have legs. The whole thing was supposed to be delivered by the end of the week.

"I know," he said, rubbing Priscilla's throat. "No more distractions."

But the first thing he did when he arrived at the workshop, a few minutes later, was look out the window. There he found Constance hunched over the garden bed. Michael Boni pressed his face to the glass, trying to read her expression. She seemed to be puzzling through what the wood and soil meant, how it might have gotten there. And then she took a small envelope from her pocket, turned it upside down, and let every last seed spill into the dirt.

For three days Michael Boni didn't talk to Constance, but he continued to watch her through the window while he worked. She'd popped the dents out of the milk jug. Several times a day she let water rain down on the new seeds. The rest of the time she waited. She'd carried a kitchen chair over to the lot, and the legs sank down into the dirt beside the bed. There she napped.

By the end of the week, Michael Boni was only a day behind schedule, and Priscilla was once again flopping onto her back to let him rub her belly.

On Saturday evening they were in the kitchen, Michael Boni warming up his dinner. There was a knock on the door. More like a hammering, the screen quaking in its hinges.

Constance stood on the porch with the dusky sky at her back. She was striking the door frame with her shoulder, spackled in dirt from nail to elbow. She held up her arms as if she were a surgeon, as if she were waiting for Michael Boni to remove her bloody scrubs.

"What'd you do?" he said through the screen.

"We need fertilizer."

"I don't know anything about that."

"Manure," she said.

Behind him, the covered pot was rattling on the stove. "Maybe your son could help you."

"Like *you* helped your grandmother?" she said, her rubber boots tromping back down the steps.

Back in the kitchen, Priscilla was hopping around on the table, agitated by the splattering pozole.

"It's all right," Michael Boni said.

He turned off the burner, and Priscilla let out a whistle that sounded like the dying throes of a teapot.

Now that they had an entire house to themselves, Priscilla had her own room, and Michael Boni had built a chicken-wire addition to her old cage. She had a duplex now, with an exercise room full of balls and plastic rings and knots of rope. But Priscilla was in her cage only when he was away or in the shop. The rest of the time she had the run of the place. Nothing was off limits, partly because she didn't understand no, and partly because Michael Boni never bothered to say no. She liked to fly to the top of his grandmother's dresser and open up the jewelry box, dropping Abuela's earrings and necklaces and rings over the edge. She loved to watch them fall.

He was sitting down at the kitchen table when the knocking started up again.

"Just come in!" he shouted.

The screen door moaned, and Constance's boots squished irritable questions down the hall. Then she stood in the doorway to the kitchen, hosed clean, her arms dripping wet.

Priscilla raised her wings.

"It's okay," Michael Boni said to the bird. "Settle down. Settle down." He scratched two fingers along the back of her head.

And then he turned to Constance. "I don't know anything about manure."

The old woman folded her arms on top of her bosom, and a darkness spread across the purple flowers. "I just need you to drive."

The truck she produced—from where, he couldn't guess—was an old blue Chevy with a red side panel. The front bumper was a pair of two-by-twelves sandwiched together and bolted to the frame. There were two shovels in the back.

"No way," Michael Boni said when he saw the tools. "You said I only had to drive."

"Get in," she said. "Don't be such a whiner."

He'd been expecting her to ask to borrow his truck, and he'd been rehearsing ways of telling her why there was no way in hell he was going to let that happen. Without his truck, the entire plan would be shot. It had never occurred to him he'd actually have to follow through.

She directed him onto the freeway, heading east. Constance explained that a woman at the drugstore had a cousin who'd worked at the Detroit Hunt Club for two summers. According to her, the stables were full of manure, free for the taking.

"Are you sure?" Michael Boni said.

She turned away, reaching down into her boot to pull up her stocking. "If you had a barn full of shit," she said, "wouldn't you want someone to take it?"

After five or six miles, they exited, and soon they were passing through a neat, shady street lined with fastidious brick cottages. The houses grew gradually larger, adding acres and stories. And then the suburban street gave way to a green pasture hemmed with whitened fence rails.

Even as they were driving up the long, narrow lane to the stables, Michael Boni thought the whole idea seemed unlikely. Someone had probably already taken one look at the truck and called the cops. But then a stable hand appeared, leading him and Constance behind the stable to a squat, glistening pile, upon which a swarm of flies danced in drunken ecstasy.

Michael Boni's disbelief changed to dismay.

"Get the shovels," Constance said.

Michael Boni went to the truck, and when he returned, he handed both of the shovels to Constance. The stable hand was a well-scrubbed college girl, someone who knew her days dealing with manure were numbered. She looked at Michael Boni and wrinkled her nose.

He raised his hands in innocence. "She said I only had to drive."

The girl rolled her eyes and said to let her know when they were done.

Constance shuffled over to the pile. The first shovel entered with a horrible sucking sound.

"Fine," Michael Boni said as he dragged his feet over to join her.

He tried to keep his eyes elsewhere. The smell wasn't as bad as he'd expected, but he tried not to think about it. The consistency of the stuff was the worst part. If he wasn't careful, half of it would stick to the shovel. Or worse yet, fall on his shoe. Unlike Constance's, his weren't made of rubber. But he found that if he used the shovel as if he were stabbing a pizza in the oven—jerking it back at the last second—the stuff slid right off, mostly.

"So tell me again why your son can't help you with this stuff?" Michael Boni said as they were driving home afterward.

Constance was leaning back against the headrest, her eyes closed.

He was tired and sweaty, and all he could smell was the stables.

Her eyelids fluttered as they hit a bump. "Clifford has certain ideas about what old ladies should and shouldn't do. His main idea is I should babysit his granddaughters."

Michael Boni had seen the girls only in passing. They were maybe ten and fourteen, and he never knew what to say to them.

"It must be nice to be able to spend time with them," he said.

Constance rolled her head to the side and gazed at him in disappointment. "They don't want someone watching over them any more than I do."

In the rearview mirror he saw that the pile of manure had slid toward the gate, like a wave frozen midcrest. Whose job was it going to be to clean it out?

"Did my grandmother ever talk about me?" he said.

"She said you made beautiful things."

Michael Boni tried to remember what his grandmother might

have seen of his work. Of course, it occurred to him now that he'd never made anything for her.

It must have been seven or eight years ago. He recalled having been in the neighborhood, a sleigh bed in the back of his pickup. He'd been working on it for months, and that was the day he was making the delivery. He'd stopped in, and his grandmother had made tea, which he hadn't touched, and they'd sat together in mute discomfort.

When it was time to go, he'd invited her to come outside. As they walked to the truck in the driveway, he remembered telling her about all the work he'd done. For once, he didn't bother to hide how proud he was, pointing out the rosettes in the headboard and the bed's four feet, which had taken him days to carve by hand. At first it didn't seem as if she were going to say anything, but then his grandmother rose to her toes and touched the cherry wood, which he'd sanded till it was smooth as glass.

"Your grandfather," she said, "he was handy, too."

"Handy?" Michael Boni repeated. Without another word, he climbed into the cab and shut the door. He was a craftsman, an artist with wood. He was so annoyed he couldn't even bring himself to wave goodbye.

"Are you asking if you're done serving your penance?" Constance said now, rolling down her window.

Michael Boni nodded.

"No."

After the manure, it was as if Constance were planting magic beans. She dropped seeds into the bed, and they seemed to shoot up on contact: lettuce, cabbages, greens, peppers, beans, and peas. Michael Boni watched her sometimes from the window while he tacked and sanded. But he was careful to stay on his side of the street. He'd finally finished the table, two weeks behind schedule. Now a contractor he'd worked with a few times before had hired him to build an entire kitchen's worth of cabinets. Michael Boni knew, even without judgmental looks from Priscilla, that he couldn't afford to fall any further behind. But it was hard to see Constance out there for hours at a time, bending, lifting. She was seventy-something, after all, and she moved as stiff and slow as a tower crane. It was easy to see why Clifford disapproved of the project. Even Michael Boni was afraid that one day he'd look up and she'd be flat on her back with a buzzard on her chest, as bad off from his help as his own grandmother had been from his neglect.

The vegetables were endlessly forgiving of the fact that Constance had no idea what she was doing. It seemed never to have crossed her mind that different plants preferred different seasons, different kinds of sunlight, different types of soil. He doubted she even looked at the envelopes before dumping them into the ground. She scattered the stuff like grass seed. The birds flew away with most of it.

For weeks he watched the plants in the bed swell to the point that it looked as if not even the mortise and tenon could hold them. One afternoon, standing at his workbench in a respirator, holding a chamois dipped in benzine, he happened to look out and see Constance's disembodied hand floating in a tangle of plants, grasping for something. It was a scene straight out of a low-budget horror film, an old woman swallowed by her garden.

Michael Boni put down the chamois and walked over to the wood bin, already knowing what he'd find. He'd used up the pine for the rafters. All that was left was the beautiful quarter-sawn oak. It would take only half an hour to get to the lumberyard and back with some shitty landscape timbers. He could fill his entire pickup for the price of just one of the oak boards.

Ten minutes later Michael Boni was crossing the street with the new frame on his shoulder. When she saw him coming, Constance set down her tools. Michael Boni lowered the oak beside the dirty, swollen pine. Constance bent over, running her finger along the buttery swirls in the grain.

"Gorgeous," she said, and she patted Michael Boni on the shoulder. "Now that's really going to piss off Clifford."

Michael Boni built a dozen frames that spring. He must have filled a thousand buckets with dirt. It didn't take long for his grandmother's backyard to run out of topsoil. By late June, all that remained was the patch underneath the old Mercury. Eventually the contractor stopped calling to ask about the kitchen cabinets.

As the garden grew larger and the harvests more plentiful, neighbors suddenly began to appear, reconnaissance missions disguised as leisurely strolls. They stopped and greeted Constance from the sidewalk, and she waved from her crouch among the collard greens. Sometimes she pointed to a bucket full of the day's pickings and told them to take what they wanted. She had no interest in exchanging pleasantries.

The only time Constance stopped what she was doing was when her great-granddaughters came by. Mostly Michael Boni saw Clementine, the younger one, who seemed to live outside, maybe in a burrow. She was always popping up among the weeds like a groundhog, wearing a second skin of dirt. She was the complete opposite of her older sister, who walked around outdoors as though on a hostile alien planet, the air poisonous to her lungs. Constance gave Clementine things to eat from the bucket, still coated in grit. He could tell where the girl had been by the trail she left of partially chewed broccoli crowns and cucumber marrows.

"Is it good?" he asked her one day when he found her sitting on a rock, gnawing on a radish.

"No." Clementine tossed the hard red knot into the dirt and wandered off.

The fact that she tried at all made her braver than him. The only use Michael Boni had for the things Constance grew was as bribes for forgiveness. All he had to do was stand at the kitchen counter chopping peas and carrots and kale, and Priscilla would dance in the sink and purr, scraping the steel with her claws.

One night Constance sent Michael Boni home with a sack of okra. While his own dinner warmed on the stove, he went to let Priscilla out of her cage. She followed him back into the kitchen, and Michael Boni got out his grandmother's slab of butcher block. With Priscilla watching beside him, he cut the okra up into little pieces, and she looked up at him with love in her eyes, or at least what looked like love, and Michael Boni could tell he'd touched something in that prehistoric dinosaur brain of hers, and that connection filled him with a primal sort of happiness, as if the universe had cracked open, and inside there was man and there was bird, living together in a state of harmony he could feel but never hope to comprehend.

That night he went to bed still feeling that warm glow, and in his sleep he dreamed of chickens.

He was awakened by the sound of a truck chugging out in the street. He got out of bed and went over to the window, pushing aside the heavy curtains. That borrowed blue Chevy was parked beside the garden, facing the wrong way. Constance stood behind the tailgate, lit up by the exhaust. It took Michael Boni a moment to make sense of what the hands on his grandmother's alarm clock were trying to tell him.

It was four in the morning.

Constance held a box. He could make out what looked like two more at her feet. The boxes were big, and they looked heavy, and she was out there all alone. Michael Boni pulled on his pants and boots.

The only working streetlight was down the block near Clifford's house. It was an overcast night, and Michael Boni felt an unexpected chill. It was early June now, and he wasn't sorry to have a break from the swelter.

Constance was standing by the fender when he arrived, wiping her hands on her coat. The canvas was smeared from the hem all the way up to the corduroy collar. Underneath she wore her purple floral dress.

"What're you doing?" he said.

"What's it look like?"

Two of the boxes already rested in the back of the truck. Michael Boni bent down and picked up the last one from the street. The cardboard sagged between his fingers. Below the loose flaps he saw something green and leafy.

"Where are you taking this?"

Constance walked over to the driver's side and opened the door, placing one foot on the running board. "Are you coming or not?"

"Does Clifford know?"

Constance rocked herself backward, and Michael Boni got there just in time to put a hand on her back and guide her up into the cab. With the door still open, she shifted from park to drive, and the transmission fell with a thud.

"All right," he said. "Move over."

The roads along the way were almost entirely empty, but the market was lit up like a movie set. It was Saturday, farmers' market day. Michael Boni had never been, but he knew about the place, an urban excursion for the weekend brunch set.

Even though the market wasn't open yet, the loading docks of the two biggest sheds were plugged with trucks, real trucks. There were six blocks of open-air stalls, six covered sheds in all. Flanneled, farmery-looking people were everywhere, shouting and pointing, shifting tables, hauling crates and dollies.

"Where do I go?" Michael Boni said.

Constance pointed to the corner of one of the smaller sheds, a spot between a loading dock and a fire hydrant. The pavement was slashed with yellow lines.

"I don't think we're allowed."

"It's fine," she said.

He pulled in as directed, and Constance reached over and turned off the ignition.

"What now?" he said.

She leaned back and let her head recline against the seat. "We wait."

When Michael Boni woke up, he was alone. The sky outside the windshield was no longer black and white. The clouds were turning caramel.

A noise had startled him from sleep. Now he heard it again, a dull scraping coming from somewhere behind him. He raised his eyes to the rearview mirror. Constance was stretching into the bed of the pickup. By the time he got out to join her, she'd already removed one of the boxes.

The cardboard had rotted even more since the last time Michael Boni had touched them. Stacked together, the boxes teetered in his arms like pillows. He had a bad feeling about all this.

"Where to?"

She started walking. He followed a few steps back, peering around the stack as best he could. He had no idea where his feet were falling.

She walked for about a block. "Here," she said from somewhere in front of him.

He shuffled in a half circle to get a better look. They were standing at the edge of one of the open-air shelters. A pillar rose from a low concrete footer.

"Where should I put them?"

She pointed to the sidewalk.

"Don't we need a table?"

She reached out toward the pillar and eased herself down. "What for?"

There were three rows of booths running through the shelter. Constance had wedged herself directly at the end of the middle row, an obstacle to anyone trying to get anywhere.

"Don't you need some sort of permit?" Michael Boni said.

Constance was elbow-deep in one of the boxes, rooting around for something.

"I'm going to go check things out," he said. If her own son couldn't talk sense to her, what could Michael Boni be expected to do?

He turned into the first open doorway he came upon and found himself standing in an enormous hangar-like space, one of the two largest sheds. He had to crane his neck to find the ceiling. Up there it was mostly girders and skylights, the early morning sun making the panes of glass throb beyond their frames.

While they'd been asleep in the truck, the market had opened. The suburban mobs were already here, a kaleidoscope of brightly colored T-shirts and canvas shopping bags. From the doorway, Michael Boni couldn't see any of the booths. There were too many bodies jammed together in slow-moving eddies, blocking his view. He stepped forward into the nearest current, letting it sweep him away.

His first impression was that the place felt less like a market than like a crowded museum, everyone around him eyeing pyramids of fruit and vegetables as if they were sculptures. A skeletal young woman in a tank top ran a finger along a stretch of eggplants and zucchini and cucumbers, never once picking anything up, as if content just to be in their presence. Michael Boni was heartened by the sight of an elderly couple, the man an old-world throwback in a felt fedora and baggy wool pants. His wife, in a plain brown dress, was frowning at a pile of tomatoes while the old man clenched a twisted root of ginger.

Michael Boni made two full circuits of the building, going up one side and then back down the other, and by the time he returned to where he'd started from, he'd seen every vegetable, every jar of local honey and preserves, every gluten-free scone, every pot of organic basil and sprig of thyme. And he realized, looking back, that every vendor in here—every member of the flannel brigade—was white. And so too were most of the shoppers. It was as if they'd somehow claimed this tiny sliver of the city for themselves. There was Michael Boni and Constance and a black guy selling ribs from a smoky barbecue and another playing spoons on the sidewalk. And then there was everyone else.

There were so many people coming into the shed now that it was hard to get back outside. He had to squeeze sideways through the double doors.

The moment he reached the sidewalk, Michael Boni heard the squawk of a walkie-talkie. Beside the pillar where he'd left Constance stood a bald, spectacled man carrying a clipboard. Constance was still squatting among her boxes, palming a head of lettuce in each of her outstretched hands.

"Ma'am," the man with the clipboard was saying, "there are procedures."

"Lettuce!" Constance's head appeared between the man's calves, shouting to everyone passing by. "Here's some lettuce."

"Ma'am," the bald man said, tapping the clipboard. "You have to go."

"Just let her be," Michael Boni said.

"I wish I could—" The man with the clipboard took a step back as Michael Boni appeared beside him.

"You can," Michael Boni said, coming the same half-step forward. "You can turn around and walk away."

"I can't do that." The bald man turned to look for something. *Someone*, as it turned out. There was a cop offering directions to the driver of a car idling in the street. "All these people have permits," the bald man said. "All of them have paid."

Michael Boni reached for his wallet. "How much is it?"

"There are forms," the man said. "There's a process."

Michael Boni realized his pockets were empty. He'd left the house without having any idea where he'd end up. He reached for the clipboard instead. "Are those the forms?"

The man jerked away. "No, this is . . . something else."

"Go get the forms," Michael Boni said. "I'll fill them out. I'll pay the fee."

"That's not how it works," the man said. The color was rising in his cheeks.

The car in the street pulled away, and as the cop turned back toward the sidewalk, it occurred to Michael Boni to wonder if their truck had already been towed. He looked down at Constance. The crumbling boxes were exactly as full as when he'd carried them here, except for the lettuce in each of Constance's hands.

Michael Boni was on unfamiliar ground. But the one thing he knew for sure was that he wouldn't be bringing the boxes back home. The stuff could be taken or eaten, by man or by rat, rained on, stepped on, or rotted into mush. He didn't care. He wouldn't be taking the stuff anywhere. Let clipboard man throw the boxes into the Dumpster if he wanted.

"Come on," Michael Boni said, reaching down for Constance's hand. She took his fingers without argument, dropping the lettuce at his feet. One of the heads tried to roll away, and Michael Boni stopped it with the toe of his boot. The lettuce had such a pleasing roundness, about the size of a bowling ball, but with just the right amount of give. He struck it with the top of his laces, just as his old soccer coaches had always instructed. The lettuce made the most wonderful sound as it exploded against the bald man's shin.

Only now, almost a year later, at the start of his second spring in his grandmother's house—the second season of Constance's garden—was Michael Boni able to see the true importance of that lettuce.

"Do you understand?" he said to Darius. "Do you get what it means?" It was hard to put such a thing—a symbol—into words.

They were sitting on a blown-out truck tire in a playground not far from Michael Boni's old apartment. It was their new meeting place, now that the plaza downtown had become too dangerous, too exposed. Here there was even a crooked lean-to near the monkey bars in case it happened to rain.

"I get it," Darius said. "I get it."

Michael Boni might have believed him, if Darius hadn't said it twice.

The chains were missing from the swing set. The seats were gone from the teeter-totter. The sandbox had been dug down to dirt. A woman had been found dead in the bushes here not long ago. Michael Boni knew better than to come around at night. But during the day it was safe enough.

"My grandmother," Michael Boni said, "she wasted away here. And I didn't do anything to help." Darius didn't need to know what a wretched soul she'd been. Anyone deserved better than what she got.

"I need to know you understand," Michael Boni said. "This lettuce . . ."

Darius nodded unconvincingly.

"All you need," Michael Boni said, "is a clean slate."

Constance had shown them what was possible. Something new could grow.

The lettuce was an opening salvo, a declaration of war.

Seven

WINDED FROM THE short walk down the corridor from the conference room, Mrs. Freeman blustered past the upraised glance of her administrative assistant and charged on through to her office. As she let the heavy oak door shush behind her, she heard a familiar voice call her name. But rather than stop, she let momentum carry her forward, all the way to the window. Having spent the last two hours sitting like a stuffed owl at the end of a conference table, Ruth Freeman decided she would rather remain there, looking out upon the city, than have to experience, so soon after the first, yet another annoyance.

The sight outside was not pretty. Indeed, the landscape was as depressing as the foreign films of which her husband was so fond. And yet Mrs. Freeman felt she might have stayed that way for the rest of the day, peacefully staring off into the horizon, through the rain and the fog, had her administrative assistant not finally, intrusively, appeared at her side.

"What is it?" Mrs. Freeman said.

"I've been going over the presentation," Tiphany said. "Your notes—I've been trying to put them together. But I notice there's nothing in here—that is, you make no mention—"

"Yes," Mrs. Freeman said, "yes," drawing out the *s* as if it were a slow leak through which her administrative assistant might escape.

"But you promised the board . . . They're waiting for your—have you gone through the reports?"

"Reports," said Mrs. Freeman, turning once again toward the window.

"Did you read Arthur's memo, Ruth?" Tiphany said, trying to move into Mrs. Freeman's line of vision. "I put it on your desk. People have been asking questions. Eldenrod at the paper. And with these demonstrations, Arthur's afraid—"

"Arthur is always afraid."

"I hope you don't mind, but I took the liberty . . ." Tiphany paused and handed Mrs. Freeman a sheet of paper.

In a glance she saw him, spread across the page: Arthur, panicking over trifles, creating pandemonium, which, in an office full of people utterly incapable of thinking for themselves, was as easy as setting fire to gasoline. And then there was her administrative assistant, who saw chaos as career advancement. Mrs. Freeman could imagine Tiphany hunched over the report, inserting her self-serving notes, and she felt herself a bit like some unfortunate king whose good nature and honesty put him at the mercy of earls and lords overendowed with hubris. Although part of her, the part that had once thought of itself as an intellectual, would have liked to be able to remember some specific king and the actual plot that had done him in, the more practical side of Mrs. Freeman was content to have remembered the gist of it.

"I mentioned we're hiring a consultant," Tiphany began again, "that we're going to discredit—"

"You'd have me deny it all," Mrs. Freeman said, waving the paper at her assistant and then dropping it back on top of the folder before turning once again to the window.

Mrs. Freeman was conscious of noises behind her, whiny ones that brushed up against her neck and made her shiver, but she found that if she concentrated her attention elsewhere, down into the alley below, for instance, the sound grew less and less irritating until finally it went away.

Mrs. Freeman knew what Arthur wanted to hear, and she could see even in a quick skimming that Tiphany had provided it: denial, obfuscation. But now, turning her gaze west toward the suburbs, in the direction of her home, where her husband was at that moment eating plain yogurt and scanning the newspaper for arcane facts with which to quiz her over dinner, Mrs. Freeman decided that this time she could not, would not, give Arthur the answer he was looking for.

"This particular catastrophe," she said, addressing the wet, misty interstate overpass outside her window, "is what was once, in more prosaic times, known as 'collateral damage.' But in recent years we have begun to think of such casualties as remnants of a primitive past—something akin to raccoon coats and flagpole sitting. We seem to have forgotten that in wars people die, and not because of the quality of our craftsmanship, but because war is distasteful."

Yes, she thought, she would say that and not a word more. The company expected her to apply a balm, as if with some possible combination of syllables she could return charred schools to their virgin state—as if it were her responsibility, as if she or the company had anything to apologize for. A story might come out in the paper. Stories were always coming out in papers. There would be no point in challenging the facts, which would undoubtedly be correct: sometimes missiles landed where they shouldn't. Sad? Yes. But scandalous? Not at all. It was simply inevitable, one of the unfortunate costs of war.

Mrs. Freeman recalled a story she had once heard from one of her more philosophically inclined acquaintances—a rare highlight from an otherwise tiresome dinner party. The story was about a Swiss engineer, a man who around the time of the First World War had come to the United States determined to answer the problem of how to drop bombs from airplanes. That is, so the bombs might hit an actual target, rather than landing wherever they might, left to guess-work and chance and the pull of gravity. It was a problem no one until then had managed to solve. The Swiss engineer's solution, after years of work, involved gyroscopes and gears and more math and physics than Mrs. Freeman could ever hope to understand. But the details were beside the point. The curious piece was the engineer's motivation: not to win wars, but to do God's will. He was a good Christian, of the old-fashioned variety. He believed a precise bomb-sight would reduce human suffering, narrowing destruction only to what needed to be destroyed. And he succeeded, introducing the precision and accuracy no one else could. And yet still one nagging problem remained, then as now: a bombsight depended, above all else, on sight. Over the last decade, HSI's engineers had developed a drone that could blow the cap off a pop bottle from thirty thousand feet. But first you still had to know where the bottle cap was.

Were it up to Mrs. Freeman, there would be no blowing up of anything. She would let the missiles rust in their weapon bays, deter-rents for worst-case scenarios. But as long as there was a need, she felt no guilt about her work; nor could she agree with those cloudy-minded idealists who had begun to pollute the plaza outside the building like so much discarded chewing gum. She would gladly add her name to any list of signatories opposed to armed aggression, but she was no longer naïve enough to believe one could dissolve an army and defend oneself instead with wishful thinking. Arthur might fret and Tiphany plot, but in this case they were beyond reproach, and with nothing left to be resolved, Mrs. Freeman saw no reason to attend to the buzz of her intercom. Let it nag if it wished. She had moved on.

"Your one-fifteen," cracked a voice over the speakerphone, Tiphany changing tacks.

"Fine," Mrs. Freeman called over her shoulder. "Send him in." And in the pause that followed, she caught herself gazing around her office, one of the few habits of her former life she had never managed to break—the need to make sure everything was in order before company arrived. But the place was as it always was, as she had aspired for it to be: good enough. It was not the largest or most impressive room in the building, but Mrs. Freeman had grown tired of offices she couldn't pace without getting winded. On the day she'd toured the third floor of the newly constructed HSI Building, scouting for the office that would be her hermitage five days a week, Mrs. Freeman had taken only one look out the windows at the front of the building, at the view of a street lined with other office buildings, all that sterile glass like dead shark eyes. That day Mrs. Freeman had determined the proper place for her was as far from all that as she could get, which proved to be a room designated to hold file cabinets, along a forgotten corridor at the back of the building. Her new office had the same full wall of windows as the rest of her colleagues, but hers were shaded, without need for blinds or tints, by the interstate overpass. Here the landscape was of empty billboards and brick walls painted with faded advertisements, all of which, even if they were only remnants, comforted her like a favorite moth-eaten sweater, reminding her of a familiar world, the very industrial wasteland where she'd gotten her start.

With the exception of her office and those belonging to the lowest rung and most unnecessary members of middle management, the rest of the rooms overlooking the alley housed files or hosted meetings with clients and suppliers no one cared to impress. The relative squalor in which Mrs. Freeman worked clearly upset her administrative assistant, whose makeshift desk in the darkest, most out-of-the-way corner of the hallway was degrading and embarrassing and was most likely the catalyst for Tiphany's designs and ambitions. But Mrs. Freeman felt she had reached an age at which her comfort, as well as her diversions, could deservedly come at someone else's inconvenience. Surely she had earned that much.

Mrs. Freeman wished now that she had told Tiphany that she wasn't ready to see her one-fifteen. There were so many things she would rather have been doing than to have to endure yet another meeting, but had Mrs. Freeman tried to tell Tiphany—whose *ph* always made her bite her lower lip a fraction of a second too long—that she was busy or indisposed or that she needed to reschedule, she knew what the young woman would have said, so well was she conditioned: *Wouldn't it be better to see him now, Ruth, while you have a few minutes, rather than later when you'll have to work around your afternoon appointments? You have a busy day . . .* Et cetera, et cetera, and, of course, Tiphany would then proceed to remind Mrs. Freeman about some other meeting, which admittedly Mrs. Freeman would also have forgotten, and Tiphany would recall to her some early business dinner with someone named Steve, one of the many Steves with whom Mrs. Freeman was always having to eat an early business dinner. Or if not dinner, it would be the symphony or the ballet with her husband, who would be sullen later were she to stand him up, and all these reminders would be delivered in such a way as to suggest that any change in plans might topple the system altogether.

"Hello?"

Mrs. Freeman turned to discover a young man with dirty blond hair standing uncomfortably in her doorway, looking as if he intended to ask her for directions.

"Yes," she said, "yes, what is it?" And she cocked her head to signal she was already moving on.

"Ruth Freeman?" The quaver in the young man's voice clashed with the bright confidence of his smile.

Her one-fifteen. Yes, of course, she remembered now. A reporter of some sort from one of the papers, a man to whom she had promised a few minutes of her time. Fine. But giving the young man a second look, Mrs. Freeman found herself growing less certain. The person standing in her doorway was a tall, handsome young man, his jaw square, his white teeth strikingly rectangular. There was a color to his skin that suggested a familiarity with sunlight. Except for the standard-issue khakis and the light-blue button-down shirt, the young man looked nothing at all like a reporter, the pale, sickly breed that generally eked out its existence under the fluorescent tubes of newsrooms.

But perhaps, she supposed, her notions about newspapermen were becoming old-fashioned. Those dinosaurs were dying, and soon, she understood, the newspapers themselves would be extinct. But how then would her poor husband fill the hours? Perhaps this young man was one of those emissaries from the Internet age, in his well-worn Chelsea boots, the only part of the ensemble that suited him.

He had called her two days before to set up this meeting, saying he wanted to talk about the protests, about the drone, about the school, about the accident. Tiphany had tried to tell Mrs. Freeman it was a bad idea.

"Come," Mrs. Freeman said, "come," and she waved the young man over to the window. But he had taken only half a step when Tiphany's voice erupted again from the speakerphone.

"I'm sorry to interrupt, Ruth," the voice lied. "I just wanted to remind you the board meeting has been moved up to one-thirty. I'm just about finished with the presentation for Arthur—"

Taking one last disappointed glimpse out the window, Mrs. Freeman shuffled her flat-heeled shoes over to her desk, cutting Tiphany off before she could say any more. The silence that followed would be fleeting, Mrs. Freeman knew, but nonetheless she smiled at the young man, and his long eyelashes fluttered in return, and for a moment it almost seemed he was he trying to flirt with her. Or did he sense the conspiracy she was inviting him to share?

Still, though, she couldn't quite shake the peculiar feeling she had about this young man, with his broad shoulders and his gelled hair. He was exactly the sort of young man she was used to seeing in five-thousand-dollar suits strutting the marble halls of investment banks, the sort of young man who at an earlier age would have been charging off Viking ships, hell-bent on rape and pillage. Every woman in her circle, it seemed, could lay claim to at least one such son. Cassandra

Boyle had two—twins even—and every time she saw them, Mrs. Freeman felt a chill.

"Come in," Mrs. Freeman said again, "and shut the door behind you." Perhaps it was the mother in her, but her first instinct, as he approached, was to look around her desk—an executive excess large enough for five or six of her employees to share—for something to offer the young man. Finding nothing other than a stale, half-filled cup of coffee with a stained rim, she frowned apologetically and directed him toward a chair.

As the young man approached, he paused to glance out the window, and Mrs. Freeman saw the rain had stopped. Some of the clouds had even parted. But now, improbably, fat white flakes appeared to be falling from the sky.

"Is that snow?" she said. And then, "It's almost the middle of May."

"You know what they say," the young man said hesitantly, and a single ray of sunshine streaked through the glass, falling upon his cheek. "Global—"

"What are you?" Mrs. Freeman asked, studying him now for the first time in profile. "Twenty-five?"

"Excuse me?"

"Your age," Mrs. Freeman said.

The young man hesitated, remaining at the window but eyeing the chair, as if torn between the two. "Eight," he said. "Twenty-eight," and his Adam's apple poked out above the top button of his shirt.

"I was thirty-seven when I got my first job," Mrs. Freeman said, leaning back in her chair. "Thirty-seven." She paused to read his reaction, but the young man seemed to have little idea what to make of this. "I'm now nearly twice as old as I was then," Mrs. Freeman continued, "but I still remember the day of my interview. I remember it vividly. On the man's desk there was a box of cigars in a fine wooden case etched with fleurs-de-lis, and I recall thinking it magnificent, like nothing I'd ever seen, representing everything I'd imagined an important businessman being. I'd never worked a day in my life, and I was starting at the bottom of the bottom. It was the year I finally finished college. My first husband and I had married young, and I was only nineteen when my first daughter was born. My second came a year later. I raised them for fifteen years, and when they were finally old enough to take care of themselves, I went to college. I had no qualms about leaving my first husband to do it. I was thirty-seven, and I'd never had a cigar.

"The man who was interviewing me was named Maxwell, I believe, undoubtedly his last name, since in those days I would never have had occasion to use his first. Mr. Maxwell was a connoisseur of fine cigars, and even kept a what-do-you-call-it . . . humidor in his office. I remember being surprised at how otherwise shabby his office was, considering that Mr. Maxwell owned a textile company, which he had inherited from his father, who had inherited it from his father, and he from his. For all I know, they brought a bolt of cloth over with them on the *Mayflower*. As Mr. Maxwell's assistant, I was obliged to take minutes during meetings with his management staff. I was the only one to whom he never offered a cigar. And do you know what?" Mrs. Freeman said, inching toward the edge of her seat. "I'm one of those managers now. I have been for a very long time. I've gone through more than thirty years of meetings since then—more than your entire life—and I've still never been offered a cigar."

Mrs. Freeman wished she had a box of her own now, a fine box to offer the young man. She knew how it was done. She had watched captains of industry guillotine the tips and light them, sucking grotesquely. She knew how they smelled. She knew everything except how they tasted.

"Coffee?" she said.

"Please."

Mrs. Freeman gestured for him to sit, and with a finger raised in expectation, she searched the instrument panel of the phone for her administrative assistant's extension.

"Would you mind getting Mr. . . . Mr. . . . would you bring a cup of coffee please, and make it black."

And then it was quiet again.

"Tell me, Mr. . . ."

"Fitch," the young man said, clearing his throat of the word, as if it were the first he'd spoken in days.

"Is that your last name or your first, Mr. Fitch?"

The young man seemed vaguely panicked by the question, and she watched his fingers walk across his shirtfront, tugging nervously at his top button, and she saw with perfect clarity that it was one he normally left undone. It disappointed her to think he had mistaken her for someone who cared about proprieties of dress.

"It's what people call me," he said, and that bright white smile of his returned.

"I see." And just as Mrs. Freeman was opening her mouth to say something more, to ask a question she hadn't yet formulated, Tiphany appeared at the door with a cup of steaming coffee in her hand. The appearance of her administrative assistant, and the all-too-obvious way Tiphany checked her watch, reminded Mrs. Freeman—as it was undoubtedly calculated to remind Mrs. Freeman—of the board meeting that would be starting in nine minutes.

Tiphany lingered there another moment, and Mrs. Freeman found herself wondering if, under different circumstances, this might be the sort of young man Tiphany would have wanted to bring home to her parents, someone handsome and tall and sturdy, someone genetically predisposed to tack and jib. Of course, Tiphany would have preferred the suited variety of this Mr. Fitch, one of those Boyle boys, for instance, who could already afford to pay cash for the sorts of cars that came in only silver and black.

"Thank you," Mrs. Freeman said as gently as she could, and as soon as Tiphany closed the door behind her, the old woman added, "She's a wonderful girl. I truly would be lost without her."

And in truth she meant it, because despite everything that came between them, Mrs. Freeman preferred to believe the girl had good within her, and perhaps the fact that Tiphany tended toward the destructive was a reflection of Mrs. Freeman's failings as much as the girl's own. After all, Tiphany had come to her young and impressionable, and if she had been blown off course, perhaps Mrs. Freeman was to blame for that prevailing wind.

The young man, for his part, seemed to have taken little notice of her administrative assistant, or of much else for that matter, notwithstanding the coffee, and when at last he lowered the mug, setting it back on her desk, it was half empty, and Mrs. Freeman wondered how he had managed to drink it so quickly without flaying the delicate skin at the roof of his mouth.

"Perhaps," Mrs. Freeman said, "we'll be more comfortable over there." And she rose and led the young man to the sofa against the far wall. When they were both seated, she leaned toward him, and in a voice just above a whisper, she said, "You know, she tried to talk me out of meeting with you. Tiphany doesn't believe I should be talking directly to the press."

"But you're—" He lowered his eyes into his hands, as if the answer were written there. "Aren't you the director? Director of corporate communications?"

"I suspect she had the board meeting moved up on purpose," Mrs. Freeman said, "just to limit our time here together."

"Your secretary?"

"Every time she comes in, I can see her rearranging the furniture in her head."

"Why don't you fire her?"

"Her greatest fear," Mrs. Freeman said, "a fear she shares with a great many of my colleagues here, is the truth. Tiphany believes the truth is something dirty, that honesty is a sign of weakness and capitulation, that one cannot speak from the heart without losing some advantage."

"You don't agree?"

In that moment, Mrs. Freeman's own greatest fear was that she had overestimated this young man, that he might not be, after all, the sort of man she thought he was, and Mrs. Freeman found herself confronting the fact that the majority of the people in the world, at least those she had met, especially those she worked with—and not excluding those she had married—never turned out to be the sort of people she hoped they would be. Mrs. Freeman wondered if she hoped for too much, or simply for the wrong things.

"Have you heard of Carl Norden?"

The young man shook his head.

"He invented the bombsight," Mrs. Freeman said. "He figured out how to make one that worked."

With some effort, the young man reached down and popped the clasps to his briefcase—a task with which he seemed almost entirely unfamiliar—and pulled out a small spiral notebook, which Mrs. Freeman could see in a glance had never been opened beyond the first page.

"Does he work here at HSI?"

"Carl Norden," Mrs. Freeman said, "thought he was doing God's will."

The young man bent over his pad, taking notes.

"They were using his sight," she said, "when they dropped the bomb on Hiroshima."

The young man's pencil abruptly stopped.

"Can you imagine the bombardier," she said, "punching in altitude, velocity, wind speed, coordinates? As if any of it mattered."

Mrs. Freeman pushed herself back a bit on the sofa, allowing more air to come between them. "But I won't bore you with any more of my prattling."

The young man appeared about to object, but Mrs. Freeman didn't give him a chance. "There were some questions you wanted to ask?"

The young man looked at her nervously.

"And which paper," Mrs. Freeman asked, "did you say you write for?"

The young man swallowed deeply. "Well—" He tried again to flash one of his expensive smiles, but it was thinner this time.

"It doesn't matter," she said, and the color returned to his cheeks in a rush of gratitude. "I will tell you," she said, folding her hands atop her knee, "whatever you want to know."

And yet her declaration strangely seemed to have the opposite effect of what she'd intended, peeling away even further at the young man's confidence. He was fumbling again with his spiral pad, turning back to the very first page, upon which it appeared something had already been written, and in blue pen, not pencil. Even with the pad upside down from where she sat, Mrs. Freeman noted something strikingly feminine about the penmanship.

"I want to ask you about these protests," he repeated, but stiffly this time, reading from the page.

"I must say, I've grown to admire their persistence."

The young man's pencil remained poised above the pad, quivering slightly in his hand. At her words, his clear blue eyes seemed to focus in on her face, and Mrs. Freeman wondered whether she had interrupted his thoughts, or whether he'd been listening to her abstractly, from a distance. And then her own thoughts returned to a cigar box and a granite-faced man with a moustache offering her her first job.

Finally the uncertain movement of the young man's lips resulted in words. "You don't, uh, dispute the facts? The drone . . . that is, I mean the school—"

At that, the tent of Mrs. Freeman's folded fingers collapsed. "It's the nature of facts, Mr. Fitch, to be correct, and there is nothing I could say to make them less so."

In Mrs. Freeman's mind flashed thirty years of meetings like these, all the petty conspiring about things that didn't really matter, all the silly memos, the secret dealings, the strategic planning. Over the years, all that changed was the quality of her chair. And it occurred to her that had her first husband respected her just a little more, she might have spared herself all this and found aggravation domestically instead. But to say she would not have missed it would have been disingenuous. She was not sorry. Not even a bit. To get here she had needed to work ten times harder than Arthur or any of the other men around her. And after all that, even with Tiphany's attempts to undermine her, what fun it was, at sixty-eight, to see her orders dutifully executed, not out of sentimental reverence for the aged but because after all this time she had become something like a sun, the center of gravity within her own universe.

"So you don't deny you blew up a school?"

Gazing down again upon the young man's hands, she saw a streak of sweat upon the pad. "How could I?"

"How long have you known about the problems with the drones?" He looked up from the page. "Or is it this bombsight you were talking about?" He seemed more comfortable going off script.

"No one has ever blown up anything," Mrs. Freeman said, "except in desperation."

"There must have been tests?" The young man sounded hesitant, almost apologetic. "You must have known there were . . . glitches?"

"Do you know what happens," Mrs. Freeman said, "when you try to bang in one those tiny, skinny nails—those finishing nails—with a full-size hammer?"

"I've never tried."

With a glance at his hands, she could tell it was true.

"You smash your thumb," she said. "And you bend the nail."

"I see," he said.

But she wasn't convinced he did. "If we really were in control," she said, "we wouldn't need bombs to make such an unholy mess."

"Maybe you'd prefer to speak off the record," the young man offered, reading once again from the page. "If there's information that's . . . sensitive . . ."

Mrs. Freeman felt an urge to reach out and pat his knee.

"For years there've been allegations against your company. Environmental abuses, reneging on labor contracts, outsourcing." The young man had found his voice. "The city gives you tax breaks, and in return it loses jobs and gets left with cleanup bills—"

"I have nothing to hide," Mrs. Freeman said, and he seemed disappointed, or maybe just confused. Suddenly he was looking over her shoulder.

Mrs. Freeman realized her telephone was ringing.

Straightening her pants and blouse, Mrs. Freeman stood up from the sofa, and with what she knew to be the grace and dignity of the old woman she had become, she walked over to the desk. And even she did not know what she planned to do until the moment she pressed her fingernail against the tab of the cord, detaching it from her phone.

There was so much she wanted to say, so much that needed to be cleared up, and whatever his story, whoever he was, Mrs. Freeman wanted this young man to know, for she had decided he was someone she could trust.

But here was Tiphany, already knocking at the door. She had come to tell them their time was up. Tiphany had played her hand well, Mrs. Freeman decided, and she couldn't help feeling a bit of pride. For decades Mrs. Freeman had held her tongue. She had quietly deferred. She had been a credit to the company but never to herself. Tiphany could be forgiven for not understanding what it had taken for her to get where she was. And Mrs. Freeman would not be the one to tell her. She envied Tiphany's ignorance.

Mrs. Freeman would never fire her. Never.

Back at the sofa, the young man was gathering his things.

Mrs. Freeman said, "I wish I had been able to give you what you wanted."

Eight

SOME PEOPLE RAN into one another in coffee shops and bars. For McGee and April, it had been picket lines and rallies.

It was 1999. They were both in their second year of college, barely more than acquaintances. McGee's plan had been to fill a bus with friends from various groups: environmentalists, pacifists, anarchists, unionists, vegans, conservationists, feminists, Buddhists, socialists, queers. But it was November, toward the end of the semester, and everyone had tests to take, papers to write, dogs to walk. McGee would've gone by herself, if she'd had to. She'd heard from people who knew that something big was going down in Seattle, a movement, a piece of history. She wasn't going to miss it.

April was the first to sign on. "Why not?" she'd said. "Sounds like fun."

McGee's second recruit was Myles. At that point they'd been seeing each other for just a couple of months, a situation they liked to think of as casual, even though their weekends together had become automatic. Holmes came along because Myles had asked him to, not wanting to be the only person there who found his mind wandering whenever McGee or one of her friends mentioned globalization or the evils of international free trade.

Fitch came because he liked road trips and because he was trying to book gigs for his band, whose western tour had so far stalled out in Ann Arbor. Also, Fitch was trying to sleep with McGee's friend Kirsten (the fourth recruit), and although his efforts were pitiful and exhausting, everyone put up with them because Fitch's van was the only vehicle they had capable of driving five thousand miles without losing a wheel.

The seventh in the group was Inez, a dour, unsmiling friend of Kirsten's whom no one else particularly liked, but they were still glad to have her, if only because seven somehow seemed like a more substantial number than six.

They drove nonstop, taking turns at the wheel, and they arrived in Seattle on a Monday night, crashing in the house of Kirsten's older sister, seven bodies laid out on the carpeted basement floor.

McGee had been in contact with one of the local groups organizing the protests, and in the morning they met up in a park. It was only a little after sunrise, and the paths were already choked. There were placards taped to light posts, bedsheets hanging from apartment windows. THE WHOLE WORLD IS WATCHING, one of them read.

The seven of them moved through the crowds as if they were rubber-banded together. Even April and Kirsten, just as experienced with protests as McGee was, wouldn't leave her side. Myles and Holmes looked alternately overwhelmed and amazed.

On a platform at the edge of the park, a black man in a green dashiki stood above a crowd stretching farther than McGee could see. *People before profit*, he shouted into his microphone, and the crowd shouted the same thing back. Here alone there must have been a thousand people, and there were thousands more all around. The protests were expected to last five days, coinciding with a meeting in the city of superpowers, industrial nations intent on slicing up the globe into their own private markets. People had come from all around the world to make sure that didn't happen. There were signs in French and Spanish, Portuguese, Korean, Chinese. Alphabets McGee couldn't even recognize.

"You didn't tell me it was going to be like this," Myles said.

McGee took his hand and led him through.

As they'd planned, McGee and the others (except for Fitch, who'd vaguely said he'd "catch up with them later") fell in with a group of students marching into the city from the north. Someone said there were four thousand of them, but McGee would have believed twice that many. It was less like walking than like getting swept along by a wave.

When they reached the city center, the police were already there, waiting. The cops had set up cordons in anticipation, but they'd underestimated the scale of what was coming. All they could do was stand and watch as marchers descended, arms linked together. Almost immediately protesters blockaded the main intersection. The scene was surreal—drummers and dancers and a man breathing fire and human butterflies on Rollerblades. Another intersection was blocked by a papier-mâché whale. Three teenage girls stood on a street corner dressed in baggy suits, monocles, and pocket watches attached by gold chains. They were passing out handfuls of money, throwing it into the air like confetti. Everyone had flyers and picket signs. STOP EXPLOITING WORKERS. DEFEND OUR FORESTS. SAY NO TO FRANKEN FOOD. RESIST CORPORATE TYRANNY. CAPITALISM KILLS. SHUT IT DOWN. STOP THE NEW WORLD ORDER. A steel drum band laid down the beat for a troupe of clowns and stilt walkers, while a parade of older, sober-looking men in trucker hats pulled up the rear. Steelworkers and teamsters, according to their windbreakers. They carried a banner on which a coiled snake snapped at the words DON'T TRADE ON ME.

On the periphery of it all, completely unamused, units of riot troops huddled in Kevlar. And Myles wanted to know why.

"It's like a circus in the middle of a war zone," he said.

Why were the protesters at the blockade wearing goggles? he wanted to know. Why were they dressed in garbage bags? Why the bandannas?

It was a strange place for McGee to feel like a tour guide. "Because," she said, suddenly feeling scarred and world-weary, "it's about to get ugly."

In truth, she'd never seen anything like this either, but she knew Myles was looking to her for answers, and it would've been worse if she'd admitted how far she was in over her head. Another battalion of riot cops had begun advancing upon one of the blockaded intersections, shields on their helmets lowered. A voice over a bullhorn was issuing threats. Everyone was to be removed—if necessary, with "chemical and pain compliance." As if these were special new products, name brands everyone would recognize from television commercials.

"This way." McGee grabbed Myles's hand, and they headed west, where the road appeared to be clear.

Cracks and booms were bursting behind them, like fireworks misfiring on the ground.

All at once the drumming stopped. McGee could hear the crowds at the blockade shouting *courage*.

Then the chants turned to screaming. The cops had swarmed the intersection, ripping off the protesters' goggles and gas masks, firing pepper spray point-blank into their eyes. Another line of cops was advancing on the scattered bystanders and picketers, shooting rubber bullets and tear gas at anyone not chained in place.

"Go back to the park," McGee said. "I'll meet you there."

"Where are you going?" Holmes said.

A concussion grenade exploded around the corner. McGee was having a hard time thinking clearly about anything.

"Just go," she said.

Myles looked at Holmes, and Holmes looked up and down the street, his eyes wide and glassy.

"All right," Myles said.

She was already turning to go when Myles leaned in to kiss her. In retrospect, it was an innocent enough thing to do. A kiss goodbye, as was their habit. But at the time it had felt like a strange moment for romance, and McGee was unprepared.

She put her hand to his chest. "Go," she said.

She could see he was hurt, not so much because she'd refused him but because of the way she'd looked at him—past him, really—at the scene unfolding at his back. She'd made him feel stupid.

And the worst part, when she thought about this moment later, was realizing that was how she'd wanted him to feel. She'd liked leading him through the streets that day, explaining what was happening. She'd liked the way he followed her, the way he listened, the way he looked up to her. Before Myles and Holmes, she'd felt like a soldier, like someone possessing a powerful secret, even though in fact what she knew of blockades was entirely theoretical. She'd never been gassed or pepper-sprayed or shot with rubber bullets. She'd never even been arrested.

McGee left them there. A block away she got caught up in a crowd retreating before a line of riot cops. There was a fog of gas and a ripple of explosions, and she struggled to stay on her feet as people around her fell and were trampled. A canister went off by a storefront a few yards away, and the last thing she saw before the gas enveloped her was the mouth of an alley. She staggered in, crumbling against the wall, her hands involuntarily pulling at her face. Her eyes had turned to water.

Someone said, "I've got you," and McGee felt hands on her hands. She kicked toward the sound of the voice.

"It's me," the voice said. Over the bullhorns and sirens she recognized April. McGee allowed herself to be lifted.

They were lucky. There was a building under renovation farther down the alley. April was able to pry open the plywood door. Once inside, McGee lowered herself onto a pile of broken cinder blocks.

A helicopter flew overhead, chopped into the distance, then returned and hovered there.

Lie down on your stomach with your hands behind your head.

April came back with a wet cloth. Beneath a hole in the roof on the second floor, she'd found a rusted drum full of rainwater.

It took nearly half an hour before the blurs became more concrete. After forty-five minutes, McGee could identify the features of April's face. She was still having trouble making out their surroundings, but it appeared they were alone.

"Where's Inez? Kirsten?"

April gestured vaguely toward the street. "What about Myles and Holmes?"

"They're okay," McGee said, hoping it was true.

She'd fucked up. Not just with Myles, with everything. All those people with goggles and bandannas had seen this coming, but she'd treated it like a field trip.

April sat down with her against the wall. It was nearly December. The building was unheated, and many of the windows were missing. Back home they would've been freezing. Here it felt more like fall than winter. But as the adrenaline left her, McGee felt a chill settling in.

"What do we do now?" April said.

The involuntary tears had drained McGee dry.

"I don't know either," April said.

In the silence that followed, McGee fell asleep.

By dusk, the helicopters and bullhorns had drifted away. The city was almost silent when McGee woke up and joined April at the window. April had enlarged a hole between the boards. She was keeping an eye on the passing patrols. Later they would learn the National Guard had been called in. A curfew was in effect.

"I don't understand," April said. "It was a peaceful protest."

McGee's eyes had finally stopped stinging. "That's not something they know how to win."

They waited until dark to crawl back out into the alley. Once they reached the street, they walked single file, clinging to the buildings, to the shadows. Twice they hit roadblocks that forced them to turn back and change directions.

Despite the curfew, there were pockets of people coming and going. Someone had thrown a trash can through the window of a bank. A Dumpster had been pushed into the street and set on fire. There were scrawls here and there of rushed graffiti. The curbs were lined with trash and tear gas canisters.

They headed west. Outside a convenience store, McGee bummed a cigarette from a woman in a rain slicker, who lit her up and quickly left. McGee and April leaned against a pair of newspaper boxes, watching helicopters sweep the streets with spotlights. McGee felt as if they'd been walking for hours. It was hard to be sure in the dark, but she thought she recognized the neighborhood.

"It's not far," she said. "The park." But what were the odds that Myles and Holmes would still be waiting? She couldn't call him. None of them yet had cell phones. Almost no one did.

April sat down next to a pyramid of windshield washer fluid. "They were arrested," she said. "Inez and Kirsten. When I reached you in the alley, I looked back. They were getting dragged away."

McGee flicked her butt into the parking lot, grimacing at the few feeble sparks.

"It would've happened either way," April said. "They would've gotten me, too, if I hadn't gone to help you."

It had all been McGee's idea, and she'd turned out to be the weakest one.

Myles and Holmes weren't at the park. McGee figured they must have gone back to Kirsten's sister's place.

Just before dawn, McGee and April reached the house. The lights were on in the basement.

Myles was talking on the cordless, taking notes on a pad of paper. He nodded stiffly when McGee and April came in.

It seemed to take forever for Myles to finish his conversation. The whole time, he wouldn't make eye contact. McGee couldn't help seeing the wait as a kind of punishment.

When he finally did say goodbye and hang up the phone, McGee came forward and put her arms around him. "I'm glad you're okay."

"We're fine," he said, as if he couldn't imagine why they wouldn't be. "We're going back out in a couple of hours."

"Who were you talking to?"

"We're getting everyone organized," Myles said. "It's going to be even bigger than yesterday."

McGee wondered who the *we* was, who the *everyone*, how in her brief absence Myles had somehow gone from being lost to being in charge. But she could see by the way he carried himself that he preferred to pretend nothing had changed, that this was the way he'd always been. And she understood that now, and for a long time to come, this was how he'd make up for that kiss.

Myles was in no hurry to explain anything, so it was Holmes who described what had happened after they separated, how they'd been driven along a huge crowd up into Capitol Hill. The state of emergency was supposed to be only for downtown, Holmes said, but the riot cops kept coming. It was a residential neighborhood, people hanging out in bars and restaurants. It was as if they were being invaded.

"The people came out to the streets," Holmes said. "A couple kids took over a city bus. The cops came after us with everything. Gas, sticks, grenades. We kept pushing them back. Every time they thought they'd stopped us, we came back for more."

"I'm sorry," McGee said. "I shouldn't have left you."

"It was amazing," Myles said. "Too bad you missed it."

Myles woke them up after just a couple of hours of sleep. He'd been making more calls. The city had gotten wind of the plans. The curfew had been swapped for a "no-protest zone" through twenty-five square blocks of downtown. Signs and leaflets were banned, and bags were getting confiscated without warrants.

"So much for the Constitution," Myles said.

It was the first time McGee had ever heard him utter the word.

The day picked up where the previous one had left off. But when they met up with Myles's new friends at Pike Place Market, it was clear yesterday's puppets and clowns and marching bands were a distant memory. The morning fog lifted; tear gas took its place.

But Myles seemed happy. Everyone around them seemed to know who he was. Now McGee was the one following him.

§

Compared to the drive that had taken them west, the drive back home seemed interminable. After five days of marching and shouting and clashing with police, the protest had ended. The WTO meeting had collapsed spectacularly. The police and the National Guard had waged war and lost. For the first time in McGee's life, she was leaving a demonstration with a sense of something having been actually won.

After all that, how could the long drive back to Detroit not feel like a letdown? She had final exams waiting, term papers to write.

Following four days in jail, Inez and Kirsten had had their charges dropped, along with hundreds of others. Myles had been among the people organizing the march that won their release. As soon as the protests ended, Fitch had reappeared, just in time for the celebration. Everyone was so jubilant, Fitch even succeeded in getting Kirsten to sleep with him.

And something that no one had seen coming had happened between Inez and April, too. There were five other people in the back of that van, but April and Inez whispered the 2,500 miles to Detroit as if they were alone.

Up in front, there was a much different kind of solitude. McGee and Myles took shifts at the wheel, alternating with Fitch. When it was just the two of them, radio stations would drift off into fuzz without either one of them noticing. Every exit on the interstate brought them closer to what McGee was already assuming would be the end.

On the second day of the drive, Myles spotted the carnival from the highway. He took the exit without asking anyone's opinion. They were in a town no one in the van had ever heard of, and the things they saw outside their windows made no sense, at least not in early December, with at least two inches of snow on the ground. Around the perimeter of a small lake, a midway of sorts had been set up, though the only ride appeared to involve horses and a wagon stacked with blankets.

But when McGee got out of the van and drew closer, she saw mittened hands tossing darts. Bundled faces squinted along the sights of air rifles, taking aim at rows of tin ducks. There were small crowds everywhere, at the bucket toss, the high striker, the ring-a-bottle.

At the ladder climb, a teenage boy in a pom-pommed hat tumbled over and over onto his ass while his girlfriend cheered him on.

Mixed in with the games were small clapboard shacks blowing puffs of steam from their hatches. They were selling all kinds of things, all of them hot: cocoa and pretzels and sacks of peanuts and caramel corn, the smells so strong they cut through the cold.

Myles took the lead, with McGee a few steps behind, the others straggling at the rear. Fitch had brought a flask, but he couldn't seem to get either Holmes or Kirsten to take any interest in it. Many of the townspeople turned to watch them come, as if seven haggard, unshowered kids off the highway were a stranger sight than a winter carnival in the middle of nowhere.

April and Inez laced their fingers and swung their arms, imitating young girls instead of lovers.

"What are we doing?" McGee said to Myles's back.

"We're having fun," he said, and he led her to a booth where dozens of fishbowls had been arranged in a flat-topped pyramid. For a dollar, a fat man with hands like tarantulas traded Myles four Ping-Pong balls. Myles offered two of them to McGee.

"You first," he said.

She shook her head.

"All right," he said, stepping up to the railing. "I'll go first."

He pitched his ball forward, and it bounced from bowl to bowl before coming to a rest in the snow.

"Your turn," he said.

But she didn't want to play. The games were rigged. Everyone knew it. So she passed the balls back to Myles, and he tossed another, and it landed again in the snow.

But on the third try, he nailed it, the ball clipping the rim and swirling down, as if through the mouth of a drain.

Myles threw up his arms and shouted, his breath exploding outward, and Fitch and Holmes and April and Kirsten and Inez closed in around him. McGee watched the carny reach under the counter, and in a moment of panic, she pictured a goldfish frozen in a block of ice. But it was only stuffed animals, a blue bear and a green dog. The carny held them in his outstretched hands, and Myles took his time considering them, examining the animals front and back, touching their shiny, fluorescent fur, each in turn. What was he looking for? What did he see?

In the end, Myles took the green dog, handing it to McGee with a satisfied grin. He'd made a decision about her. Ever since then, she'd wished she knew what it was.

Nine

WHEN HE THINKS back on it, the trip to Mexico feels like a beginning. But it is also an end. Six years past, but he remembers every detail, as if part of him were still there now. A long, narrow side street submerged in the murky darkness. The tall brick walls on either side funnel exhaust from the boulevard, and he coughs into his sleeve. Somewhere within his body, it's as if a lever has been pulled. Something, he's not sure what, has been set in motion. He can feel the sensation even now in his memory, almost like vertigo. He stands in front of a nondescript steel door. A single light burns on the outer wall. Shadows move about on the sidewalk, closing in. The door suddenly grates open. An elderly woman in large, pirate-like hoop earrings looks Dobbs over skeptically and steps aside.

Número diez, she says. Number ten contains a narrow bed and a wobbly table balancing a cloudy water pitcher. The carpet looks like matted dog fur. The ceiling is low, and upon stepping into the room,

Dobbs immediately ducks, mistaking the brown stains overhead for some falling object. Even in his memory, he can smell the dampness seeping from every surface.

The proprietress is slight and stern, and one of her eyebrows seems permanently arched. "You wait," she says in English. No one ever expects him to speak Spanish. It's his hair. Wild, curly red hair. Hair that doesn't inspire confidence. In his own unnecessary pidgin, Dobbs says, "I wait." Already his body is leaning toward the bed like a divining rod. His bones feel hollow, his veins bloodless. The proprietress backs out into the hallway, and Dobbs recalls his descent toward the mattress, lightheadedly trying to remember what he might have eaten to make him feel this way.

He has just turned twenty, still a young man. Since neglecting to register for his junior year of classes, though, he's been feeling a great deal older. He was never really going to be an environmental engineer or an ecologist or a marine biologist. Those were his parents' dreams, efforts to translate his fears into intellectual ambitions. So far in this unofficial and thoroughly unsanctioned year abroad, he's been questioned and scrutinized, sniffed and swabbed. And every moment of it has been exhilarating, the German shepherds and border guards bringing him closer than he's ever been to understanding what he's been seeking: the stripping away of false reassurances, the discovery of a path through the world to come.

But first comes the sweating; first Montezuma must have his revenge. If Dobbs concentrates hard enough on gathering his strength, he can remove a single blanket during a single round of consciousness. This he does three times, until the blankets and the coarse, heavy sheet slip to the floor. He's never expended so much effort to achieve so little, but the practice is important. Soon, he knows, though he doesn't know exactly when, he'll be called upon to get up out of this bed and go somewhere, and somehow he'll need to do it. The man they call Sergio will be waiting.

Sometimes, in his fever, he feels as if he's stepped outside himself, watching himself on film, but either his brain is working too quickly or the film is playing too slowly, and all he can see are the blurs between frames. His shirt comes off in three stages—a sleeve at a time and then once over his head. It's as though he's wearing mittens when he tries to unbutton his pants. The sun has only just risen when he makes his first tentative tugs at the zipper. By the time he's kicked off his second pant leg, the room is filled with light.

In his delirium, his mind wanders backward, coming to rest in his body seven years before. He knows the number precisely because it is the summer he turns thirteen lying in a hospital bed, his arm tethered to an IV drip. He feels a fuzzy, floating sensation, as if he were a piece of pineapple suspended in Jell-O. His femur rests in a sling of wires and pulleys, and he recalls feeling as if the leg were no longer attached, as if the pain his broken bones radiate is no longer his. He remembers wishing, more than anything else, for the morphine to fade, for a taste of the pain to come back. And along with the pain, that brief but tangible feeling of truly flying—his own birthday gift to himself—leaping off the roof of his parents' garage and into the neighbor's wading pool.

He's been assured that Sergio is eager to meet him, that Sergio is a man of the world, someone who understands that even young men from stable homes can be awakened, can come to see past the comforts upon which they've been suckled. Dobbs senses that despite the different worlds they come from, Sergio will understand him. Perhaps he will understand even those things that Dobbs does not, for which he has images but not words. For instance, a butcher's case, its thick, glistening tiers of animal parts nestled in shaved ice. And how the sight always makes Dobbs's own internal organs ache. He is not squeamish, but there's something about the magnitude of the slaughter. The numbers make no sense. Two dozen cases of meat and fish and pig and bird in every average town, a thousand towns in every state, fifty states and hundreds of countries and seven continents and seven billion people. He does the math emotionally, the only way he knows. How could any of this possibly be made to last?

Dobbs is eager to meet Sergio, too, but the time has not yet come. Here in número diez, when he's finally ready to remove his undershirt and boxers, he feels as if he's peeling skin. He doesn't bother with the socks. His feet might as well be on the other side of the room.

His first attempt to meet Sergio, two weeks before his arrival in número diez, comes when Dobbs is left in the care of the beautiful people, friends of friends, contacts of contacts, none of whom he knows. He's not even sure of their names, although one might be called Polanco, or maybe that's the name of the place they're taking him, these friends of friends, these beautiful people driving him down a lovely tree-lined street past embassies and art galleries and windows draped in thousand-dollar handbags. There are five of them in Polanco's Mercedes, everyone so thin it feels as if they could fit three more in the backseat. The beautiful people are all his age, college kids, but that's the only thing they have in common. The girls wear shimmery blouses that look as though they've been woven with precious metal. The beautiful people call him Red. *Rrred* is how it comes out. He doesn't call them anything at all, except in his head, where he thinks of the beautiful people as a rare sort of ethnic tribe. The beautiful people speak perfect English. They are the children of oil and telecom tycoons, and when the Mercedes reaches the club, the beautiful people tow Dobbs past a battery of bouncers, and inside there are still more beautiful people, stacked chest to sweaty, beautiful chest. The drinks all come with enormous straws, and standing on the edge of the dance floor beneath strobing spheres of light, Dobbs feels as though he's basking in the rapturous glow of a UFO. Women in half-shirts and other nearly invisible garments pause in their bumping and flailing to marvel at Dobbs's hair. When the search-lights hit the long red curls dangling before his eyes, his hair looks even to him as though it's on fire. The women's fingernails clatter across his scalp, and sometimes he feels a tug, as if they're testing to see if it's real.

But here in the bed in número diez, all he feels are the chills, and he can do nothing more than roll onto his side and gaze at the pile of clothes and bedding just out of reach on the floor. The sun burns through the gauzy curtains, thin as the knees of old jeans, and Dobbs gives in to the waves of shivering and shuddering as he crawls in and out of consciousness.

His mind sways like a kite, and once again he is thirteen, at the center of a crowd of doctors and nurses, his parents and Jess in his small hospital room, balloons and candy, his leg in plaster from hip to toe. And a moment comes, by some strange chance, when everyone seems to forget he's there—the nurses having finished what they came to do, the doctors leading his parents out into the hallway to discuss his condition, his sister flipping through the fuzzy channels on the small TV bolted to the ceiling. Suddenly it's just Dobbs and the bottle of Percocet he's been refusing, which someone left behind on the side table. The two dozen pills fit neatly into a tissue twisted and stuffed into the top of his cast. His only thought: Be prepared. Someday you might need them.

Two weeks later, out of the hospital, even the memory of his earlier pain eludes him. In frustration, he flushes the pills away.

Beyond the enclaves of the beautiful, Mexico City is like a dingy basement arcade, sticky and loud and prone to testosterone rages. He's never been anywhere either so vast or so claustrophobic. The place is impossible to fathom more than a block at a time, the ruins of the Aztecs choking in the fumes of motorbikes and VW microbuses. The markets are cities unto themselves, with every imaginable flesh cleaved and hung without modesty for all the world to see. More seemingly endless supplies, all of it false. Brooding in judgment over everything are cathedrals more magnificent than anything he's ever believed to be within the power of man to conceive. And yet what seems to tie all the disparate pieces together is not faith but its exact opposite, chaos.

He awakens with chills every few minutes, every few hours. Sometimes in these moments, he imagines himself as a child back home in Minnesota, watching the snow sifting past his window, feeling the cold at a cellular level.

Sergio never shows at the club. The beautiful person Dobbs thinks might be named Polanco is so drunk afterward he can hardly stand, but he has no trouble driving, and they wind up Los Lomas to a hill-side mansion of stucco and glass, where a guard holds open a gate for them to pass through. The beautiful people tramp upstairs, collapsing onto a white leather sofa, and Dobbs goes alone out to the balcony. Removing his shoes, he stands there, barefoot on the terra-cotta tiles, staring down at the hovels stapled to the hillside below as thick as a forest. As for actual trees, virtually none. Something like twenty million people live down there. At his back, the beautiful people are taking turns guiding their shaved, perfect noses toward a mirrored tray, and Dobbs can't help marveling at the seemingly endless absurdity the world seems able to accommodate as it hurls toward collapse.

His childhood in St. Paul has not prepared him for chaos. He's grown up accustomed to heated buses stopping precisely at every block, to the efficient choreography of front-end loaders and dump trucks disappearing mountains of snow, to the humane practicality of skyways, connecting together the tidy burrows of civilization. Until his arrival in Mexico, chaos has been for Dobbs just an anomaly, a temporary condition, the rule of law broken down. But here he's discovered chaos is not an aberration, not a consequence of failure. Chaos is an entity, a living system, a force. Chaos is the sea upon which the raft of civilization floats. And the future, Dobbs now believes, will belong to those who strip themselves bare, enduring the sting of the water, and swim.

A week after the club, a week before número diez, another meeting with Sergio is scheduled, this time at the Palacio de Bellas Artes. But once again Sergio doesn't show.

For days, he's not sure how many, the proprietress is Dobbs's only company, her hollow, distant voice visiting him clandestinely from the vent above the toilet. The even hollower reverberations ring around the tiled bathroom, singing to him while he hunkers in the shower, trying to keep cool. Sometimes the vent makes her voice rumble like a stadium crowd. She multiplies exponentially. In his delirium, Dobbs imagines applause each time he moves his bowels, cheers when he empties his stomach. He sits on the porcelain for twenty minutes. He sits for an hour. He falls asleep sitting.

He dreams he's in a grocery store, selecting a box of cornflakes with the help of an old friend. For the first time in days, he wakes up in número diez and he isn't sweating.

Slowly his head is clearing, his body parts gradually coming back into focus. He is thirteen again, awakening from a long sleep in his hospital bed, his broken leg still in traction. He is alone. It is daytime, or so the clock says, but the summer sky outside his window is inky gray, radiating angry swirls of violet. The wind is louder than the night janitor's vacuum, and each raindrop lands upon Dobbs's windowsill like a water balloon. What awoke him, he realizes now, are the emergency broad-cast tones and the staticky, officious voice emanating from a radio in some neighboring room. If Dobbs rolls his head all the way to the right, he can see the trees at the edge of the hospital grounds do things he didn't know trees could do. There is a pine in the distance taller than the hospital itself, and Dobbs watches it bend like a noodle. On the news lately he's been hearing more and more about violent storms like these, how they once were rare but are becoming ordinary. Dobbs watches each bend and swerve of that one tall pine, high up above all the rest. He's witnessed such storms before. He's seen his mother's car crushed in the driveway by a fallen limb, and yet there's something about this particular tree that makes Dobbs swell with sadness. He can't look away. Even through the roaring wind and the pounding rain, he can hear the very moment the trunk—three-quarters of the way to the top—finally snaps. All the green needles arrayed at the canopy, all at once, fall away, hitting the ground with a crack and a thump. Just then a shadow expands upon the wall—someone approaching his open door, and Dobbs closes his eyes, not wanting anyone to see what's happened to him. He knows he wouldn't be able to explain. And in the morning, when at last the traction comes down and he's free to go, the landscape all along the route home is littered with branches and twigs and even entire trees. Silent corpses. The power is down throughout his neighborhood, but all Dobbs can think of are the losses, that new seeds—at least as far as the span of human existence is concerned—will never catch up with what's been destroyed. The coming end only quickens, Dobbs thinks—it never slows.

His fever subsides, and the next day the proprietress comes upstairs and hands Dobbs a note. He puts on a set of clothes from his back-pack, wrinkled but clean-smelling clothes, and he emerges unsteadily from behind the steel door, into the blistering daylight.

§

Sergio meets him that afternoon in a dingy playground in San Pedro el Chico. Sergio is not one of the beautiful people. He is unshaven and wearing the half-apron of a waiter.

"I just quit," Sergio says in English as they shake hands. Dobbs's palm feels like a damp sponge.

"Quit what?"

Sergio says, "What's it look like?"

It looks like there's been some mistake, is what Dobbs is thinking. Or is he still in bed in número diez, feverishly dreaming?

"I need to find a new direction," Sergio says.

Dobbs says, "Me too." He can feel the sweat gathering along his brow.

"I used to live in California," Sergio says, wandering over toward the swing set. "Right on the bay. I was a waiter there. That's where I made most of my connections."

And Dobbs wonders if there's been some misunderstanding, if he's mistakenly been led to the kingpin of busboys.

"The nicest people I've ever known," Sergio says, "were the friends I had at that restaurant. We used to go out drinking together, smoke weed together. It was nice."

They're walking side by side, and when they reach the teeter-totter, Sergio offers to buy him a beer.

"Sure."

"Let's go this way," Sergio says, turning away from the main road. The cafés, he says, are too expensive.

They head north, past a school. Dobbs's heels seem reluctant to lift off the sidewalk. Balance is suddenly not something to be taken for granted.

They're in a residential neighborhood, small concrete boxes with gates and courtyards just off the street. It's pretty and quiet, but it's nothing like where the beautiful people live.

"I had a good friend named Sammy," Sergio says. "He had the most beautiful girlfriend I'd ever seen."

Sergio is glancing down a side street that appears to Dobbs to offer more of the same.

"His girlfriend wanted me," Sergio says, "and Sammy knew it, but he didn't care. He used to let her come over to my place and drink and do whatever. You can't find people like that here," he says, pointing to the word CORONA painted on the side of a small store. "I miss my old friends."

The beer comes in a plastic sack with a straw, to save on the deposit, and Dobbs finds himself holding what looks like a sandwich bag full of frothy urine.

"*Salud*," Dobbs says, bouncing his bag off Sergio's.

"Cheers," says Sergio.

One sip, and Dobbs's head is swimming.

"Do you have a girlfriend?" Sergio says between slurps.

When Dobbs says no, Sergio asks why not.

"I've been focusing on other things."

"I couldn't live without my girlfriends," Sergio says. He tells Dobbs he has two.

"My wife and my son are away in Spain right now visiting her family. I miss her," Sergio says, "but you can't expect a man to just sit around and wait." Sergio works the straw into a fold at the bottom of the bag. "We have to find you a girlfriend."

Dobbs's socks are soaked in sweat.

For the next half hour, Sergio tries his best to procure that missing girlfriend. As they walk, he whistles and follows and sometimes even calls out to different women, but nothing seems to work.

"I don't know what the problem is," Sergio says.

Dobbs realizes it's been days since he's looked in a mirror. If he looks at all like he feels, he must resemble a strand of overcooked spaghetti, the very tip dipped in sauce.

"Did I ever show you pictures of my son?" Sergio says, as if the forty minutes they've spent together have somehow stretched into decades.

"I'm pretty sure you haven't."

Sergio has four pictures, two of his son and two of his wife. All of them are small and rectangular, like the kind that come from photo booths. Sergio's son looks to be around twelve, older than Dobbs expected.

"After I got kicked out of the States," Sergio says, "I worked as a tour guide. I rode around in one of those luxury buses talking about churches and parks and things. I had to say everything twice," he says, "first in Spanish and then in English. That's where I met her."

"Why didn't you go to Spain with her?" Dobbs says.

"I had to work," Sergio says.

"When did they leave?"

They're standing at a curb, and Sergio tosses his empty bag to the ground. Dobbs looks down to see that countless other people have done the same. A gutter lined in tangled, muddy plastic. Dobbs thinks of the floating continents of trash churning out in the Pacific, dolphins and pelicans choking to death on bottle caps and disposable lighters.

"A year ago," Sergio says.

As they cross the street, Sergio yells something Dobbs doesn't understand to a woman in tight jeans walking farther up the sidewalk. She doesn't pay Sergio any attention, but he looks at Dobbs and smiles anyway, as it to say, *We're making progress.* Dobbs tries to smile too, but his lips feel very far away.

"Will they be coming back soon?" Dobbs says.

Sergio reaches into the pouch of his apron and brings out a ring of keys. "Yours are waiting for you up north. Paid up. Ready to go."

Dobbs steadies himself against a light post.

"Most kids take up smoking, drinking," Sergio says. "They get tattoos. That's how they"—he pauses to remember the word—"rebel."

"You don't know me."

Sergio leans in closer, the kindness fleeing from his face. "You understand this is serious business. These are serious people."

Dobbs says, "I'm serious, too."

Sergio stretches out his arm toward Dobbs's hair.

Dobbs's senses are too dulled to flinch.

"They'll see you coming from miles away," Sergio says. "But who'd ever think to stop you?"

Dobbs thinks about the German shepherds, about the border guards with their guns, about a van full of concealed strangers. He reminds himself borders are arbitrary, imaginary. The future has no place for them.

Dobbs lets go of his empty beer bag, watches it fall into the street.

"I'm just a middleman," Sergio says. "For there to be a middle, there has to be a bottom."

The keys are weightless in Dobbs's hand. It's only adrenaline now keeping him standing.

Then Sergio points to a group of young girls standing in front of an ice cream stand.

"What do you think about them?"

Dobbs says, "Let's go."

Ten

JUST BECAUSE SHE was a kid, they assumed she didn't know anything. Like the world was so complicated and mysterious, and unless you were the kind of kid that got straight As, you had no hope of understanding it. But Clementine knew plenty of things. Of all of them, she was the only one that paid attention. Her mother was always tired when she got home from work, and all Pay ever noticed was the bits of leaves and grass and dirt by the door, which he tweezed with his fingers, shouting *isittoomuchtoaskthatyoutakeoffyourshoesinmyhouse*? It was always *his* house, and it always would be, even if Clementine and her mother and Car lived there for the rest of their lives.

Since she got sick, May didn't see much of anything. She couldn't even tell Clementine and Car apart anymore. Clementine felt sorry for her and all, but even a blind person could see Car's tight, skanky pants from a mile away. And Car was too far up her own ass to notice anything at all.

Even though she was the oldest, May-May noticed a bit more than the others. She lived down the street, away from the hysteria of Pay and May's house, and at least once a week Clementine yelled over everyone else's yelling that she was going to move in with her great-grandmother, even though everyone knew May-May would never let her. May-May liked her peace and quiet, but most of all she liked her garden. Lately the garden was all she seemed to notice.

From the empty lots around May-May's garden, Clementine could see everything for blocks. She kept track of cars as they came and went. She knew the ones that belonged to the neighbors. There weren't many. Most of all she watched for the slow ones, rolling along like they had no place to be. Some were sightseers, even though there was nothing much to see. And then there were the ones Pay called hoodlums, looking for a place to set up where no one would notice them.

"Set up what?" Clementine asked him once.

"Never mind," he said.

As if she didn't know he meant drugs—guns and drugs and women with hollow eyes and bad teeth who dressed just like Car. As if everyone didn't know. There were exactly thirteen houses in the neighborhood, four of them empty. Pay said there used to be hundreds, but the rest had been torn down or burned. The burning was something Pay said they did for fun, lunatics with cases of beer and gallons of gasoline. Well, Pay's idea of fun was walking around the yard wearing spiky shoes, because *ithelpsthegrasstobreathe.*

As May-May said, to each her own.

While she patrolled the lots around May-May's garden, Clementine liked to imagine that not a single door or window in the neighborhood ever opened without her knowing it, but while she was stuck at school, stuff happened and no one was there to notice. Like the day she flunked her fractions test and came home to find a big gray pickup parked in front of the house on Bernadine Street. Of all the empty houses, the one on Bernadine Street was Clementine's favorite. She liked it because it was old and weird, like a cross between a castle and one of Car's old dollhouses, dragged through the mud. Nobody ever went inside the house on Bernadine Street. No one except Clementine. It was where she kept her magazines, because Pay wouldn't allow clutter in *his* house and *whatdoyoucareaboutmusclecars-anyway?* She only had one magazine about cars, but it was the one she'd made the mistake of leaving on a chair in the kitchen.

The day she saw the truck in front of the house on Bernadine Street was clear and sunny, the warmest so far that spring. All day during class she'd cheered herself up thinking about how she'd spend the afternoon in the house organizing her periodicals, like they did in the library. But then she got there to discover the truck and the door to the house wide open. So Clementine set her book bag down in the weeds across the street and waited.

After a while, she got bored and rolled onto her belly and pulled out a magazine. It was a new one, a science magazine, less than a year old. She'd found it in the trash on her way to school, and she'd spent almost the entire lunch period reading it. Science was her favorite. It was the nice thing about eating alone, that no one was there to interrupt her, and so while she'd chewed and smacked a crustless PB&J wrapped in cellophane, she'd read a story about eyes. About the evolution of eyes. About how there were a bunch of different kinds of eyes, people eyes and insect eyes made up of bunches of little tiny eyes, and octopus eyes, which were the opposite of people's eyes. And the story was about how for a long time scientists had thought the fact that there were so many different kinds of eyes meant that eyes were an ordinary thing, that even though they seemed complicated, everything over time eventually grew them, in one way or another. Maybe in another million years, worms would be squirming around in sunglasses.

But then, the story said, scientists eventually discovered all those different eyes had something in common, a gene, and that a creature a billion years ago had that gene, which meant that one creature was where all the eyes in the world came from. So eyes weren't ordinary at all. In the whole history of the world, they'd happened only once, and over time they'd changed, until every animal got the eyes it needed. If it hadn't been for this one creature, this prehistoric slug or whatever it was, there wouldn't be any eyes at all. Here was another thing Clementine knew that the rest of her family didn't.

Lying there in the weeds, she flipped through the rest of the magazine. Her stomach was growling like crazy. When the guys with the gray truck finally came out of the house on Bernadine Street, she felt let down. They were wearing identical brown jumpsuits, like mechanics. One was fat and one was short, and they were both white, and there wasn't a single interesting thing about them, except the short one had flames tattooed all up and down his arms, but even they were boring, like the stickers on the doors of Matchbox cars.

But then the fat one shut the door of the house on Bernadine Street, and Clementine heard the sliding of a bolt. That was something new. They pulled away from the curb, and Clementine closed the magazine and put it back in her bag. From her crouch, she watched the truck get smaller and smaller, and when it was gone, she got up and crossed the street.

It wasn't just new locks they'd put in. There was a whole new door. Now when she put her knuckles to it, the door didn't sound like a dead, hollow tree. She walked around the back and slipped in through the kitchen window. Dummies.

She was lucky her magazines were still upstairs, just where she'd left them. It had been so long since anyone other than her had been in the house on Bernadine Street that she'd stopped hiding them. They were sitting in the corner of the second-floor room that looked like a castle tower. It was her favorite room. On rainy days when she had nothing else to do, she liked to go up there and pretend she was a knight and the squirrels were an invading horde, and she drew back her bow and arrow and—*thwunk, thwunk, thwunk*—they dropped from the telephone wires. She took the new magazine out of her bag and added it to the pile. Then she gathered up the whole stack and crammed it into the hole behind the loose paneling. When she was done, she went downstairs, and with her favorite marker, a fat red one that looked like it was bleeding when it touched paper, she wrote *hahaha* right beneath the peephole.

She was home in time for dinner.

At first it seemed she'd scared them off. A week passed, and the men in brown jumpsuits didn't come back. No fat man, no flame tattoos, no gray truck. Nothing else changed at the house on Bernadine Street, except that some paper went up over the windows one day when she was at school.

She got bored sitting and waiting. She'd read all the magazines and shot all the squirrels a thousand times. Besides, she reminded herself, she had the whole neighborhood to patrol. She couldn't go spending all her time in just one place.

So she moved on, and for a few days she managed to forget all about the house on Bernadine Street.

But then one afternoon later that week, she was passing through the lot on her way home from school, and someone new was standing on the porch, the new door and the shiny deadbolt open behind him. But there was no truck at the curb, nothing but him. He was tall, and coils of red hair flopped around his head like ribbons. He was dressed in worn corduroys and a heavy coat that fit him like a tin can on a beanpole. He was so pale he almost disappeared in the glare of afternoon sunlight. He was looking right past Clementine, as if she wasn't even there.

She knew four different ways to get into the house on Bernadine Street. Not to mention that she'd seen the short man with the flame tattoos hide the key in the drainpipe. No matter how hard she tried, she couldn't see anything through the papered windows, but eventually she figured out that during the day the guy who looked like a sickly clown left the back door open, probably for light. From the empty lot behind the house, she could sometimes catch a glimpse of him moving around inside. No matter how hot it was, he was always wearing the same heavy coat buttoned up to his chin.

After that first time on the porch, she never saw him outside. But somehow he managed to get furniture: a table, a chair, a mattress. She didn't know what else. At just the right angle, she could see him moving the stuff around, trying different spots. As if it mattered, as if the place wasn't a complete dump. He ended up leaving it all in the living room. She would've put the furniture up in the tower. If he was the kind of hoodlum with guns, the tower would've given him the clearest shot. For any kind of hoodlum, that was the smart place to be.

That weekend Clementine was supposed to be helping May-May in the garden. Clementine usually didn't mind helping, but Car was there too, and she was being the word Clementine wasn't allowed to say but everyone knew Car was. The two of them were shoveling compost, and anytime a speck touched her shoes, Car would shriek and stomp her foot until it fell off.

"What will the other skanks think," Clementine said, watching the routine for what felt like the thousandth time, "when they hear you've been standing in horse poop?"

"What will your friends think?" Car said, flexing her blood-red talons. "Oh wait—you don't have any friends."

"All right," May-May said, "all right." And she came over and lifted the wheelbarrow by the handles. "You're both excused."

"She's acting like a baby," Clementine said.

May-May had already turned away. "I'd rather do this alone."

Car gave Clementine a nasty look, her face even more hideous than usual.

"Go text somebody," Clementine said as her sister walked back toward the house.

"Go play with yourself!" Car shouted over her shoulder.

As she watched her great-grandmother weave the wheelbarrow among the raised beds, Clementine thought about how furious Pay would be. It had been his idea that they help. He thought May-May was too old to be out here all alone.

"I'm sorry, May-May," Clementine said, picking up her shovel again. "I want to help."

May-May wouldn't even look at her. "You're all done for today."

Pay would be waiting for her at home, and Car would already have blamed Clementine for everything. So she went in the opposite direction, passing through the garden and into the empty lot. She was halfway across when she lifted her eyes and saw something strange on the porch of the house on Bernadine Street: the tall, gangly, clown-looking guy, slumped against the house, as if he'd been shot. But even from the top porch step, Clementine didn't see any blood. Unless his coat was hiding it.

"Are you dead?" she said.

His eyes opened slowly, and it seemed to take them a moment to focus in on her.

"What's your name?" she said.

He righted himself, pushing his palms against the peeling porch floor. "Dobbs."

She came another step closer and stood there looking down on him.

"What's yours?" he said.

"Clementine."

He leaned his head against the dirty siding. His eyes looked as though they might close again. "Really?"

"You got a problem with it?"

He pressed a thumb into each of his temples. "It's just unusual."

"There's a song," she said. "There's a fruit. It's more usual than yours."

"How old are you?"

She put her hands on her hips and thrust out her chest, her trade-marked impersonation of Car. "Too young to be your girlfriend."

"I figured."

Her gaze wandered over the surface of the porch. It was all so much more depressing now that someone was actually living here. "Your house is terrible."

He shrugged. "Where do you live?"

"Wouldn't you like to know?"

He got up slowly, one hand against the wall for support. "Are you like this with everyone you meet?"

"Just suspicious people."

He moved toward the open door.

He'd dumped the mattress in the middle of the floor. Against the wall were the table and chair. His junk was all over the place, a few pieces of clothing, a flashlight, wrappers, and cans.

She said, "It's even worse on the inside."

She lost him for a moment in the glare and the shadows. When she found him again, he was standing at the table, lifting a plastic jug to his lips. The water seemed to miss his mouth completely, pouring down the front of his coat.

"Why are you wearing that?" she said. "It's not winter anymore. Aren't you hot?"

His right eye twitched. And then the twitch traveled to his nose and on to his other eye. It was like a tremor spreading across his face, making every stop along the way.

"I think you might be dying," she said.

He groaned into his chair, which rocked on uneven legs. "Just tired."

"Weren't you just sleeping?"

"Was I?"

"You're weird."

Clementine turned to look out the open door. From the tower upstairs, she could see past the brush and shrubs to May-May's garden and, past the garden, to May-May and Pay's houses. From down here, though, she couldn't see anything.

"What kind of hoodlum are you?" she said.

His head fell sideways. "How old are you?"

She stepped back out onto the porch. "I have to go."

On Monday a cat Clementine had never seen before crawled under the pricker bush in the lot beside May-May's garden. She waited two days before poking it with a stick.

Science! Would the cat shrivel up and turn to dust? Would rats come and pick its bones? Would she get to see what it looked like on the inside?

For the rest of the week, she raced to the pricker bush after school with her notebook.

Day 3: *It stinks. Looks the same.*

Day 4: *It stinks even more. Fur is falling off. Flies all over the place.*

Day 5: *Something ate its butt. It smells disgusting. Covered in ants.*

On day six, her mother found out about her fractions test, and Clementine was grounded until day nine.

By then the cat had lost almost all its fur and its stomach was puffy, and Clementine was afraid that if she poked the cat again, it would explode, and she'd get covered in guts.

On day ten, she spent the afternoon at home watching cartoons. Car, for a change, was somewhere else.

The next morning Clementine was on her way to school, less than a block away, with exactly two minutes to spare, when Dobbs appeared, turning the corner at the old fire station, coming straight toward her. Clementine was wearing shorts and a T-shirt, and he was in the same heavy coat as always. There was no one else on the street but the two of them. She waved, and he kept right on going, like she was invisible.

He turned onto Bernadine Street, heading home. She thought about following him, but the bell was going to go off at any second, and she knew what would happen if she got another tardy.

The next morning the same thing happened all over again: Clementine going to school, Dobbs going the other way. Same time, same place.

It occurred to her he must've been out all night. And he was only now returning home.

But where in the world could he have been?

§

Her mistake was saying she felt sick before asking what was for dinner. When she sat down at the table that night, there was spaghetti with garlicky bread, and her mother had even made meatballs. Clementine knew if she made a pig of herself now, her mother would see she'd been lying. So instead she picked at her plate while Mama and May and Pay and Car twirled birds' nests on their forks and crammed them into their mouths. They were so busy stuffing themselves, they didn't notice Clementine slipping pieces of bread into her pocket.

As Car went back for a second helping, Clementine clenched her stomach and moaned. "May I be excused?"

Pay looked like he was going to give her his usual *you'regonnastayin yourseattileveryone'sdone*, but then he raised a paper napkin to his lips and nodded toward the stairs.

Clementine went up and then straight out the window and over to Bernadine Street.

★　★　★

It was dark by the time Dobbs finally appeared on the porch, shutting the door behind him. Clementine's knees were woven with the impressions of grass and twigs. It was getting cold, and she wished she'd brought a sweatshirt.

He was easy to follow. She didn't even have to be directly behind him. Every once in a while he disappeared in a screen of trees and bushes, but she never lost his trail, even with blocks of empty lots between them. She knew these streets better than anyone.

But after a few minutes, they'd left the neighborhood behind. She couldn't see Pay's house anymore. There were empty homes and storefronts, but they weren't the ones she was used to.

They must have gone twenty blocks. Most of the street signs were missing. She kept track of the turns using landmarks: broken fences, burned-out cars, heaps of junk. Just when it was starting to seem like they were wandering aimlessly, Dobbs turned down a narrow alley. At the end of the alley was a warehouse, two stories tall. Brick and cinderblock, all of it old and crumbly. Around the side there was a garage. Clementine was close enough behind him that when he lifted the overhead door, she saw a big van parked inside.

The door rattled shut behind him.

There were windows, but they were too high for her to see through. On the ground all around were scraps of metal. They were sharp and cold and rusty and boring and they didn't look like anything. The only sound was the drone of the highway coming from she couldn't tell where.

She hugged her arms across her chest. She'd given up spaghetti and meatballs for this?

Then it started to rain.

Everyone else was downstairs watching TV when Clementine sneaked back inside. She dove under the covers and took out her book. Through the floor she could hear the laugh track laughing hysterically to itself.

Her favorite book. Life, she read for probably the thousandth time, had begun on earth with single-cell organisms that lived in the sea. Almost four billion years ago. It took millions of years for those first single cells to attach to other cells. After all that time and hard work, the ice age came, and 440 million years ago most of those early organisms froze themselves to extinction.

When the ice melted, what remained were plants, mosses, and algae. As the Earth warmed, insects appeared. Corals in the oceans built reefs. But the oceans were hit hard again around 374 million years ago, and the reefs suffered the worst of it.

There were five mass extinctions in all. The one that wiped out the insects came 252 million years ago. That was the biggest extinction of all, killing virtually everything on land and sea. It took tens of millions of years for life to recover. During that time, amphibians and reptiles first appeared, but most of them were killed in the fourth mass extinction, which cleared the way for the dinosaurs. But the dinosaurs eventually got theirs, too. Whether it was an asteroid or volcanoes, no one knew, but whatever it was blotted out the sun. First the plants died, then the animals that lived off the plants, and then the animals that lived off them. What survived were the scavengers.

And then we came, appearing recognizably human about two hundred thousand years ago, and even though we came last, we behaved as though we'd been here forever, as if we were the goal everything else had been leading to. But most scientists, including the author of Clementine's favorite book, believed a sixth mass extinction had already begun.

All a person had to do was go outside and look around.

§

The warehouse door was so solid that when she knocked, she barely made a sound. There were no lights on inside, but she knew Dobbs was here. She'd set her alarm to go off two hours early, and she'd left May and Pay's house when the sky was still thick as gravy.

She knocked again. Overhead, between the trees, a pair of bats twirled like a twist tie. She pressed herself up against the door. Last year her class had taken a field trip to a bat sanctuary. She knew these were probably brown bats. Harmless. Living bug zappers. But they were still ten times more disgusting than even a hundred dead cats.

A moment passed, and she noticed a shadow—or maybe a reflection—gliding past one of the windows. She tried to watch it, but without taking her eye off the bats. She banged again on the door, and the shadow advanced the length of the building a window at a time. It stopped on the other side of the overhead door.

"Let me in," Clementine shouted as the bats swooped low. Their species was dying off from some sort of disease. No one knew why. But who would ever miss them?

The overhead lifted with a jerk. Dobbs stood before her in jeans and a T-shirt. Without his coat on, he looked like a wet dog. His skinny arms were shaking under the weight of the door.

"What are you doing here?" he said.

"What are *you* doing here?"

He jerked his head to show her the way. "Are you coming or what?"

Even though the garage was enormous, entering it felt like squeezing down the narrow stairs into Pay's dirt basement. The darkness and the damp and the cold hit her from all sides. But Dobbs didn't seem to feel it. There was pink in his cheeks. Coils of red hair were matted to his forehead with sweat. There was a smear of dirt along his jawline. His palms were nearly black.

A broom leaned up against the wall a few feet away. Next to it was a mound of dust and debris. There was still more grit beneath her sneakers. She toed at the cement floor, and a chunk popped loose.

He brushed the wet coils of hair from his eyes. "You shouldn't be here."

She walked past him. The garage area was attached through a wide doorway to the warehouse, which seemed even bigger from the inside. Everywhere she looked, there were more mounds of dust and dirt, but everything still seemed dirty. He could sweep all he wanted, and it would never get clean.

In the warehouse were piles of all sorts of junk: hunks of cement block and broken glass and more of those metal scraps she'd seen outside.

The overhead door squeaked back down. The sound bounced through the building, and Clementine was happy to imagine the confused bats smashing into each other midair. Then it was silent again.

In the middle of the warehouse, overshadowing everything else, was an enormous pile of floppy-looking slabs of something. As she came closer, Clementine realized it was a pile of mattresses. Dozens of them.

"Shouldn't you be in school?" Dobbs said.

She shrugged the backpack off her shoulders. "Not yet."

Clementine walked over and gave the bottom mattress a kick. She felt an urge to jump on top of them, but even she could see they were gross and smelly and disgusting.

"What are these for?"

He opened the passenger door of the van, and the dome light came on. "I found them there."

She reached out and touched one of the mattresses, carefully, as if it were alive. And it probably was, full of bedbugs. The case was dirty and stained, but not with the dust and grime that covered everything else in there.

"What are they *really* for?"

He twisted the cap off a water bottle. This time he managed to pour it into his mouth. "People, I guess."

If this was what he left out in the open, she wondered what he was hiding in the rest of the piles.

"What people?"

His sigh was barely more than a breath, but in that huge, empty space, it sounded like her grandfather's bellows.

"Are these people friends of yours?"

His tired footsteps clopped toward her. He was carrying her backpack. He was wearing his coat.

"Come on." He handed her the bag and started back toward the garage.

"Who are they?" she asked again.

He squatted down to lift the overheard door. "I don't know."

"Why don't you know?"

"Because it's none of my business."

He hoisted the door onto his shoulder. The pink had drained from his cheeks. He seemed to teeter slightly as she approached.

Halfway under the door, she paused and pointed at the truck. "Why don't you drive?"

"It doesn't work."

He wouldn't look her in the eye. She could see tracks from the parking lot leading straight inside. She wasn't stupid, but she didn't really care either way. She didn't mind walking. He was the one dragging his legs like heavy suitcases.

The muddy windows in the warehouse had made it seem like it was still night. But once she got outside, Clementine saw the morning sun had already chased the bats away. The trees were backlit, and she could see birds—soft, feathery, nondisgusting birds—perched in the branches. It was hard to believe they'd once been dinosaurs.

The moon was up there too, but it was fading.

"What time is it?" she said as they walked down the alley to the street.

Dobbs shrugged.

"You don't have a phone?"

He kept walking.

She paused to stomp on a Styrofoam cup. "Who doesn't have a phone?"

"Do you?"

"I'm a kid. I'm not supposed to."

"I don't like them," he said.

"How do you call people?"

"Let's go," he said, waving her on.

"How do you call people?" she asked again.

"I don't."

"Jesus," she said. "You're weird." She caught up to him after just a few steps. "My sister would die without her phone. She uses it instead of a brain."

"You're the neighborhood watch?" Dobbs said.

Just as quickly as she reached him, now he was falling behind. "I keep an eye on things."

"Who else are you watching?"

She said, "There's this cat . . ."

"And have you told your parents about me and the cat?"

"They don't notice anything," Clementine said.

He kept slipping farther and farther back. But she didn't need him to lead the way anymore. She already knew a shorter route than the one she'd seen him take.

He stopped. He seemed to be struggling to catch his breath. There was a chain-link fence running along the sidewalk. He let his weight fall against it.

"Are you okay?" she said.

"I'm fine." The coils of hair on his forehead had dried into greasy springs.

"You look like you're about to fall over."

The top rail was missing from the fence. The linked chains were cradling him like a hammock.

"Don't you ever sleep?"

He gazed back at her blankly.

Clementine grabbed his elbow. "Come on." She could see he'd never make it home without her.

It should have taken only ten minutes to reach the house on Bernadine Street, but by the time they got there, the moon was gone. She could tell by the light in the sky that school had already started. There'd be trouble when she got there. It was just a question of how much.

She steered him up the path to the front door. He removed the key from his pocket, and she took it from him and fit it into the lock. Once inside, she pushed him toward the mattress.

"I don't want to lay down," he said, but his knees were already folding beneath him.

"Too bad," she said. "I have to go."

She got detention, of course. The moment she arrived at school, she was steered straight into Ms. Crossman's office, and she had to sit on her hands and wrinkle her nose and try not to sneeze at the old lady's perfume as she pounded out a speech about *responsibilityandmaturity* and Clementine's *educationalfuture*. All the while Clementine watched the hands on the wall clock tick away even more of her precious *educationalopportunities*.

From experience she knew the worst thing about detention wasn't detention itself but what would happen when Pay and her mother found out. But today in particular the punishment also meant she wouldn't get out of school until after four o'clock, and by that time who knew what might have happened to Dobbs.

The day rambled on endlessly, and when they finally opened the doors to let her go, Clementine stuck out her tongue and sprinted down the street, backpack crashing against her with every stride.

When she reached the house on Bernadine Street, she was relieved to find Dobbs sitting on the back step, hidden by the overgrown shrubs.

"You still look terrible," she said. In truth, though, she'd half-expected to find him dead.

"Might as well get used to it."

She pulled a bright red slip from her backpack. "I got detention, thanks to you."

He barely glanced at the paper flapping in front of his face.

"What kind of hoodlum are you?" she said.

He squinted past her into the sun. "I help people."

She waited for him to laugh. Instead he looked at her crookedly. "Who could you possibly help?"

"No one." He gave her a shrug. "I was kidding."

Yet another person who assumed she was dumb.

Clementine tried to picture people sleeping on those mattresses in the disgusting warehouse. It was their own stupid fault, asking for help from someone who lived in a place as crappy as this.

"Where do they come from?"

"What does it matter?"

"Why would they want to be *here*?" she said.

"It's better than where they're from."

Clementine found that hard to imagine. She tried picturing one of those landscapes from the movies, brownish-purple skies crackling with electrical storms, and people living beneath the earth in things that looked like submarines, hiding from their killer robot overlords.

"This is your job?"

"It's not about money," he said.

"Pay sells cell phones. He could get you one."

Dobbs looked down at her, the way everyone else did when they wished she would go away.

"What?" she said.

Dobbs stood up, drifting into the sunlight. The wide, bright rays looked like a tractor beam trying to pull him into the sky. "You're better off without one."

"It's all my sister does, play with hers."

"People take them for granted," Dobbs said.

"Everyone has one, except you and me."

"They're full of metals," Dobbs said. "Rare ones. And there aren't enough."

"They're going extinct?"

"We've mined the easy ones. The rest, it's too expensive."

"Good," Clementine said. "I can't wait to tell her."

"Electric cars, solar panels, wind turbines, batteries. All the stuff that's supposed to save us," Dobbs said. "They all need these metals."

"I've been reading this book," Clementine said. Then she changed her mind, reaching out and grabbing his hand. She gave him a tug. "You're coming with me."

"Where?"

She pulled him forward, and he stumbled after her down the steps. She led him through the yard, not letting go until they'd made it all the way around to the front of the house.

"Come on!" she yelled over her shoulder as she launched herself across the street and into the empty lot.

She was surprised when he did what she said.

She'd never seen him move so quickly. High-stepping into the weeds, he looked like a different person. It was as if it had never occurred to him there was a way to get places that didn't involve sidewalks. She felt like a rabbit, and he was the fox. But even with this sudden burst of energy, he couldn't keep up with her. After half a block, she had to pause to make sure he was still behind her.

She stopped again when she reached the pricker bush. The cat had been there for two weeks now, and its skin was almost completely gone, except for the caramel-colored tip of its tail. The carcass was mostly bones and black stuff swirling with flies and white wormlike things she thought were larvae.

Dobbs's footfalls were heavy for someone so skinny. She raced off when she heard him coming.

A lot and a half away Clementine stopped at another of her favorite spots. Buried in the grass was a low concrete elbow, a piece of some sort of foundation missed in the bulldozing of whatever had been here before. In the corner was a little nook where Clementine kept a collection of things she'd found out here: a metal spring, a ceramic mug covered in poppies, a pocketknife so rusted the blade wouldn't open. She stood up on the concrete, using it as a step. From there she could see Dobbs still back by the pricker bush, bent over the cat. Then he looked up and saw Clementine here, and the chase resumed.

From the elbow she sprinted across another overgrown field to a thicket of scaly red bushes skirting a squat silvery tree. She got down on her knees. There was an opening in the thicket, and inside was a big hollow space, like an igloo made of sticks. Once inside she couldn't see Dobbs anymore, but she could hear his heavy footsteps. The sun was beating down on the bushes, and when Dobbs got there, he was a long, dark shadow blocking out the light. Through the webbing of the thicket, she could see his feet and legs.

He bent down. There was a blue metallic wrapper along the path. He turned it over, tossed it aside. And then he was on his hands and knees, peering through the opening.

"What are you waiting for?" Clementine said.

He poked his head through the hole. He pushed at the upper arch, trying to make more space. A few twigs snapped, but the hole barely moved. Dobbs took a deep breath, sliding forward on his belly.

They sat across from each other in that tight, domed space. This was where she kept her most favorite things, even better than the magazines. There was a coffee can of her favorite rocks. And there was a tree stump table spread with acorns and thorns and sharpened sticks. Around it sat her lieutenants, a blue rubber bear, an armless Spiderman, a fat little robot with dingy lights, a pink-skinned princess wearing a dress of mud.

"I love what you've done with the place," Dobbs said.

For once, she didn't know what to say. No one knew about her igloo—not Car, not her mother, not May-May, definitely not May and Pay.

"I know your hiding spot," Clementine said. "Now you know mine."

His eyes were still adjusting to the dark. She saw him focusing in on the far corner. There was a nasty old sleeping bag and a blanket she usually kept wrapped up in a garbage bag, but it hadn't rained in more than a week. At the sight of them, Dobbs's smile began to fade.

"Is this where you live?"

She rolled her eyes and pushed him aside, and then she crawled past him through the opening. She waited until he backed out, and then she took off again. He was walking strangely, his legs stiff from the squatting. In no time, she'd put another lot between them.

When she looked again, he was still standing beside the thicket. He was turning around and around, but she could tell it wasn't her he was looking for. He was trying to find his house. He had no idea how close it was, tucked away behind a phone pole and a couple of trees. He'd never seen the city from the inside before.

From somewhere up the block, she heard the thump of a stereo. It took another moment for the car to appear, a big black SUV with tinted windows.

Glancing back to where she'd left him, she saw Dobbs ducking down, hidden in the weeds.

Was it someone he knew? she wondered. Or was he afraid how it would look to strangers, chasing a little black girl through an abandoned field?

Once the truck was gone, Dobbs was back on his feet again. Now he picked up his pace. Clementine flew around the beds of May-May's garden in crazy batlike swerves and loops. Dobbs stopped to watch, as if unsure whether he was supposed to follow. In one great swoop, she ran to the edge of the lot and leaped over the weeds, and then she sprinted down the block and into her own backyard. Without stopping, she bounded up the steps and through the clattering screen door.

Her mother, in the kitchen, looked over her shoulder and let out a sigh as Clementine ran past. Clementine glided into the living room, weaving around Pay's brown recliner and past the lamp, then hopped onto the couch, where Car was watching TV and thumbing texts to her imaginary friends. Clementine bounced onto the cushions, and Car started to scream. The phone dropped down into the springs, and Car flopped after it like she was drowning. Clementine went climbing onto the arm of the couch and hovered there, midair, before crashing down to the floor.

On her way back to the screen door, Clementine passed the kitchen again. Her mother was standing in the doorway looking cross, about to open her mouth to yell, when Clementine pressed her lips against the metal mesh and shouted, "Are you coming?"

Dobbs had made it only as far as the edge of the neighboring lot, up to his knees in grass. He seemed afraid to come any closer than the swing set.

"Who are you talking to?" her mother said.

Clementine could tell from the tone of her voice that her mother didn't really want to know.

"A friend!" she yelled, loud enough for Car to hear.

Dobbs must have seen her mother appear at Clementine's side, because after inching forward another step, he suddenly stopped, dead in his tracks.

Her mother took Clementine by the shoulder and pushed her aside.

"Who are you?" she yelled through the screen.

Dobbs looked up at her. Her mother might have been taller than him even if she hadn't been inside the house.

He took a step back. "I'm sorry," he said.

"Clementine." Her mother's voice dipped to that low place she went when she wanted to show her disappointment.

Clementine started to push open the screen door. "I invited him over for dinner."

150

Her mother reached out for the handle. There was cheesy laughter from Car's stupid show. But when Clementine turned around, her sister was standing at the opposite end of the hallway, watching and listening.

"He's my friend," Clementine said again, even louder this time.

But now Dobbs was backing away. "I'm sorry," he said. "I'm leaving."

Clementine wedged herself past her mother. "Don't go." She got as far as the top stair before her mother grabbed her shoulders.

Her mother's voice was rising now, as it did when her disappointment turned to anger. "How exactly are you and my daughter friends?"

"We're not," Dobbs said. He took another step back. "Not really. We're neighbors."

Her mother came down and joined Clementine on the top step, still not letting go. "Where do you live?"

Dobbs started to gesture over his shoulder, but then he must have remembered he was lost.

"Over there," Clementine said.

Dobbs squinted at where she was pointing. From there, even he could see the crazy tower rising above the trees. She could tell he was surprised that Bernadine Street was so close.

The news didn't change her mother's expression.

"We've run into each other a couple of times," Dobbs said.

Clementine felt her mother shift her weight from one foot to the other.

"Do you normally hang out with ten-year-old girls?" she said.

Dobbs lowered his head. "Not usually."

Her mother responded with that slow, heavy shuttering of her eyelashes. Clementine rarely got to see it directed at someone else. "What's your name?"

"Dobbs," Clementine answered for him.

"What kind of name is that?"

"I should be going," Dobbs said.

He took another step back toward the weeds.

Clementine's mother did too, descending to the next step. "How long have you lived here?"

Dobbs's fingers were scratching at his chin. "A couple of weeks?"

"Strange place to move to," she said.

"I'm sorry," he said again. "Clementine told me to come with her, so I kind of just came. I don't know why."

Her mother palmed Clementine's head, letting her nails dig in. "She can be hard to say no to."

"I don't think I even tried." Dobbs turned around to face the empty lots. "She was showing me some of her favorite places."

Her mother sighed. "She thinks the whole neighborhood is hers."

"Can he stay for dinner?" Clementine asked.

The laugh track rose up again.

"I have to go," Dobbs said.

Clementine's mother climbed back up a step. "He has to go."

"It was nice meeting you," Dobbs said over his shoulder as he waded back into the weeds.

Her mother's hand scratched down Clementine's head to the base of her neck. "Pay will be home soon," she said. "You can tell him about your new friend."

Clementine tried to wave goodbye, but Dobbs didn't look back.

Pay grounded her for two weeks. No TV, as if that was something she'd miss. But she also wasn't allowed to leave the house except to go to school.

That night, lying in bed, confined to her room, she took out her book again. She'd checked it out from the library months ago. Eventually, she guessed, they'd stop sending notices, asking for it back. Feet on the wall, she turned again to her favorite part. The sixth extinction, already under way. She'd read this chapter a million times. The planet heating, ice caps melting, species dying, ecosystems collapsing. The sixth extinction would wipe out everything now living, changing the world forever.

Through her window, she watched the sun set behind the empty house next door. The roof looked as though it were engulfed in flames. The heat was rising. The new ice age was coming, and Clementine imagined a girl slapping at a cell phone with fins instead of fingers, a kinder, gentler version of Car.

Eleven

THE LECTERN WAS cut from a refrigerator box, a slab of cardboard creased twice to form three sides. They'd topped it with a square angled slightly toward the back. There Myles had laid his single sheet of paper, just a little too far away for him to be able to read it clearly. But if he were to lift the sheet or the hand that was holding it, everything would have blown away—paper, cardboard, and all. Almost Memorial Day, and a storm had blown in overnight from what felt like the arctic, blasting through the flat, open plaza in front of the HSI Building. The lectern clung to Myles's legs like a terrified child. The hand that wasn't pressing down on the paper hovered above his head, above the dancing locks of his powdered wig. The loose sleeves of the black robe snapped around his upraised arm.

Over the snapping, over the screeching wind, over the rumble of the traffic, over the hurried patter of leather-soled shoes, there were the shouts of interrupted cell phone conversations.

Hold on.

Hold on.

Wait.

I can't.

The wind, I can't.

Hold on.

Their heads were lowered, hunkered down. Nobody so much as glanced Myles's way, which meant, to Holmes's relief, that no one noticed him, either. Too busy, too cold, too busy.

It was Friday, just before nine in the morning, and the eastern edge of the HSI Building was aglow. Holmes stood several paces to Myles's right, aware that he was visibly swaying but unable to do anything about it. His problem had nothing to do with the wind. He barely felt the cold. He was focused instead on trying to keep his knees from giving way beneath him.

Myles was the judge. Holmes was the bailiff, a plastic star from the dollar store pinned to his chest, an army surplus patch on his sleeve. Shiny black thrift store tie to match his shiny black thrift store shoes. Every piece of the ridiculous costume felt as though it were pressing in on him, cutting off his circulation.

All this had been Myles's idea, another little surprise for McGee, another bit of theater. Holmes had spent the previous night trying to talk him out of it, as he had earlier with the video. Stunts like these never worked, especially on McGee.

"But she's tired of picket signs," Myles had said. "She told me. She thinks we should try something else."

"Fine," Holmes had said, "but I don't think this is what she had in mind."

"Then what?" Myles had demanded. "What?"

And Holmes had been able to see his desperation. How could he say no? His oldest friend. A pointless action was one thing, but love was something else. And underlying everything lately was Myles's fear he was losing her.

Across the plaza, the revolving door of the HSI Building slowly

155

turned, and out of the gap stepped an unsettling vision. Holmes had to look and then look again to make sure it was real: his twin, a black man dressed in an almost identical getup of polyester and vinyl, right down to the patch on his sleeve.

But not really a twin after all. When the guard turned and the wind stopped billowing into his shirt, Holmes could see he wasn't as big as he'd seemed. But he more than made up for that with the gun holstered on his hip.

Holmes felt himself teeter. It was now or never. He nodded to Myles. At least he tried to nod, but his head was so heavy he couldn't be sure it moved.

There was an excruciating pause, and then Myles cleared his throat:

"Today, before this gathering of witnesses,
Here in the shadow of this great obelisk of capital,
We find thee guilty of avarice, of arrogance, of deception, of murder,
Of pressing benevolent tools into the service of enmity.

"For thou hast filled thy belly at the tables of tyrants.
For thou has lent thy back to indiscriminate burdens,
Not as a servant, but as a mercenary.
For thou hast reaped profit in damnation.

"We, the jury of thine infamy, have espied
Thee building empires upon the swollen catacombs,
Have beheld thy bitter seed
Aborting thy neighbor's fertile pastures,
Have heard thy chants and prayers
To summon storms of poisoned rains.

"For thou art duplicitous.
Thou art both pillar and pillage.
And we, those of us gathered here upon this solemn day,

And those whose headstones pave
The paths of thy secret gardens,
Are ready to receive thine head and hands
Into this, our hallowed pillory.

"May God have mercy on thy soul."

Throughout Myles's recitation, the world to Holmes had seemed to stand still. The wind, the traffic, the shoes, the chatter—all of it had melted away. Even Myles's words had seemed distorted. Holmes had been aware of him speaking, or at least of Myles's lips moving, but there was no discernible sound. Now, however, the indictment had been read, and now Myles's lips had stilled, and now the world began to reawaken a bit at a time. First there was the piece of paper flopping like a fish in Myles's hand. And then the suits and the leather soles became animated again. But the bodies wearing them were different from before. The revolving doors of the HSI Building continued to suck them in. The guard had left his post by the entrance, heading straight toward Holmes.

Holmes realized now, in fact, that almost nothing had stopped, that almost no one had noticed anything. Aside from the guard, there was only an older white woman in a burgundy skirt who stood a few yards away, the only still body in the entire plaza. The suits swerved around her. Even the wind appeared to leave her alone. A strange expression consumed her face—a cramped, bemused smile. She was looking from Holmes to Myles and back again. She seemed to be waiting to see what would happen next. It was only when the guard reached her side, and she turned slightly to speak to him, that Holmes recognized her. Hers was the face from the picture Fitch had shown them. This was the woman McGee had been coaching him to meet.

Ruth Freeman had hair like a librarian: gray and short, boyishly sweeping across her head. She held her briefcase in both hands, like a child with a basket full of eggs. And in the moment the guard came forward to grasp Myles's arms, the woman's expression changed to something that looked to Holmes like pity.

In the scuffle, the powdered wig slid across the dome of Myles's head. Freed from his legs, the lectern pirouetted once in the wind, then shot across the plaza like a luge. The speech swirled in some invisible vortex.

As the guard pulled him away, Myles pointed to Holmes and shouted, "Bailiff! Take away the prisoner."

Despite the quiver in his fingers, Holmes managed to remove a pair of handcuffs from his pocket. And with the guard distracted, he strode over to the entrance and locked his own wrist to the handle of the nearest door.

§

McGee was calling it a party. But what the hell was the occasion? As best Holmes could tell, they had nothing to celebrate. A couple clips of their arrest on the evening news? Snarky, pompadoured anchors who couldn't even be bothered to mention what the protest had been about? From what Holmes had heard in the hour he'd been out of jail, the local stations had been playing Myles's performance for comic relief, a fuzzy cell phone video shot by someone passing by. It was hard to imagine McGee impressed by such cheap notoriety. But here she was, throwing a party.

Maybe Myles had gotten what he wanted after all.

Fitch had delivered the invitation when he came to bail them out. But he didn't seem to know anything either.

"All I heard was 'party,'" Fitch said, scrawling his name on the clerk's forms and returning them unread. "But something tells me there's not going to be a lot of dancing."

Fitch's response to the situation was vodka. It was his response to everything. He'd been medicating himself with the stuff almost nonstop since his own charade a few days before with the woman Holmes had seen in the plaza. The encounter had left Fitch unnerved.

"I still don't know how she did it," he said as he drove Holmes and Myles from lockup to the loft. "Some kind of Jedi mind tricks."

Fitch had been insisting he'd done everything he was supposed to do, asked the woman every question McGee had written down for him. And still Ruth Freeman had revealed nothing.

"I told you I wasn't cut out for this stuff," he said to Myles in the rearview mirror. "I told McGee. I barely even know what this shit is about."

Holmes was having a hard time feigning sympathy. "We've only had like a thousand meetings to talk about it."

In the backseat, Myles sat silently.

"It's complicated," Fitch said. "There's too much shit to keep track of."

"Especially if you're asleep." Holmes looked to Myles for agreement, but he was looking out the window, not even paying attention.

"I've got a lot going on," Fitch said. "That new demo . . ."

"Have you even started recording?"

Fitch glared back. "I don't remember you leaping to volunteer for Myles's little . . . Shakespeare-in-the-park."

Myles turned his head briefly at the sound of his name, then drifted back to wherever he'd been.

"I still did it," Holmes said.

"So did I."

"Yeah," Holmes said, "but yours isn't going on your criminal record."

"Stop!" Myles shot forward, hovering over the center console.

"I spent the night in jail," Holmes said. "I'm not done complaining."

"Stop the car." Myles was pointing to a store at the corner. "I want to get some cookies."

Fitch elbowed Myles softly in the head, nudging him back into his seat. "Grown men in a van don't stop for cookies."

"For McGee," Myles said. "They sell her favorite kind."

"Jail's not enough?" Holmes said. "We have to buy her cookies?"

"For the party."

"Should we get balloons, too?" Fitch said. "Is someone turning seven?"

"Don't be a dick," Myles said. "Pull over."

The next logical stop after cookies was the liquor store. Fitch's supply had run out.

The bottle he picked was squatting alone and dusty in the bottom corner of a buckled aluminum shelf, no brand name, just the word VODKA printed in bold block type across a coat of arms dominated by an eagle wearing a sarcastic smirk. The bottle was the size of a bullhorn. Holmes didn't drink and never had, but as they drove the rest of the way to McGee and Myles's loft, he started to feel attached to the weight of the brown paper bag in his lap, and he could imagine clinging to the bottle for the rest of the night.

But he never got the chance. The moment they arrived, Fitch ripped the vodka from Holmes's hands. The paper bag fell to the floor, and that was where Fitch left it. Still standing in the doorway, Holmes stared at the crumpled sack, debating whether to pick it up, feeling his mood grow even darker.

"We brought you something," Myles said, handing McGee his latest offering.

She took the package, looked at it sideways. "Cookies?"

"Lemon!" Stepping over the dropped bag, Myles put his arm around her shoulders, and she turned her cheek into his kiss.

No *How was jail*. No *You must be tired*. Not to mention *hungry*. McGee just walked toward the kitchen, and everyone followed. April was already inside.

Holmes had always hated coming here. Two steps past the threshold was all it took to remind him. The place, when McGee and Myles found it, had been an industrial graveyard haunted by the ghosts of sad machines. It had fallen to Holmes to try to make the space livable. His reputation as a handyman had been built around a very limited repertoire, but it was more than any of the rest of them had. He'd never understood how Myles and McGee could possess so much energy and so few actual skills.

Holmes had picked up what little he knew from his father, a locksmith and drunk and general tinkerer. And his uncle, a halfhearted slumlord. Also a drunk. But their work was and had been mostly just fixing whatever was broken. They'd never built entire new rooms or routed new plumbing. So Holmes hadn't either. He'd tried to tell Myles and McGee that he knew exactly as little about that stuff as they did, but McGee had said, "I have faith in you," as if that and a tool belt were all he needed.

They got what they paid for: a shower stall squatting awkwardly almost in the middle of the room, surrounded by crooked walls. It looked like an outhouse. Every time Holmes walked in the front door, this depressing sight was waiting to greet him.

It wasn't as if the city had run out of vacancies. McGee and Myles could have bought a whole house with the change in Fitch's ashtray, but they enjoyed living like this. Or they wanted to enjoy living like this. Sometimes it was hard to tell the difference. Holmes sensed they liked imagining themselves storm chasers dashing into the eye of a tornado everyone else was fleeing. That Holmes himself had fled two years ago, when Fitch offered to let him freeload. Fitch's parents had bought him a condo in Grosse Pointe Woods, and Holmes had packed up his stuff and moved into the spare bedroom, not giving a shit if anyone called him a sellout. If he wanted to, Holmes had a whole childhood full of shitty, derelict apartments in the city to feel nostalgic about. But why the hell would he? Of course, Myles did, too. They'd grown up down the street from each other. But Myles had McGee, and they seemed to feel some imperative to stay. So did April and Inez, though at least they had an actual apartment, with actual rooms and actual doors.

In the kitchen Holmes poured himself a coffee cup full of cranberry juice. Above his head, the fluorescent lights hummed.

"The men's room was empty," Fitch was saying, as Holmes took a seat next to him on the sofa.

April sat on the opposite couch.

"What the hell are you talking about?" Holmes said.

"Empty," Fitch repeated as Myles came over to join them, "except for this one guy standing in front of the urinal on the tips of his toes."

"Why are we talking about urinals?" Holmes said.

Fitch gave him a peeved look. But before he could answer, there was a jostling at the other end of the sofa; Myles seemed to be struggling to pull himself out of a pit.

"What are you doing?" Fitch said.

Myles was holding on to the arm of the sofa as if it were a life vest. "Broken spring."

"It's your own couch," Holmes said.

Myles shrugged. "I forgot."

"Why don't you sit on the other couch?" Fitch said, interrupting his own story. He pointed to the cushion next to April, who sat all alone, her legs crossed like a swami's. Between them was a steamer trunk they were using as a coffee table.

Myles scratched at his stocking cap. "It's a love seat, not a couch."

"I don't care if it's a fucking pumpkin," Fitch said. "We were here first, and now you're squeezing us out."

Myles rocked forward and back, like a cork stuck in a bottle, and Fitch tried to help his vodka ride out the commotion by holding his mug directly above Holmes's lap.

Once Myles was finally resettled, Fitch elbowed Holmes to move aside, and a few drops of vodka bloomed on Holmes's thigh.

"He's standing there on the tips of his toes—" Fitch said, drifting back into his story.

Holmes was chagrined to glance up from his juice and discover Fitch looking directly at him, as if this were all somehow for his benefit.

"What the fuck are you talking about?"

"He's standing there at the urinal, on the tips of his toes," Fitch said, even more dramatically now that he was sure he had everyone's attention. "And he's totally stiff—"

At the sound of the word, something caught deep down in Holmes's chest, and the next thing he knew, he was doubling over, a mouthful of cranberry juice spraying out between his teeth in a fine purple mist.

April, sitting directly across from him, let out a shriek and shot into the air, but it was too late. The juice was splattered across the front of her white sweatshirt.

"Shit, shit, shit, shit, shit," she said, flapping the fabric away from her skin, as if it were on fire.

Holmes waved his arms in surrender, feeling as though he'd swallowed gravel, and everyone—even Fitch—turned wincingly toward McGee, expecting the worst. She was in the kitchen, leaning over the table, making sandwiches, and when she saw what had happened, she turned away without a word, thrusting her hand into a bag of sandwich bread.

By now, April had wrestled the sweatshirt over her head, rushing toward the sink, whimpering, "Shit, shit, shit."

"It's just a crappy sweatshirt," Fitch said. "What's the big deal?"

April grabbed a balled-up towel from the sink and began dabbing at the purple spots. Even from across the room, Holmes could see it wouldn't do any good.

"I borrowed it from *Inez*," April said.

"So it's *Inez*'s crappy sweatshirt," Fitch said. "Who cares?"

April rolled her eyes. There was no need to answer. Everyone knew it was Inez who cared. Even Fitch knew, though he pretended not to.

"She's going to kill me," April said.

Holmes rasped, "Don't tell her it was me."

"It's a fucking hoodie," Fitch said. "She probably got it at the thrift store," which everyone knew to be both perfectly true and completely irrelevant.

"And who the fuck buys a *white* sweatshirt," Fitch said, glancing from one to the next, waiting for someone to echo his indignation.

Holmes rushed to the outhouse and returned with a wad of toilet paper. As soon as it touched the stain on the love seat, the tissue turned pink and began to stick to his hand.

"Maybe you can flip the cushion over," Myles said, not bothering to get up from his seat.

"The thing was hideous anyway," Fitch said as he made his way toward the bullhorn of vodka in the kitchen.

"Do you have any dish soap?" April said. The sweatshirt had turned into a fetal pink blob in the sink.

Fitch came up behind her, peering over her shoulder. "Seriously?"

"Laundry detergent, dish detergent," April said. "It's all the same, isn't it?"

No matter how much Holmes dabbed at the cushion, it didn't seem to make any difference. "Maybe it won't look as bad when it dries," he said with a sigh.

"She'll still see it," April said, not realizing Holmes wasn't talking to her. She turned off the faucet and let the soggy hoodie flop into the sink.

"I'm sorry," Holmes said.

Over in the kitchen, McGee was slapping slices of soy cheese onto the bread with far more force than necessary.

"Anyway," Fitch said, more loudly now, as he and his cup swerved back to the sofa, "I meant his *body* was stiff."

"Why are we still talking about this?" Holmes said.

"Because it's interesting," Fitch said.

"The only one who's interested," Holmes said, "is you."

Fitch shrugged and turned toward Myles, who seemed to be staring at the wall. He'd been out of it all day, ever since they got bailed out, as if his head were still back in that jail cell.

"The guy looked like a mannequin," Fitch said. "He was standing on his toes, ramrod straight, his ass cheeks tight as fucking walnuts." He stood to demonstrate.

Holmes muttered, "Jesus."

"There was a stream coming out of him like a fire hose," Fitch said, tapping Myles on the knee, trying to get his attention. "It's like the guy was drilling a hole in the back of the fucking urinal. It was like a fucking laser beam. And he had this serene look on his face, like he was channeling the energy of the entire galaxy into his cock."

McGee, who'd been knocking a knife around inside a jar of mustard, paused to listen, but Myles still looked as if he'd fallen asleep with his eyes open.

"This is the last time we let you stop at a liquor store," Holmes said.

Fitch sat down at the edge of the sofa. "I was at the sink washing my hands when the guy finally ran out," he said. "Behind me I could hear him moaning."

"Jesus," Holmes said again, and Fitch's eyes flashed toward him.

"Why don't you just let me tell the story?" Fitch's gaze was clear and steady. Maybe he wasn't drunk at all. Maybe it was just this loft that made people crazy.

"When he came over to the sink," Fitch said, more measured now, "there was sweat along his hairline."

"Maybe he had kidney stones," April said weakly. She was sitting on the arm of the love seat in only her T-shirt, rubbing her arms for warmth.

"The guy splashed a couple handfuls of water on his face," Fitch said, "and then he told me I should try it."

"It?" Holmes asked, already wishing he'd kept his mouth shut.

"It?" April repeated.

"What?" asked Myles, his eyes suddenly coming into focus.

Fitch raised his cup to his lips, savoring the anticipation. "The secret Taoist method of urination."

Holmes fell back with a groan.

"He says it strengthens the kidneys," Fitch said with a grin.

"Great," Holmes said. "Can we talk about something else now?"

Fitch said, "It's like a fire hose."

"And why," McGee said, rising now from the table with a stack of sandwiches on a plate, "would you want to pee like a fire hose?"

Fitch stood there openmouthed, seemingly stunned by the question.

"I mean," McGee said, "is it really necessary to turn even something like peeing into a competition?"

"The fire hose," Fitch said, "is just an added benefit. The real point is your kidneys. When your kidneys are strong, you function better—sexually." And Fitch patted his stomach, as if trying to figure out where his kidneys were.

"You talk about your dick like it's a sports car," McGee said.

Holmes was relieved he was no longer fighting this battle alone. "He'd put mag wheels and a spoiler on it if he could."

Fitch flashed his famous smile, the long, glinting eyeteeth. "You'd like that, wouldn't you?"

"Flames and racing stripes too," Holmes said. "You've got me all figured out."

Fitch tugged gently on one of his sideburns, and his eyes moistened with laughter. "You're such a weepy drunk."

"I'm drinking cranberry juice," Holmes said. "You're the one that's drunk."

Fitch raised his empty glass. "That's even worse."

April went back to the kitchen table and returned with the vodka bottle.

"Don't," Holmes said. "He's had enough."

April poured.

Fitch said, "What are you, my mother?"

"How can you drink that?" Holmes said. "It smells like it was distilled in a rain barrel."

Fitch sprang up from the sofa and pirouetted around the steamer trunk. He grabbed April by the hand, and she let out a shriek.

"'Save your sobs for thunderstorms,'" Fitch sang out in his raspy voice, "'and your tears for when it rains.'"

"It's been raining all day, you idiot," Holmes said.

"It's stopped now." April had wriggled free of Fitch, escaping to the wall of windows at the back of the apartment. "Why does it only rain when *I'm* outside?"

With a glance in her direction, Holmes saw it had grown dark. But inside the apartment, under the fluorescent lights, nothing had changed. He wondered sometimes if it ever would. It was possible, wasn't it, to love one's friends and be driven crazy by them, too? People couldn't spend this much time together without occasionally dreaming of murder.

McGee had taken the empty spot on the love seat next to Myles, ignoring the wet cushion. The two of them looked like an old couple on a park bench, lost in thought and memory as the world went by. For all their differences lately, it was one thing they still had in common, the ability to be absent even in the midst of a crowd.

On the wall above McGee and Myles's heads hung a painting, one of the ugliest things Holmes had ever seen. The canvas looked like a lunch tray on which the remains of a thousand meals had permanently congealed. Over the top someone had smeared a layer of something thick and shiny, the texture of fossilized gravy. Everything about the piece was revolting, and yet it demanded to be touched. The painting called out to Holmes every time he was here, and the only way to resist was to avert his eyes, to turn away, even if that meant having to look at the crooked outhouse he'd built. But for once Holmes couldn't seem to take his eyes off the canvas.

"Where did this come from?" he said.

"She used to have a studio here," McGee said, "the woman who painted it. She left it behind."

"I can see why," Fitch mumbled into his cup.

"It's supposed to be this building," Holmes said. "I just realized that. After all this time."

167

Fitch said. "I thought it was meatloaf."

"It looks like trash," April said, not judgmentally.

"Those are wrappers," McGee said. "Bits of newspaper and parts of containers and packages and advertisements. It's made of stuff she found on the street outside. Then she put paint on top."

The whole time she was talking, Myles was shaking his head.

"What?" McGee said, glancing at him sideways.

"It's just, I mean"—Myles looked at her helplessly—"of all the things to use to describe the place you live," he said. "Trash."

"You think she should lie?" McGee said. "Sugarcoat it?"

"It's like giving up," Myles said. "Accepting the worst."

"I think it's more of a reminder," McGee said. "To keep you going."

Fitch broke out in a fit of laughter.

April looked up. "What's so funny?"

"Nothing," Fitch said. "Nothing at all. It's all so deadly fucking serious."

Fitch fell down onto the sofa with all his weight, and Holmes, as if on the other end of a teeter-totter, immediately sprang to his feet. He didn't know why at first, other than that he'd been sitting there too long, and suddenly the space seemed so small, the high ceiling pressing down on his head. And also, he realized now, he needed to take a piss, but he didn't want to go in that outhouse. He'd rather go outside in the alley. He'd rather go out the window. He'd rather go anywhere but there.

"That reminds me," McGee said, and her voice was supposed to sound offhand, casual, as if she'd just managed to retrieve something before it slipped away from her memory. She stretched out her legs and reached deep into the back pocket of her jeans, pulling out a piece of paper, a crumpled printout, which she unfolded on the steamer trunk. Holmes leaned forward to look. The words were upside down, but even so they were immediately clear: HELP WANTED. The address, he couldn't help noticing, was the HSI Building. What, exactly, had reminded her of this?

"Custodians?" Holmes said.

McGee's enormous eyes were wide, and a smile was forming in the corners of her mouth. And Holmes knew, without having to ask, that this, whatever this was, had nothing at all to do with what they'd been talking about a moment before.

"No," Holmes said.

McGee frowned. "You don't even know what it is."

Holmes leaned back against the sofa, arms folded across his chest. "I don't need to."

"What is it?" April said.

McGee handed her the page. "It's perfect."

Holmes realized then that the occasion for the party had been hiding in her pocket all along.

There was a long silence as the inevitable question, the question Holmes had decided he himself wouldn't ask, went unspoken among the others. And Holmes found himself hoping the silence might go on forever, or at least as long as it took for them all to gather their coats and belongings and head for the door.

But then April, sweet April, handed the page back. "Perfect for what?"

McGee lifted the ad weightlessly between her fingertips. "This is how we'll bring them down."

"Oh, God," Holmes said.

Over in the love seat Fitch broke out in more drunken laughter.

"Just listen."

And McGee explained her plan. She was going to get a job there. She was going undercover.

"As a cleaning lady?" Holmes said, no longer able to remain quiet.

"Let her finish," April said.

Once inside, McGee would get into their files. "I'll grab everything I can find," she said.

"About what?" Fitch shouted from his reclining position. "What do you think they're hiding?"

"Everything," McGee said, "going all the way back to the begin-ning. Every toxic spill they've hushed, every environmental report they've squelched, every pension they've cheated, every corner they've cut, every compromise, every casualty they've written off."

For months and years, she'd buried them in information about the company's crimes: exposés uncovered by shoestring nonprofits; hunches chased by alt weekly reporters; arcane pie charts issued by obscure agencies; blog posts by unaffiliated Ph.D.s.

"But why *them*?" Fitch's drunkenness seemed to have miraculously vanished. "There's a million other companies doing this stuff. If not worse. Why are you so obsessed with *them*?"

"Because they're here," Myles said. "And they're all that's left. The others are gone."

McGee rewarded him with a partial smile. "And everyone's afraid they'll leave, too. So they don't say anything, don't hold them account-able. Why do you think the city keeps giving them tax breaks? They move another plant down south to get away from unions, and the city gives them more handouts. The company threatens bankruptcy so they can slash wages, and then they give their executives a two-hundred-percent raise. No one says a word. The city council wouldn't give them a jaywalking ticket, they're so afraid they'll pack up HQ."

"City councils don't give out tickets," Holmes said.

"It's a parasite," McGee said, ignoring him, "destroying this place."

"You actually think this is stuff they've just got lying around?" Holmes said. "All these revealing documents?"

"Filed under D," Fitch said with a deep, throaty air of mystery, "for diabolical plans."

"That," McGee said, turning to Holmes, "is where you come in."

"No," Holmes said, "no, it isn't."

It was all a simple matter of locks, she said. And locks had simple answers: picks. "You," she said, coming up to Holmes's side, "just have to teach me how."

"Have you forgotten where I woke up this morning? Me and

Myles?" Holmes looked over to find Myles had returned to his staring game.

"Since when are you afraid of getting in a little trouble?"

"There's trouble for a purpose," Holmes said, "and there's trouble that's just stupid. His interview—" Holmes pointed to Fitch, who promptly rose from the sofa, eager to sneak away. "What did it accomplish?"

"If it'd worked," McGee said, "we wouldn't be having this conversation."

"What makes you think they have this stuff at all? These reports? These memos? Why on earth would they keep them?" And why, Holmes wondered, looking around the room, had everyone else fallen so silent? Fitch diving back into his cup. Myles off in a daydream. April at the sink, bent over her sweatshirt. Why was no one taking his side?

"Because they're arrogant," McGee said. "Because they think they'll never get caught. Especially your new friend." McGee nodded toward Fitch, and he swallowed deeply. "If Ruth Freeman really doesn't fear the truth, like she says, then she's got no need for a shredder."

"What if you get caught?" April said.

"I'll make sure I don't."

"What's there to say?" Myles finally lowered his eyes from the painting. "It's not like we can talk you out of it."

And of course, Myles was right. McGee wasn't asking their permission. She was informing them of what she'd already decided.

"This isn't us," Holmes said. "This isn't what we do."

"Like you said,"—McGee turned back to Holmes—"what we do isn't working."

April had drifted over from the sink. "I should get going." The ball of pink cotton cupped in her hands looked like a dead rabbit.

"It's early." McGee's smile reappeared. As if she were trying to remind them this was just a party, an innocent party.

Was it early? To Holmes, the hour suddenly felt ancient, as if they'd been frozen in these positions not just for the evening but for eternity, like a dark parlor scene painted by an old master in a world before industrial ruins—before trash could be glued to a canvas and passed off as art. It was time for some new kind of scene. A landscape, a seascape. A nude. It didn't matter. He'd gladly settle for even less than that, for a vase of cut flowers, a still life with fruit.

Twelve

SHE CALLED HERSELF Zolska Zhronakhovska. For her hair, she found a dye to turn the brown hay-colored blond. She had April cut her bangs straight across and iron out the waves. From the front, it looked as though she were wearing half an iceberg lettuce on her head.

She practiced speaking so it sounded as if her mouth were full of ice cubes. Only ever the simplest of words. *Yes. No. Okey-dokey.*

According to the placard, the woman in the basement was the "Head of Facilities Maintenance," a fancy title for someone whose office was a cage. The woman's name was Dorothy, and Dorothy shared the cage with mops and buckets and jugs of pastel cleaning fluid. Dorothy was slim as a cigarette. Her red plaid shirt fit her like a cape.

Beneath the low-hanging fluorescent strips, Dorothy asked McGee questions about her experience and about her immigration status, and McGee smiled and scratched her head and blinked. At the thrift store,

April had dug up a pair of toothpaste-white orthopedic shoes. McGee's pleated, acid-washed jeans closed at the ankle with zippers and bows.

"Okey-dokey," she said, knowing perfectly well the legal formalities were a bluff.

Dorothy pointed to a square in the calendar. McGee would start the next night.

Never had she ridden in anything capable of moving so fast without seeming to move at all. When the elevator doors opened at the third floor, McGee thought at first that she'd forgotten to press the button and was still in the basement.

But the view had changed. Dorothy's cage was gone. There was a tiny black woman squatting with a rag before a set of double glass doors. Beyond the doors was a suite of inner offices.

McGee was right where she'd intended to be.

But already there'd been complications. This was a forty-story office tower, and not until after Dorothy had hired her had it occurred to McGee to wonder what the odds would be that she'd be assigned the precise floor she wanted. One in forty, April had pointed out in her innocently helpful way. And sure enough, McGee had shown up tonight for her first night of work, and Dorothy had handed her a scrap of paper bearing the number twenty-four. From there she was supposed to work her way up, not down. McGee had no contingency plan, and the sight of the number twenty-four had shut off something in her brain. If she'd been capable of thinking anything, she might have thought to turn around and walk home—give up right then and there. But she'd managed to suppress her instinct to flee, and then she'd managed to suppress the unwanted information too, crumpling the number in her pocket and getting on the elevator and pressing the button for three instead.

Now here she was, her brain still numb, with a woman glaring at her, annoyed by the interruption. The woman's ID badge said her name was Calice.

"What is it?" Calice said, already turning back to her work.

Trembling slightly, McGee picked a bottle at random from her cart. "Okey-dokey."

"What are you doing?" Calice said as McGee approached the glass.

McGee smiled, and she was raising the spray bottle to the glass when Calice grabbed her arm. She was small but strong.

"No, no, no," Calice said. "What are you doing?"

It was difficult to guess the woman's age. There were no wrinkles anywhere on her face, but her hair was threaded with gray.

"This is my floor." Calice's teeth were big and square and clenched. She took McGee by the arm and led her over to the elevator. Calice pointed at the forty numbered lights above the elevator doors. The third bulb was lit. Calice motioned toward that one, then pointed at herself.

"You see?" she said.

Every last bit of moisture in McGee's mouth had evaporated, but she swallowed deeply anyway. "Okey-dokey," she said, turning around again and squirting a faint yellow mist onto the glass.

Calice's mouth fell open. "All right," she said, shouting with the first syllable, already calming with the second. She stopped her tongue between her big square teeth. "I don't know what your problem is," she said. She came right up to McGee's chin, so close she could smell the citrus in the woman's shampoo. "I don't know what country you're from that you don't understand *no*. Babies understand *no*. Dogs understand *no*. Are you dumber than a dog?"

McGee didn't know whether it was the chemicals in the air or the misery of the charade, but she suddenly felt like crying. Yellow drops were streaking down the glass.

The woman opened the glass door, and the yellow drops swerved toward the bottom.

The scene McGee overheard Calice narrating into the receptionist's phone was not flattering, but there was nothing she could think to do to about it.

Then the numbered lights above the elevator fell—3, 2, 1, B. And then back up they came, 1, 2, 3, and McGee felt her pulse rise with each digit. The elevator doors parted, and Dorothy burst between them, unbuttoned plaid shirt flapping behind her.

Throughout the cursing and pointing that followed, McGee stood silent and dumb, offering nothing in response.

Was it minutes? It felt like hours. She didn't know. Eventually Dorothy and Calice gave up and went away. They must have decided it was easier to retreat.

McGee waited alone in the reception area a short while longer, wobbling in her orthopedic shoes, but the women never came back.

She needed to get moving. Too much time had already slipped away. Skipping the cubicles, McGee headed straight for the corridors of private offices. As she went, she read the etched bronze nameplates on the thick oak doors. None of them belonged to Ruth Freeman. So back she went again to the beginning, but she was finding it hard to focus. The names passed under her eyes, and she forgot to read them.

Back to the beginning again, once more. Slowly, slowly this time. Concentrate. Nameplate after nameplate, but it still wasn't there. No Ruth Freeman.

Fitch had been useless. She'd interrogated him repeatedly in the days leading up to this. But he'd been such a wreck when he'd been here before, he couldn't remember anything about the layout. They might as well have blindfolded him.

McGee wilted backward into the spongy wall of the nearest cubicle. Was it possible Fitch had given her the wrong floor number?

On her way back to reception, to the cleaning cart she'd left behind, McGee passed a poorly lit corridor in a corner far removed from the other offices. In a glance, it looked unused, if not forgotten, space set aside for some unknown future. Most of the doors along the darkened corridor were unlabeled. Only a few of the rooms had windows overlooking the hall. Peering inside as she went, McGee saw conference rooms, long tables circled with chairs.

She was moving quickly, not watching where she was going, and as she turned a corner, she slammed her shin at full stride into the metal leg of a desk. The pain was so exquisite, she couldn't even cry out, her breath stuffed in her mouth like cotton. She crumpled to the floor, holding her leg, biting her lip until she tasted blood.

She stayed there several minutes, squeezing her knee to her chest. When the pain finally subsided enough that she was able to lift her pant leg, she found a scarlet welt along the ridge of her shin. What kind of place was this for a desk, anyway—this dim, narrow hallway? Had it been left there to be thrown away? And would she be the one responsible for getting rid of it? But no, the computer on top was hooked up and plugged in, as was the phone. There was a pile of papers in a metal tray. A rubber stamp lay on its side in the center of the desk. McGee picked up the stamp and held it before her eyes. The letters were a backward-slanting cursive. Ink had rendered them almost indistinguishable from the background. McGee pressed the stamp into the pad and untucked her shirt. On her belly, she tattooed herself with Ruth Freeman's signature.

Of course. Of all the offices, this one, tucked away in the shadows, was by far the most villainous.

She left the desk limping, but she'd already forgotten the pain in her shin.

McGee's training had consisted of an hour spent sitting in front of a TV/VCR combo in the basement. On a tape drained almost entirely of color, a pair of actors in extravagant perms had demonstrated the art of dusting and vacuuming and mopping (coil the head before pressing!), and when it was over, Dorothy had turned the lights back on and handed McGee a flip chart full of colorful pictures and a schedule of which things she was supposed to clean on which night:

light switches, light fixtures, keyboards, computer screens, telephones, windows, floors and carpets, door handles, door frames, windowsills, blinds.

McGee made her way back toward Ruth Freeman's office, in what she hoped would appear to the guards watching on the security cameras as a natural progression, touching her cloth to everything in sight but never stopping.

In the private offices, with no cameras, she skipped steps that seemed unimportant. But in these places there were far more steps to begin with. The executives had bookcases and shelves and tables and chairs and file cabinets, collections of glass elephants and tennis trophies, awkwardly posed family photos with the same frosty blue backdrop—as if the rich all lived somewhere up among the clouds.

And then at last, McGee stood in the doorway of Ruth Freeman's office. The office was less spacious than the others but had the same furniture: the polished tables and chairs, the hardwood desk so large it looked like an aircraft carrier. The room, at least, was just as Fitch had described.

Ruth Freeman didn't decorate. Little in the office suggested anything about the woman who worked there. But that in itself said a lot. The anonymity could have been a sign of bland taste. But more likely it was the hallmark of a woman who liked to keep secrets. The only object at all revealing was a small photograph in a simple cherry frame propped up in one corner of the desk. In it a man and woman posed on a cliff overlooking the ocean. Behind them the sun was setting, the sky streaked with crimson. McGee had long imagined Ruth Freeman as middle-aged and underfed, desperately trying to cling to her youth, a wearer of pantsuits with shoulder pads and too much makeup, hair chemically stiffened to the texture of funnel cake. But as Fitch had said, the woman in the photo was older than middle age, her hair gray. She'd made no attempt to color it. Her skin collected in wrinkles around her mouth and eyes. Her smile was friendly. But of course, the Ruth Freeman in the picture was on vacation. The Ruth Freeman who sat in this chair, at this desk, was someone else entirely.

The man standing beside her in the picture was younger, lean and handsome, dressed in khakis and a white linen shirt, the top three buttons undone. On his face McGee recognized the smile of someone at ease with himself, someone well acquainted with comfort.

As she'd expected, Ruth Freeman's file cabinet was locked. In vain McGee searched the one unlocked desk drawer for a key. But as it was, she didn't yet have a plan for handling the files once she found them. And not until dawn was blandly announcing itself though the tinted windows of the corridor and it was time for her to move on to the next floor, did McGee come across the room housing the photocopier. By then all she wanted to do was go home to bed.

Myles didn't even roll over when she came in. There were no grunts when she fumbled to join him under the covers, still dressed in her horrible jeans. She was too tired to deal with zippers and bows.

Sometime later—hours later, maybe—McGee became aware of Myles's lips on her forehead, but she had no strength to do anything in return. And then he was gone.

At one o'clock in the afternoon, her phone rang, and she let it go to voice mail. A few seconds later the ringing started all over again.

"What happened?" April asked, even before McGee had a chance to say hello. She was calling from the bookstore.

"There was this video," McGee said with a yawn, describing the actors and their perms, and then she told April about the cleaning cart and about how Calice and then Dorothy had yelled at her, and then about the glass elephants and the trophies and about the desk and her shin, which now looked as if there were a mouse hiding under her skin.

"You mean it actually worked?" April said.

Until that moment, the thought had never crossed McGee's mind. Despite everything Holmes and Myles and Fitch had said, their insistence that she was crazy even to consider it, the plan had actually worked.

Holmes came over with his picks later that afternoon, and he and McGee practiced on an old dented file cabinet. She'd underestimated how difficult it would be to get a feel for pins and tumblers. She'd thought it would be like learning to juggle or to perform a card trick, just a matter of getting down the motions, the sleight of hand. Every dozen or so tries, she got the lock to pop, but she never understood why. It would just happen, the sequence of steps buried somewhere inside the metal casing.

"Try again," Holmes said each time. "Try again."

He never lost patience, but he also never took off his coat.

"You understand it's a felony, right?" he said. "Just getting caught with them."

"I'm not going to get caught."

"Just having them on you."

"You're worse than Myles," she said. "When did you guys get to be such pussies?"

Holmes stood up and checked his watch. "I've got to go."

After four hours, it was the first mention he had somewhere to be.

That evening, riding the bus into the downtown twilight, McGee was jittery, her feet pumping the pedal of some imaginary machine. Twice on her way from the bus stop to the building, she nearly stepped directly into oncoming traffic.

In the basement, she got her cart and went through the motions of checking her supplies. She was waiting for the elevator when she heard footsteps behind her.

"Zolska, Zolska."

Not until the fourth or fifth time did she recognize her name.

It was one of the guards, the black one with the kind face, the mouth that even at rest seemed to settle into a smile. The same expression was there on his ID badge: Darius.

"They told me to help you upstairs," he said. And then, "to your floor." There was no meanness in his voice, and yet as he hooked two fingers to the front of her cart, steering it toward the elevator, she felt flattened. Together they stepped inside the car. Darius pushed the button for the twenty-fourth floor. But while his head was tipped back to watch the numbers change, McGee pressed the button for the third floor. And when the doors opened there first, she rushed out, rocketing the cart before her. She was already removing supplies when Darius realized what had happened, sticking his foot out just in time to stop the doors from closing.

McGee's second confrontation with Calice was even more unpleasant than the first. Calice cursed. Calice waved her arms. Calice made every threat she could think of. McGee felt genuinely sorry to have caused this woman so much trouble. But there was no room for regrets when so much was at stake.

In the end, it was good that Darius *had* come up with her. He was the one who finally managed to coax Calice and her cart onto the elevator, reassuring her she was right. A simpler task, presumably, than arguing with a woman incapable of understanding what you were saying.

As soon as they were gone, McGee hurried to Ruth Freeman's office, skipping all the pretenses from the night before. She knew she had only a few minutes before Darius returned to his security cameras in the lobby.

She slid the leather case from her pocket. Inside, the picks looked like dental tools, thin and delicate and all neat in a row, shining and sterile. Holmes had told her the desk would have a wafer lock, like the one in her cabinet at home. So she did what she'd spent hours practicing, inserting the tension wrench and then raking at the wafers with the ball pick. After a couple of tries, she could feel the wafers rising, one at a time, but she couldn't get the cylinder to turn. Her fingers were getting sweaty.

Holmes had prepared her for this as well. Deep breath. Then

another. Remove. Start over. In again with the wrench and the pick. Again she felt the wafers move against the springs, but no matter how much she wiggled and pressed, the wrench wouldn't turn. She wished she could call Holmes, but it was too risky to bring her phone. The Lucite clock on Ruth Freeman's desk told her ten minutes had already passed. She had no choice but to get on with the cleaning.

The hours that followed were some of the longest of her life. It wasn't the cleaning she minded. It turned out she liked vacuuming, enveloping herself in the drone of the machine, how it cut out every other sound, the way being underwater reduced the outside world to a harmlessly diffused suggestion of light. But her mind kept returning to the lock, to what she'd done wrong. She replayed the sequence in her head, and in tandem she replayed Holmes's lessons, looking for mistakes. But she was sure she'd done exactly the same thing tonight that she'd done with Holmes that afternoon.

She called Holmes as soon as she got home the next morning. It was five A.M., and he was sleeping. So was Myles, just a few feet away from where she stood with her phone.

"I need you to come over."

Myles snuffled into his pillow.

"Are you kidding me?" Holmes said, the words coming out in a croak.

She told him what had happened, that she needed his help.

"I'll be over later," he said.

Through the phone McGee could see him closing his eyes. "No," she said. "Now."

Myles was sitting up on the futon, squinting. "What's going on?" he said.

"Nothing." She sat down at the computer. "Go back to sleep."

★ ★ ★

"It must be a double wafer," Holmes said. It had taken him three hours to make the twenty-minute drive. She smelled coffee on his breath, eggs and bacon. Myles had left for the store.

"What does that mean?"

"The things inside that make it lock," he said. "They move in both directions, not just one."

"So what do I do?"

Holmes picked up the black leather case from the steamer trunk. He pulled out what she guessed was a wrench, but different from the one she'd tried the night before, a pair of sharp tines poking out from one end. "Two-prong wrench," he said, and then he pulled out a pick shaped like a snowman. "Double-ball pick."

He showed her how to rake the pick along the wafers. "It's not enough just to do the top," he said. "You have to do both. Top and bottom."

He sounded confident, but he'd been just as confident the day before. "You're sure this'll work?"

He was already walking toward the door. "I'm not sure of anything."

McGee slumped down on the love seat. "Are there locks that can't be picked?"

"Everything I know," Holmes said, "I learned when I was fifteen."

McGee ran her finger along the contours of the snowman. "What do I do if it doesn't work?"

"I've given you everything I've got."

McGee knew better than to trust the quiet. That night no one stopped her as she collected her cart in the basement. Not Dorothy, not Darius. No one escorted her to the elevator. And no one, not even Calice, was waiting on the third floor when she arrived there.

Maybe they'd all given up, but that didn't mean they'd stopped watching.

Ruth Freeman's office was only thirty paces from reception, but that night it took McGee an hour and half to get there. She was slow. She was methodical. She gave the third floor the most thorough cleaning of its existence. As she dusted, she lifted every stapler, every pen. She vacuumed not just around but even under every chair. She aspired to be the most boring thing ever seen on a security monitor. She wanted to make Darius, or whoever was watching, fall instantly asleep.

By the time McGee finally reached Ruth Freeman's office, there was no reason for anyone to suspect anything at all. She stopped her cart, unlocked the door, grabbed her duster, and went inside, tools already sheathed in her pocket. She kneeled down in front of the desk. At first she felt as though she were trying to find an unfamiliar light switch in a pitch-black room. She ran her pick along every edge, feeling her way. Whatever was in there, it wouldn't line up. She reached for the double-prong wrench, and then she slid in the snowman pick. It met no resistance. When she angled the tip, she could feel the wafers rising and lowering in their grooves. And then all at once, the wrench turned, and it kept turning until the lock clicked.

McGee's breath fell short and shallow as she reached for the handle. The drawer rolled open on liquid wheels. There were folders inside. She reached in and touched them, just to make sure they were real.

Out in the corridor, she swapped her duster for the vacuum. She forced herself to move slowly, full, deliberate motions with pauses in between. On the threshold she stopped to wipe off the doorknob and run her cloth along the jamb. And then, at last, she was back inside, heading directly for Ruth Freeman's garbage can. She removed the bag. It contained almost nothing, a few tissues and crumpled notes. Then she opened the desk drawer again. She pulled out the files and put them in the garbage bag. She carried the bag through the doorway, lowering it into the belly of her cart.

The photocopier was in a room on the same poorly lit corridor as Mrs. Freeman's office. McGee stopped her cart just outside the door.

Using another wastebasket for cover, she smuggled the files inside. With the papers snug in the automatic feeder, there was nothing left but to press the start button and hope. She closed the door, just as the first burst of green light leaked out from around the edges of the copier lid.

Back in the corridor, she turned on the vacuum. The drone drowned out the whoosh of the copier. Choking the handle with two clenched fists, she tried to keep her eyes on the carpeting, but there was an irresistible pull in those quick flashes of light in the crack under the door.

Even at her most optimistic, she'd never imagined the plan would work so well. Lately it seemed to be the nature of plans to go wrong. Or if not the nature, then at least the tendency. But maybe they'd been having so little success recently because they'd stopped taking risks. They'd fallen into routines. This was her reward for pushing, for making them go further than they'd been willing to go.

McGee drifted off. And when, minutes later, she gradually drifted back, she found herself staring, hypnotized, at the copier room door. She'd forgotten about the vacuum. She'd forgotten about her disguise. She was simply standing there dumbly, waiting for the copier to stop.

A shadow appeared along the edge of the corridor, moving.

The vacuum slipped from her grip.

As Darius came closer, his reflection skated across the surface of a framed landscape—a mountain, a valley, a distant lake. The fallen vacuum was still running, masking the thumping in her chest. Then Darius was beside her. Her hand was shaking. The vacuum vibrated, rattling against the baseboard. Darius bent over to pick it up for her, and he was about to switch off the power when she snatched the vacuum back.

Furrowing her brow, she bent into the machine, rolling it over and over again across the same few square feet, as though she and the carpet were engaged in a fierce tug-of-war. Darius leaned against the wall, watching the brushes spin.

"I don't want—I hope I'm not making you nervous," he said when she finally killed the switch.

McGee unplugged the cord and whipped it around the vacuum.

"I noticed—" He gestured over his shoulder. "I think you missed something in the reception. One of the windows . . ."

McGee hoisted the vacuum back onto its platform, then wheeled her cart down the corridor, speeding away from the photocopier room.

"But you're doing fine, though," Darius said, jogging to catch up. "You'll get the hang of it."

She stopped short, and he stepped on her heel.

"Did you do this where you're from?"

They'd reached reception, and she headed over to the windows.

"You're not—are you going to use *that*?" Before she could spray, he'd wrenched the bottle from her hand. The first time that had happened, with Calice, McGee had only been able to watch helplessly. This time she had to uncurl her fist to keep from hitting him.

He went over to the cart. After a brief search through its contents, he replaced the bottle with something more to his liking. "It's just they expect everything to be perfect."

He sprayed. His finger followed the course of a drop running down the window. When McGee made no move to stop it, he sopped it up with his sleeve.

While he was distracted, she tried again to get away, but Darius caught up with her outside Mrs. Freeman's office. Not at first realizing where she was, McGee turned and went inside. Then it was too late. She had to do something, but her mind was blank. Darius stood in the doorway looking at her, or looking past her. She couldn't tell which.

"Cobweb." He was pointing at a corner of the ceiling. "A cobweb."

The silky thread was a high wire about a foot and a half long, passing from one wall to the other. McGee stared at it, enjoying the stretch it allowed her neck.

"You can use this," he said, and his touch awoke her with a jolt. For a brief, blissful instant, she'd been able to forget he was there.

He stood behind her with a broom in his hands. He held it out to her, and when she didn't take it, he extended it toward the ceiling. After several swipes, not a trace of the cobweb remained.

"Cobweb," Darius said, pointing at nothing now. "Cob-web."

McGee got to work on the blinds.

For the next hour they continued on this way, Darius talking, McGee looking for escape.

"At home I do a lot of the cleaning," he said at one point. "Vacuuming, dishes. I don't like to dust."

She made no effort to listen, but it was impossible to tune him out completely.

"My wife cleaned for a while," he said. "For work, I mean. But not here," he added. "At the college. Just after high school. Years ago."

He seemed especially interested in talking about his wife, and at first McGee found this sort of endearing. He told her how they'd met as children, how they'd been friends for a dozen years before finally marrying. But then he started in on their apartment and their neighbors, about a girl who lived upstairs. He had a lot to say about her, this girl, how she fought with her mother a lot, was constantly coming to see him. She was young, wore tank tops and stretch pants. She filled them out, McGee could tell, the way Darius's eyes glazed over as he described her. He spoke of the girl as a nuisance, which was clearly contrary to what he actually felt, and McGee found it troubling that he would bother lying to someone he believed couldn't understand him in the first place. But he was calm and soft spoken. He seemed happy just to talk, as if it were some form of therapy.

The files remained in the photocopier, and the thought of them nauseated her. McGee kept telling herself that if he didn't leave, she would. The plan would be a loss, but she wasn't about to let herself get caught.

Her savior, it turned out, was Darius's partner, calling from the lobby to say Darius was needed downstairs.

187

Darius looked apologetic as he headed toward the elevator, as if this were a date they'd both be disappointed to end prematurely. "I'll be back in a little while."

The moment he was gone, she sank into one of the waiting room chairs, nearly numb with exhaustion.

Darius must have run out of time or found someone else to bother. He never came back, and McGee was able to return her cart to the basement without running into him. Without looking over her shoulder, she was cruising out the door, a cool sheath of paper cutting into her belly.

Over breakfast that afternoon, McGee gave April the details.

"You're crazy if you're thinking about going back," April said. "What if he does it again?"

McGee had already wondered the same thing. "He probably does that to everybody," she said. "He's just lonely. There are forty floors and I don't know how many people cleaning."

"Is it worth the risk?" April gestured toward the manila folder McGee had left on the table, which contained Ruth Freeman's files. "Was what you got that great?"

McGee lifted her empty cup and watched a few coffee grounds slide across the bottom. "Worthless."

She'd spent the last several hours going through every page. Reports about budgets and memos about policy changes and personnel moves. It was the most boring pile of nothing McGee had ever forced in front of her eyes.

April sat silently across the table, looking as if she were afraid to speak.

"Two hundred pages," McGee said. "Probably more. All completely useless."

"What are you going to do?" April said in her tiniest voice, the one she reserved for her friends' darkest moods.

McGee had been asking herself the same thing all morning. "Maybe I'm just not looking in the right place."

§

By the end of her first full week, McGee had begun to develop a routine. There was a logic to cleaning. If she waited to dust until after she'd vacuumed, she ended up spilling filth back onto her clean floors. And trash bins were better emptied all at once. Collect them all—do that first, before exhaustion set in, and then dump the bags near the elevator. Otherwise she ended up carrying all that extra weight, hour after hour.

On her sixth night, Darius appeared as she was wiping down the conference room table. She wasn't happy to see him, but she wasn't afraid, either. By then she'd already done what she needed to: picked, copied, and returned. Three nights in a row now, she'd pulled it off, getting in and out of Ruth Freeman's files without any trouble. Stealing, it turned out, was easy. The problem remained finding something worth taking. As with the first files she'd brought home, the stashes from the last two nights had been useless: memos and spreadsheets and mountains of meaningless data. If Ruth Freeman's main job was obfuscation, she was incredibly good at it.

All night, as she cleaned, McGee's thoughts had been returning to that conversation days before with April: what if there was nothing in this batch of files, either? Then she'd have to move on. There was no shortage of files. The main filing room was down the corridor from the photocopier, a space bigger than her whole apartment, row upon row of cabinets. In Ruth Freeman's office, with its few drawers, McGee could copy everything. But confronted with an entire room of files, where would she even begin?

As usual, Darius announced his presence that night when her back was turned, as if hoping to catch her by surprise. "Here you are," he said, leaning in the doorway.

As if she weren't in the same place as always.

189

For a change, though, he didn't seem especially happy to have found her. He looked tired, the jamb doing most of the work of keeping him upright.

She brushed past him, refusing to meet his eye. Out in the corridor, she began on the windows. He seemed distracted, watching without his usual enthusiasm. Next thing she knew, he was slumping down in the corner with a dramatic sigh.

"I don't know what to do," he said. "Violet—" He looked up pitifully, giving McGee a meaningful look, the meaning of which she made no effort to understand. She moved on to the next set of windows, wishing she could get even farther away. She'd had enough of Violet, the girl Darius liked to pretend was such a nuisance. His latest report, several nights before, was he'd finally told her to quit stopping by in her skimpy clothes. As if that were the problem, not Darius himself.

"I didn't see her for two days," he said now, trailing McGee with his eyes. "Two days," he repeated, pausing, as if to allow time for applause. "I don't know," he said, pulling his knees to his chest. "I'd started thinking maybe everything would be all right."

McGee remembered him having said the exact same thing the night he broke it off with her, too, that maybe now his problem was solved. She hadn't believed it any more then than she did now.

"Yesterday I got home from work," Darius said, "and I saw something in the stairwell. One of those things you put in your hair, you know what I mean? One of those things." He made a vague circle with his hands. "It looked like something I'd seen her wear. I thought maybe she'd dropped it. So I brought it upstairs. I wanted to leave it outside her door, but I don't know," he said. "I must've hit the knob or something."

Right, McGee thought. Or something.

"She must've heard me. She opened the door, and then I had to go in, and . . ."

He trailed off, but McGee had no trouble filling in the details he'd left out.

It seemed to McGee as if they were hours into his sordid soap opera before Darius finally excused himself to go to the men's room. In the sudden silence, she thought she could feel her nerves stretching out, returning to a state of calm. Each breath seemed to carry all the way to her toes.

Knowing she had only a minute or two, she moved quickly, hurrying from the lobby to Ruth Freeman's corridor. Past the old lady's office she went, past the photocopier room.

She let herself into the main filing room with her key. She flicked on the light.

She'd been here before. She knew what the room contained. But she needed to see it again. She needed to see it now, to measure it, to think about what it would really mean to try to find something here. A couple hundred cabinets, at least. Labeled, but the labels helped only if you knew what you were looking for. Even if she managed five hundred pages a night, it would take her decades to get through it all.

She made it back to her cart just ahead of Darius.

She let him load the heavy bags of trash into the elevator. Once they reached the basement, he picked them up again and carried them out to the loading dock. As he tossed the trash into the Dumpster, McGee stashed her papers underneath.

For a moment afterward, while Darius collected a few Styrofoam cups and candy wrappers from the pavement and tossed them into the bin, she allowed herself to watch him with a smug sort of pleasure. No matter how close he followed, he'd never catch her.

As he came toward her now, she gazed at the files just visible underneath the Dumpster, daring him to look. But was that it? A game of chicken, until hopefully, maybe, she got lucky? Found something useful?

Darius sat down beside her on the loading dock. McGee sucked on her cigarette as if it were made of pure oxygen. But no matter how deep she pulled the smoke into her lungs, calm kept eluding her.

"She came downstairs again." Darius toed a loose bolt onto the railing at the edge of the dock. "This morning."

McGee inhaled again, let the smoke linger even longer.

"I told her, 'I said you shouldn't come here anymore.' And you know what she said?" Darius paused, shaking his head. "She said, 'Yeah, but you came upstairs yesterday.'" Darius gave the bolt a solid whack with his heel.

"I said, 'Yeah, but that was different.'" Darius looked again at McGee, as if waiting for her to agree. "I told her, 'That was because I needed to return your thing, your hair thing.' But she came in anyway, and I don't know," he said. "I don't know how to make it stop."

McGee was glad she couldn't speak, that she didn't have to be the one to point out the obvious, that he didn't actually want it to stop.

It was a strange thing, though: on behalf of his wife—on behalf of women everywhere—McGee wanted to punch him. But he was so helpless, so pathetic. A grown man undone by a girl barely out of her teens. He was a child, sitting beside her with a loaded gun.

He was still fidgeting. "See that light?" he said. He was looking at the parking garage across the alley, pointing toward a gap between the garage and the building next door. "It's hard to see. That one right there. The red one."

Perhaps half a mile away, a red light flashed, high in the sky, attached to a smokestack or some sort of tower.

"They used to have factories all over the city," he said, gesturing to the building at their backs, HSI.

No kidding, McGee wanted to say.

"The stuff they sell," he said, "they made it right here. Washing machines, laser beams, I don't know what all. You can still see what's left of it. The factories, I mean. Ruins."

McGee flicked her butt off the dock, and Darius watched it go, grimacing. For a moment he seemed to be debating whether to go retrieve it.

"They found cheaper places," he said. "Cheaper workers. That red light," he said, pointing again, "that's the last one. I don't even know what they make there."

Compressors, McGee said to herself, lighting another cigarette. They make compressors. She knew more about HSI than anybody. For all the good it had done her.

She breathed out a heavy column of smoke, and the red light briefly faded.

Darius picked up a pebble from the loading dock and tossed it into the alley. He seemed to have given up on the bolt. "They're shutting it down, too. The last one."

McGee lifted her eyes to his face, forgetting to hide her surprise. No, she wanted to say, you're mistaken.

"It's true," he said, as if he could hear her thoughts.

She took another drag. No, it wasn't.

Whatever else she thought of it, the company was too smart ever to leave the city completely. Even if the factory was a money pit, it was HSI's one token gesture to the place it'd been fleecing and poisoning for generations. That factory wasn't going anywhere.

"China," Darius said. "They say it's moving there by the end of the year."

Of course, China. It was always China's fault.

"Another ruin," Darius said, and then he turned to face her. "Where's the future in it?"

She was surprised by how sincere he seemed, as if he were genuinely waiting for an answer.

"My friend Michael Boni," Darius said, "he's got a plan. He says we should clear it out, all these ruins."

Plans, McGee thought. I had a plan, too. And there it lay, under a Dumpster.

"Enough's enough. That's what Michael Boni says."

Off in the distance, the little flash of red was all there was to see.

Darius rose to his feet. "A clean slate, he says."

McGee thought again of the file room the size of her apartment up on the third floor. In her head she counted all the cabinets it contained. Hopeless.

Darius was walking past her now, back to the building.

"How would you do it?" she said.

Darius stopped midstride, and he remained there, frozen.

"How would you do it?" she said again. "Clear it all out?"

When he turned to face her, Darius's expression was perfectly blank. "Michael Boni knows."

"This stuff about the factory," McGee said. "Where'd you hear it?"

He blinked at her slowly. "I don't remember."

So much for clever plans. She got up, brushed off her pants. She might as well keep going, not stop until she reached home, leave the useless file where it lay with the rest of the trash.

"Everybody knows," Darius said. "I heard it from everyone." He was staring at her now, trying to process what was happening.

Well, that made two of them. After everything she'd gone through, after all the chances she'd taken, here with a stricken look on his face was what she'd been looking for all along. This guy—who treated his wife so abysmally, who spilled his guts to strangers, who cared so irrationally about the cleanliness of a stupid building—he was the one with the answers.

"Then I guess we've got two choices," she said. McGee moved over to the railing, and it wobbled beneath her.

"The one I prefer," she said, "is that I help you and you help me."

When she got home that morning, McGee pulled off her orthopedic shoes and let them hit the floor with all their weight.

Myles shot up in bed, his eyes as big as moons.

"Have you heard anything about them closing the last factory?" she said.

Myles blinked, rubbing his eyes.

She said, "We've got a new plan."

Thirteen

HE WAS ON a bench in a plaza outside Caesars Palace, near a concession stand that sold frozen, sweetened alcohol in yardstick-size glasses. This was summer, eight months ago, and the Nevada heat had been punishing. But Dobbs hadn't gone there for pleasure. In his foreseeable future, he knew, there'd be no stage shows, no five-card draw. If anything, the odds seemed to favor him ending up on a blindfolded drive back out to the desert. He accepted those odds, and the people who'd brought him here knew it, which was why they hadn't bothered posting anyone to watch him, to keep him from getting away.

Dobbs was waiting for Gordo to come and tell him their fate. He would wait all day, if necessary.

The fuck-up had been Gordo's, not Dobbs's, but these were not the sort of people who sat around splitting hairs. The problem was that

Gordo, his partner on this particular job, had a little side business of his own, one that didn't compete with the business they'd been hired to do but certainly benefited from it, allowing Gordo to take advantage of certain efficiencies in logistics management, as he later said, filling transport space in the truck that otherwise would have gone empty with cargo of his own.

Dobbs hadn't known about any of this until it was too late, but the secret had apparently gotten out to others. The night before, somewhere east of Barstow, a mismatched pair of plus-size Fords had overtaken them, forcing them off the road, and the truck had overturned. Dobbs and Gordo were okay in the cab, but the same couldn't be said for the people in the back. Two of them were already dead when Dobbs and Gordo extracted themselves from the wreckage. There were broken bones and agony among the rest. Even then Dobbs didn't understand what had happened, not until he and Gordo were kneeling in a patch of gravel spotlit by the Fords' high beams, squared-off Glock barrels pressed into the backs of their skulls, and under his breath, as if no one else could hear, Gordo admitted he would've told Dobbs sooner but "I thought you'd say no, Doc."

At that moment, with the jagged rocks pulverizing his kneecaps and the diesel fumes swimming in his brain, it had pleased Dobbs to imagine Gordo was right. There were lines Dobbs had drawn. And in heroin there was no imperative, moral or practical. Gordo had been operating purely for profit.

In truth, though, when had Dobbs ever said no to anything? From the start he'd gone along with whatever jobs Sergio offered him, no questions asked, trusting in an unspoken pact. He chose to believe Sergio understood Dobbs was different. Not a criminal. A Conscientious Independent Contractor.

But Dobbs's commitment seemed to make no difference. There was still something about him the others didn't trust. Gordo treated Dobbs's two years in college as the equivalent of a medical degree, and nothing Dobbs said could convince him otherwise. Why would

Dobbs be doing work like this, Gordo wanted to know, when he could've had a house with a pool, a fleet of Cadillacs, a Rolex, a beautiful wife?

Dobbs accepted that to the others his presence was hard to understand. But for himself, it all made perfect sense. The world was changing, borders were dissolving. The rich were still rich, and everyone else was in free fall. Those jobs that Gordo imagined coming with a college degree, they didn't exist anymore. And there was so much worse to come. Drought throughout the West. Hurricanes from the Gulf to the Atlantic. These were just teasers. But people denied what they were too scared to face. They went on dreaming of beachfront condos soon to be a mile under the sea. They stuck umbrellas in the sand and burned.

So Dobbs had aligned himself with the survivors. Bottom-feeders had always been the most adaptable of species.

Then came the accident. But not an accident, really. A transaction. One of the costs of survival. Outside Barstow, with a Glock to his head and carnage all around and the pitiable moans of the wounded, Dobbs discovered he'd gone numb. He could no longer feel anything at all.

The men who'd intercepted Dobbs and Gordo on the highway were so efficient, so confident, they didn't bother wasting bullets. They took the drugs and left. But it would've been easier, in certain ways, if they'd been less merciful, sparing Gordo from having to make the phone call, to admit what had happened. "It's like ordering your own execution," Gordo said as it rang.

In the hour it took for help to arrive, Dobbs tended to the injured as best he could. There was so much blood it was hard to make sense of what he was seeing—what was severed and what was broken. There was screaming and praying, and Dobbs couldn't understand a word. His Spanish was still just as bad as during his first trip to

Mexico. He went from one to the next saying, "It's going to be all right," and he hoped the language barrier meant they couldn't hear the tremor in his voice.

"I should've just called the cops," Gordo kept saying. "Better off taking my chances with them."

If there'd been anything for a hundred miles other than heat stroke and dehydration, Gordo would've taken off on foot. But Dobbs had decided to stay, no matter what.

Fifteen minutes before the three black Suburbans appeared on the horizon, a third person died, a woman maybe forty years old. Pink theme-park T-shirt, not a speck of blood. Not even a bruise. Dobbs had given her barely a glance, thinking she had no need for him. There one moment, gone the next.

They were the first people Dobbs had ever lost. All this time he'd thought he was good at what he did. Now he understood he'd just been lucky.

He and Gordo were tossed into the back of one of the Suburbans, and everything Dobbs saw on the way to Vegas, and everything since, had been a blur. It was as if his eyes had forgotten how to focus. And here on this bench outside Caesars Palace, the scorched cement radiating through the soles of his shoes, he felt not just his eyes but his entire body growing hazy, as if he were becoming absorbed in some sort of mirage. The Eiffel Tower at his back, a showgirl's ruby thong, four stories tall. The palm trees along the boulevard were pert and happy, but all of it was smeared now with a film of blood. Dobbs kept watching for Gordo, for his inverted straw basket of hair bobbing among the crowds, for his big, goofy smile. Why did Gordo have to be so stupid?

Dobbs thought back to his first meeting with Sergio, to that frothy bag of beer. It was all so much farther from Minnesota than he'd ever dreamed. But even now he couldn't imagine not having made that trip.

It wasn't that he'd hated school or had no aptitude for it. He'd been a perfectly mediocre student. He just hadn't understood how most of it mattered. And not in the way other people said it, the cliché about the real world being more important than books. The people who said that kind of thing just weren't very smart. They needed to believe in simple things.

But that simplicity—if it had ever existed—was gone. Dobbs's professors, his textbooks, his parents, they'd all been products of the old world, preparing him and everyone else for something that remained only in their memories. He'd felt this certainty since he was a kid. He'd seen what the future held. The empty mines and lumber mills surrounding his grandfather's cabin. All those old rural towns, abandoned. It came for the cities next. He'd traveled with his family, seen what was left of Indianapolis, St. Louis, Cleveland. He had cousins in Buffalo. Ruins.

A few months before that first trip to Mexico, before all the business with Sergio began, Dobbs had gone north to his grandfather's cabin. He'd told no one. By then his grandfather was dead. He'd passed away the year Dobbs started high school. Even though they'd hated the place, his parents hadn't bothered trying to sell the old lake house. Possibly they'd forgotten all about it.

On the long drive there, Dobbs had taken mental inventory of his grandfather's possessions, the things he'd cataloged as a kid and now, as an adult, felt ready to claim: a liquor cabinet full of Canadian Club, a Remington 870 in a velvet-lined case. And hovering on a winch above his grandfather's dock, an aluminum fishing boat with the fifty-horsepower Evinrude.

The first night in the cabin, bent over the porch railing, Dobbs purged himself of the Canadian Club.

The next morning, still woozy, he took the Remington and all the shells, stacking them neatly in the prow of the boat. Pulling away from the dock, he steered the outboard motor toward the far shore of the lake, half a mile away.

As soon as he was clear, he opened the throttle. The fifty-horsepower bought at best a gallop across the still green water. When he was maybe twenty yards from the steep, rocky bank, he dove starboard, surfacing just in time for the impact.

There was no explosion as the boat struck the sharp limestone, no ball of fire. No broken bones, either, that time. Dobbs kept treading, the pistons in his heart still firing, as the boat filled with water and tipped to the bottom of the lake.

Two months later he arrived in Mexico. He hadn't been back to Minnesota since.

Dobbs had been sitting on the bench outside Caesars Palace for two hours when someone finally appeared, swimming toward him through the refracting waves of heat rising up from the concrete. Like everything else in his field of vision, the figure was a blur, but it wasn't Gordo. The waves settled into something less distorted, something dark-haired and trim, and Dobbs allowed himself to believe he was seeing—could it be?—Sergio himself. His trouble really must be serious, Dobbs realized, if suddenly Sergio seemed like a comforting friend. Years had passed since Dobbs had seen him in person. Five, six? It seemed even longer ago. This time Sergio—or the figment of Sergio—had traded his apron for a business suit, but Dobbs would still have known him anywhere. With every stride, Sergio grew larger and more fixed, the black of his suit more saturated, but still Dobbs couldn't be sure what he was seeing was real. Even when Sergio sat down beside him and took off his sunglasses, even when Dobbs saw the lines on Sergio's face, he had doubts. But then a pair of girls strolled by in nearly transparent white capris, and Sergio turned to Dobbs and said, "Found yourself a girlfriend yet?"

Dobbs's mouth felt as though it were full of ash.

"Let me buy you a drink," Sergio said, and he led Dobbs over to the concession stand. Once there he pulled out a stool for Dobbs to sit. His every move was slow and solicitous. "I would've picked different circumstances," Sergio said, "but it's good to see you again."

From the girl behind the counter, Sergio procured two glasses of perfectly normal proportions, and he set one down in front of Dobbs. No plastic bag, no straw. With his first sip, the beer seemed to sizzle on Dobbs's tongue. The first thing he'd put in his mouth all day.

Sergio seemed unfazed by the heat, there in his black suit without even a glaze on his skin. He was turning the glass between his hands, his fingers wet with condensation. He looked sad, and Dobbs couldn't help wondering if he'd been talking with Gordo. Had something been decided?

Sergio reached out and patted Dobbs's hand, a gentle, fatherly gesture. A big gold watch peeked out from under his sleeve.

"There's something I've always regretted," he said.

Dobbs felt his arm turn to ice under Sergio's touch.

"That day in the park, in Mexico," he said. "I never asked what it was you wanted. We talked about so many things, but not that."

There was a baseball game playing on the TV above the bar, the sound turned off, a slow, awkward pantomime. Dobbs could already feel the beer going to his head.

Sergio leaned closer. "Money, adventure. I should've asked."

"What's going to happen to them?" Dobbs said. *Them.* The people in the truck. He couldn't bring himself to give them a name. He wondered what sort of explanations Gordo had offered, what kind of apologies and promises he'd made for the future, whether any of it had mattered.

Sergio folded his arms, and the gold watch disappeared. "What's going to happen," Sergio said, "is I'm giving you one chance to pay me back. This kind of thing is very bad for business. What's the word?" Sergio said. "You've *tarnished* our reputation. I'm giving you one chance to make up your losses."

Dobbs filled his lungs, and the air burned going down. He couldn't begin to imagine how math like that could even be calculated. His glass, he suddenly realized, was empty.

A tall, dark-skinned woman strolled by in a clingy summer dress, and Sergio's eyes followed her down the steps to the street. But Dobbs went a different way, returning to that roadside in the middle of the desert, to the jaundiced moon looking on dumbly as he laced his fingers behind his head, the first two dead bodies lying in the brambles along the shoulder, the men Gordo claimed not to recognize stacking soft white bricks into their idling SUV. Was Dobbs the one who'd been naïve?

And then Sergio's voice brought him back. He was saying something about Detroit, about Dobbs's next assignment.

"Detroit?" Dobbs said, thinking he must have misunderstood.

Sergio slipped his sunglasses from his breast pocket. "It's the new frontier."

"Detroit?" Dobbs said again.

"The new Old West."

It would be the closest Dobbs had been to home in years.

"You can't afford any more mistakes," Sergio said, rising to his feet.

Dobbs was no longer sure he could afford even the mistakes he'd already made.

Sergio was slipping away, moving across the plaza.

"Whatever happened to your wife?" Dobbs called to his back. "Your son?"

Sergio paused, already partly dissolved in the heat.

"Memories," Sergio said. "Just like Gordo. You have to be able to let them go."

Fourteen

RUTH FREEMAN HAD never cared for cars. At least not in the way her brothers did. When they were teenagers, it had all been about fins, the roads swollen with schools of these absurd terrestrial fish. The power, the speed—she got all that. She just never understood why there needed to be so many different kinds, so many she could never tell them apart. Whatever the distinctions were between a Dodge and a DeSoto, they meant nothing to her. She simply wanted one, she didn't care what kind.

In 1956 her father brought home a brand-new two-tone Roadmaster with a grille like a sleeping toad. Her brothers got their turns first, and when they were done, Ruth slipped under her father's arm and into the driver's seat, wrapping her slim fingers around the knotty wheel. She was sixteen and had never driven before, but she had the posture and the gestures down pat.

"Will you teach me how?" she asked her father, who stood with his hand on the door, the smile wiped from his face. With a stiff laugh he said no, no, no, her brothers would take her wherever she needed to go. And then he reached in and removed the keys from the ignition.

She made up her mind that very moment that she would never ask anything from him again.

Her father brought home a new car every couple of years. Her brothers inherited the old ones. In '58, Gus got the Roadmaster. By then his friends were driving Corvettes and Thunderbirds—fish transformed into torpedoes—and the Roadmaster was already as boxy as a casket.

As for Ruth, she might not have cared so much about having nothing to drive if she could have taken a streetcar, but they'd ripped up the last of the tracks in '53. And there was no dignity in a bus. So she did what any girl would do, and that summer when she turned eighteen, she told Francis Statler she'd go steady with him as long as he let her drive. He wasn't the brightest boy, but he had dimples and held open doors and called everyone *sir* and *ma'am*. Besides, she'd known him forever. They lived only a few blocks apart in Palmer Woods, and although he went to Kingswood-Cranbrook and she went to Girls Catholic Central, their circles were more or less the same. They saw each other at socials and dances, at Tom Clay's Saturday night balls at the armory. Francis was always staring at her through the bottom of an empty punch glass. In the summer they'd mingled deck chairs at the pool of the Detroit Golf Club, where their fathers shot rounds together. Her father worked in management at Ford, slowly edging his way up. Francis's father was at GM, already a big cheese. On the fairway, Ruth's father said Mr. Statler had a hopeless slice, but that didn't stop the club from giving him his very own brass plaque at the top of the donor wall.

Francis Statler meant well, but he could never quite keep up, despite his father's money. He wasn't unattractive. Besides the dimples, he had deep hazel eyes and the straightest teeth Ruth had ever seen. His face was warm and inviting, but he parted his hair just like his father, and he'd been wearing the same plaid shirts since grade school.

Francis was either indifferent to fashions or unaware of them. He always stood out, the one boy clinging to cotton twill slacks in a world that had moved on to blue jeans. In '58, when every teen in the city was coveting sport coupes, Francis bought a turquoise Edsel. At least it was a convertible. From the front, the car looked like a disgruntled koala bear, but all Francis cared about were the frills: touch-button transmission, glowing cyclops-eye speedometer, power windows and seats. He could afford every option they offered.

Some of her girlfriends expected Ruth to be embarrassed to be seen in something so uncool. "Doesn't everyone stare?" Donna asked, but Ruth simply shrugged. Anything was better than nothing. And besides, people really didn't stare at Francis. He somehow managed to get away with being strange. Were anyone to ask him his secret, Francis wouldn't even have understood the question. Before Ruth took him up, Francis had no close friends. Hours might pass at the pool without anyone speaking a word to him, and yet the dopey dimpled smile never left his face. It was impossible to exclude someone who didn't notice he was being excluded. Whatever was happening, Francis was always there. He became a sort of mascot, though no one could have said exactly what it was he represented. He rarely spoke, never danced, didn't drink. And yet by the time he and Ruth made their arrangement, a belief had spread throughout both their high schools that the dullest parties were the ones from which Francis Statler happened to be missing. For every gathering, someone was invariably dispatched to ensure Francis's arrival, after which Francis would spend the entire evening by himself, examining the host's parents' collection of ivory statuettes until it was time for someone to take him home.

For Ruth, the best thing about Francis Statler was that he didn't mind handing her the keys. When they were together, the Edsel was hers. It was Ruth cruising Belle Isle with the top down, Ruth roaring north to the charred remains of Jefferson Beach. And there was Francis, grinning beside her with the wind in his teeth.

The only exception was Friday night. When they pulled into Ted's drive-in, it would be Francis behind the wheel. Ruth insisted. As a ritual, Ted's was sacred: the trays on the windows, Frantic Ernie Durham shouting his strained rhymes through the radio: *Ernie's Record Racks! Whale of a sale! Whale of a sale!* Ted's was a place where, for better or worse, boys had to be boys. Although of course Francis never seemed to notice all the jockeying and revving. He was the only one not craning his neck to watch each tight sweater flouncing by. Ruth supposed he was in love with her.

Everything in Francis was forgiven. It helped that he was rich. But that was another thing he seemed unaware of. She would always remember one night when she was fifteen, entering the dining room at the club to begin an excruciating meal with her family, and there was Francis Statler helping a busboy pick up the shards of a broken plate, the two of them kneeling side by side, searching among feet and legs, their heads thrust under the tablecloth together, like a pair of old-fashioned photographers. Francis's father was ruddy with embarrassment, tugging at his son's armpit, trying to pull him up. Unlike his son, who was quiet as a giraffe, Mr. Statler was incapable of speaking in anything less than a shout, and even the dishwashers could probably hear him repeating "That's enough, son, that's enough." But Francis didn't stop until every last piece had been collected, just as anyone other than his own father would have known to expect. Alfred P. Sloan himself could have been in the room, and even he would have said, "Oh, it's just Francis Statler."

But it wasn't that Francis was a saint. Nor was he a savant. He was more a like a traveler in a foreign land who understood neither the language nor the customs but was quietly, respectfully accepting of everything he saw.

One July weekend, as was the tradition, Francis took Ruth (or rather she took him) to watch the hydroplanes skip like stones across the murky Detroit River. Everyone they knew was there, and while the other boys shouted and clapped one another on the back, Francis sat with his hands folded in his lap, transfixed, as if God himself were presiding over the rumble and the wakes. Legs folded beneath her on the green plaid blanket, Ruth felt certain she saw the other girls, Donna among them, looking at Francis and then at her. She saw in their eyes not jealousy or judgment but a kind of distrust. They didn't want to date Francis Statler themselves, but they didn't want anyone else to, either. It wasn't that he was like a brother to them—he was more like a newborn baby, someone vulnerable and helpless and in need of constant protection.

Maybe these girls didn't believe Francis could be loved. Maybe Ruth didn't believe it either. By then they'd been together three months, and he hadn't made a single move.

One Sunday afternoon they were strolling the glass-domed paths of the Belle Isle conservatory, Ruth pointing out all the most beautiful orchids, when she realized Francis was no longer beside her. She doubled back through the rows of blooms and found him near the entrance, gazing up at the glass. There was a small bird trapped inside, flapping among the rafters, trying to find a way out.

"We should help it," Francis said.

He started to whistle, as if he and the bird shared a common tongue. A young couple she didn't know stared at Francis as he offered his finger as a perch. Meanwhile Ruth inched away, lowering herself onto a little iron bench tucked away in a tiny alcove. She would have liked to disappear completely.

With Francis, there was always waiting. He had a child's sense of wonder, and it was peculiar how often Ruth's adventures with him produced in her the feeling of returning to childhood things. That day on Belle Isle, after Francis was finally forced to give up on the bird, they went next door to the aquarium, which Ruth hadn't visited since she was a little girl. She was struck by how small the aquarium felt that day, the single arched gallery seeming to close in on her from all sides. The place was dark and tight, and each recessed tank was framed in stainless steel, as if it were a porthole—the people imprisoned and the fish utterly free, swimming there of their own accord. She felt as though she were leagues under the sea in some sort of Gothic bathysphere. Francis was captivated by the four-foot-long electric eel that slunk across the tank with its jaws a crude rictus of malevolence, its dead eyes fixed on some nonexistent prey. Ruth caught just a glimpse of the horrible creature, and then she had to turn away. But Francis couldn't seem to get enough. He was still standing there a few minutes later when some sort of food was dropped into the water. The tank was rigged in such a way that when the eel ate, the current it produced surged to a light bulb affixed to the wall. As the light began to glow, Francis's eyes grew wide, and Ruth couldn't help wondering what the others would think if they were to see this side of Francis Statler, not the charmingly oblivious young man but the guileless, naked boy.

Before the eel could finish, Ruth slipped her arm in the crook of Francis's elbow and pulled him out the front door. His head came last, eyes still locked on the display. She reached into his pocket then and pulled out the keys to the Edsel. He climbed into the passenger seat without a word. Without waiting for him to fully close his door, Ruth squealed out of the parking lot, swerving into the oncoming lane as she entered the road along the southern shore. Francis didn't ask where they were going, and in fact she didn't know herself until they got there, to the massive marble fountain about a mile away at the western end of the island. When they arrived, she got out of the car alone and walked briskly toward the fountain. She felt propelled by a great sense of purpose, but what the purpose was, precisely, she couldn't have said. In defiance of nature, lions and turtles together spouted a froth of water into the already humid air. Ruth stood there in silence, looking past the fountain and out over the river, toward the city. She'd known from the start that her relationship with Francis

Statler was not meant to last, but it had only just occurred to her that perhaps this fact had escaped him. It was a troubling realization, but what could she do about it? All she could think was how the other girls would judge her when that time finally came.

And so they stuck together, Ruth and Francis, even after the thrill of driving had worn off, after Ruth found herself more and more often sitting cross-legged in the passenger seat on their weekend drives to Walled Lake.

The night he finally kissed her, they were at the Gratiot Drive-In. It was August, and they were about to enter their last year of high school. A group of them had caravanned up there together, and they were only a short way through *Gigi* when Francis put his arm around Ruth. Maybe he could sense how bored she was watching Maurice Chevalier do his shuffle in topcoat and tails, thanking heaven for little girls. As Francis leaned in, Ruth was thinking about the irony of watching such silliness in a city that had done so much to destroy the French language, turning Bois Blanc to Bob-Lo and Gratiot into Grash-it, not to mention Detroit itself. And then in a flash, Chevalier's walking stick was replaced with Francis Statler's nose, shiny with grease and terror.

She didn't try to stop him. She was pleased to be done with the horses and carriages and silly parasols. And yet she couldn't help being aware of the many eyes turned to face her. She and Francis were surrounded on all sides—Donna and Robert to her right, and she didn't remember who else, but there had been at least five cars. Soon a cheer rose up. That was the moment Ruth pulled back, wiping the damp from her mouth. Taking Francis by the hand, she pulled him out of the car, past the box offices, and a minute later they were alone outside the theater. Alone, but it hardly felt private out there. There was so much light all around them, it felt like midafternoon. The sky pulsed at their backs with every flashing image on the screen. For Ruth, the Gratiot Drive-In wasn't really about the movie. Especially when the movie was something like *Gigi*. There were plenty of places closer to home: the Bel-Air, the Eastside, the Ford-Wyoming, the Town. But none of them had what the Gratiot had, the movie screen built onto a one-hundred-fifteen-foot tower, from the top of which, on the highway side, cascaded an actual waterfall—the spray illuminated by a kaleidoscope of colored bulbs. It was both beautiful and absurd, surely the world's only liquid marquee. It was the spectacle she marveled over, the ambition so peculiarly placed. It was said the construction had cost four hundred thousand dollars. Ridiculous! But could she say the money had been poorly spent? Here she was, after all, gazing up at the red and yellow mist. And as they stood by the railing in front of the pool into which the water fell, Ruth saw that Francis Statler was trembling. At first she thought he'd somehow gotten wet. But that wasn't it, and it wasn't just nerves anymore, either. Although it might have flattered her to think so, she understood he wasn't shaken by an overwhelming passion. He was miserable. Leaning against the rail, she pulled him toward her, and he collapsed onto her shoulder.

"It's okay," she told him. "It's okay." That was the moment it occurred to her to wonder if perhaps all of this wasn't complicated for him, too, and in ways she couldn't imagine.

When they got back to the car, the others were poised for celebration. Good old Francis had finally done it. Even the other girls looked upon Ruth with respectful warmth, as if she'd now proven she would not hurt this gentle boy no one else wanted.

At Ruth's insistence, Francis Statler took the wheel, and the others marked his triumph by making him lead the way to the Totem Pole, grandmaster of their small parade. Ruth squeezed next to Francis on the bench seat, their bodies combined into one shadow, but down in her lap, where no one else could see, Francis's hand had gone limp.

At the Totem Pole, Francis ordered a burger, but he seemed distracted, and Ruth had to be the one to remind the waitress to bring his customary extra pickles. As the other boys squeezed his shoulders and mussed his hair and called him Casanova, Francis contorted his bendy straw into unrecognizable shapes. Stuffed beside him in the overcrowded booth, Ruth quietly sucked on a cherry-flavored ginger ale, a drink she loathed but had ordered anyway, feeling somehow it was what she deserved. With every sip, her tongue became more sharply preserved in the cloying, medicinal sweetness. And when the glass was empty, she realized she'd inadvertently erased every trace of Francis Statler's kiss from her lips.

For the rest of the night, she clung to his side, smiling whenever he looked her way, but there were no more kisses. At eleven, Francis pulled up to the curb in front of Ruth's house, the Edsel still running. With lowered eyes he wished her goodnight. Francis lived on Balmoral too, the biggest house in the neighborhood, an eight-bedroom colonial with presidential-looking columns and an English garden in the back. Ruth's father passed the Statler mansion every morning on his way to work, never tiring of the view.

Ruth's house had a circular drive, but Francis never used it. He seemed to prefer having a buffer of yard between him and her front door, as if he were afraid of falling within her father's reach. She could have told him there was nothing to fear, that Ruth's father worshipped the Statlers, that Francis himself could do no wrong. But that was something Francis could never know. Ruth let her fingers linger on the door handle, giving Francis one more chance to take the cherry from her lips, but his gaze would not budge from his lap.

The summer faded into fall, and fall quickly dissolved into winter. All at once, it seemed, the excursions to the club to swim and play tennis were replaced with parades downtown and skating at the pond at Palmer Park. A week before Christmas, Ruth and Donna took a bus downtown to buy presents for Francis and for Richard, Donna's new boyfriend. The city had painted the bus in white and red stripes, like a candy cane, and the driver wore a matching vest. Ruth knew she was too old for such things, and she made a point of rolling her eyes at Donna as they boarded, but secretly the one time she loved to ride the bus was at Christmas, high above the snow and slush, watching the tinkling lights and laurels strung from all the buildings. Nothing made her more sentimental than Christmas, and Christmas at Hudson's Department Store most of all.

Every year after Thanksgiving when she was a child, Ruth had gone with her mother to Hudson's to do the Christmas shopping. At any other time, she would beg and plead to stay home, dreading the boredom and exhaustion, dragging bags up and down twenty-something stuffy floors. But at Christmas everything changed. Hudson's became a place of infinite possibilities and endless riches magically transformed: a life-size diorama of carolers floating from the ceiling amid a dusting of snow; a frosty Cinderella descending an icy path to a twinkling carriage; holly wreaths and floating angels and chandeliers done up like ornaments. Ruth could remember being eight years old and sitting in her very own chair beside her mother in the Christmas card shop on the ninth floor, flipping through the catalogs, imagining the day when all this would be hers. And now it was. Ruth and Donna were women now. For the very first time, they were here to shop for men.

They got off the elevator on the second floor and strolled the disorienting racks of suits and ties and French-cuffed shirts. Ruth felt the salesmen watching her, preparing to come forward and offer assistance, and it made her feel powerful to have their attention. A tall, angular man with a jutting chin was the first to step into their path, and with a distracted, harried air borrowed from her mother, Ruth raised her nose in his direction and said, "Where might I find the Levi's?"

With the help of Donna and the salesman and an embarrassed stock boy roughly Francis's size, Ruth picked out a pair that looked as if they might fit, admiring each heavy seam, every shiny rivet. Afterward, the handle of the bag tingling in her fingers, she followed Donna down to the salon on the fourth floor.

Donna left the salon with a new compact, and together they went up to the thirteenth floor. At a table overlooking the river, they ordered Maurice salads and Coca-Cola, and while they ate, they talked of nothing. Nothing, at least, that Ruth would later be able to recall. She would have liked to think of the two of them, there on the cusp of adulthood, discussing what the future held, a world full of possibilities. Their last year of high school was nearly halfway finished, and what then? There was college and marriage. They must have discussed Richard, whether he would propose, and would he like the pebble-grain wallet Donna had chosen for him? In fact, in little more than a year, Donna would become Mrs. Richard Galt, and the two of them would buy a new brick rancher in Royal Oak.

But what about Ruth? Did Donna ask what might happen between her and Francis? If she did, how did Ruth respond? The relationship would end, of course. Everyone knew it would have to end. But Ruth herself could not yet see the end. She was too young to be able to see the end of anything. At eighteen she was less like a young version of her adult self than like some primitive ancestor. There would be many crude steps along the evolutionary path before she became what she was now. And it bewildered her still to look back at this young girl, so lacking in ambition, teenage years spent wanting nothing more than to be her own driver. And having achieved that simple goal with the help of Francis Statler, she found herself tapped out of ideas. There would be college, one wasted year of it in Ann Arbor. And there would be a marriage, almost two decades' worth of unhappiness and frustration.

But then again, if she had then already possessed the notion to make something of herself, things might not have turned out half as well as they did. At eighteen, the best she could have hoped for was to be taught to type, and no one then wanted to employ a girl who thought she deserved better. Of course, no one did fifteen years later, either, when Ruth's aspirations finally surfaced. But by then the two daughters she had loved and coddled had taught her patience, and her husband had taught her how to humor men less intelligent than herself.

But such change would not come to Ruth alone. Nor would it always come so slowly.

On July 23, 1967, when the children were four and six years old, the only city Ruth had ever really known would suddenly be set alight. Of course, there would be nothing sudden about it, except that neither Ruth nor anyone else she knew had seen it coming. But that didn't mean the tinder hadn't been sparking for years.

Even four decades later, she would remember the day vividly. It was early Sunday morning when the riot broke out. They heard murmurs on the radio of something happening miles away on Twelfth Street. Hours before dawn, police had raided an unlicensed bar, arresting eighty-something patrons, all of them black. In the hours since then, black people across the city had been expressing their anger with fire and bricks.

Having witnessed a few similar flare-ups years before, Ruth and Tom assumed that this one, too, would pass. They were living then not far from Palmer Woods, and at nine-thirty they left for church, their route taking them down Woodward, where they were alarmed to find the street already trashed, all those precious cars overturned like stones. Everything was on fire.

Later that day came reports of a fireman shot dead by a rooftop sniper. The National Guard took up positions—terrified boys who had never seen anything like this. And then, at last, came the tanks and the infantry troops fresh from Vietnam. It took five days for the streets to clear.

And once the streets were cleared, they never really filled again.

Forty-three people died, most of them black. More than a thousand people were injured. The blacks called it a *rebellion*, claiming they were fighting back against police brutality and discrimination and all kinds of other iniquities, but it would be years before Ruth could understand what that meant, before she could feel anything other than anger. Only then would she come to see them as something more than a mob hell-bent on destruction.

Within a year, all of Ruth's closest friends (the ones who had not gone already) left the city for the suburbs. For a while, the people she had known were replaced with others she didn't. Black doctors and lawyers and executives moved into neighborhoods that had always been completely white. Ruth was ashamed sometimes to remember how much she and Tom fretted for their safety, for their prosperity, how they watched moving trucks through curtained windows, wondering where it all would lead. It didn't take long to find out. At the time, they felt lucky to have gotten out when they did, when it was still possible to sell a house for something. There were only so many black doctors and lawyers and executives to go around. The city emptied faster than it could be filled. First one house at a time went empty, and then entire streets, and then entire blocks, and then entire neighborhoods, and eventually entire zip codes. And nothing would ever be the same again.

§

All that had happened long ago, to someone else, to someone that Ruth, at sixty-eight, truly felt she barely knew. As she looked out now over the river from the third floor of the HSI Building, it occurred to her that the eighteen-year-old girl who had left Francis Statler to stand alone by herself at the Belle Isle fountain would have been staring then at the very spot where she currently sat. Of course, the tower hadn't been built then. That was a different city in 1958, the sort of city that could still afford to maintain a conservatory and an aquarium and a lavish fountain that shot water forty feet into the air.

Ruth had gone back to Belle Isle for the last time the previous fall, wanting to share the aquarium with her granddaughter before it was permanently closed. Her younger daughter had brought her family in

215

from Connecticut for the weekend. Ruth and little Hannah found the island dead, the casino and the children's zoo already shuttered. The shoreline roads she'd cruised as a girl were empty, the bushes overgrown, the sidewalks disintegrated. The parking lot in front of the fountain was barricaded, the water shut off. It was fall and overcast, and the leaves were off the trees, and on all the battered grass there wasn't a single dog or child to be seen. Ruth felt as if she were the last cold war spy, sent to some vast, desolate place for an exchange of top secret microfilm. Even her favorite orchids in the conservatory weren't enough to mask how far the place had fallen. The bark of the palm trees had been carved up with initials. Squares of plywood covered the broken panes of greenhouse glass.

Hannah kept saying, "Grandma, I think we should go."

"It didn't used to be like this," Ruth tried to explain. But eyes can't be talked out of what they see.

On all of Belle Isle, only the yacht club had been kept up. It didn't belong to the city. In its latest manifestation, the building was a Spanish Colonial stucco anomaly with it own private wooden bridge. Ruth couldn't help suspecting the club had chosen this least logical of architectural styles precisely in order to signal its detachment from the rest of the city. Her second husband was a member, as was virtually everyone else in their circle, as were all the other HSI executives. It was the only reason any of them came onto the island anymore, the place to go when one wanted to feel as though one were somewhere else.

Everything was gone. Hudson's, where she'd spent almost as many hours as she had at school, had been imploded years before, 2,800 pounds of explosives turning the twenty-eight stories—more than two million square feet—into 330,000 tons of rubble.

The Gratiot Drive-In, where Francis Statler had finally kissed her, was a strip mall now. It was hard to say if that was better or worse than remaining an abandoned hulk, a freestanding waterfall run dry.

And the cars, which had been all anyone cared about then—the city largely imported them now. They were someone else's pride and joy.

There were more than ten thousand empty houses in the city. Her childhood home in Palmer Woods was one of them. The last time she drove by—for no reason other than curiosity—the roof wore an immense blue tarp, and the glass was gone from the windows, even in the small dormers in her brothers' old bedrooms. She couldn't bring herself to stop. A few other houses in the neighborhood looked just as bad, but as a whole Palmer Woods was still one of the best neighborhoods in the city. On the way back out to Woodward, she passed Francis Statler's house. It, at least, was as presidential as ever, the lawn still perfectly manicured. Someone else owned it now.

For weeks after that drive through Palmer Woods, Ruth had debated buying her old house on Balmoral Drive. She'd gone as far as to have a contractor acquaintance of her husband's go through it to see what it might take to restore the place. Nearly half a million dollars was his estimate, all for a house that in her lifetime would never be worth even a fraction of that. David, her second husband, would never agree to live there. She knew better than to ask.

For David, there was no city. As far as he was concerned, the whole place had been bulldozed decades ago, leaving nothing but an immense blank he sometimes needed to pass through to visit friends in Grosse Pointe. That Ruth consented to come here every day to work was for him just another mark of her eccentric character. Her colleagues would have been mystified to learn that at home she was in this regard the hopeless romantic, and that David, despite his full-time devotion to leisure and exotic produce, was the practical one.

Ruth was not ashamed to admit that part of her lived in the past. David was content to live in the eternal present. Nothing was permitted to remain in his life longer than a couple of years. Periodically he would cast away every last piece of furniture, and she would come home to find last year's Asian transformed into this year's rustic modern. He'd never worn down the heel of a shoe or the tread of a tire. Things came and went. It was a wonder he hadn't yet grown tired of her, although without her he could never have afforded such profligacy.

She rarely complained.

At thirty-three, Ruth Freeman had decided to remake her life. And unlike the city, she had succeeded. And that was why she sat here now, in a walnut-lined boardroom surrounded by a phalanx of balding men in boxy suits impatiently waiting for her to sign off on the proposal before her, to add her rubber stamp to theirs.

The presentations were over, their case laid out. All they needed, all they had wanted for the last hour, was her okay. She could not blame them for their irritation. For decades she had been training them to imagine they had her agreement, her consent. Without that, she never would have made it to where she was, the only woman among their ranks.

But it was impossible for her not to think back on her old life. And on the other lives she might have lived. If not with her first husband, whose vision of her was only as large as the kitchen and the bedroom, then with Francis Statler, that strange, gentle boy. Sometimes she wondered if he had ever found a world in which he fit. His family had moved away while Francis was in college back east, and Ruth lost track of him after that. He never resurfaced for reunions, never appeared in any corporate profile. She could have found out, of course, if she had wished, but in truth she liked it better this way. She wanted to leave the past as it was, as it remained in her memory, with Francis showing up at her door unexpectedly at the end of August 1958, the week before he was to leave for college, and announcing it was over.

"We've had a lot of fun," he said, reaching out for her hand. "But it's time to move on."

And as he strolled back down her walkway, she wept, quietly at first so he wouldn't hear. But as soon as he was gone, she let it all go, burying her face in her pillow, glad for once of the din of her brothers in the room next door. That letting go was the first of many, and it was important to her that it be preserved.

She let go of the house on Balmoral, too. Some things were beyond saving. By now it was probably gone for good, scooped into Dumpsters, another blight erased. As if somehow emptiness could hide what had been there before. And now the neighbors who remained tossed grass seed onto the filled-in foundation and tasked their children with keeping the lot mowed. They did not want to think about the contagion, that with every passing year their own homes were worth less and less.

Where did it all go, the rubble they swept away? Where was there a landfill big enough to swallow an entire city? What sense would they make of it, archeologists two hundred million years from now trying to sift through these layers of sediment and reconstruct what had happened here?

Almost nothing remained, but it wasn't nostalgia she felt for the city of her youth. Nostalgia was for coping with the passage of time, with the inevitability of decay. Nostalgia was the Motown they played on the radio. But nostalgia had no answers for a tragedy of this scope. That was what David couldn't seem to understand, the way her heart prickled sometimes at the thought that things could have been different, that in some ways she felt herself to be at fault. And that she and everyone else she had known back then had awakened too late, and by the time they realized the destruction they'd set in motion, all the accent walls and fresh coats of paint in the world could not undo it.

From her teenage years, only the cherry-flavored ginger ale remained, that dreadful stuff. It still made her tongue curl.

And the other executives continued staring at her, waiting for her to complete the circle of ayes.

"The factory's redundant," Arthur was saying yet again. "And given what it would cost to repair and modernize, we don't have any other choice."

"What about the city?" Ruth said, her eyes drifting back to the shuttered island out the window. "What about that?"

"There comes a time," Arthur said, "when you've got to accept you've done everything you could."

"A drop in the bucket," Ruth said. "An investment, PR."

Arthur frowned with fatherly disappointment. He was eight years younger than she. "We've talked about all that, the costs and benefits."

Quietly in the corner, pencil poised as she took the minutes, Tiphany was nodding.

"You have all the votes you need," Ruth said. "If you want to shut it down, shut it down."

"The board prefers consensus."

"Well," Ruth Freeman said, rising from her chair and letting her pen clatter to the table, "they're not going to get it."

Fifteen

HUDDLED TOGETHER IN the still, dark night, staring off at the same distant point, they must have seemed they were waiting for something exciting to happen. Thirty yards away, down the alley behind the HSI Building, the door of the loading dock was open, its shadow slightly shortened by a single overhead bulb.

April had discovered it was hard to maintain her balance, biting her nails while squatting. Her legs had grown so wobbly, she wondered whether she'd be able to get up and move when called upon to do so.

April, Holmes, and Fitch, dressed in black, pressed themselves up against the low alley wall, just out of range of the surveillance cameras. They were so silent that for long stretches the entire outside world seemed to fade away, making it feel to Fitch as though he were completely alone—just him and the relentless thumping in his head.

McGee had reported that the loading dock was where the custodians and the guards came to smoke. It's where she'd gone herself. To avoid having to disable the alarm every time someone needed a break, they left the door open, even though it was against company policy. By now, nearly morning, the custodians were gone, but the door remained open.

April, Holmes, and Fitch had their orders. They were to wait.

While she waited, April thought about Inez, who was at home, undoubtedly wondering why April was so late in coming back from the meeting. April didn't like to lie. And really, she'd told only a partial lie. Technically, there *had* been a meeting, but it had lasted only fifteen minutes, just long enough for them to go over the plan for the last time. It was the plan itself April had neglected to mention. But by morning Inez would know where April had really been. By then it would be all over the news. And then what?

And then April would never lie to her again.

Too brief, Holmes thought, too brief. Fifteen minutes hadn't been enough time to check everything he needed to check. His tools. What a disaster it would be to get inside and realize he hadn't brought the right tools. It was too dark now and too late. His eyes remained fixed on the building, but his mind built an image of the inside of the black case where he kept his picks. He could picture them, their curves and edges, but he couldn't be sure each one was in its place.

Wedged between the others, Fitch leaned his head back against the wall. Trying to clear his mind, to quiet the thumping, he found his thoughts drifting to a girl. There were so many girls he'd forgotten, and he would've been happy, as he stared at the open door of the loading dock, to think of any of them, with the single exception of the one girl who came to mind. Even in his memory her face wasn't pretty. She'd been seventeen, two years older than him, and when she walked, her hips had swayed like a woman's. But what he remembered most acutely, besides her body, was that she'd made him feel like a coward. And now, with the HSI Building looming above him, Fitch was beginning to feel that way again.

As the three of them waited, a solitary figure turned the corner at the back of the building, approaching the loading dock. They leaned forward.

April, smiling, whispered, "McGee."

Fitch closed his eyes.

Holmes squeezed his case of picks and licked the sweat from his upper lip.

Everything was going according to plan. The three of them had scaled the wall and dropped down at the end of the alley unseen. McGee was right on schedule, and her disguise—or at least what April could see of it from fifty yards—gave her reason to smile. McGee's clothes were tattered, a wig of dirty blond dreadlocks swinging from her head. Hunched and shuffling behind a shopping cart, she moved so slowly that, to the guards inside watching her through the cameras, she must have seemed like a slug captured by time-lapse photography.

But would they really buy it? Fitch wondered. Wouldn't the camera pick up the shopping cart's modifications? What if the wig slipped? What if they recognized her? And then McGee suddenly stopped, and Fitch's stomach clenched. What if she lost her nerve?

McGee bent over to pick something up—maybe a coin—and put it in her pocket. She resumed shuffling. Fitch could hear her cursing at the wobbly wheels of the cart, which seemed to be following a course of their own. What if the cart overturned and Myles fell out, tumbling from the hole they'd cut in the side? McGee paused beside the loading dock. Despite his conviction that the plan would go horribly wrong, even Fitch had to admit he never would have noticed Myles slipping out the side of the shopping cart, had he not known what was coming.

Slide, pull, glide. Slide, pull, glide. Three fluid movements: slide out of the cart, pull himself up onto the dock, glide into a corner of the receiving bay. Myles could remember only the anticipation. His body had performed without his mind, had carried him into the shadows, leaving no memory of the steps as he'd actually taken them. Only the anticipation: slide, pull, glide. Then wait.

When April opened her eyes, it was over.

For Fitch, it seemed minutes had passed between breaths.

As he watched Myles tuck himself inside the receiving bay, it came back to Holmes in a flash, the pick he'd forgotten: the snake tip. Of course. He'd taken it out of the case to clean and wipe down with silicone. In his mind he could see the empty slot where he'd forgotten to put it back.

The crashing of the shopping cart into the side of the Dumpster was not unlike a gong, and it seemed to Fitch an appropriate commencement for such a doomed undertaking.

Unable to look away, April winced as McGee clambered up the side of the Dumpster and rolled, feet first, inside and out of sight. McGee reappeared again a moment later, a lumpy trash bag raised above her head. With a tremendous grunt, she shot-putted the bag into the alley, where it slumped awkwardly, end over end, before softening to a stop. The heavier bags she had to push up and over the side, like a beetle rolling a ball of dung.

April rose up slightly, balancing on the balls of her feet. She might have gotten up entirely and crossed the parking lot to help her struggling friend had Holmes not held her back. But then McGee must have found some lighter bags, because suddenly the trash went sailing farther out into the parking lot, expanding the radius of the mess.

With each broken bottle, each rattling can, Fitch slunk deeper into the shadows along the wall. The noise seemed to go on forever. Over time McGee's yells grew softer, and bags flew out of the Dumpster with less frequency.

Fitch began to wonder if the guards weren't watching, or if they recognized such an obvious setup. He put his lips to April's ear. "Maybe we should call it off."

The sound was so faint to April that it was as if the air itself were speaking. Fitch's bottom lip brushed against her lobe. She shivered, shook her head, pointed. One of the guards—the white one—stood in the doorway of the loading dock. Where the guard trained his flashlight into the mouth of the Dumpster, Fitch and Holmes and April could only just barely see the top of McGee's head.

"What the fuck do you think you're doing!" the guard yelled.

April had to force herself to remember the guard was speaking to McGee, that this was all part of the plan.

The booming voice of the security guard was Myles's cue. Looking through a gap in the stack of pallets, he saw the man at the end of the dock, facing the other way. The path was clear to the next door, the one that would get him inside the building. To reach the door was easy, a simple matter of putting one foot in front of the other. But Myles's feet were still. All the guard had to do was turn around, catch a glimpse of him out of the corner of an eye, hear the squeak of Myles's sneakers on the smooth concrete floor. That door was the point at which his first real crime would begin. Trespassing, breaking-and-entering. What was to stop him from getting shot? A black man in a dark corner. It was ridiculous.

But after everything he and McGee had been through together, how could he say no, no matter how badly he wanted to? The two of them didn't often talk of love. Their relationship rose above such banalities. So instead here he was again tonight, using the most complicated means to say the simplest of things.

The corridor on the other side of the door was so bright that at first Myles saw only spots of light. Momentarily blinded, his other senses awoke. Over the charging of his heart, he caught the pin-drop silence. He smelled an absence. Where were the bleaches, the concentrations of fake lemon and pine? McGee had said the custodians cleaned the lobby and the ground-floor corridors first, but the dull floor at his feet showed a day's wear.

"I swear to God." Darius's partner hovered at the end of the loading dock, one shirttail untucked from his pants, surveying the mess McGee had made. "You ever come back," Carl said, "I'll shoot you till I run out of bullets."

He cut at her with the beam of his flashlight as McGee rattled the shopping cart away. She'd never felt so filthy. The hunch she'd affected to make herself look older pressed her nose toward her reeking clothes. And she was tired. Tired of getting yelled at. She was ready to do some yelling of her own.

April, Holmes, and Fitch watched McGee shuffle away, back in the direction from which she'd come. When the wheels of the shopping cart were barely perceptible squeals, they examined one another's faces. April was the only one who managed a smile, and even for her it didn't come easily.

Holmes unclenched his fists, untied and retied his shoes. How had he let McGee talk him into this again?

Fitch slid the phone from his pocket and waited for the text.

In the lobby, Myles crouched behind an enormous stone pot, out of which rose a tall, narrow tree with a shiny trunk and small, five-pointed leaves that looked like the hands of a child. Across the broad expanse of marble, this was the only cover.

Down the corridor behind him, a door slammed, followed by the jangling of keys. The guard coming back inside. Myles raised his eyes to the edge of the pot and watched the white guard enter the booth, joining the other one, the black one. Just as McGee had said he would, just as she'd planned.

No one would ever know, Myles decided. He could tell them anything. He could say the guards had separated, that they saw him and chased him out. Whatever. It occurred to him, as he watched the booth, feeling something in his bowels loosen, that he'd never actually thought he'd have to go through with this, that it would come this far. The one time he'd secretly hoped for failure, things had gone almost impossibly perfect.

"Are you ready?" Holmes said. "Any second now . . ."

Fitch checked his phone. He said, "It's not too late to change our minds."

But everyone knew it *was*.

Myles seemed to cross the lobby in a single step, sliding to a stop against the booth as if it were a base he'd just stolen. The guards must have heard or seen him coming. But before they could do anything, Myles had pressed Holmes's nail gun to the door and pulled several times at the trigger. The nails went in deeply, effortlessly. Teeth clenched, he kept squeezing. Whoosh and pop, whoosh and pop. With each squeeze, the plan slipped further back in his memory. He found the sound of nails biting into the wood door unexpectedly pleasing, and he would've liked to keep firing them, happily ignoring what was supposed to come next. He might have gone on forever, had he not run out of nails.

From his backpack he removed the hammer, and with two quick blows he punched a hole in the wall of the booth. In spite of his hurry, he found time to note how uncannily accurate McGee's instructions had been. Phone and data lines nakedly exposed. He just hoped she was right that the men had to leave their cell phones in their lockers.

With two quick snips, the ends of the wires separated like the sections of a drawbridge. My God, he thought, sitting on the floor with his knees to his chest, my God.

The text flashed onto the screen of Fitch's phone. Beyond the wall, somewhere behind them, a barge was making its sluggish way up the river.

April parted her lips, mouthing *goodbye* to Inez, at home in bed.

Fitch, the one staying behind, thought April's *goodbye* was for him. But he couldn't seem to find the strength to return it.

Holmes was the first to stand, picking up one of the duffel bags, handing the other to April. "Well . . . ," he said.

Fitch smiled, offering what he hoped looked like encouragement. Or maybe optimism. Or anything, really. Just so long as April and Holmes couldn't see his relief—relief that he didn't have to go with them.

Somewhere in the bottom of the shopping cart, her phone played a marimba. McGee brought the rattling wheels to a stop. The text had taken longer than she'd expected to arrive, and she'd begun to revisit her second guesses about depending so much on Myles. And what about Darius? Had she been wrong to trust him, to believe him when he said he wouldn't get in her way?

McGee had already circled around to the front of the building. The surface of the plaza was pale in the moonlight and looked almost like sand. Into the cart she tossed the wig and the outer layer of clothing, the filthiest. The stench had already spread to the bottom layers, but as she ran back around to the rear of the building, bag in one hand, phone in the other, she could smell nothing but the humid night-going-on-morning air.

★ ★ ★

They lined up on the same side of the stone pot, only just barely enough room for their eight combined hands. Together they managed to push the tree across the lobby, up against the door of the guard booth.

When they were done, Myles leaned against the pot, breathing irregularly, mopping his forehead with his sleeve. He hadn't thought it would be so easy to get swept up in the excitement.

McGee reached out and squeezed Myles's hand.

April checked the time.

Holmes opened the black case and ran his finger over the picks and the single gap, the one missing piece.

On the other side of the window, the white guard had drawn his gun, but he seemed to be having a hard time deciding whether to point it at Myles or Holmes.

"Don't you fucking move," he said, muffled by the bulletproof glass.

Darius stood still and silent beside him.

"We're not going to hurt you," McGee said.

Carl cocked his pistol, and even McGee couldn't resist the instinct to duck.

"I'd like to see you try," Carl said.

"This isn't *Die Hard*!" Holmes shouted from his crouch. "You can put that away."

"I'll put you away."

"Good lord," Holmes said with a roll of his eyes.

"It's fine," McGee said. "Everything's going to be fine." But what to make of Darius's expression, eyes flicking furtively in her direction? As if he had something to tell her.

McGee knew she'd taken a chance coming clean to him that night on the loading dock. But without his help, none of this would have been possible. He'd been the one to tell her what to do. It had become his plan as much as hers. But she'd made him promise not to tell his friend. And in return she hadn't told Myles or anyone else about him. It was simpler that way. But what would she have said if she could? How could she begin to explain him? Darius's loyalties were hard to untangle. In the time she'd known him, his commitment to clean windows and cobwebs seemed to run deeper than his convictions about the city. And his teenage girlfriend trumped them both. Though she couldn't help noticing he'd stopped talking about Violet once he realized McGee understood English.

"It's over," he'd said the last time she'd asked about his affair, her final night of cleaning. "I told her no more. I told her I'm a new man now."

A new man—it seemed to have become his trademark line.

The first time they'd met to discuss the logistics for tonight, she'd asked him, point-blank, why he was helping her, siding against an employer he seemed to adore. "That was the old me," he'd said. "That was before. I'm a new man now."

Later she'd asked if Sylvia knew anything about his plans with Michael Boni. Darius had said, "She can see something's different— that I'm a new man."

As if through repetition it might come true. And each time he thumped his chest where this new man apparently resided.

But tonight in the lobby of HSI, looking through the glass into Darius's eyes, McGee sensed he was trying to say something different now, his head moving subtly side to side, as if he were telling her no.

McGee said, "Does everyone know what to do?"

§

Fitch had met her at a party. Her name was Abby and she was seventeen and alluringly unattractive. There was her long, dark, unclean hair, the bags under her smoky eyes, the pale skin, her emaciated body. She'd been in rehab several times. Alcohol and harder drugs, too. She explained it all to him indifferently, as if it were someone else she was talking about. And she told him about her friends— Angel and Bertrand who'd OD'd, Hua who'd gone straight, and Moss who'd killed himself with a shard of glass. She knew a cast of characters longer than movie credits.

It all started at the party, and Fitch was afraid it would end there, too. But then the next night Abby showed up at the door of his parents' house and asked him to come for a walk. He'd wondered briefly if she was high on something and had mistaken him for someone else.

They walked for miles, eventually turning onto a dark industrial highway where Fitch had never been before. Abby told him the road reminded her of the one she'd been on the time she skidded on a patch of ice in her father's BMW and landed upside down in the ditch. The first thing she did when the car finally stopped moving, she said, was take a drag from the cigarette, still smoldering between her fingers.

Abby smoked the entire time they walked, and each time she lit up, Fitch regretted having said no the first time she offered. Now it was too late. Abby said smoking helped her avoid thinking about drinking and all the other things she wasn't supposed to think about, which might also have been why she took the time to explain the art of making espresso, how to build a bomb with gasoline and a snake-bite kit, how she'd once watched her best friend drown in the undertow on the Gulf of Mexico, how she'd once traveled to Costa Rica with a married man and his infant son (who was probably actually someone else's son), whose baby seat, on the return trip, served as a carrier for ten pounds of cocaine, the very cocaine that got her hooked, that would have led to who-knows-what had the man not disappeared, presumed dead, after a mysterious boating accident, again, in the Gulf of Mexico. Abby told all this in a tragic, breathless voice, as if her whole life were a sigh, and Fitch was in awe, not so much because of what she was saying but because there was so much of it, like a train with no caboose in sight, and you wondered how it was possible a single engine could pull it all.

At a certain point, Abby explained where they were going, but Fitch hardly cared. They were somewhere near the river. He would've followed her anywhere. When she turned onto a small gravel side road, he went with her, not giving it a second thought. The side road led to a factory, a sprawling compound, all lit up against a starless black sky. The gray-shrouded buildings resembled the sheet-covered furniture haunting Fitch's family's lake house during the off-season. Even the lights gave off gray light, even the windows were gray, even the dead trees were blanketed with a gray, dusty film, which it turned out had something to do with the concrete the factory produced. Or so Abby claimed. Peering through one of the dirty windows, they saw the main building was as large as an indoor stadium. It was two or three in the morning, and there were people inside working.

Fitch had thought the factory was only a stop along the way. Along the way to what, he didn't know. As Abby told him about her curiosity, talked about how much fun it would be to break in and walk around inside, Fitch studied her small breasts, trying to decide if she was wearing a bra. He continued to follow her around the perimeter of the building, not realizing she really meant to go inside until he saw the open door she'd found—a dock door like the one April and Holmes and McGee had just gone into—a chink in the factory's armor.

"Let's go," she said.

"There are people—"

"Are you afraid?"

"No," he said, "but it's late . . ."

"The door's open," she said. "It's okay if the door's open." Abby took him by the arm, and Fitch did what he hadn't thought possible. He resisted her. He said no. She must have seen that he was afraid, genuinely afraid, because without putting up a fight, she said, "Okay. Fine, okay."

And they walked in silence away from the doorway, away from the factory, away from the gray trees. The seat of Abby's jeans was worn and frayed in a broad smile just beneath each buttock. Fitch thought about how soft the material would be, how soft the skin beneath. By then it must have been three or four in the morning. It was either exhaustion or he was lost in her body, but he didn't notice when she flagged down a car on the main road. She took his arm—he tingled slightly at the touch—and directed him into the backseat.

On the ride back to Grosse Pointe, she told the bearded man who was driving how she'd once been hitchhiking out west and was picked up by a guy in a blue Ferrari. Occasionally the bearded man glanced at Fitch in the rearview mirror. Abby went on talking about the blue Ferrari, about the police and the high-speed chase across the desert. The driver's mouth, hidden somewhere in his beard, was silent.

The chase and the story went on so long that Fitch was asleep before it ended. He was still almost entirely asleep when the man dropped them off at the entrance to Fitch's neighborhood. And as Abby walked away in the wake of the departing car, having said goodbye and goodnight, having untruthfully said she'd see him later, Fitch wanted to be able to take it all back, to do whatever she asked, but he knew it was too late, and anyway he knew he couldn't. And although he'd managed to change a great deal about himself since he was fifteen, he was dismayed to discover, as he watched the loading dock of the HSI Building, that he was still a coward.

§

Myles removed the elevator's control panel. The wires, each one as meaningless to him as the next, he disconnected. He flipped every switch. But he was careful to damage nothing. What he'd done to the door of the guard booth and to the phone and data lines had been unavoidable. They weren't reckless. They didn't destroy for the fun of it.

Taking one last look around the lobby, it struck him that the guard booth resembled an aquarium, the two guards a pair of ridiculous fish, blinking at him dumbly. He hadn't forgotten their colleague who'd arrested him, cuffing him roughly. He supposed he should feel pleased with himself for having gotten them back. But as he moved toward the stairs, blocking the door behind him, he couldn't help thinking about the cops and robbers movies he'd watched as a kid, how they always ended with the bad guys trying to climb their way to freedom—up stairs, up towers, up scaffolding, fences, whatever; they never seemed to realize the higher they went, the more difficult it would be to escape.

Of course, in this case it didn't matter. McGee's plan left no room for escape.

The floor tile was dull, the carpets foot-printed, the bathrooms littered with paper towels. Monday night, and the custodians were gone, Dorothy too. McGee had timed things so they would be. But by all appearances, the custodians had never been here in the first place. McGee checked several floors and found every one of the custodians' closets locked. And that wasn't all: Holmes had spent a full minute trying picks on the door to the main office before realizing it was already unlocked.

"Let's get to work," McGee said, and she sent Holmes to the main filing room to get started opening up the cabinets. He came back a moment later wanting to know which ones.

"Anything new," she said. "Within the last year. Starting with the factory."

"How am I supposed to know which ones are new?"

"Look at the labels, the dates."

Holmes led her down the hall and into the room and over to the cabinets and showed her row after row of tall metal cases from which the labels had all been removed.

For a moment McGee stood there with her hand over her mouth.

"Just start opening them," she said.

His father had always said locks were like people. They had weaknesses, and if you could learn to exploit those weaknesses, you could control them. As with anything else, you got a feel for locks. You learned to dance with the pins, allowing them to lead. You used all your senses: you felt the stiffness of the springs, you heard the clicks and scrapes. Your nose would tell you how recently a lock had been greased. Your eyes focused inward, on the image of the inside of the lock that was inside your head. You learned to concentrate, remaining relaxed and flexible. From lock to lock you carried a physical memory of the proper tension for your muscles to apply, the correct pressure in your wrist, the torque, the resistance. And then there was the moment when everything clicked.

Holmes wondered what his father, who'd always been so upright, so law-abiding, would have thought had he known to what end his son applied these lessons. Growing up at his father's side, going along on calls, Holmes had spent years watching him open trunks and safes and doors. The work had seemed like magic then, and it had always made him proud, the way his father's customers stood there watching, too. But with the white customers, there was often something different, a nervousness that entered their gestures, a sucking of teeth, a clenching of hands. It was years before Holmes realized what it meant, that they watched not with fascination—as he did—but with fear, wary of a black man who could pick a lock as easily as untying a knot.

§

April had taken a job at the computer lab during her second semester at college. That was where she'd met Jane, who seemed to come every night, dressed in a T-shirt commemorating some special event: bake sales, softball championships, company picnics, blood drives, mayoral campaigns, state fairs, public radio fundraisers, pie-eating contests, sack races, badminton tournaments, charity car washes, graduating classes, band tours from before she was born, birthday milestones she hadn't reached, Fourth of July celebrations, supermarket grand openings, go-cart rallies, philatelist conventions. She had dozens of T-shirts celebrating family reunions, each bearing a different family name, none of them her own. She was a full foot shorter than April, and she had dark, almost black hair with streaks of blue. Shy, though she didn't look it. But after the first time, asking April for help with the computer became her nightly ritual.

Several weeks into the semester, April volunteered to fill the grave-yard shift no one else wanted. Jane made the switch too, and soon she was coming to the lab even when she didn't have any work to do. She needed to get away from her roommate, she said. She and April hung out together all night. In the morning, they ate breakfast together in the cafeteria. Afterward Jane was often so in dread of seeing her roommate that she went home with April, whose own roommate had moved in with her boyfriend. In the following weeks, Jane's belongings—T-shirts, books, records—began to take up resi-dence in April's room.

Jane got the letter from the school during spring break. They'd both stuck around, looking forward to a quiet, empty campus. The letter came on official letterhead, watermarked and printed with a colored seal. Through watery eyes, Jane read it to April, a past-due bill for tuition. There was trouble at home, she explained, her parents splitting, money tight. If she didn't pay up, she'd have to leave.

Two nights later April and Jane let themselves into the computer lab. They stole six computers, loading them into Jane's roommate's car, to which Jane had somehow gotten a key. The next day Jane drove them into the city.

It didn't take long for the school to figure out April had been the only person on campus over the vacation with access to the lab. There were no signs of forced entry. Staring at her breasts as he spoke, the dean told April that if she returned the computers, he'd forget the whole thing. She'd be done at the lab, but he wouldn't kick her out of school.

But Jane said it was too late, the computers were gone, and so was the money, and soon so was Jane.

The quiet of Ruth Freeman's office helped to ease some of April's queasiness, but it did nothing to erase the memory. April had never told anyone the real reason she'd been expelled. She didn't need to be told what an idiot she'd been, didn't need Inez making fun of her for being so gullible. She wondered why it was that she was forever getting herself involved in things like these, sacrificing herself for other peoples' causes. It wasn't that she didn't believe, that she wasn't committed. If anything, she believed too much, believed in everything, every voice so reasonable, so cogent and clear. Sometimes she just wondered who she'd be if only everyone would be quiet for a moment.

In a few hours, there would be news crews outside and police downstairs trying to break in. And would Inez forgive her?

Taking a deep breath, April pressed the power button on the computer. She waited a few seconds for the flash of lights, for the *dong* and the flicker on the screen, the spinning of the hard drive. She waited.

She pressed the button again, harder this time.

And waited.

Under the desk she found the power strip. There were plugs for the lamp, the printer, a radio, a cell phone charger. Nothing at all for the computer.

The news knocked the breath out of McGee.

Myles dropped the banner he'd been unrolling. "Can't you do something?"

"It's the cord," April said. "There's no cord."

Then Holmes appeared, and April was relieved to have their attention shift to him.

"In one of the cabinets," Holmes said, "I found rental contracts for the office equipment."

"What good will that do us?" McGee said. "What's in the others?"

"Empty," Holmes said. "All of them. Empty."

"I don't understand," McGee said.

Holmes flopped down in a chair. "They knew we were coming."

"It's okay," McGee said. "It's fine. We'll be fine."

Holmes fainted back, draping his arm over his eyes. "I said this was a stupid idea."

Myles came over from the window. "We all agreed."

By which he meant no one had said no. After all this time, April thought, still no one could tell McGee no.

Okay, fine. It would be all right. It really would. McGee had hoped for more. Details, secrets. But they could get by without it. She'd still have plenty to say when the news cameras arrived. She could break the story even with just what Darius had told her, HSI abandoning the city once and for all. What mattered was breaking the scoop before Ruth Freeman had a chance to spin it into silence. Myles would fly the banner. McGee would e-mail the press release. April would help make the calls. The point was the occupation. The point was the attention, asking questions, and asking them loudly, forcing the company to answer.

McGee said, "We can still do what we came here to do." She picked up the phone and dialed the first number on the list. It wasn't until she put the receiver to her ear that she realized the phone was dead.

Okay, fine. It didn't matter. She would use her own.

At first Fitch didn't see them. He'd been watching for flashing lights and listening for sirens. Four sedans appeared, headlights turned off. The cars were black, sweeping into the alley as ominously as storm clouds. The men who stepped out were invisible in their dark suits. Fitch could see them only as dull blotches against the cars' shiny finish.

One at a time the men hoisted themselves up to the dock. Fitch could hear them talking quietly to one another. One of them crushed out a cigarette. Another laughed, and then another, and the sound was so unexpected that Fitch found himself nearly laughing, too. And then the men disappeared inside, and Fitch steadied his hands just long enough to send McGee a text to let her know someone was coming.

Sixteen

THE TRIP TO New Orleans was now two years in the past, but Tiphany had relived it in her mind so often that it was less like a memory than like an obsession. She'd been twenty-two and fresh out of college when Mrs. Freeman hired her as her administrative assistant. It was Tiphany's first full-time job, and her very first task on her first day in the office had been to make the travel arrangements for the convention. This she had done without help from anyone, and because of that, there was no question about whom to blame when they arrived at the hotel in New Orleans a month later to find only one room reserved.

"I don't suppose you've another?" Mrs. Freeman inquired. But before the pockmarked young man at the desk could confirm what all three of them already knew—that with such a large convention, the hotel was booked beyond capacity—the old woman drifted off toward the elevator, leaving Tiphany to get the key.

Not wanting to embarrass Mrs. Freeman in front of the bellhop,

Tiphany kept her apologies to herself. The upward movement of the elevator went straight to her stomach, and she was unable to avoid her own pale reflection in the mirrored walls.

Even after she stepped out of the elevator, Tiphany couldn't seem to get away from herself. There were mirrors along the corridor and mirrors in the suite. Never had she seen such a hotel room. Actually it was several rooms: bedroom, living room, kitchenette, and even a small dining room. Most incredible, however, were the two bathrooms. Seeing them gave her hope. Maybe there was another bedroom behind one of the closed doors. But the doors led to closets. There was only one bed. One bed, two women.

In the mirror above the bureau, Tiphany caught another glimpse of her own face, blue veins throbbing through translucent skin. Oh well, she tried to tell herself, it's only a job—a job you never really liked anyway.

Remaining always a step ahead of Mrs. Freeman, the bellhop ripped open the blinds with such drama, it was as though he were revealing a fabulous prize. And it *was* a prize of sorts—a view of the lazy river dozens of stories below. Then he showed them the bar with its selection of fine liquors, and he commenced a tutorial on operating the air conditioner. Mrs. Freeman teetered into a wing chair. Tiphany supposed it would fall to her to offer the man a tip, and preferably soon, before he moved on to the rudiments of the television remote control. She had no idea what was appropriate.

The bellhop accepted the ten dollars she offered with neither open gratitude nor scorn. But perhaps it was in a mild gesture of appreciation that he returned to the living room, where Mrs. Freeman sat with her eyes closed, and removed the cushions from the sofa, exposing the bed folded up underneath. Tiphany was so relieved, she would have given him another ten, but her wallet was empty. She hoped she'd be reimbursed before Mrs. Freeman fired her.

As soon as the bellhop was out the door, Tiphany began preparing her apology, assembling ideas for possible acts of penitence. But then again, she wondered if it wouldn't be best to say nothing at all—to avoid annoying the old woman any further.

"The room's big enough for three anyway," Mrs. Freeman said, as if reading her assistant's mind. Tiphany knew better than to believe she meant it, but she took it as a hopeful sign that Mrs. Freeman also wished to put these unpleasantries behind them.

"Yes," Tiphany said, stalling as she tried to think of something witty and self-deprecating to say. "Yes."

Mrs. Freeman got up to mix herself a cocktail. "Have I ever mentioned how much I hate coming to these things?"

The question was clearly meant to sound rhetorical, but to Tiphany it was like something from one of those personality tests she'd taken when applying for retail jobs in high school. One of the questions was always something like "There are occasions when an employee might be justified in taking something without paying for it." The answer was always *strongly disagree.*

"I'm looking forward to it," Tiphany said.

"You'll see soon enough." Mrs. Freeman swung her feet onto the ottoman and kicked off her shoes. "It's like walking into a crowded men's room."

"Oh," Tiphany said, as if she understood.

No one had ever made her as nervous as Mrs. Freeman. Tiphany was pretty sure she'd done the right thing saying she was happy to be here, but she also knew one right answer wouldn't be enough to make her boss forget whose fault it was that she now had an unwanted roommate.

In the morning, while Mrs. Freeman ate breakfast, Tiphany read and reread the schedule of the day's events. She felt nauseated, watching the old woman chew her eighteen-dollar over-easys and toast. She supposed her nerves were to blame. Her nerves and her boss's silence. All night, and so far this morning, Mrs. Freeman had persisted in hiding her anger. Tiphany was beginning to think she might prefer the old woman simply yell at her and get it over with.

The morning's meetings were closed to all but the most senior members and officeholders. Even among them, Tiphany had observed, Mrs. Freeman enjoyed a position of doting reverence. After breakfast, Tiphany led the old woman downstairs to the hotel lobby and from there down a twisting corridor to a darkly furnished room polka-dotted with bald and gray heads. There Mrs. Freeman assumed the burden of her briefcase, telling Tiphany to return for her at two o'clock.

"Call me if you need anything," Tiphany said as Mrs. Freeman walked away. She could only hope the old woman wouldn't take her up on the offer.

Once outside, Tiphany felt her nerves finally settling. They seemed to settle all the more the farther she got from the revolving door and the taxi stand and the luggage trolleys. Soon her pace had increased so much, it must have seemed she was fleeing some kind of conflagration.

Several blocks from the hotel, she came across a square bordered by cafés and small shops. It was early, but the place was already choked with tourists. In the center of the square was a small elevated park enclosed by a wrought-iron fence, upon which hung row after row of paintings, most of them streetscapes. The artists themselves—there were perhaps a half dozen—sat languidly in the shade.

One artist in particular caught her attention. Maybe he looked a bit like Sasha, with his wavy brown hair and several days' worth of stubble. He wore tight, paint-spotted jeans and a thin, almost pulpy shirt. His fingernails were dirty, his forearms blue with ink. His display consisted entirely of representations of the portion of wrought-iron fence and the foliage behind it that passersby saw when they looked at the display of paintings on the wrought-iron fence with the foliage behind it or, more precisely, that they would have seen had the paintings on the wrought-iron fence not been obstructing the view of the foliage.

Thinking back on it now, Tiphany could remember the paintings so clearly because at the time she couldn't stop thinking how Sasha would have made fun of them. Sweatshop art, he called it. Down the conveyer belt it went, dab a few butterflies and fluffy clouds, and then on to the next.

While she was standing there watching, a man and woman in ventilated safari shirts approached the display, and the woman pointed at one of the pieces and asked the price. Tiphany didn't hear the artist's answer, but a few moments later she observed the exchange of cash, one tattooed forearm driving a thick wad deep down into his threadbare pocket. If only Sasha were here to see it.

As she watched the couple walk away with the canvas wrapped in paper, Tiphany recalled being at a party once with a bunch of Sasha's artist friends, and Sasha going on about rich people with more money than taste, dragging home monstrosities from galleries, hanging them in the gilt "foy-yays" of their McMansions, forcing their children to look at them day after day, torturing them with garish, derivative clichés, and how the kids would grow up to wear pleated khakis and boat shoes and despise art and everyone who practiced it. Sasha had been drunk, acting out the parts, a tube sock as an ascot, and Tiphany had laughed so hard, she snorted a burning jet of rum and Coke.

But really, the paintings in the square didn't seem that bad. A little boring, maybe. But she wasn't an artist like Sasha. Tiphany didn't exactly know what she was. A secretary, an assistant? No one important. Not like Mrs. Freeman. It was strange. Tiphany knew she shouldn't, and she knew she could never admit it to Sasha, but in truth she actually kind of liked her boss. The old woman was smart and opinionated and didn't seem to care what anyone thought of her, which made it all the more amazing that powerful people listened to her and took her seriously. And now Tiphany had let her down.

When she looked again, the landscape artist had filled the gap in his display with an exact duplicate of the one he'd just sold.

★ ★ ★

That afternoon Tiphany ate lunch alone and then met up with Mrs. Freeman in the main conference room. But it was too loud in there, too congested with the crowds of jovial, back-slapping men. The old lady pushed her way out to the corridor, where she and Tiphany could talk in peace.

"How is it outside?" Mrs. Freeman asked, leading Tiphany to a quiet corner.

Tiphany made a point of glancing out the window. "Warm, I think."

Mrs. Freeman cocked her ear, as though hard of hearing. "You think? Good lord, go outside. There's no reason for both of us to suffer in here."

Tiphany nearly took the bait, nearly confessed. "I was going over your material," she said. "For your panel. I wanted to make sure everything was there."

"Go have some fun," Mrs. Freeman said. "Be young."

Then a man emerged from a plume of cologne and put his hand on Mrs. Freeman's shoulder, asking if she was ready to get started.

Mrs. Freeman sighed. "If we must." She moved off before the man could take her arm, forgetting to say goodbye.

It took Tiphany several hours to finish Mrs. Freeman's tasks, tying up loose ends from a project they'd left unfinished back at the office.

By the time Tiphany finally made it back outside, the landscape painter had left, taking his canvases with him. The crowds of tourists had started to thin. Lethargy had settled over the square. A palm reader wearing sweatpants and a head scarf had fallen asleep at her card table. Reclining on a park bench, a four-man jazz band played ragtime for an audience of two little girls, their pink, sparkly sneakers flashing strobes of red light every time they tapped their feet. At a souvenir stand on the corner, two college-age boys flipped through a rack of postcards, grinning grotesquely at an enormously fat woman posed in the nude, strapped to a pair of vintage roller skates.

This was the farthest Tiphany had ever been from home. Compared to Detroit, New Orleans almost seemed like a different country. She could picture Sasha rolling his eyes at how crass it all was. Tourist bullshit, he'd say. He was all about grit these days, Detroit the only authentic place on earth. Dirty and raw and real, and if you didn't like it, get the fuck out. Tiphany wasn't quite so sure, but she liked Detroit, too, all the old buildings and neighborhoods. It was where she'd been born, about the only place she really knew. Sasha had been there less than a year, since he finished college, but he was already saying he'd never leave. Tiphany supposed that meant she wouldn't either.

Soon after arriving at the square, Tiphany had spotted a girl lounging on the steps of what appeared to be a courthouse. The girl was younger than Tiphany, but only by a couple of years. She was clearly in bad shape. Even from several yards away, Tiphany could see her eyes mapped in red veins, her greasy hair congealed into a sort of fin. As Tiphany passed the courthouse, the girl had gotten up from the steps, and for the last several minutes she'd been following Tiphany everywhere she went. At first, Tiphany had tried to ignore her, but the girl clung so close, Tiphany could smell her, a mix of patchouli and rancid butter.

Tiphany had made it almost all the way back around to the palm reader when she slowed down, shortening her stride. The girl stumbled into her, and Tiphany reached out to keep her from falling. "Are you all right?"

The girl grinned, baring her teeth. "They're planting dreams in my head." White spots glistened on her gums.

Tiphany tried asking the girl her name and where she was from, and in response the girl mumbled something Tiphany didn't understand. And then Tiphany didn't know what to do, but she couldn't bring herself to walk away. She was looking around for help, maybe a police officer, when she happened to spot the mime.

The mime was in whiteface and black tights, sauntering toward

246

Tiphany and the girl, moving against the flow of tourist traffic. He seemed heavy for a mime, his black-and-white-striped shirt clinging to his belly, exposing a patch of hair just below his navel. When he was only a few steps away, the mime leaned in toward Tiphany's ear and pointed at the girl, who was now laughing quietly to herself.

"At least someone's having a good time," he said.

The mime was smoking, and his words had curled around and up Tiphany's nose. Then they were gone, and she wondered if only she had heard them. In midstride she stopped and turned, as if to verify that what she thought had just happened *had*, in fact, just happened.

The mime said nothing else. Having reached the entrance to the park, a few yards away, he too came to stop. There he stood for a moment, his back to the low stone wall, savoring a final drag of his cigarette, as if a firing squad awaited.

Slowly, reluctantly, the mime pulled the cigarette from his mouth and let it dive, filter first, onto the sidewalk. Somewhere behind Tiphany, the girl continued to laugh.

Eyes cast downward, the mime watched a thread of smoke twist up from the ground, thinning to nothing before reaching his knees. Tiphany thought she read resignation in the curl of his lower lip. A few inches above the butt, the mime's heel began its descent upon the embers. Clearly he meant to grind it out, nothing more complicated than that. And yet the moment his foot touched the cigarette, it immediately recoiled, as though his heel had landed on a loaded spring. With exaggerated outrage, he raised his foot a second time, stomping again on the cigarette. Again his foot bounced back.

Sensing some sort of performance, passersby began to slow. A few people at a time, a small crowd gathered. Unsure what was happening, they watched the mime glower at the sidewalk, and they looked too, trying to find the object of his fury. Chest puffed, the mime faked another stomp, as if hoping to catch the cigarette off guard. Then for a moment, he seemed to give up, content to let the cigarette smolder. He turned his back on it. But this too was only a ruse. His plan was to lull the cigarette into a false sense of security. And then he spun around, and then he leaped. Not just one foot this time—he raised both knees to his chest. Swiftly and heavily his feet hit the ground. His aim was perfect. But something went wrong. The instant he landed, his feet sprang back up again, rising higher as the mime toppled over backward. When he hit the cobblestones, Tiphany thought she heard something inside him crack.

The show was over. On his back on the sidewalk, the mime watched with boredom as the last of the spectators wandered away. Into his hat, which he'd lost in the fall, an old woman in a wig tossed a few coins. Seeing that no one else remained to help him, Tiphany came forward and extended her hand. The mime waved her off, preferring to pull himself up by an invisible rope.

That evening, sitting alone in the hotel restaurant, Tiphany nursed her second beer and marveled at the world in which she'd found herself. A day had passed in which only four people had spoken to her: Mrs. Freeman, a fucked-up street kid, a mime, and finally her waiter. The first hated her. The second was barely conscious. About the third she could only guess. Judging by his neglect of her, the fourth seemed to have already decided Tiphany's tip wasn't worth the effort. For anyone else, she was sure, such encounters came easily. For anyone else, the trip would have been simple. A free vacation. A per diem. A break from Detroit's endless winter.

When she got back to her room after dinner and found that Mrs. Freeman wasn't there, Tiphany gave Sasha a call. The thing she wanted to talk about most was the mime.

"'At least someone's having a good time.' That's what he said."

"If a mime's going to speak," Sasha said, yawning into the phone, "he must have something pretty important to say."

"He was right. I don't belong here," Tiphany said. "And she's probably going to fire me when we get back."

"So you have to share a room," he said. "She's old. She probably won't even remember."

"You're not helping." It was always the same. He offered jokes when she was looking for comfort. The day after she'd told him she'd be going on this trip—the first business trip of her life—he'd gone to the thrift store and bought her a beat-up attaché case, which he monogrammed himself with a permanent marker.

She'd been planning to tell him about the landscape artist and his paintings, but now she just wasn't in the mood.

Tiphany was getting ready for bed when Mrs. Freeman returned, stepping out of her shoes before even shutting the door.

"Would you mind making me a drink?" the old woman said, crumbling into the chair. She seemed to fall instantly asleep. But at the sound a moment later of the clinking ice beside her ear, Mrs. Freeman opened her eyes and gratefully took the glass. After a few sips, she'd recovered enough to sit up straight and answer Tiphany's questions about her day.

"Buffoons," she said, "blowhards, posses of chittering monkeys. They left their brains at home to save space for their golf clubs."

"Some of the panels were interesting, I thought," Tiphany said, hoping Mrs. Freeman wouldn't ask for examples.

Mrs. Freeman rattled her ice and waited for the last drops of gin to reach her tongue. "I hadn't realized you were so interested," she said. "You should come with me tomorrow. Frankly, I wish you'd take my place."

There was nothing Tiphany would have liked less. But as she unfolded her bed, she couldn't help feeling she'd made some slight progress toward amends.

Having been unable to think of an excuse for backing out, Tiphany began the next day at Mrs. Freeman's side, and there she remained up through lunch. There were six of them at the restaurant, the four men old friends and colleagues of Mrs. Freeman's. Tiphany forgot their names the moment she was introduced.

They spent much of the meal discussing their favorite resorts. Mrs. Freeman seemed especially fond of a hotel in Haiti, of all places. Tiphany kept quiet, ashamed to admit the hotel she was in right now was the most exotic place she'd ever been. But as the conversation wore on, she kept feeling everyone was looking at her, waiting for her to say something, anything. Finally, in a moment of desperation, she choked down a gulp of frigid ice water and, turning to a ruddy-faced man who'd just concluded a long, boring story about a trip abroad, said, "I can't remember—what part of France is Belize in?"

All at once, it seemed, everyone reached for their napkins, dabbing at their lips so as to have an excuse not to answer. After a moment Mrs. Freeman reached across the table to pat Tiphany's arm. "I can hardly remember myself sometimes."

After that Tiphany was sure every time she opened her mouth, she was making a fool of herself. But what could she do? They were smart and successful and sophisticated, and she was just a glorified secretary. She'd obviously embarrassed Mrs. Freeman as well, and that was why the old woman was so desperate to get rid of her when the meal was over, claiming she had business to attend to alone.

Despite having spent the day sitting down, at the end of it Tiphany was more exhausted than the day before, when she'd walked for miles. For the second night in a row, she had dinner and drinks in the hotel restaurant. Afterward, depressed and slightly drunk, she went upstairs and called Sasha.

"I miss you," she said. "I wish you were here."

"Me too," he said without sincerity. She couldn't blame him.

She told him about lunch, how she'd embarrassed Mrs. Freeman in front of her friends.

"Who cares?" he said, interrupting. "These people are animals.

You should never have taken the job. I mean, it's repulsive. They're vile. A fucking military contractor. Spewing toxic waste all over the place. They're a scourge."

"A scourge?"

"It's immoral," he said. "Working there, you're part of the problem."

In the background his stereo was blasting his favorite band, the Chicken Tongues, and she just wanted to close her eyes and listen.

"We need the money."

"Which is more important?"

It was his way, when he didn't want to talk about something, often simply because talk bored him, to reduce it to the most simplistic of terms. Yes or no. Either or. The fewer the choices, the shorter the conversation. But what sort of job could she have taken that he wouldn't find objectionable? Just about everybody sold something, and nearly all of it was garbage in one way or another. Yes, the company made weapons and drones. But it also built toasters and fetal heart monitors and solar-powered water filtration systems. She'd applied for the job in the first place for the same reason she'd applied for everything else: because it was there. She'd gone to the interview without even the faintest sense of optimism, not so much assuming she wouldn't get the job as almost hoping she wouldn't. She'd had a brief office internship in college, and the thought of spending her life doing something like that had filled her with something even more debilitating than dread.

And so it had come as a surprise to Tiphany that during the fifteen minutes the interview for the job had taken, Mrs. Freeman had voluntarily, without any provocation on Tiphany's part, acknowledged each and every one of her fears. She had said the position Tiphany had applied for was tedious and unglamorous, that the people she'd work with would often be tiresome, that the company itself could be exasperating. But she'd added that she herself had fought her way up from the bottom, a woman in a man's world, and that she'd come to HSI because she'd seen great potential, potential she saw still.

251

"We do good things," she'd said, "but sometimes we do them badly." And as far as Mrs. Freeman was concerned, there was no point getting up in the morning if there wasn't something—and for her the company was that something—in one's life worth struggling to make better.

"We get to be the conscience," Mrs. Freeman had said that day, seeming to enjoy the idea of the two of them conspiring in her office. "These men need us, even if they don't know it."

And Tiphany had admired not just her honesty but the confidence with which Mrs. Freeman had voiced her convictions and her condemnations. Even before the fifteen minutes were up, Tiphany had decided that, if she was lucky enough to be offered the job, she would take it.

But she knew if she'd told Sasha any of this, he would've said she was a sellout. So she kept it to herself.

§

All throughout the next day, Tiphany found it impossible to concentrate. She couldn't get out of her head the thought that tomorrow she and Mrs. Freeman would return to Detroit and she'd find herself out of a job. Then she'd have to start all over again.

Toward the end of the afternoon, she gave up on her work altogether. Desperately needing to get out of the hotel, she changed into her grungiest clothes, a pair of jeans and the T-shirt she'd been sleeping in. For the first time since her encounter with the mime, she returned to the square. Standing beneath a café awning, she scanned the kids on the long steps of the courthouse. She was looking for the girl with red-veined eyes. But what would she have done if she'd found her?

Neither did Tiphany see any sign of the landscape painter. His peers were in their usual spots, with their displays hanging from the wrought-iron fence. But his space was empty.

Coming upon the park entrance, Tiphany thought she spotted the mime, but it was a different one, tall and lean. She guessed the odds weren't good that he'd be a talker, too.

As she walked away from the square, she found herself wondering what Mrs. Freeman would have made of all this. The old woman had seemed so determined for Tiphany to get out of the hotel and experience it. Was it possible her boss would've found it fun, enjoying the place for the spectacle it was?

Back at the hotel, the desk clerk was holding a note for her.

Dinner at 8, it said. Well, Tiphany thought, death row inmates get a final meal—why not me?

The waiter who greeted them wore a black T-shirt and black jeans and a yellow pencil behind his ear. The interior of the restaurant was almost as dark as his clothes. The place was decorated with dead, brittle flowers. Tiphany recognized almost nothing on the menu.

"I come here whenever I'm in town," Mrs. Freeman said. "It's the one place I know I won't run into anyone."

Tiphany made it to the last page of the menu and then started over. Perhaps she'd simply order whatever Mrs. Freeman was having.

"Are there interesting sessions tomorrow?" she said.

Mrs. Freeman barely glanced at the wine list, and then she was done, ready to order. "Every year I promise myself I'll skip the last day," she said. "Of course, I never do. I don't know what it is—some weakness of character, I suppose. Everyone else plays golf."

"Do you play?"

"If I were Supreme Dictator," Mrs. Freeman said, taking up her martini, "I'd outlaw that hideous addiction. My husband's a fanatic. Does your boyfriend play?"

"He doesn't really play sports."

Mrs. Freeman seemed relieved. "Personally, I don't consider golf a sport," she said, "but that's another matter. What does he do? I don't believe you've ever mentioned."

Tiphany chose that moment to take a long, slow sip of water. It wasn't that she was exactly ashamed—she just wanted to avoid any more uncomfortable conversations. "Plumbing. He's a plumber. Actually an apprentice. But he's really a sculptor . . ."

Either she wasn't listening or she was busy thinking of something else, but Mrs. Freeman suddenly fell silent. Tiphany fully expected her to change the subject—hoped, in fact, that she would.

"Nothing wrong with being a plumber," Mrs. Freeman said. "It's far more noble than doing nothing, which is my husband's sole profession. He's quite good at it, though. Don't ever get married," Mrs. Freeman said, sipping again, "At least make sure you know what you're getting into. Your generation has broken many of my generation's bad habits. You test each other first. You have trial runs. You sleep around. I don't mean *you* in particular, of course. For us—some of us, anyway—marriage was something that just happened, like menstruation. You learned to accept it. I don't even remember how we met, my husband and I. My second husband, anyway. My first I prefer not to think about. With my second it was never love. We knew each other through others, mutual friends. It's hard to remember how it began. I guess these things seem less exciting when you're older, these opening volleys of a relationship. When I think about it now, I think of it as being at a party—one of those god-awful parties where you get stuck talking to someone for hours on end. Not necessarily someone you hate. Maybe it's just that you don't know him very well, but because you've met him before—probably at some other god-awful party—it's easy to fall into conversation. There are things you both know that you can talk about. It may not be the most stimulating conversation in the world, but it's better than sitting by yourself in the corner. And of course he's a little attractive. All right, more than a little. So there's that. But then what happens is you get stuck. No one comes over to say hello. And the conversation isn't so painful that you want to go out of your way to come up with an excuse to escape. You don't want to offend him. It's just that you don't particularly want to spend the entire evening with him. But that's exactly what happens. At a certain point you look around and discover that you and this man are the only people left. You can hear voices coming from the patio. People are laughing. You know there's something interesting going on out there. Maybe the host is showing off his new outdoor theater. Or his professional-grade grill that runs on briquettes of ancient sequoia trees. Whatever it is. The point being that you like this man, more or less, but really you'd rather be outside with everyone else. At the same time, though, the two of you being alone together has already begun to feel natural and inevitable. Next thing you know, you're married, and you realize you'll never again have a chance to go out to the patio to see what all the hubbub was about."

Mrs. Freeman raised her glass to her mouth, and then she seemed to smirk—or was it a smile? Tiphany couldn't tell. She'd long ago lost track of what Mrs. Freeman was saying, and she'd been sitting in terror for several minutes, dreading the moment when she'd have to respond. Uncertain what to do, she raised her salad fork to the light of the candle between them on the table and rubbed her thumb over some imaginary watermark.

When she looked again at Mrs. Freeman, Tiphany saw it was a *smile* on the old woman's face, and she understood the moment had come, the final reckoning. But she also realized the moment brought with it one final chance. If she could just figure out the right thing to say, Mrs. Freeman might perhaps forgive her. Maybe they could, after all, put everything else behind them.

But nothing came. Not the right thing. Not even the wrong thing. Tiphany kept rubbing the fork, as if a magic genie might pop out to save her. She couldn't imagine Mrs. Freeman having floundered like this when she was her age—when she was any age, for that matter. The old woman must have thought her a complete imbecile.

And so it was with great relief that Tiphany looked up just then and saw the waiter approaching. She took that opportunity to glance once more at her menu, and she settled at last on the coq au vin. She didn't know what the *coq* was, but she was certain she needed as much *vin* as she could get.

Mrs. Freeman ordered the same thing, but the words rolled off her tongue as if she'd been saying them all her life. When the waiter left, Mrs. Freeman also seemed to have forgotten what they'd been talking about. In retrospect, Tiphany didn't remember much else about the meal, perhaps because she'd worked so hard to repress the many ways in which she'd embarrassed herself. Unnecessarily, entirely out of kindness, Mrs. Freeman had given her a second chance. Tiphany had blown that one too.

Embarrassment was Tiphany's principal recollection of that entire trip. Embarrassment and disappointment. Disappointment because she discovered she liked Mrs. Freeman even more than she'd expected. She liked Mrs. Freeman so much, in fact, that in the years following the convention, as she grew more settled into her position, she ceased to debate with herself about whether it was right for her to be working for a company that profited from pollution and war and destruction. As Mrs. Freeman said, they were the conscience.

Mercifully, the old woman had let her keep her job. She'd even reimbursed her the ten dollars she'd tipped the bellhop, without Tiphany having to ask. And yet it was clear to Tiphany that the old woman's feelings for her had changed. The more she tried to make up for her mistakes, the more Mrs. Freeman seemed to resent her.

The morning the investigators showed up at Tiphany's apartment, the trip to New Orleans was two years in the past, but for the last hour she'd been able to think of little else. She wasn't surprised to see the men in their dull gray suits, though she wasn't quite ready for them either. It was eight-thirty, and she hadn't bothered to dress for work. Sasha had already left for his studio. Tiphany was still trying to understand the story she'd seen on the news. Last night, extremists— terrorists of some sort—had broken into HSI. They'd taken the guards hostage and barricaded themselves on the third floor. *Her* floor. When Tiphany had left for the day, Mrs. Freeman had still been working there. Tiphany had left her all alone.

"Is she okay?" Tiphany said, looking from one man to the next. "They didn't hurt her, did they?"

One of the investigators opened his briefcase and took out some photos. They were mug shots of five or six people, all close to Tiphany's age.

"Have you seen any of them before?" one of the men said.

"Have you noticed anything out of the ordinary?" said the other.

Was it possible, Tiphany wondered, that she'd somehow failed Mrs. Freeman again?

Summer

Seventeen

SYLVIA REMEMBERED THE first time, waking in the night, thinking *something's missing.*

Looking at the empty half of the mattress beside her, the discolored pillow, thinking, *There was something here that's gone.*

And then, in the morning, she found him asleep beside her, breathing through his mouth, like the boy she once knew.

But still there was that feeling: *Something is missing.*

All day long at work, on her feet, trying to understand what it might be.

Eighteen

HE MISTOOK THE sound at first for birds. He was blocks away when he heard the chirps, several of them at once, floating in from different directions.

But on second thought, the sound was too dull, the edges of the notes too static. There was no music in it. And it was the middle of the night.

As he drew closer, he saw the forklifts, crawling through the streets, pushing and pulling pallets stacked high with produce, beeping as they went.

It was Saturday, market day. Dobbs had lost track. The sun was nowhere near risen yet, but the overhead doors of the hangar-like buildings were open. Inside he could see vans and panel trucks and pickups. Harsh fluorescent light leaked out from every opening. Everyone was busy, brigades of exhausted-looking people ducking in and out of the backs of trucks.

One of the enormous sheds was in the process of being transformed into a greenhouse, waist-high terraces of pink and white and yellow and red, all in rows, stretched out like the stripes of some exotic flag.

In the other buildings, in the open-air stalls, there was so much produce, it hardly seemed like food. Potatoes were tossed together like rocks; the unwashed carrots and turnips looked like grotesque deep-sea creatures, with their tentacle roots.

No one seemed to notice Dobbs. His exhaustion was indistinguishable from theirs. From the sidewalk he picked up a small, empty crate. As he went, he filled it. Something here, something there. He didn't know what half of it was. His hands did his thinking for him. No one thought to stop him.

This time the note was stopped up in an empty water bottle, cast onto the porch, as if it had made the voyage here by sea.

Dobbs fished the slip of paper through the neck. *Delay*, it said. *Four weeks.*

He tossed the note into the corner with the others.

It was late June. By now Dobbs was supposed to have been done and gone.

But there'd been problems. First it was *ten days*. Then *two weeks*, then *three*. What did they even mean when they said "delay"? It wasn't as if they were running a factory. There were no raw materials to run out of, no supply lines to get tangled, no labor disputes, no bureaucratic holdups at customs. The entire business had only one piece: take people from here and move them to there. What did that leave? It didn't take months to change a flat tire.

He'd already spent almost all the money they'd given him in advance, the setup funds. There'd be no more until the shipment arrived.

In the meantime, he'd done everything he could with the warehouse. Sweeping alone had taken weeks. A strange, dense dust had filled the place: crumbling block, flaking paint, shards of rust and glass.

His broom had moved across the floor like a shovel through mud. It was as if the floor were made of this—sediment and nothing more.

And he'd spent more weeks clearing away the junk and rubble: cable spools as tall as he was, piles of rusty disks and rebar. Everything was deceptively heavy. Even scraps of wood seemed to have doubled their weight from the damp.

In addition to the mattresses, he'd gathered food, every dented can he could find within twenty square miles. And he had half a dozen syrup barrels, swiped from a bottling plant. He'd filled them with water at the sewerage department.

And now he had four more weeks to wait.

He dreamed he was in an ice cream shop. It was a clean white space. Lots of small tables, matching chairs. Every seat was full. The customers were men, each one dressed in the same tan linen suit. There must have been at least twenty of them, identical but for their ties. The ties came in reds and blues and burgundies. None of the men were eating. They sat perfectly still, brown paper napkins draped across their laps, as if waiting to be served.

Dobbs was minding his own business, bent over the ice cream case, trying to choose what he wanted. But he didn't recognize a single flavor. The names were typed onto plastic cards, but they made no sense. DON'T BE AFRAID, one of them said. Inside the tub was an orangey soup. Deep within the next tub Dobbs saw a forest, a copse of trees bending in the breeze. LOOK BEHIND YOU, the label read.

It was the girl from the bookstore, from the demonstration. McGee. She was directly behind him. She was even smaller than he'd remembered. There were butterflies now beneath the glass, flitting among the ice cream tubs.

When Dobbs looked again, the men in the tan linen suits had gotten to their feet. They stood shoulder to shoulder now, brown paper napkins tucked awkwardly into their collars. Side by side with their backs to the counter, Dobbs and McGee were surrounded.

"Don't be afraid," McGee said, patting his arm.

Beside the cash register was a Lucite box. Inside the box, on the very top shelf, a row of cardboard cups were arranged by size, from small to large. On the shelf below sat a pair of cones, one sugar, one waffle. As McGee reached inside, Dobbs saw the cones weren't real. They were plastic, for display only. McGee placed the sugar cone in her palm, pointy side up, and then she turned to the nearest man, driving the cone into his open mouth, impaling him with a single jab.

"What do you have against light?" she said.

Dobbs opened his eyes, and the chair teetered beneath him. He caught his balance just in time.

The ice cream shop had vanished. He was back in the house, sitting at the table, a small pile of carrot tops in his lap.

Clementine stood in the doorway to the kitchen, sun blasting at her back, book bag slung over her shoulder. Dobbs hadn't seen her in more than a month, since the run-in with her mother.

He closed his eyes again, but McGee was gone.

"You shouldn't be here."

Clementine let her book bag slip to the floor. "Afraid you'll get me grounded again?"

He stood up, carrot tops spilling to the floor. "I was thinking more of myself."

He walked over to the crate. He'd already eaten the more appealing things. Among the remains were some sort of bulbous purple root and something big and green and leafy that didn't quite look like lettuce.

"I wanted to make sure you're still alive."

Dobbs rooted around until he found a cucumber, something that could at least be eaten raw. "Want any of this?"

Clementine lifted her bag. "Come on," she said. "There's someone I want you to meet."

"Not this again."

She came over and grabbed the cucumber and dropped it back into the crate. "Trust me."

It was too easy to forget how young she was, like a tiny adult in cheerful clothing. He still couldn't bring himself to disappoint her.

She didn't run this time. There was no treasure hunt through the weeds and brambles. Instead, Clementine led him in a straight line across the field from his house.

Over the last several months, the lots had turned into meadows of wildflowers, tall green stalks wearing tiny lace caps. The foundations and even much of the trash had disappeared. The trees that had surprised him when he first arrived had swollen into pockets of plush green jungle. In the early spring he'd been able to go upstairs and see for miles, but now the view was everywhere interrupted by explosions of foliage and vines.

Evening was coming across the sky in streaks.

Clementine had come to a stop. "What do you think?"

They were standing beside a garden. The last time he'd followed her they'd passed this way. But since then everything had gone from brown to green.

At the far end of one of the garden rows, an elderly black woman was backing out of a tangle of little red balls, the tiniest tomatoes Dobbs had ever seen.

"May-May," Clementine said.

The old woman tilted her head in their direction. Then May-May was ambling toward them in rubber boots and a long summer dress, a dubious expression on her face.

"Our neighbor," Clementine said.

When the old woman brought her hands together, they sounded like sanding blocks. "Your grandpa told me."

That was Dobbs's cue. Digging his heel into the ground, he pivoted back in the direction from which they'd come.

Clementine grabbed his arm, holding him there. "He needs food."

"Thanks," Dobbs said. "But I've got everything I need."

The old woman came forward, handing him a bucket. Inside, a head of lettuce poked out of a web of green beans.

"Come back if you need more."

"I will," he said, knowing there was zero chance he would.

§

His clothes that night came off like Band–Aids, sticky with sweat. He sat on the mildewed tile of the water and sewerage department locker room, a frigid rain falling on him from the showerhead.

Wake up, he told himself. Wake up. Think of the cold, the numb in your toes, the goose bumps prickling your arms.

Hunger is temporary. It's all a test, to see what you're made of.

He reached up to turn the handle, but the cold was already open as far as it would go.

He dried off with a fresh jumpsuit from the supply closet, leaving his own clothes soaking in the sink.

In the van he ate the last four green beans from the bucket.

§

He was leaning against a wooden pallet when she found him.

"Sleep well?" she said.

The sun was up, puddled in the arms of a sprawling oak at the edge of the lot.

Dobbs had a vague memory of a chase on top of a moving train, leaping from car to car. Who'd been doing the chasing, he wasn't sure, but he was certain McGee had been there beside him, her clothes stained with someone else's blood.

But the dream seemed far-fetched now, down here in the dirt.

The old woman leaned over him, wearing a smirk he recognized from her great-granddaughter. He remembered having arrived at the garden in the middle of the night, ravenous. But he didn't remember what he'd picked, didn't remember sitting down or anything else that followed.

The old woman squatted beside him, picking up the half-eaten green pepper that must have fallen from his hand.

"I don't want to get Clementine in trouble," he said.

"Is this all you've eaten since the beans?"

"I should've asked first."

She lifted a plastic milk jug full of water, offered him a drink. "It's a lot easier to see what you're doing in the daylight."

Easier for everyone else to see what you were doing, too.

§

That night he was in the van, driving to the warehouse. On a side street east of Warren, he saw her. McGee.

He recognized her tiny figure peeking out the front door of an old tenement building as he passed by. Hood pulled up over her head, despite the heat. Those bright anime eyes of hers scanning for something.

He stopped, slamming on the brakes. But by the time he'd turned the van around, she was gone.

He parked. He got out. There was no sign, inside the building, that she'd ever been there.

Back in the van, he changed direction, heading north instead. He remembered the way.

But the bookstore was closed. This time, for good. A sign in the window said OUT OF BUSINESS. Just those three words, no other explanation of where everyone had gone.

He drove to McGee and Myles's apartment next, following the same route he'd once walked.

From the street, he couldn't see anything. No lights. No movement. He climbed onto the roof of his van and from there onto the roof of the building next door. Beyond the bars on McGee and Myles's windows, there was only emptiness, the place stripped bare.

§

Constance stood in her rubber boots, pouring water from her milk jug onto the globe of an eggplant.

"I thought they drank through the roots," Dobbs said.

It was early for him, twilight casting shadowy stripes along the garden rows. But he'd decided to take her advice, to arrive before she went in for the night.

She came over and handed him something, a tool of some kind. Wooden handle, metal shank split like a serpent's tongue.

"What's it for?" he said.

She knelt down and gestured for him to do the same. She found a weed and lifted up the leaves, pinching them between her fingertips. And then she plunged the metal tool into the dirt below, like a dagger to the heart. The weed rose with a pop. She lifted it up for him, showing Dobbs the twisted, trunklike root and the branching hair-like veins. "If you don't get it all," she said, "it just grows back."

"Got it."

She slapped the tool into his palm and returned to her jug. She found another globe and poured. "You've got to make them work for it," she said. "Put the water where they want it, they just get lazy."

"Is that true?"

She looked around. "See anything dying of thirst?"

There was no water source at the garden itself. Constance had to keep crossing the street to fill her jug. There was a house over there with a spigot below a curtained window, almost entirely obscured by a pair of overgrown shrubs.

Dobbs watched the old woman come and go, back and forth, back and forth. She must have been almost eighty years old, but she never seemed to tire. Sometimes Dobbs thought he saw a head peeking past the window curtains, watching. He couldn't make out much, just a dark form and a wedge of white T-shirt, too big to be Clementine.

"Is that your house?" he said.

She came over, scowling at his meager pile of weeds. "That the best you can do?"

Constance didn't talk about herself. She barely talked about the garden.

"Get those," she'd say. Or "You missed that."

He learned about her plantings only when he asked.

"Is that spinach?"

"Kale."

"Zucchini?"

"Cucumber."

"How about this?" he said one evening, pointing to some tufts poking out of the dirt.

She tottered over to look, wiping her hands on the front of her dress. "Not a clue."

Dobbs kept coming back, always waiting until sunset. He still did most of his work in the dark, after she'd gone home to bed. She didn't ask why he did all his gardening at night. But sometimes he caught her watching him when she thought he wasn't looking.

One evening he was picking tomatoes, twisting them off the vine as she'd shown him. He could feel himself fading. Everything he reached for seemed to bob from his grasp.

"Hey!" Constance shouted across the garden. "Wake up."

"I'm fine."

"You look like a cat about to fall from a windowsill."

He poked himself awake with the weeder, drawing blood.

Constance wasn't the only one watching. He was aware of Clementine out there sometimes, too, spying from the weeds, even after dark, when she was supposed to be asleep. But she never came close enough to talk to him. She was just a head in the tall grass, moonlight bouncing off the beads in her hair.

One night in early July, Dobbs arrived to find Constance waiting for him. She handed him a blade, a wood-handled steak knife with a broken tip.

"Broccoli," she said.

There was almost a full bed of it, low dark plants with broad green leaves.

"How do you know it's ready?" he said.

Constance pointed to several spots on one of the heads, florets turning yellow. "And here." With her finger she lifted up a small yellow bloom.

She did the first one herself, gripping the head and slicing it right at the bottom of the stalk. "Nice and clean. Leave everything but the head," she said. "More will grow in its place."

With her standing beside him watching, Dobbs did the next one, pushing down the giant leaves, sawing through the coarse green stem.

She set a bucket at his feet. "The rest is yours."

"How'd you learn to do all this?" he said.

She shrugged, shuffling off to her end of the garden.

"I can't believe I never thought of it," Dobbs said. "Of all the things you need to know how to do. It's the most basic there is."

"You're getting the hang of it."

"It just makes me wonder what else I missed."

The next couple heads came off as cleanly as the first. But after that Dobbs could feel his arms growing tired. Or maybe the blade was getting dull.

The knife slipped. He split one of the stalks in two, almost all the way down to the roots.

"A body can't survive without sleep," Constance said, hovering above him.

"I'm fine."

She reached out and took the knife. "I'm not going to have you butchering my broccoli."

In her other hand she held a canvas bag, stitched on the side with a bright yellow sunflower.

"You can carry this instead."

"Carry it where?"

She said, "We're going shopping."

Constance led the way. For an old woman, she was steady on her feet.

"Where do you go shopping at this hour?" Dobbs asked her.

"Where do *you* go?" she said.

He'd noticed several times before that she had the habit of hinting at little things she knew about him. He assumed Clementine was her source.

Their destination turned out to be a quarter-mile away, three squat rectangular buildings arranged at the end of a horseshoe-shaped driveway. A housing project maybe, but strangely quiet, even for the hour. Every window was dark.

"They just shut it down," Constance said.

"Why are we here?"

She started up the drive without him.

"Is this a good idea?" He didn't like the looks of the shadows, all the dark corners.

In the courtyard between the buildings loomed several piles of junk, some of them five or six feet tall. Together they looked like the sort of thing desperate villagers might construct to keep out an invading army.

"Where did all this come from?" he said.

Constance stepped forward onto the grassless lot. "Inside."

"What are you looking for?" Dobbs said.

"Let's see what there is."

So she went from mound to mound. Three-legged tables and sagging box springs, gaping screens, unstuffed chairs, blackened pans, cracked pots, shattered mirrors, leaning shelves, beer-stained coolers, headless trophies, deflated footballs, unwound cassettes, melted toasters, boxes of boxes, grills without grills, knobless TVs, twisted umbrella frames, end tables scarred with cigarette burns, lamps without shades, dented bed frames, dusty fans, moldy lunch boxes, commemorative mugs, warped oars, splintered cues, broken belts, ripped posters, chipped vases, tattered bedsheets, unwoven baskets, piss-stained carpets, sofas with fleas, tarnished silver, wilting plants, hingeless trunks, dented colanders, crusted jars, knotty wood, rickety ladders, caked pie plates, gilt frames, AM radios, veined platters, velvet paintings, greasy pillows, ratty blankets, shoes without laces, Hawaiian shirts, hula hoops, wobbly strollers, floppy-headed dolls, scratched records, mildewed dictionaries, oily boots, stained ties, puzzles with who knew how many missing pieces.

Dobbs sat down on a balding corduroy love seat to rest.

Who knew how long she would've gone on if it hadn't started to rain.

"Let's go," Dobbs said, holding the canvas sunflower bag over her head as they made a dash for the bus shelter at the corner. They sat down together on the bench.

"You didn't find anything you wanted?" Dobbs said.

Constance was looking outside through the clear plastic wall, gouged and scrawled with initials. Still taking inventory of whatever was out there.

"Clementine tells me you've got a truck," she said.

"A van."

Constance folded her hands in her lap. "We can't let all this go to waste."

He dreamed that morning that he and McGee were in a field, knee-high grasses and wildflowers bending in the breeze. Down the hill, a pond glinted in the sunlight, a rowboat perched on the bank. They were looking out over the water as dragonflies zipped in and out among the reeds. The men, as he and McGee should have expected, were lying in wait, popping out of the weeds and grass. The men's faces were smudges, like thumbs pressed in ink. As each one rose, Dobbs and McGee took off his head with a scythe, their swings clean and precise, leaving not a drop of blood on the blade.

When Dobbs opened his eyes, there were two men standing over him.

"Wake up," one of them said.

One of them—maybe the same one—jabbed a shoe into Dobbs's side.

The men were dressed in brown jumpsuits. They had faces, with features. There were name tags embroidered on their chests in gold script: MIKE and TIM.

Mike was the short one, the sleeves of his jumpsuit rolled. Limp flames licked at his forearms.

"What is it?" Dobbs said.

"It's almost time," Tim said. He was fat, and his crooked nose whistled when he breathed.

Mike folded his arms together, and the flames seemed to extinguish one another. "Sergio says you'd better be ready."

Nineteen

THE KID WORKING the counter at the feed store had a long, downy swan's neck and an Adam's apple that bounced along like a Ping-Pong ball.

"What kind of chickens do you want?" he said, voice bending like a rusty hinge.

Michael Boni hadn't come prepared for questions, and he found it hard to believe a kid like this could possibly know any more about birds than he did.

The Ping-Pong ball bobbed and swerved. "Meat or eggs or both?"

The kid was leading him down the hall to a garage-like space in the back. There was a shift in the air, a tanginess like a crowded bus terminal, but not entirely unpleasant.

The birds were huddled together in a wire pen laid with sawdust, chirping like cheap watches. The pen was even cruder than what Michael Boni had made for Priscilla. Inside, the chicks were tumbling over one another, white and yellow and brown. There were red warming lamps with aluminum shields and some sort of contraption on the floor the birds were huddled around. Whether it was food or water, he couldn't tell. Just the sight of it made Michael Boni realize how little thought he'd put into this.

But how hard could it be? He'd been thinking of crusty old farm women tossing apronfuls of seed here and there in the dirt, the same lazy way Constance planted her garden. What was a chicken compared to a caique? Priscilla, his spoiled princess, more dog than bird. A chicken was like a goldfish that laid eggs.

"See any you like?" the kid said.

Michael Boni came another step closer. "They're so small."

"That's the idea."

With Priscilla, the choice had been simple. Michael Boni hadn't been looking for a pet, least of all a bird. One afternoon he'd gone to the store to pick up some new saw blades, and in the parking lot there'd been a man in work boots standing beside a truck. When he saw Michael Boni coming, the man had held up the smoldering nub of a cigarette, like a torch to guide the way.

"I've got something for you," he'd said.

The man was wiry and unshaven, and his jeans were torn at the crotch. He lifted a tarp in the back of his truck, and there were three cages in the bed, the thin metals bars dull and dented. The bed itself was scraped and battered, raw steel showing through the red. Maybe the dinginess of everything else was what made the birds look so beautiful, with their patches of green and yellow and orange. There were two in each cage. To Michael Boni, they looked like parrots, but they were smaller and peculiar. The pair that caught his eye were hanging upside down from their perch, like bats. The smaller of the two had a flame-orange crown, and she looked at Michael Boni with her head cocked, as if he were the unusual sight.

Michael Boni came closer, and the man pulled the tarp all the way back. On cue, the tiny bird with the orange crown righted itself, hopping down to the floor of the cage. Its partner did the same.

A moment later the two birds were on their backs, wrestling like kittens. Michael Boni had the sense he was watching some sort of vaudeville act.

"What are their names?"

The man rolled the extinguished butt between his fingers. "Whatever you want them to be."

Michael Boni gave him twenty dollars for the pair, cage included.

As the truck's engine rumbled and caught, hacking in place, Michael Boni drifted over to the open window. "What do they eat?"

"Bird food?" the man said, reaching for the crank, closing the gap. Then he was gone.

Michael Boni named the one with the orange crown Priscilla, a name fit for a princess. The black-headed one was Caesar.

Forgetting the blades, he went straight to a used bookstore near his apartment, and in the third book he tried, a hardcover branded with library stamps, he found a picture of a twin to Priscilla but with a bit more yellow at the throat. It was the first he'd ever heard of a caique.

Two days after Michael Boni took the birds home, Caesar began plucking feathers from his chest. Michael Boni brought him seeds and fruit, but Caesar wouldn't eat. The book didn't explain why. Michael Boni might have thought it was normal, but Priscilla's appetite was good. She ate her share and Caesar's, too.

The next morning Michael Boni found Caesar on his side on the bottom of the cage, breathing heavily. The bird didn't object when Michael Boni picked him up. He seemed to like being cradled, nestling his head in the warmth of Michael Boni's armpit. They passed the day that way.

Twenty-four hours later Caesar was dead. There was no hiding what had happened from Priscilla. When Michael Boni carried Caesar outside, leaving Priscilla alone in the cage, she responded by flinging herself against the bars.

Michael Boni buried Caesar in the yard. Afterward he came back inside. Priscilla was flapping and strutting around angrily. He opened the door to the cage, wanting to hold her, to comfort her. The nip she took from his hand later healed into a crescent-moon-shaped scar.

A week passed before she would let him touch her again.

The baby chicks in the pen at his feet had none of Priscilla's personality. Maybe that would come later. So Michael Boni picked five that looked energetic and healthy. The kid also gave him a sack of rations and another of scratch.

"What else do you need?"

There was a long silence as Michael Boni squinted at the balls of fluff in the box. Only now did it occur to him to wonder what Priscilla was going to make of this.

The kid kept staring at him, waiting for an answer.

By then, spring was over, and the hot soup of Michigan summer had begun, Michael Boni's second in his grandmother's house. Unlike his old apartment, which at least had a window unit, his grandmother's place had no air-conditioning at all, no escape from the swelter.

Carrying the box of chicks inside from the truck, Michael Boni thought about the red bulb at the feed store. Was it really possible the birds would need even more heat than this? The book he'd bought to learn about caiques was strictly exotic. Nothing at all in it about chickens. So Michael Boni brought the box into the bedroom, pressing it against the radiator.

Down the hall, Priscilla was pacing. He could hear the clatter of angry claws on the bottom of the cage. How did she know? He'd come in through the front door to avoid passing her room. Could she smell the chicks? Could she hear the muffled cheeps?

"I'll be there in a minute," Michael Boni said, hoping the sound of his voice might calm her.

There was no way to get to his workshop without passing Priscilla's door. He darted past as fast as he could, but the moment she saw him, Priscilla let out a squeak.

"A minute," he said. "Just a minute."

He returned from the shop with a garbage bag full of sawdust. Priscilla followed him with her beak, wailing like a siren.

"Just a second," he said.

He sifted the sawdust into the box a handful at a time. The five chicks fled into the farthest corner, huddling, whistling their own alarmed tune. He nestled a ramekin of water and another of rations into the sawdust.

As soon as he turned on the heat, the pipes began to thunk, seeming to ask if he was sure. It was a good question. During his first winter he'd discovered the radiator could be as cold as a sewer pipe one moment and then bolting like a steam engine the next.

Back in the bedroom, he pulled off his socks and shoes, and then he waited, curled up on the floor.

It surprised him how helpless he felt.

Wobbling around on their ridiculous legs, the chicks couldn't seem to find the food. Michael Boni kept thinking about the tiny, cold weight of Caesar, the ever fainter rise and fall of his scabby, featherless breast. He tapped at the seed with his finger.

Cheep, cheep, cheep, he said. The chicks tripped over his finger as if they were blind. Maybe they were. It was impossible to tell what was going on behind those tiny black specks.

One at a time, he picked up the chicks and dipped their beaks into the food and water, and several of them stayed behind for a meal.

Within an hour, the house had turned tropical. Sweat was speeding down his spine and pooling beneath him. He got up to check the thermostat. Ninety-five. He stripped down to his briefs. In the other room, the siren still wailed. And now Priscilla was slamming her rattle against the bars of the cage, sounding like an ambulance crashing over a curb stacked with garbage cans.

"Okay," he said. "Okay. I'm coming."

The moment he appeared in her doorway, the siren faded to a whistle.

"Here I am," he said. "Here I am."

Her head wove back and forth in sharp, halting jerks.

"It's okay," he said. "It's okay."

She took a step back from the door of the cage. He took that as a sign she was ready to be calm.

The moment he opened the door, her beak came down like a spike.

"Fuck!" Michael Boni leaped back, pressing his hand to his mouth, a spot of sour blood on his lips.

Priscilla hopped from the cage to the bureau to the desk. He realized she was making for the hall.

"Oh, no you don't," he said, getting to the door just in time.

Priscilla watched with tilted head as he shook the pain from his hand. Smugly, it seemed to him. She barely reached his anklebone. He could have crushed her with one foot, but she stood her ground.

And then, with a single swift jab, she sank her beak into his toe.

The chicks didn't sleep. Not all at the same time, anyway. They seemed to take turns keeping guard, at least two of them constantly peeping. That first night Michael Boni never managed to close his eyes.

For the next several days it was the same. Sweat ran down him like rain from an umbrella. The bandages on his hand and foot swelled into sponges. Meanwhile he could hear Priscilla down the hall. He hadn't tried to put her back in the cage. It wasn't worth the bloodshed. Now she was shredding his grandmother's drapes. Her claws scraped grooves in the floor.

Twice a day he slid green beans and lettuce, delivered by Constance, under the door.

Every couple of days, while the chicks were distracted with fresh rations, Michael Boni turned the thermostat down a degree. By the beginning of the second week, he got it down below ninety for the first time. He was able to wear an undershirt again. But the evening the house hit eighty-eight, he found the birds huddling in the corner of the box like balls of socks. When he squatted down to talk to them, they wouldn't even look in his direction.

"All right," he said. "I get it."

Back up the thermostat went to ninety-two.

By then, Michael Boni hardly heard the chicks anymore. The peeping was his white noise.

Since moving in, Michael Boni hadn't touched his grandmother's yard, her borders and hedges. The time for that would've been when she was still alive. The good grandson, coming over every weekend to mow and trim. Now the bushes were in a late stage of swallowing the house, another reminder of how much he'd failed her.

From the bedroom, Michael Boni's view of Constance's garden was mostly obstructed by an overgrown juniper. But he could catch the occasional glimpse of the old lady through some of the dead branches.

These days Constance was so busy planting and weeding and harvesting, she didn't seem to have noticed he'd disappeared. She still left a bucket of vegetables on his porch every couple of days, but she never knocked, never came inside. And he hadn't left the house since coming home with the chicks. They were still so small and fragile, he was afraid to leave them.

One evening just before dusk, someone new appeared in the garden. Michael Boni was sitting by the window, and a guy he'd never seen before stepped out of the weedy lot, Clementine at his side. A white guy, pale, with wild red hair. His stay was brief. Constance sent him off with a bucket.

Two nights later the guy was back. And again the night after that, always just as dusk was falling. Constance put him to work.

Just like that, Michael Boni saw he'd been replaced.

But didn't he get some say, a vote? After all the work he'd put in, wasn't the garden almost as much his as hers?

What worried Michael Boni was the hours the guy liked to come. The evenings soon became nights. Michael Boni would wake up in the black of morning to check on the birds, and there the guy would be, peeling lettuce leaves and picking beans by moonlight. By dawn, he'd be gone.

Soon Michael Boni was staying up all night to watch him. More than once, when the guy disappeared into one of the juniper's blind spots, Michael Boni even crept out to the workshop to get a better view. The last thing Michael Boni needed was strangers poking around his business.

By late June, the cotton balls had acquired distinct new parts, wings and necks. Michael Boni got them a larger box. A week later they needed something even bigger. He began taking them outside during the day. The birds liked to peck in the grass. They seemed happy there, chasing bugs and kicking dirt. When he wasn't napping to make up for lost sleep, Michael Boni was watching over them, feeling like an old mother hen.

One afternoon a week or two later, Michael Boni and the chicks were in his grandmother's bedroom, and he glanced out the window and saw Constance alone in the garden.

He knelt over to the box by the radiator. "I'll be back in a minute."

Constance was on her knees, sprinkling mulch. She didn't bother raising her eyes. "I was beginning to wonder about you."

Michael Boni stood beside a patch of something new and leafy, something he didn't recognize. "I've been busy."

Constance tilted her head toward his grandmother's garage. "You got some fancy new saws that don't make any noise?"

"A different kind of project."

"Is that so?"

He didn't know what stopped him from saying the rest. Wasn't that why he'd come over, to tell her about the chicks? Hadn't he gotten them in the first place just for her? But in a strange way, he and the birds had begun to feel like a family, Priscilla the bitter older sister. And it was Michael Boni's role to protect them.

Then again, he hadn't told her about Darius, either. He just hadn't found the words yet, a way to put it so she'd understand. But in his mind, it was all about Constance and his grandmother, different pieces of the same thing.

"You've got a new helper," he said.

Constance stabbed her little shovel into the dirt. "I'm not sure how much a help he is."

"Who is he?"

Constance shrugged. "One of Clementine's strays."

"He seems to be here a lot."

"Is that right?"

"It's strange," Michael Boni said. "Don't you think? Gardening in the middle of the night?"

A fly was circling Constance's face, and she blew at it from the corner of her mouth. "You tell me what's strange."

"What do you think he wants?"

"Green beans?"

Michael Boni could sense she knew more than she was letting on, but the way she was looking at him now, it seemed she was thinking the same about him, that he was also holding out.

"I've been thinking of expanding," Constance said, breaking the silence.

"I don't really have time right now to be making any more beds."

"Who asked you to?"

"I just figured," he said.

"Who said I was even talking about the garden?"

Christopher Hebert

"Okay," he said, regretting now that he'd spoken at all. "All right."
Constance picked up her shovel again. "Are you just going watch?"
Michael Boni turned back toward the sidewalk. "Later."
She gave the soil a whack. "I won't hold my breath."

Later that night and into the early morning, Michael Boni sat in the chair by the bed, waiting and watching through the dead juniper branches, but the redhead didn't show. The chicks kept him company, while down the hall Pricilla slept among the shredded remains of his grandmother's drapes.

The chicks' peeps had lost their urgency. Now they sounded something like music.

They looked almost like real chickens now, feathers and all. Still small, but they'd outgrown their last box, the biggest Michael Boni could find. He'd already built them a coop of sorts. He'd stuck with what he knew. Their new home looked a lot like the set of kitchen cabinets he was supposed to have made the previous spring. The birds could have moved in a week ago, but he wasn't quite ready yet to let them go.

Through the window, through the bush, Michael Boni watched the first streaks of burned orange and gold spill above the garden. He'd been awake all night.

By the time the doorbell rang, sometime later, the morning shadows had retreated from the yard. But he didn't feel the least bit tired, rising to his feet to peer through the peephole.

Darius stood on the porch in his wrinkled uniform, dark bags under his eyes.

"You're early," Michael Boni said.

Darius checked his watch. "I'm right on time."

The morning had come more quickly than Michael Boni had expected. His mind felt as though it were still in the chair, watching, waiting.

Darius was looking past Michael Boni, into the interior of the house. He wore a strange expression. "This is where you live?"

Michael Boni realized he'd never let anyone other than Constance come inside.

As Darius passed the threshold, his eyes latched onto the foyer table, a burled walnut half moon holding a porcelain Virgin Mary.

"My grandmother," Darius said. "She had something just like that."

Michael Boni put a hand on his back, pressing him forward. "Down the hall. Toward the back."

Darius took a step and lifted his nose, trying to make sense of what he was smelling.

It was a straight shot down the hall, but along the way they passed the bedroom. Inside, the chicks were chirping. A few feet farther, Priscilla was flinging what Michael Boni guessed were his grandmother's earrings against the door.

"What is that?" Darius said, edging toward the far wall.

Michael Boni kept walking, never looking back.

With the lights turned off, the garage felt like a cave. Michael Boni led Darius into the far corner. There he lifted up the tarp.

Each of the components was in a separate crate, and in the middle was the sack. Michael Boni reached into the bag and pulled out a handful of small white pellets. "It's not what I expected," he said. "Like tapioca."

Darius took a step backward, knocking over an empty can of acetone.

"Fertilizer," Michael Boni said. "It's just fertilizer."

Darius squinted into Michael Boni's palm.

"Go on." Michael Boni came forward. "Touch it."

"I believe you."

"You think it's going to explode?"

Darius cast his eyes over some unfinished cabinet sections sprawled on the floor. "You made these?"

"You're afraid."

Darius fell silent.

"You're afraid," Michael Boni said again.

Darius put his finger to his lips, tilting his ear toward the door. Outside, a robin was whistling unevenly in the hickory.

Then Michael Boni heard it, too. Footsteps, and they were just outside.

He froze.

Before he could think of what to do, the door to the shop was creaking open. A triangle of light cut across the floor. A shadow head poked through the opening. Michael Boni tried to make out the silhouette, expecting to find a mess of red curls.

"Hello?" she said. A girl, a woman.

Not Constance. Not Clementine. Not the other great-granddaughter, either. She was peering into the darkness, hadn't spotted them yet.

Michael Boni reached out and picked up his hammer.

Darius took a step forward. "I wasn't sure you'd come."

The woman let out a gasp, reaching out for balance. "I wasn't expecting a surprise party."

Michael Boni looked from Darius to the girl and back again. "What the fuck is this?"

She moved in front of the window, a small figure but with a woman's voice. It was impossible to make out her face.

Then Darius was standing next to her. "This is McGee."

Turning to Michael Boni, she said, "I've heard a lot about you."

He could feel the pellets turning to powder in his fist. "Are you crazy?"

Darius brought her closer, slowly, as if he were the father of the bride. "She wants to help."

"You're inviting fucking strangers—?"

"She's not a stranger."

Michael Boni tipped his palm back into the sack and dusted his hands clean. "She is to me."

He could see her a little better now, a white girl—a kid. Hoodie, faded jeans. On a field trip from Ann Arbor, maybe. "What is it with you and teenage girls?"

"It's not like that," Darius said.

"I'm not a teenager," she said.

Michael Boni could see that now, but so what? He set the hammer down.

"Don't be mad at him," the girl said. "It was my idea. I'm on your side."

"This isn't the Salvation Army," Michael Boni said. "This isn't a canned food drive."

She was peering into the fertilizer sack. "I know what it is."

The girl was standing among the crates, lifting the tarp with the toe of her boot. "Do you really know what to do with all this?"

"We haven't tried yet," Darius said.

Michael Boni tugged the cloth free and put it back where it was.

"I broke into HSI," the girl said. "Me and my friends."

"Right," Michael Boni said, certain clouds parting in his head. Darius had mentioned it. The vague outline, at least, conveniently leaving out the part about knowing who was involved.

"And how'd that work out for you?" Michael Boni said.

Darius and the girl exchanged a glance, and there was no warmth coming from either direction.

But what it all meant, Michael Boni didn't care. He said, "I'd leave that off your résumé, if I was you."

"They got lucky," she said.

"These photocopiers store everything now," Darius said. "What's being copied. When."

Michael Boni leaned in closer. "They went to a lot of trouble to make you look stupid."

The girl turned away, looking toward the window. "He told me about Constance, about the garden. About your grandmother."

It was a good thing Darius wasn't in arm's reach, that Michael Boni wasn't still holding the hammer. "You don't know when to keep your mouth shut."

"We all want the same thing," she said.

"I doubt it."

She shrugged. "Our interests overlap. Even if our reasons don't."

She was so small standing before him, toe to toe. Michael Boni could see the holes blooming along the seams of her shirt.

Outside there was a flash of purple, Constance passing into the window frame, wading in a reef of waist-high lettuces.

"This isn't a club," Michael Boni said, returning McGee's gaze. "We're not open to new members."

Her eyes didn't waver. "The secret ends with me," she said. "I've got no one left to tell."

Maybe she was just a kid, but Michael Boni already saw more guts in her than he'd ever seen in Darius.

Out in the garden, Constance was staring cockeyed at the sun, as if daring it to do something.

Meanwhile Darius stood several paces away, half in the light, half in the shadow, looking to Michael Boni as if he were measuring the distance between himself and the door.

Twenty

It was ten-thirty in the morning, and Violet was wearing only one shoe as she burst out of the apartment to all the usual pandemonium—shouting and banging and the motherfucker directly below whose God-given right it was to blast his bass so he could feel it in the shower. But right now she couldn't care less about adding to the racket, slamming the door behind her, glad at last to have a solid object between herself and her mother.

Solid*ish*. Cheap, hollow wood. And her mother's voice still carried through. *Raised you . . . Never forget.* The missing words easy enough to fill in. She'd heard them a thousand times in the last two days alone. That's how long it had been since her mother had gone fishing for something in her purse and found ten bucks missing. Two days for ten bucks! Not that Violet wouldn't have been pissed. Ten bucks was two hours work, after taxes and all that. But was it worth two days of crazy?

Violet had never pretended she was an angel. There was the time she was nine, the bracelet with the turquoise stars from the display stand at the drugstore. But to steal from her own mother? It was just easier to yell at Violet than to accept the obvious, that the ten bucks had disappeared the same way everything else disappeared from the apartment—crumpled bills and pocket change and anything still in a box that could be returned; and the old broken watch and the hideous old necklace that had belonged to Violet's grandmother, neither of which was worth the effort of pawning, except to somebody already beyond help, like Victor.

Everyone in the building knew about Victor. But still they had to play this game. When her mother shouted, for all the neighbors to hear through the cardboard walls, what an ungrateful thief of a daughter she had, the only thing for Violet to do was to pop in her earbuds and wait it out. But sometimes she couldn't help wondering what exactly her mother gained from this drama, why she thought it was better for the neighbors to believe she had two fuck-ups for children, rather than just one.

With the door closed behind her, Violet could choose to imagine the crazy voice inside the apartment belonged to someone else, someone with a good reason for this despair, someone, ideally, she wasn't related to, didn't even know.

But now she was about to be late. Hopping on one foot, she reached down to pull on her other shoe. That was the moment she realized she'd grabbed the wrong one. A black clog and a white sneaker. Not even close.

She was so exhausted, her first thought was *Fuck it. Go back to sleep.* Rest her head right here on the mangy carpet, stare at the bug-bottomed globe of the ceiling fixture, pretend her mother was screaming a lullaby.

It had been only six hours since Violet had finished the closing shift, her third that week. Five hours since she'd gotten into bed. But Sheree was sick, and someone needed to fill in for lunch, and an hour spent at work, no matter how dead on her feet, was an hour

Violet didn't have to spend here. And when she got in, she could stick her mouth under the Mountain Dew dispenser until everything on her twitched.

On the other side of the door, the shouting had faded. Ear to the keyhole, Violet calculated how quickly, how quietly, she could duck in, get the other shoe. It didn't matter which one.

"What is it this time?"

She nearly jumped at the sound of the voice, spinning around to find Darius sitting on the top step at the end of the hall. He was still dressed in his work clothes.

"What'd he take?" Darius was all scrunched up, hunched over, as if he'd been huddled there for hours.

"What are you doing here?"

"I got in late," he said. "Everyone's gone. Sylvia, the kids."

Violet pulled on the black clog. "I'm going to be late."

"Nothing worse than an empty apartment."

"Want to trade?"

"I haven't seen you in a long time." Darius's eyes were red, his shirt half untucked.

If she didn't know him better, she might have thought he was drunk. "That's what happens," she said, "when you tell a person you don't want to see them anymore."

She hobbled forward, her feet at different heights. Just as she reached the banister, she heard something new coming from behind the apartment door. Something almost too soft to catch over the rest of the noise vibrating up from the lower floors.

"She's crying," Violet said. And crying, unlike everything else her mother did, in a way not intended to be overheard.

"What are you going to do?"

"I'm late."

Darius stretched his legs out across the top stair, and Violet stepped over them.

"Don't you want to know where I've been?" he said.

291

Christopher Hebert

She reached the landing. "Not really."

"I'm in trouble," Darius said.

From down here, he looked even more pitiful. She could no longer hear her mother crying. "Why don't you tell Sylvia about it?"

Darius rose on unsteady legs. "I made a mistake."

Maybe so, but Violet had done exactly what he'd told her to. For almost two months now she'd stayed away.

"I've got to go."

But now he was coming toward her down the stairs, and then she felt his heaviness on her, and then she was holding him. He was nearly limp, all arms and dead weight.

"Something bad's going to happen," he said. "Something—"

"It's going to be fine," she said. "Everything's going to be fine."

At his door she felt in his pocket for his keys.

"I don't know what I was thinking," he said. "I didn't realize—"

"Go to bed," she said. "Get some sleep."

His arm was still around her shoulders. "Don't leave."

"We agreed," Violet said. "You were right."

He took her hand. "Please."

From his bed, a half hour later, Violet texted Sheree: *:-(sick 2.*

292

Fall

Twenty-One

APRIL DIDN'T KNOW if the cancellation had anything to do with the weather. It was just as possible the bus had broken down somewhere. The other, more irritated passengers speculated more wildly; they suspected a cover-up. Why was no one from the station volunteering information? At this hour, most of the employees had gone home. The public address system simply informed the irritable occupants of the waiting room that their bus wouldn't be coming. The hurried, monotone voice offered no explanation. It suggested they return in the morning, and then the station fell into silence.

The people around her took out cell phones. April could hear them making their apologies for calling so late, asking for a ride home, a place to spend the night. A line formed at the pay phone. There was a bustling trade in bills for coins.

April took out her cell, looked at the time, then let the screen go dark again.

Inez had dropped her off an hour before. She'd been so upset, she wouldn't return April's kiss. Didn't even take the car out of gear.

"Don't do this," she'd said.

"I have to," April had told her.

The car was Inez's first, a subcompact that stalled whenever she slowed.

"One thing," Inez had said, one hand on the stick, the other on the wheel. "Just name one thing you've done for her you didn't come to regret."

"It's complicated," April had said. Everything with McGee was always complicated.

There was nothing comforting about the nearly empty station. But April found she appreciated the ambiance of the place, its high ceilings and buttresses and columns hiding doors that never seemed to open. She guessed the station hadn't always been a station. It had been constructed at another time, for another purpose, with a clientele in mind that would appreciate such excesses. Half an hour before, the room's deep acoustics had echoed and preserved every one of the other passengers' curses—toward the bus company, toward its employees, toward the rainy late-August night. There was something about the station's impractical dimensions and ostentatious design that made the place seem almost holy. In their simplicity and arrangement, the rows of oak benches looked like pews. Replace the ticket counter with an altar, and April could have imagined herself sitting in a church. She hadn't been in a real one since she was a child. She'd forgotten how intimidating they could be.

She would spend the night. That would be easier than going through everything all over again with Inez.

Through the narrow windows, April could see the rain pouring down, but the thick stone walls muddled the sound to a soothing drone.

Three other people remained in the station. She couldn't be sure if they were passengers or if they'd come in to get out of the rain. There was a woman talking to herself by the pay phone, agitated, jerking her head and sighing. By the restrooms, an old bearded man in a folding chair appeared to be reading. The obese guy in the shrunken fatigue jacket beside the windows looked as though he were asleep.

As she paced the imaginary boundary of her quarter of the station, April read and reread McGee's letter.

Thanks so much for writing. It's nice of you to offer to come and visit my parents with me. Things are always so difficult with them. I'd rather not have to do it alone. Uncle Xavier put together a package and asked me to ask you if you can bring it with you when you come. He'll drop it off sometime soon, if that's alright . . .

No matter how many times she read it, the letter made no sense. It was the first April had heard from McGee in the nearly three months since she'd left. What was April supposed to have written? She didn't even know where McGee was, aside from the Detroit postmark. And McGee hadn't seen her parents in years, even though they lived only a couple of miles away. Things between them definitely were difficult; that much was true. But there was no Uncle Xavier, at least not that April had ever heard of.

Then there was the simple fact that McGee had written a *letter*. An actual, physical, pen-on-paper, stuffed-in-an-envelope-and-stamped letter. Who did that anymore? But no return address on the envelope, just instructions about when and where they would meet upon April's arrival.

April had tried to find out what was going on, but no one else seemed to know anything either. Myles hadn't heard from McGee. Neither had Holmes or Fitch. But April wasn't surprised.

Everything had fallen apart so quickly.

In custody, the morning after the fiasco at HSI, they'd refused to give their names. But the men who'd arrested them already knew their names. These were guys straight out of the movies, cheap suits and mirrored sunglasses. Were they federal agents? Cops? Private security? April never thought to ask. The men who'd arrested them already knew everything, carrying out their interrogations only as a matter of course. After just a few hours, Myles and McGee and Holmes and April and Fitch were free to go, like children caught shoplifting. No charges. The men who'd arrested them didn't say why, but they didn't need to. The company didn't want the publicity. For their effort, the five of them received only a warning. Next time, and the kindly agents sincerely hoped there wouldn't be a next time, each of them would pay for everything he or she had ever done—of which the men were well informed—and for a few other things as well.

The rest had unraveled in stages. Inez had been applying to grad schools. After what happened, she couldn't get out of town fast enough. And given the long, exhausting battle April had had to wage to win Inez's forgiveness, how could she not go with her?

The move to Portland had originally been Fitch's idea. But he didn't have a hard time convincing Holmes to come along. Myles hadn't planned to join them. Not at first. He was going to stay in Detroit, work things out with McGee. But within a month, the two of them were hardly speaking. At the bookstore he finally hung a sign saying it was closed for good.

McGee had been the only one who stayed, but she'd left the loft and no one knew where she'd gone. Other than underground. But why?

The one thing the letter didn't say was the one thing April understood: McGee was in trouble and needed help.

Inez had been incredulous when April told her she had to go back to Detroit.

"What does she think you've got left to give her?" Inez wanted to know.

April had no answers. McGee had made her into some sort of spy, extracting orders from a complicated code.

Back at the apartment, April had been packing her bag when there'd been a knock at the door. A pale man with a puff of a moustache had stood in the hallway in cutoff jeans, his legs little more than bones and completely hairless.

"She wanted me to make sure you're coming," he'd said.

"Who are you?"

"Xavier."

He'd handed April a small package tied with a green ribbon. Then he'd stalked away on his birdlike legs.

So April had become a courier too. But whatever the package was, neither McGee nor Uncle Xavier had said anything about not opening it. And now, here in the station, she had nothing but time.

The ribbon was knotted. She had to use her teeth, her fingernails chewed down to nubs. Beneath the paper was a white cardboard box. April untucked the flap and lifted the lid. Inside was a lump of aluminum foil. A clump of chocolate chip cookies.

"What the fuck?"

"Do those have nuts?"

April looked up with a jerk into a bearded, smiling face—the man who'd been reading by the bathroom. From up close he was decades younger than he'd seemed across the station. He reached into the box and took one, biting into it tentatively.

"Good, no nuts. I'm allergic to nuts. Peanuts, walnuts, pecans, pistachios, walnuts. All kinds. Doctor once told me to stay away from nuts unless I wanted to end up in the hospital again. Been back to the hospital plenty of times since then. Had nothing to do with nuts, though. These are good. Make them yourself?"

"No," April said uncertainly. "Uncle Xavier—"

"Your uncle makes a good cookie. Nice and soft. Lots of brown sugar."

April watched him swallow, not knowing what to expect. It crossed her mind that he might choke on something hidden in the batter and she'd have to save him.

"Aren't you going to have one yourself?"

She wasn't, of course, but she couldn't think of any easy explanation. Taking up the box and paper, she struggled to put the package back together. When she got to the ribbon, he offered his finger. Around it she tied a bow.

"Think nothing of it," he said, though she was too flustered to thank him.

The obese camouflaged man in the pew across the room was still asleep. The agitated woman by the pay phone seemed to have dozed off, too, her head resting on the plastic-bound yellow pages. Nowhere in the enormous station was there a single excuse for getting up. There was nothing to do, nowhere to go, and April didn't want to offend someone who had so far done nothing but invade her space.

"I hope you won't take this the wrong way," the man said, sitting down beside her. "I was sitting over there watching you. You're a very pretty woman. You probably hear that all the time."

He must have noticed the look in her eyes, because he shook his head apologetically. "I'm sorry. That's not what I meant. It's just you seem like a very nice person. You can tell even from across the room. But I should know better than to bother a pretty lady all alone in the middle of the night. Lord knows you meet enough crazy people when you ride the bus."

"It's okay," April said, forcing a smile. "It's all right."

"To tell you the truth," he said, "usually I don't find pretty people all that worth talking to. They're usually so dull. But there's something about you. You see people all the time, walking around, thousands of them a day, and what do you know about them? Nothing. Not a damn thing. You live in the same city, walk the same streets, breathe the same air. It's a shame we should all be such strangers. You shouldn't need to know a person by name to say hello. You shouldn't look at someone suspiciously just because he asks how you're doing. Do you know what I'm saying?"

She nodded.

"It seemed to me there's no good reason for you and me to be sitting all alone. Especially in a place like this." He gestured with his hands toward the ceiling. "It reminds me of the church I went to when I was a kid."

"I was thinking the same thing," April said.

"One of those old-fashioned churches, so big and heavy it seems like it must've been built by giants. The kind of place where you really feel the presence of a higher power. Do you know what I'm saying? You feel like you're in the hands of a mighty god. Not like these new churches you see around, with the neon signs and the vinyl siding. They look like dentists' offices. What sort of god would hang out in a place like that? Do you know what I'm saying?"

April nodded noncommittally. She was wary of the direction the conversation was turning. She looked out the windows onto the dark platform, imagining herself climbing onto the bus.

"It's these benches," she said. "They look like pews."

"That's right," he said. "That's right." And then, after a pause, he added, "I remember one time talking with a minister from one of those dentist-office churches. We were talking about sin. He asked me how I decided what was right and what was wrong. A minister, of all people." The young man shook his head. "But that's what happens when you preach in a building covered in vinyl siding. I remember saying I was surprised to hear him ask such a thing. He should have known it wasn't for me to decide. What's right is right, and what's wrong is wrong. I would have expected him of all people to understand that. Do you know what I'm saying?"

"Yes."

"Do you believe in God?" the young man asked.

April looked off into the corner, where the young man had been sitting just moments before. He'd left no luggage there, hadn't brought any over with him.

"I don't know," she said.

"You should."

301

He reached into his pocket, and even before he extended his hand, she was shrinking away.

He held out a roll of mints.

She declined.

"Nothing lonelier than a red-eye," he said, mint clicking against his teeth.

After that, neither one of them seemed to know what to say, and April sat in nervous silence, waiting for whatever would come next. But aside from occasionally asking her the time and smiling mildly, the young man kept to himself, quietly reading beside her, apparently comforted just to have her near him.

Throughout the night, the station grew colder by degrees. Every time she awoke, April's pulse set off pounding in her collar. But everything was always fine, her bag and the cookies still at her side, the others still in their corners.

Not long after daylight, just after the first new passengers arrived with the dense scent of the cool morning in their clothes, the station suddenly filled. Employees seemed to materialize at the ticket counter. An old lady with a loose cough settled in behind a coffee urn and a display of packaged Danish.

Among the crowd April recognized several faces from the night before. They seemed less angry now, but they still insisted on speaking brusquely to the clerk—a different one from last night—in order to convey their right to be irritated.

On the bus, April rolled a pair of jeans into a pillow and placed them against the window. Stretching her legs across the empty seat next to hers, she closed her eyes. It was worth a try, and for several minutes she could hear other passengers coming on board and pausing at her row before moving on.

She must have dozed off for only a moment. When she awoke again, the bus still hadn't started moving. A boy with softly spiked blond hair was standing in the aisle staring at her. He must have been twelve or thirteen, his nose scrunched up as if he were trying to keep a pair of invisible glasses from falling off his face. A lumped, over-stuffed backpack rested at his feet. He held a pile of poorly folded newspaper sections in his hands.

"Could you hold this for a thanks—" Without waiting for a response, the boy dropped the papers into April's lap. She pulled her legs reflexively toward her chest, and the boy took that opportunity to flop down into the seat beside her.

"I was afraid somebody'd be sitting here. I kept telling my brother we had to get to the station, but he had diarrhea or something and he was in the bathroom for hours, and I kept telling him we'd miss the bus, but he said there's no way he'd let me miss it. I like to show up early to get a good seat. I'm R.J."

He'd already finished shaking her limp hand before she registered what he was doing.

"Your papers," April said, lifting them for him to take.

"See that guy over there—?" R.J. pointed out her window to a hefty middle-aged man, bald on top, smoking beside a pickup, eyes fixed to his watch.

"That's my brother Franklin. I don't think he can see me waving. You can wave, too, if you want. He's not even looking. See, we're directly in the middle. Twenty-second row. Twenty-one in front of us, twenty-one in back. If we get in an accident, we're the least likely to get crushed."

April swallowed the news in bewilderment.

The door of the bus creaked shut. The air brakes released. They started to move.

"Would you mind taking—?" April dropped the pile into R.J.'s lap, and he commenced flipping through the sections.

"I was just reading about this train crash where all these people

303

died. The train just like fell off the tracks. I mean, have you ever seen train tracks? They're like just these little pieces of metal. I'm surprised trains aren't always falling off." He paused and pointed out the window again. The bus passed a billboard upon which a jet was rising majestically over a palm-tree-lined beach, ESCAPE IS NOT AS FAR AS YOU THINK spelled out in bamboo lettering.

"I've never flown before," R.J. said. "It's like a hundred times safer than riding in a bus, even though it's the plane crashes you always hear about. Probably because they're so bad when they happen. I mean, a plane crashes, and you're pretty much . . . well, I mean, what good is a life vest when you're about to crash into a cornfield or something? Most people get hung up on that and forget how rare it happens. People die like every second in car crashes."

April rose up slightly in her seat and scanned the other rows. There wasn't a single empty seat. She watched the posts of the guardrail flick by as the bus merged onto the highway. The rain had picked up again. Cars passed on the wet pavement, and the sound was like paper tearing. The grassy median seemed to draw nearer. April imagined she could feel the bus losing its traction. She thought of herself back at the station, lying on the pew. She thought of being home, of Inez's new blackout blinds, which sealed the bedroom off from every ray of sunlight.

What in the world was she doing here?

"I'm going to try to sleep now," she said.

"There's a report in here that most people die because they don't buckle up," he said, tapping her on the knee. "And this bus doesn't even have seat belts. We should write a letter to the company."

April closed her eyes, trying to will away the sound of his voice. When that didn't work, she focused on the splashing of the passing cars. She wondered if the bus had caught up with the storm from last night, or if another storm had met them coming from the opposite direction.

R.J. tapped April on the shoulder. "There's also an article in here about all these buildings that are blowing up and nobody knows why."

"If you read too many newspapers," April said, massaging her temples, "you start to think the whole world is on the brink of disaster."

R.J. crinkled his eyebrows at her in disappointment. "My sister Samantha says what's wrong with people is they don't read the papers. That's why they're going out of business. People don't know what's going on anymore."

The sky had turned purple. Rain was lashing at the window. April stood up on unsteady legs. In her stomach, she thought she could feel the tires start to skid. She reached into the overhead compartment, removing a book from her bag.

She blew through an entire page before realizing she'd finished even a paragraph. The words came and went like passing cars. Somewhere in the back of the bus, a man was talking so loudly it seemed he must have wanted everyone to hear. Pages vanished like the words themselves. The man in the back of the bus accused the driver of being drunk. April wondered whether the man himself was drunk. He grew louder and louder, until April could no longer hear the scratching.

"If this was a boat, we'd be on the bottom of the sea!" the man hollered. "If it was a plane, we'd all be wearing life vests!"

The clouds and the rain had grown so thick April could no longer see the highway on the other side of the median. Hazy lights swam past unattached to anything. The bus had slowed, as had the traffic surrounding them. Everyone around her was holding on to something, everyone but R.J.

"Afraid of a little rain," the man in the back snickered. "Worse thing you can be when you're driving is afraid."

"Please keep your voice down," a weary voice crackled over the loudspeaker.

April clenched her book to keep herself from standing and yelling at the man to be quiet. She couldn't understand why nobody else, nobody sitting back there with him, hadn't already told him to shut the fuck up.

"Say the word, and I'll go up there and take over. If not me, somebody, anybody. I'll send my eighty-year-old grandmother up there. Blind in one eye, but I'd sooner trust my life to her."

"Please keep your voice down."

"Look up, ladies and gentlemen!" the man in the back of the bus thundered, his voice carrying the fever of a revivalist preacher.

"Look up into the sky above you! You can't see them, but somewhere above the clouds rich people are coasting along with their feet up, munching on complimentary peanuts!"

"If you don't shut up, I'll throw you off the bus." The loudspeaker fuzzed and then went dead, a much less measured tone this time.

April started another chapter without realizing she'd finished the previous one.

"He's right," R.J. said after a long silence. "If I died right now, I'd be pissed. I mean, if you're going to die, shouldn't it be for something good? I want to die doing something fun, but it almost never happens that way. I mean, we could die right now. Look at it out there."

She was better off not seeing.

"Where are you going?" R.J. said.

"To visit a friend," April said curtly. "But right now I'm going to try to get some sleep."

"And if you ended up dying on your way to see this friend, how would you feel? I mean, wouldn't that suck? Or maybe you wouldn't mind. I mean, maybe this is a good friend, and you have to die sometime, right? But what if you're driving to the store for like bread? I mean, can you imagine dying for a loaf of bread? Maybe if you're starving, it would be different. I'm going to see my sister Beatrice. I don't even like Beatrice. Maybe if I had to choose, I'd rather die before I went. At least that way I wouldn't have to stay with her. She bakes sugarless cookies and reads books about Jesus. Her husband can't talk about anything except what a great baseball player he almost was. I'd hate to think the last thing I ever did was something I didn't want to do. My mother died of cancer, but there was nothing anybody could do about that. For a couple of years, she couldn't even leave her bed. But my father—I mean, he died when I was little. He'd always wanted one of those little trees. You know the ones I mean? The little miniature kind. So one year my sister Phyllis got him one for his birthday—she had to order it from like, I don't know—and then he died of a heart attack before she could give it to him."

"I'm sorry."

"Yeah," R.J. said. "The tree died too."

April had no brothers or sisters. She'd barely known her own father. But hearing R.J. talk about his family made April think about Fitch and Holmes and Myles. In the months since they'd gone their separate ways, they'd e-mailed every once in a while, but it was hard to know what anything they said really meant. They had jobs in Portland. At least Holmes and Myles did. Holmes was pulling espresso. He was seeing somebody, a guy who did PR. Someone stable, professional. Myles was working at a bookstore. A manager. Shiny, clean new books this time. And Fitch was assembling a new band and living off his parents. Until he got "settled," as they called it, which they were still willing to believe might happen someday. The three of them talked about the weather, the food, the music, the people. Everything about Portland was fabulous. But it was the things they didn't say that made her wonder. No regrets, no mention of McGee. April knew all those years together couldn't be so easily forgotten, no matter how much they wanted to put Detroit behind them.

But she was guilty of the same sort of silence. She'd told them about Inez; school hadn't even started yet, and Inez was working so hard that April rarely saw her. About herself, though, there was much less to say. She was doing freelance stuff when she could, websites mostly. She hadn't told them she was going to see McGee. Maybe she was afraid they'd try to talk her out of it.

In her e-mails, she always left out how much she missed everyone. Not because she didn't want them to know, but because every time she caught herself bringing it up, she couldn't help sounding nostalgic, as if she wished things could return to the way they'd been before, the five of them together again. And in a way, she truly did wish this, but she understood it was no longer possible. And anyway, she knew no one else would agree.

They'd started out wanting to save the world. Then they'd scaled back, settling for saving the city. But they couldn't even do that. Maybe they'd gone about it the wrong way. April wasn't sorry they'd tried. But then again, for her the cause had always been the smallest part. She'd believed in McGee more than she'd believed in politics. The five of them could have organized a bowling league and April would've been satisfied, as long as they did it together.

Whenever she caught herself thinking this way, April tried to tell herself that missing the past didn't mean she regretted having chosen to leave with Inez. But sometimes she couldn't help feeling Inez was unhappy with her—as if, having won April away from her friends, she'd come to discover the prize was less enjoyable than the fight.

And was that why she was on this bus now? April wondered. Not for McGee but to force Inez to fight for her again?

A commotion woke her, a screech and a shudder. April looked outside. It took a few moments to understand they were at a bus station.

"Where are we?" she asked.

R.J. had turned to face the back of the bus. "Police."

With a start, April spun around. There was a cop standing at the last row.

"Up," he was saying, "now." He was gesturing at one of the passengers, his other hand hovering at his hip, just above his holster.

At the front, another cop, a woman, was talking to the driver.

Quietly, impossible to hear over the chatter of her radio. Suddenly the female cop looked up, meeting April's eye.

April ducked behind the seat in front of her.

"What are you doing?" R.J. said.

Beyond the edge of the seat, April could see the cop up front coming toward them. Slowly, studying everyone as she passed. As if she were looking for someone. Or something. April's first thought was Uncle Xavier's package. When the cop reached her, April felt as pale as the mist on the window.

But the cop passed her by.

"What's wrong with you?" R.J. asked.

"Nothing."

In the back of the bus, the two cops together raised a short man in a lime-green sweatsuit to his feet. Together they dragged him backward down the aisle.

"This is unconstitutional," the man hollered as he struggled to grip a seat back. "I have my rights. I paid just like everyone else. You can't do this. Hey, what's your name? Give me your names. You're all witnesses. We have to stand up together."

As he passed April's row, the man's flailing arm smacked R.J. on the back of the head.

"I'm going to sue your ass off. I want my money back. Driver. Driver—"

The man fought to free himself from the cops' grip.

"Is it my fault you can't drive?"

At the top of the steps, the man attempted to lunge at the driver, but the cops held him back.

The driver's hands were shaking as he levered the door shut. Not until he'd released the air brakes did April feel sure the police wouldn't be back for her.

Within a few minutes, they were back on the highway. Half an hour later, the bus stopped again, this time at a rest area. April got off with everyone else, but while the others were still in line for food and coffee, she returned to the bus, intending to collect her bag and find a new seat before R.J. got back.

But he was already there, row twenty-two, sitting with his head between the pages of the newspaper.

April didn't have it in her to hurt his feelings. She lifted her backpack from the overhead bin and sat down beside him with a sigh. She held the bag in her lap. Somehow it seemed safer pressed to her body.

"I guess you're not going to visit for too long if that's your only bag," R.J. said. "I've got a whole suitcase. Plus this." He pointed to his own misshapen backpack. "My brother Simon taught me this trick where if I put the strap around my leg, no one can swipe it. I mean, without taking me with it."

Before she could stop him, R.J. had taken April's backpack from her lap. Then, as though her leg were his own, he lifted it and lowered it again into the center of a strap. He smiled at what he'd done.

"No thanks," she said, to his clear disappointment, returning the bag to her lap. She didn't want to let the package out of her sight.

"So who's this friend?" R.J. said. "Is it like a boyfriend or just a friend?"

"Just a friend."

"So like where'd you meet this friend? Is this someone you knew from when you were a kid?"

R.J. removed a piece of paper and a nub of pencil from his bag. "When was the last time you saw this friend?"

"Are you taking notes?" she said. "Are you a spy?"

R.J. smiled enigmatically. "Do you want to play tic-tac-toe?"

She didn't. He commenced to draw. The bus resumed its course.

In the center of the paper, R.J. sketched a large rectangle, twice as wide as it was high. Inside he drew a door. Then came the windows, which he crossed with thin veinlike lines, to indicate they were broken.

"Why do you think they're doing it?" he said.

"Doing what?"

"Blowing up buildings. In that story I was telling you about. This is like the second one."

"I don't know," April said, turning away. "I don't know anything about it."

"Just to scare people?"

"I don't know."

"Does it scare you?"

"I guess so. Maybe——"

"Do you like scary movies?"

"You ask a lot of questions," she said.

"That's what my brother Freddy says. He says people don't like to think about everything they do. He says sometimes people just do things, not for any reason."

Well, April thought, if that's what Freddy believes, then Freddy's wrong. Or Freddy knew it was pointless to try to explain something so complicated to someone so young. There were always reasons for what people did. Sometimes they were just bad reasons. Or deceitful reasons—sometimes self-deceitful. In this, she considered herself an expert, and nothing Freddy could say would dissuade her. All her life she'd been doing things, pretending they were for herself, when really they were for others.

"What are you going to do while you stay with your friend?" R.J. asked, looking up from his drawing.

"I don't know," April said, waving him off. "I don't know."

R.J.'s drawing had expanded. The city in the picture had undergone gentrification. The first building was now one of many, rising into a sky that seemed never to have known a cloudy day. Motionless on the sidewalk, stick figures stood wide-legged and open-armed, as if bewildered by the beauty of the scenery. A small boy with unbending legs rode a bicycle. Each of their faces held an impossibly wide grin.

A squarish car with no steering wheel sped down the street, past the buildings and pedestrians, lines like a jet stream shooting from its back tires. A man, defying gravity, hung three-quarters of the way out the driver's side window, one arm raised, as if to throw something or as if in warning.

"What do you think?" R.J. said, lifting it up so April could get a better look.

As he raised his picture, another appeared beneath it, a photograph on top of the stack of newspapers. In a glance, April could see the photo had been his model, though only loosely. The place R.J. had drawn first was in this photograph a mangled wreck of debris. Ceiling caved in, walls collapsed.

April had to squint to read the caption, something about an old, shuttered grocery store.

"That's what I'm talking about," R.J. said. "A couple weeks ago it was something else, a place that used to make shoes."

On the sidewalk, firefighters picked through a small pile of rubble, while a stooped man in a wrinkled suit watched over their shoulders. Beyond a police barricade, just at the edge of the frame, stood several onlookers. There was a stocky Hispanic guy with a ponytail. And there was a black man April vaguely thought she recognized. And between them, as if April had known all along, stood McGee, dressed in the same wig she'd had that night at HSI, blond hair reaching down to her shoulders.

"Oh God," April said, placing her hand over her mouth. "Oh God."

"What?" R.J. said, scanning the page.

"What has she done?" April tried to stop them, but one of her tears got away, blazing a trail of blurred ink down the newspaper page.

R.J. saw her tears, too, and April could tell he didn't know what to say.

Twenty-Two

IN HER NOTEBOOK McGee kept two lists. If she opened it in the front, spiraling back the tattered, duct-taped cover, there were addresses. The addresses came to her on scraps of paper—receipts and wrappers and corners of magazines. She was in charge of the master list, a column spreading down the left-hand margin, all in the same blue pen, all in her tidy rounded print. Every day, the list grew.

Michael Boni seemed to work by memory, adding places that for one reason or another had pissed him off: a garage that had sold him a worn-out clutch; a bank where the tellers had always looked at him funny; a grocery story where he'd once gotten a can of bad ravioli; the club where he'd been robbed.

Though he later admitted he hadn't actually been inside the club when the robbery happened. He'd been walking past, on his way to get a coffee, someone in a puffy coat sticking a nine millimeter in his ribs. The club hadn't even been in business at the time. But still it made the list.

It felt wrong to her, humoring such petty grievances. But they had to start somewhere. Otherwise there was just too much. And anyway, the places were all empty now, the people who had wronged Michael Boni long gone. For all she knew, the owners themselves had their own bad memories they'd just as soon see forgotten.

Darius's additions to the list were just as arbitrary. To her at least. They were places he passed on the bus on his way to work, depressing sights that caught his eye. Obstructions in the skyline—towers full of gaping windows, like spent candy Advent calendars; and smokestacks caked with dead soot. They were offenses to the eye, which meant they were often large and prominent and hard to get rid of. On their first try, still working out the kinks, they'd managed to inflict barely more than a blemish.

To the entire list, she'd contributed just one address. And she was saving it for when they were ready.

If she opened the notebook in the back, the plain brown cardboard holding on by just a few untorn tabs, she could see the other list, the dozens of letters she'd begun and then abandoned.

Dear Myles:
I love you, though you think I don't.

Dear Holmes:
I know it was you who broke my mug, the one with the glazed yellow sun. I forgive you.

Dear Myles:
You always smelled best coming in from the cold.

Dear Fitch:
Last New Years Eve I laughed so hard I peed on your couch.

Dear Holmes:

I was the one who broke your watch, the one with the peeling leather strap.

Dear April:

I tried to like Inez. I really did.

Dear Myles:

I don't know what to say.

Dear Fitch:

Did you know, the first time we met, that your cousin was trying to set us up?

Dear April:

I also question your taste in men.

Dear Myles:

I know that you don't understand. I'm not sure I do either.

She meant every word. And that was why the letters were impossible to send.

Only one had she succeeded in signing and folding into an envelope, addressed to April, three states away. That one had been easier—also full of things she meant, but all of them comfortably buried in a lie. A lie somewhat softened, she hoped, by cookies.

Twenty-Three

THE KNOTTY PINE booth came from a private club in Hamtramck, a dingy, subterranean dive pretending to be a mountain lodge, bear traps and beaver pelts mounted to the walls.

The bright red molded-plastic booth looked like a piece of playground equipment; she'd found it in a hamburger joint on Woodward.

The third booth came from an east side diner, marbled laminate edged in imitation chrome.

"I was in a library," Dobbs was saying as they staggered across the floor at either end of a wrought-iron patio table. "I had one of those encyclopedias—you know, the big, heavy kind." With a melodramatic shiver, he fell silent, implying what she supposed was more of his grisly comic book violence.

He liked to talk about his dreams. He was the palest, unhealthiest person Constance had ever known, but he dreamed blockbuster action movies: explosions, chases, high-wire fight scenes. The villains were interchangeable, but Dobbs was the indestructible hero. Except of course there was nothing heroic about him. Even the table had him gasping, nearly breathless. More than forty years younger than she was, and he let down his end first. At this rate it would be days before they finished.

"The thing is," Dobbs said, "I've never even been in a real fight."

Constance said, "No kidding."

By the time they were done for the night, it was three o'clock in the morning. The place didn't look half bad. They'd managed to squeeze in six tables, three in the center and the three booths along the back wall. No two of them matched. And there was a van full of chairs and lamps and assorted stuff from the housing project, still waiting to be unloaded.

Dobbs sat down at the red booth and poured himself a cup of coffee. "What are you going to call the place?"

Constance came over to join him, her bottom nearly slipping out from under her on the slick plastic bench.

"How about Constance's?" he said. "Simple but classic."

"I'll leave that to you."

Dobbs lifted his cup, waved it vaguely around the dining room. "This is the future, you know. When everything else collapses—"

"You make it sound romantic."

"People will remember you," Dobbs said. "What you started."

"I prefer when people don't talk like I'm already dead."

Dobbs raised his hands in protest.

"Tell me about your parents," Constance said.

"My parents?"

"These dreams of yours . . ." Constance said.

He gulped his coffee like water. "You think I'm damaged goods? The product of a troubled childhood?"

She shrugged. "You don't have to if you don't want to."

"They're lovely people," he said. "There's nothing to tell."

"All right," Constance said. "Then let me tell you about mine."

In 1941, Constance said, when she was six and Darrell, her brother, three, her family moved into the Brewster Projects. Getting into Brewster then was like winning the lottery. The place was a marvel, clean and shining and new, the same age as Constance. For a family even to be considered for an apartment, at least one parent needed to have a job. Constance had only one parent, and as far as she knew, her mother had never worked a day in her life.

Constance measured her childhood by her mother's illnesses—birthdays and holidays entertaining herself in dark, curtained rooms. When her mother was away in the hospital, it was Constance's job to take care of the apartment and of Darrell. This was when most of Constance's happiest memories took place. Left to themselves, Constance and Darrell slept curled up together in their mother's bed. In the morning they strolled to school singing "Chickery Chick" in off-key harmony, and each night they ate lukewarm soup in front of the radio until they dozed off, fully dressed. But the bliss never lasted. As soon as their mother was discharged and sent home, Darrell turned feral, tearing at the couch cushions with his teeth and nails, charging at his mother and sister, butting their legs with his head until their mother shouted, "I guess I have to do everything!" and then closed the door to her bedroom until it was time for Constance to bring her dinner.

Her aunts didn't believe Constance's mother was really sick. They thought her illnesses were just a way of getting attention, now that she'd lost her looks. Her mother had been pretty once, the best-looking of all her sisters. Constance had seen the photos herself: tall and generously curved, almond-shaped eyes. But now her skin looked like the dust Constance let gather in the far corners under the dresser.

The doctors must have had a name for it, but Constance's mother referred to her sickness only as "my condition." Her condition required meals in bed. Her condition made it impossible for her to work or wash dishes or buy groceries or do anything strenuous. Her condition responded well to foot massages and heavy doses of rest. Her condition made noise intolerable, except for when she needed to shout orders at Constance through the bedroom door.

Constance did whatever her mother asked. It had never occurred to her that she had a choice.

"And that," Constance said, "is everything you need to know about my mother."

Dobbs was slumped in the corner of the plastic bench, half asleep.

She got up to refill the coffeepot. "These dreams are your conscience," Constance said. "You know that, right?"

"Yeah," Dobbs said. "I know."

§

Constance got the oven from Michael Boni. She traded him her old microwave. The stove had been his grandmother's, and he had no use for it. Everything he ate came straight from a can. He treated eating as if it were a burden.

But the oven still needed to be moved, and only she and Michael Boni were there to do it, now that Dobbs had disappeared.

She hadn't seen Dobbs since the night he'd helped with the booths and tables. She'd known him only a couple weeks, but she'd gotten used to him, had made the mistake of counting on him to show up. But for three nights in a row, he'd failed to appear at the garden. And Constance wasn't the only one who'd noticed. Last evening, while she was out watering peas, Clementine had emerged from the weeds, saying, "I know where he is."

Constance had waved her off. "We'll manage," she'd said, though in fact the list of chores she'd assembled for him was already longer than she could remember.

"I can take you," Clementine had said, offering her hand, determined for some reason not to give up. "There's these mattresses—"

Constance had cut her off with a shake of her head. "I don't want to know."

"He's getting things ready," Clementine said. "They're almost here."

"It's okay," Constance had said. "We're fine without him."

Michael Boni was shifty too, but he was almost always there when she went to pound on his door.

They'd set out from his house with the stove an hour ago. He was able to hump the old hunk of steel about three yards at a time before having to stop and rest. So far they'd made it about thirty feet, to the middle of the street, where Michael Boni now squatted with his head between his knees, trying to catch his breath. It was a good thing there wasn't any traffic.

"Does your son know about this?" Michael Boni said, reaching around to massage his own back.

Constance opened the oven door and peered inside. "Are you sure this thing works?"

"It better."

She let him rest another couple of minutes. Then Michael Boni wrapped his arms back around the oven and grunted. They made it maybe nine more feet before it all came crashing back down.

"Why do you even want a restaurant?" he said, gasping again for air.

He was doing a lot of whining for someone who still had another whole block to go.

"Did I ever tell you about Charles?" she said.

Charles, Constance said, was one of those people everyone knew. Not just the whole school—the whole neighborhood. But Constance had always been a grade behind him, and Charles had no reason to notice Constance until she turned seventeen and inherited the figure her mother had lost.

There was an intensity to Charles that drew people toward him. He wasn't athletic or outgoing. He wasn't exactly handsome, but he was striking, his brow and his cheekbones so pronounced that his small, deep-set eyes seemed to disappear between them. Even standing face to face, Constance sometimes couldn't tell where he was looking. It made her uneasy, not knowing if she had his attention. That was Charles's allure. His gaze was like a gift.

Her only problem with Charles was his friends, James and Bobby. James and Bobby were large and shovel-faced and enjoyed cornering girls in stairwells. Like anyone with any sense, Constance had long made a point of avoiding them. But suddenly they were everywhere she was. Charles and his friends spent most of their time hanging out at the rec center, Constance now in tow. James and Bobby were both trying to become the next Joe Louis, but James was too slow and Bobby's left arm was stiff as a broom. When the two of them met in the center of the ring, they looked like pigeons tussling. But Charles took their training seriously. Charles took everything seriously. While the boys sparred, Charles would stand at the ropes and take turns waving them over and whispering in their ears. Charles didn't know the first thing about boxing, but Constance found his confidence transfixing. Watching from a bench in the corner, she was prepared to believe he could do anything.

Michael Boni scraped the stove up onto the sidewalk. "Is that right?" he said, lifting his shirt to wipe the sweat from his face.

"We got married the summer I finished high school," Constance said, but Michael Boni wasn't paying attention. He sat down on the curb, looking as though he were about to pass out. "How much farther?" he said, though he knew perfectly well all they'd managed so far was to cross the street.

Where had she found such feeble men? "We'll finish it another day," she said.

Michael Boni looked up at her with hopeful eyes. "The stove or the story?"

"Both," she said.

Michael Boni sighed. "Better hope it doesn't rain."

§

Constance found the paint at a secondhand building supply store. The cans were half and three-quarters full, with spills on the labels showing what color they were. Mostly white and off-white, but that was okay. They would make the place look clean and bright.

There was more she'd wanted to say about Charles, but not all of it was fit for Michael Boni's ears. For instance, she remembered being in bed at night, newly wed, with Charles above her, and how sometimes she'd felt as if she could be anyone, that he didn't see her there. She was just a body. He took what he needed, and all he gave in return was soon flushed away. But she was just a girl then, and the feeling of isolation had seemed like a small price to pay. After all, Charles had saved Constance, freeing her from her mother. In return, how could she not give herself to him completely?

§

The lights were from a junk shop, left in a bin out front, full of stuff free for the taking. Dobbs had spent the last couple of hours trying to hang them, but the fixtures were old and the wires were loose and Dobbs, it had become clear, had no idea what he was doing. Now he and Constance were sitting at the red plastic booth, drinking coffee, gathering strength for a second attempt.

He'd shown up tonight for the first time in almost a week, and now he was strangely quiet, preoccupied.

"You haven't told me about a single dream," she said.

"I've been busy."

Constance refilled his cup. "Clementine was telling me something. About some people you've been waiting for."

Dobbs looked away, held up one of the light fixtures, wires dangling like a wind chime. "Are you sure these aren't broken?"

Constance took the light from him, set it down. "Did I ever tell you about the night Charles was arrested?"

Dobbs squinted at her from somewhere far away. "Who's Charles?"

It was June, she said, and Clifford had a cold. He'd just turned a year and a half. It was the middle of the night, and Constance was in the kitchen filling a cup of water to settle Clifford's cough. There was a knock at the door. The next thing she knew, the cops were kicking Charles, curled up on the living room floor. He was handcuffed, wearing nothing but boxers, shouting "I'll fucking kill you!" between blows.

Constance had never heard Charles make so much noise. She was in her nightgown and Clifford was crying and one of the cops said something about a stolen truck. The cops were all white. There were three squad cars parked out front with flashing lights. They pushed Charles into the back of one of them, and he looked so small as he rode past her, his face turned away from the window.

Constance stood there paralyzed. They'd taken him away before he'd had a chance to tell her what to do.

By the time she got to the station, the charges had expanded to armed robbery, assault, grand larceny, conspiracy. Constance tried to get the desk clerk to explain what was happening, but nothing he said made any sense. There was the clatter of typewriters and the clanging of cells. There was no space left for words. Someone eventually led her to an interrogation room, where Constance sat down, smoothing her skirt. When she looked up, Charles was being handcuffed to the table.

She'd never felt so helpless. As she had so many times before, she tried to meet his gaze, searching for some sort of reassurance. She'd failed so often to see anything there that she was unprepared for what now appeared. In those bright overhead lights, she could see pink in the whites of his eyes.

"What are you looking at!" Charles shouted, and then he was pulled into the hall and back to his cell, and Constance waited for someone to take her away, too.

"He sounds like an asshole," Dobbs said.

Constance frowned. "It's more complicated than that."

"But tell me about these lights," Dobbs said. A bouquet of loose wires bloomed out of his fist. "How badly do you really need them?"

§

She'd found the scraggly white birch in the back room, growing up through a crack in the slab. That was how she knew this was the perfect location. It helped, too, that the building was only a block from her house and had been abandoned so long, no one would notice or care if she made it her own. The tree was just the right touch, a bit of garden brought indoors.

Constance and Michael Boni were in the kitchen now, the birch hanging overhead. Michael Boni was on his back, his flashlight strobing the stove's undercarriage. His toolbox was stuffed with screwdrivers and wrenches whose battered edges inspired confidence.

"What seems to be the problem?" she said.

"The problem," he said, "is I'm a carpenter. I don't know shit about appliances."

She poured him a cup of coffee and led him out to the dining room. He stood in the doorway, shaking his head. She'd needed help with the booths, the heavy stuff. But she'd done the rest herself—the paintings, the plants, the knickknacks. It was his first time inside, his first sight of the tables and chairs and decorations. "Where'd you find all this stuff?"

"Oh, here and there."

He walked into the center of the room, turning around and around. "When I was a kid, it was a dairy." He pointed to the far wall. "That's where they had the ice cream."

It wasn't a bad idea.

He came over and joined her at the knotty pine booth, blowing steam from his cup. "You never finished your story."

"My story?" Constance tried to remember where she'd left off. "Charles," she began, "he did eight years . . ."

But from Michael Boni's expression, Constance could tell she'd lost track of things, that she'd told the piece about prison to Dobbs instead.

"It doesn't matter," she said. "The day he got out, I took the day off to go to Jackson to pick him up. I got there just in time to see him get in a car with a woman slathered in eye shadow. I never saw him again."

Michael Boni had turned back to peer at the vanished ice cream cases. "Sounds like you were better off without him."

Constance spooned sugar into her cup. "I'm going to tell you a different story," she said.

After Clifford was born but before Charles was arrested, Constance said, she and her husband almost never went out together. Charles was working only part time then, filling orders at a warehouse. The war was over, and so was the boom. Charles always said they couldn't afford dinner or dancing, though that didn't stop him from disappearing almost every night with James and Bobby.

In retrospect, she would've liked to think at least a part of her knew they were up to no good. But in truth she was still a child then. A mother, but still a child.

One night a couple of months before he was arrested, Charles came home and announced they had plans for Saturday night. He'd already bought her a new dress, and he gave her money to get her hair and nails done. She didn't know what the occasion was, what they were celebrating. She was afraid if she asked too many questions, he might change his mind.

The dress he'd bought was blue, a size too big, but Constance pinned it in as best she could. And when Saturday night came, she was so excited, she didn't even care that James and Bobby showed up at the house with unfamiliar women on their arms. It was a triple date, and James and Bobby wore new suits. Constance had never seen them in anything but jeans. The girls looked young enough still to be in high school, swaying their narrow hips through the doorway.

James and Bobby and their dates took one car, a borrowed Buick. Constance and Charles were alone in theirs. It was their first car, a salt-corroded '47 Dodge prone to vapor lock. Charles had bought it just two weeks earlier, another display of wealth she'd chosen not to question. As they drove south on Woodward, Charles balanced his hand on Constance's knee. His fingers were dry, but she didn't mind. Just to be with him, to be the center of his attention, made her willing to forgive anything.

The Sparrow Room was packed, nothing but elbows all the way from the door to the dance floor, but somehow there was a table waiting just for them. And the drinks that night came in endless rounds, Charles simply wagging a finger whenever they needed more. James and Bobby, across the table in their pin-stripe suits, were as calm as bankers. They'd turned their chairs to watch the band, a jazz quintet. She'd never heard Charles or James or Bobby listen to jazz, but that didn't matter. Everyone was someone else that night. Charles held her hand, and she could see sparkles of candlelight in his eyes. They were rich and beautiful, every single person in the club. That night was a fairy tale, and Constance was the servant girl transformed into a princess, discovering the world where she'd always belonged.

★　★　★

"But that was a different time," Constance said now to Michael Boni, sitting opposite her in the knotty pine booth. "I was a different person." Someone capable, she thought, of mistaking a blue dress for love.

Michael Boni nodded distractedly, as if he weren't even listening.

"Let me show you," she said.

She reached into the pocket of her cardigan, taking out a newspaper clipping. Slowly, careful not to rip it, she unfolded the paper, smoothing it out on the table, directly in front of Michael Boni. There were two pictures side by side on the page, both of them black and white. Michael Boni saw them, but he didn't yet understand.

The first shot was from more than half a century ago, a picture of a downtown building at night, glossy cars parked on the street out front, long swooping Cadillacs and Lincolns and Packards. There was a crowd on the sidewalk, the men all wearing suits and hats. The building's marquee was aglow, spelling out THE SPARROW ROOM in bright white bulbs.

This was the "before" picture. The "after" was only a day old, a smudgy shot of crumbled walls, a weedy lot circled with police tape. Nothing recognizable, and yet the place felt just as she remembered it.

Pointing at the rubble, Constance said, "This was the corner where the bandstand was. Over there, the bar."

And here, she said to herself, was the table where she and Charles had held hands, where James and Bobby had given themselves to the music, where Constance had lost the last piece of her innocence.

Now the place was gone. The night before, someone had come along and blown it to pieces, leaving little more than a crater.

"I know about the others, too," Constance said, staring into Michael Boni's eyes. "The grocery store, the shoe place. They're not just buildings, you know. They're memories. They have meaning."

"What makes you think I know anything about it?"

"You men," she said, "you think you're so mysterious."

"Think of the gardens," Michael Boni said. "Think of the possibilities."

She jabbed at the clipping with her finger. "This isn't what I want."

"Who said it's for you?"

"Buy flowers for her grave," Constance said. "Say you're sorry. There are easier ways to make up for having been a shitty grandson."

Michael Boni folded the scrap of newspaper back into a square and pushed it toward her. "They're burdens," he said. "We're better off without them."

Twenty-Four

THE FIRST ONE, a week ago, had been small and quiet as explosions go. The target had been a derelict old building, a former shoe factory. No one seemed to know what had happened. The news reported it as an "accident," but they were short on details. Dobbs had no TV, no radio, no Internet, but there were trash bins and bus stops where a fat, damp wad of newspaper could still be counted on.

The story he'd happened to spot, buried in the metro section, had barely stood out. By now he'd been here long enough to know old abandoned places were always going up in flames. He was lucky no one had gotten around to torching anything of his.

The night he read the story, after finishing his work at the warehouse, Dobbs had gone to check it out.

Beyond the police tape, the building had still been standing. The only damage was to the wall facing the highway. There was an old advertisement painted onto the brick, an enormous brown loafer: BRINKLEY'S—COME WALK A MILE IN OUR SHOES! Over the years, the paint had aged just like real leather, losing its buff, turning gray. As bricks crumbled, even the sole appeared to have worn low.

Dobbs had wandered through the wreckage for a few minutes, and then he'd climbed the embankment to the highway and stood on the shoulder among the broken bottles and fast food wrappers. He couldn't help wondering about whoever had set the explosives. Either they had no idea what they were doing, or they had a sense of humor—the hole they'd blown was at the toe. Now the loafer was a hobo's shoe, worn through with age and left unrepaired, just like the city itself. So prominent was the building, so close to the highway, anyone entering the city from the west couldn't help but see it and take note. A wry sort of welcome sign.

With the second blast, a few days later, they'd grown more serious. Or more competent. From a single punched hole to complete demolition. The place this time around had once been a grocery store, vacant when it blew. Vacant like every other grocery store in the city, just rows of empty metal shelves and a floor flaked in onion skins.

According to a woman in the neighborhood Dobbs later met at the scene, it had been one of the last of the markets to leave the city, selling off its stock at half price. In the remaining days before the store soaped its windows, the woman said, everyone with a coin to spare had shown up and bought as much and more than they could afford to, knowing it was the last time they'd be able to buy food in their own neighborhood. Afterward they'd pushed their cans and boxes of groceries home in the store's rickety carts, commandeering every last one: a wagon train of settlers in housedresses and sleeveless undershirts.

Even ten years later, at the time of the explosion, Dobbs was able to stand at the roadside and see parts of the trail they'd blazed, over-turned and wheelless shopping carts, scattered like the remains of mules that died along the way.

★ ★ ★

Two days after the supermarket was destroyed, the delivery Dobbs had been waiting months for finally arrived. Mike and Tim had given him a four-hour window in which to expect them, and he was at the warehouse, sweeping away the latest accumulation of dust, when the truck pulled up.

It was five in the morning, and they'd cut it close, just barely beating sunrise. Dobbs raised the overhead door, and the truck pulled in. It was a large panel truck, plastered in pictures of appliances, shiny stainless steel refrigerators and dishwashers and washing machines. Mike and Tim climbed down from the cab in their brown monkey suits and came around to the back. Even with the engine off, there was a bounce in the springs, weight restlessly shifting.

With the turn of a handle, Mike swung the cargo doors open. The response inside was instantaneous, a collective recoiling. But they were packed in too tightly, nowhere to go. They had to shade their eyes, even in the dark garage.

Tim, the fat one, was waving them out, wheezing *Come on, come on, what are you waiting for, come on*, through his crooked nose.

When still no one moved, Tim banged his fist on the bumper and shouted, "I said, 'Come on!'" As if volume were the problem.

Mike, the short one, came over to join Tim in the waving. Maybe it was something about the sight of the flames licking his arms that made the people inside understand it really was time to go.

Dobbs watched them step down from the truck, disoriented and wary, legs uncertain as they worked to find sure footing. He wondered how long they'd been standing. Most of them needed help, and Mike and Tim grabbed them roughly under the arms, like a grade school bus drill. Except what Mike and Tim did was really more like dropping than setting down.

Once they were standing on firm ground, Dobbs could see them looking around. He tried not to be disappointed by the quickness of their eyes as they took in the dirty floors and blackened windows. He wanted to tell them all the things he'd done, what the place had looked like before. But they stayed huddled beside the truck, even as Tim tried to shoo them away. Turning to Dobbs, he said, "Are you just gonna stand there?"

Dobbs came forward, stepping into the circle of bodies. "It's okay," he said, as calmly as he could. "Come with me." And he pointed the way through the doorway into the warehouse.

For the first time now, he could see their faces. Some were Asian, he thought. Others maybe Middle Eastern. More specifically than that, he couldn't say. But definitely not Mexican, not from anyplace south. It seemed Sergio's business was expanding.

The man beside Dobbs was tall and thin, wading around in an oversize shirt, a scar like a question mark just above his cheekbone.

"Where are you from?" Dobbs said, and the man kept walking.

Behind him came a teenage girl wearing a pair of men's dress pants folded over at the waist. She was moving slowly, favoring her left leg. "Are you all right?" Dobbs said.

"You're not here to pick out a date!" Tim shouted from the truck.

By now there must have been at least fifty people gathered around him. Dobbs showed them the mattresses, laid out in a grid on the floor. In the moonlight coming through the high windows, their faces didn't change expression.

Over in the corner, a woman was laying a bundle out on a blanket. A baby, tiny, no more than a few weeks old, wrapped up in what looked like a windbreaker.

Dobbs bent down to get a better look. "What's her name?" He was extending his finger toward the baby's fist when someone stepped in front of him, batting his arm away.

A man hovered over him, looking down, yelling in a language Dobbs didn't understand. Then there were hands on his shoulders, and others were closing in.

"It's okay." Dobbs raised his hands, took a step back. "I just wanted to look."

"What the fuck's going on?" Tim and Mike stood in the doorway, side by side, watching over the scene. And then they parted, turning sideways, making room for Sergio.

Dobbs hadn't heard him arrive. But now he saw the sedan, parked alongside the truck. Sergio must have been driving with the headlights off.

Tim and Mike went back to the truck, resumed lowering people down.

Sergio nodded for Dobbs to follow him outside. "Let's take a walk."

Sergio wore a different suit from the one in Vegas. A lighter fabric, with a shine to it like silk.

"What took so long?" Dobbs said.

Sergio signaled to Mike, and the overhead door came down with a rattle and shudder. Now he and Dobbs were alone in the gravel lot. It was quiet out here, as if someone had switched off the sound.

Sergio hooked his arm in Dobbs's, and together they walked toward the weeds at the edge of the lot.

"I thought something went wrong," Dobbs said.

"Everything's fine."

"But why did it take so long?"

"You of all people," Sergio said. "You shouldn't be complaining."

"I was worried."

"It's a messy business."

Dobbs tried to loosen his arm from the awkward angle Sergio held him in. "It doesn't have to be." He nodded back toward the garage. "They don't have to be so rough."

At least five inches shorter, and Sergio still somehow seemed to be looking down on him. "You know," he said, "we don't run into a lot of idealists out here."

"I'm a realist," Dobbs said. "But you can still have a conscience." He stopped himself. "I don't mean *you* specifically."

Sergio came to a stop under a leafless tree, all bark and hollow branches. "All this conscience of yours," he said, "and you didn't think you should tell me?"

"Tell you what?"

From the inside pocket of his jacket, Sergio removed his phone. He pressed a button, and an image materialized on the screen. The demolished grocery store, reproduced in miniature.

"The second one, I'm told." The screen went black again.

"It's just old buildings," Dobbs said. "Ruins."

Wrinkles appeared at the corners of Sergio's eyes. "Nothing to be concerned about?"

Dobbs shrugged. "The new Old West—isn't that what you told me?"

"There were no explosions at the O.K. Corral," Sergio said.

"But it's what you wanted, isn't it? Distractions, a little chaos?"

"When things start blowing up for no good reason," Sergio said, "people start paying attention. They start looking at what's going on inside empty buildings. You understand what I'm saying?"

"It's going to be fine," Dobbs said.

"I gave you this chance as a kindness."

Something had changed in Sergio. The friendly wingman from Mexico was gone. Even the avuncular boss from Vegas, the one who'd given Dobbs this second chance—he, too, had vanished.

"I've done everything you asked," Dobbs said.

Sergio jerked his thumb toward the street. "Go get some sleep. You look like shit. And don't come back unless you hear from me. In fact," he added, "go home, shut the door, and don't go anywhere until things calm down."

Dobbs glanced back toward the building. He'd have to be a bird to see down through the high windows, to know what was going on in there.

"This was supposed to be mine," Dobbs said. "I set it up."

"You've earned a vacation."

"I don't trust them."

Sergio took Dobbs by the elbow and turned him around, back toward the street. "Show me I can still trust *you*."

"You can."

"I want to believe you," Sergio said, "but what I see is someone cracking. I think the strain is getting to you. I see a man that's breaking down."

"I'm a survivor," Dobbs said. "Just like you."

"I'm a businessman," Sergio said. "And right now I see a man putting my business in danger."

§

That night, huddled in the stuffy house, Dobbs studied his palms in a sliver of moonlight, wondering if there really was something the lines could tell him, something about the future or even about the present.

The boom came without warning, out of nowhere, a low distant rumble. It didn't sound like much, and in a moment the sound was gone, dissolving into the roar of the cicadas.

From the upper floor, Dobbs could see smoke. A small plume to the west. On a second glance, he spotted a low, gathering cloud to the north, too. From somewhere came the blistering wail of sirens, but they could've been headed for still more smoke Dobbs couldn't see.

He was at the front door, turning the knob, when he remembered. "Okay, Sergio," he said. "You win." He slid the bolts back into place.

Dobbs broke a twig from his most recent broom, this one cut from the maple in the yard. The branch had turned brittle. Instead of sweeping, it left trails of chipped leaves across the floor.

In the weak yellow light of the paper-covered windows, he peeled off the bark. Sitting down at the table with his dull pocketknife, he set to work.

He thought about his grandfather, those long summer nights at the cabin on the lake, especially after his grandmother had died. Without electricity, there'd been few distractions. Dobbs's parents had never really been able to take a vacation from their research, opting to squint at books by flashlight. His sister had relied on a backpack full of batteries to keep her music playing.

His grandfather hadn't been much of an outdoorsman. He was always breaking ax handles, trying to split firewood. The fish he caught and cooked were all scales and bones. He'd been in real estate all his life. Maybe he'd thought he had something to prove. Every night when the sun went down, he set to work with a block of wood. His goal was a duck. A mallard, specifically, but why he'd picked that particular bird, Dobbs never knew. Throughout his childhood, there'd been flocks of all kinds of things around the lake, but he couldn't remember a single mallard. Maybe his grandfather couldn't either. Maybe that was why, by the time he died, his collection of carvings resembled a lot of things—from mastless Viking ships to gravy boats—but there was nothing that looked at all like a duck.

Dobbs's aims now were more modest. By the time the next day passed once again into night, he'd carved himself a pencil. Not far off from the stick he'd started with, but eight squared sides and a fine, sharp point. His eraser was credible, round on the sides and flat on top.

When he was done, he set the pencil down on the table and spent a moment admiring it.

Then he got up and walked out the front door.

"I was beginning to wonder," Constance said, standing beside the greeting station as he passed inside.

Since he'd been here last, she'd transformed the place even more. There were pictures on the walls and a plastic fern beside a folding screen. A real restaurant, unmistakable. He'd never asked how she managed to get electricity here.

Constance went into the kitchen and reappeared a moment later balancing a mug and a thin, twisted log on a chipped china plate. "Bread?"

The coffee was instant, as always, but it would do.

Taking a sip, Dobbs glanced again around the restaurant, at all the random pieces she'd somehow assembled. "How did you know?" he said. "How did you know this was what you had to do?"

"I did what I felt like doing."

"You had a vision," he said.

She shrugged. "I was bored."

"It's more than that," he said. "Most people just hunker down. But you—how do you go outside, in all that emptiness—how does it not get to you?"

"I'm old," she said. "How's it going to hurt me?"

"You don't feel dread?"

She took something from her pocket and slid it to him across the table. A newspaper clipping, crisscrossed with fuzzed edges from being repeatedly creased. She pointed to a picture of rubble.

"Last night," he said. "I heard it."

This time it was an old jazz club. The article he read, as Constance watched, was long and elegiac, brimming with nostalgia. Below the fold was a photo spread of the club's once glorious past, a marquee aglow with the names of bands and stage shows he had never heard of but would have looked impressive anywhere up in lights.

"Did you know it?" he said. "Had you been there?"

Constance gazed at the photo. "Maybe once," she said. "It doesn't matter."

Dobbs picked up a piece of bread, crammed it in his mouth. He stuffed two more in his pocket. "I've got to go."

It had started to rain while he was at Constance's, but the day—the entire week, really—had been oddly hot and humid, unlike any Midwestern fall he'd ever known. He would've liked to lie down among the weeds, spread out like an angel, letting the rain wash over him.

He found the place easily. From a block away, he could see the limp yellow police tape bouncing as it caught the falling drops. Drawing closer, he could make out the scorched grass and muddy rivulets studded with boot prints, where the fire hoses had run off. The club was nothing more now than a cordoned-off heap. The remaining boarded-up buildings on either side of the street looked like a Potemkin town turned around—the braces that kept everything standing rotting in the rain.

The city was silent as a fallow field.

"I know you."

Dobbs spun around on the wet concrete. McGee stood on the opposite sidewalk, directly behind him. She'd dyed her hair blond, but there was no mistaking her eyes.

"It was raining last time I saw you, too," she said. "You had a newspaper over your head."

How could he tell her that lately he'd been seeing her constantly, that he was with her almost every time he couldn't keep himself from falling asleep?

In the rain, her oversize clothing hung off of her like a wet tarp. "Sightseeing?" she said.

He turned back toward the rubble. "I keep trying to figure out what it all means." The street lay between them, and Dobbs wondered if he should cross, or if she would.

"I think they're trying to help," she said. Her hands were in her pockets, her eyes fixed on the ruins. "They're trying to do the right thing."

Dobbs put his hand in his own pocket, felt around for the bread. Aside from the crust, it had turned to mush. "Is this the right thing?"

She shrugged. "Maybe it feels like the only thing left."

And then she was walking away from him.

"See you later," Dobbs shouted. But the words came out sounding hollow, as if he already knew they might not be true.

★ ★ ★

The rain had slowed to little more than a drizzle by the time he reached the house. He left a trail of shoe prints across the cracked, weathered porch.

The first things he saw, when he opened the door, were Mike and Tim standing side by side, perfectly still at the far end of the living room. Their jumpsuits were dry. They'd been waiting a long time.

The two men broke toward him in the same instant. The door was still open behind him, but Dobbs didn't bother trying to run.

"You brought this on yourself," Mike said as the flames on his forearms danced in Dobbs's eyes.

And then Dobbs was on the ground, and there was a stampede on his ribs and spine.

Tim, standing by the door watching, said, "This won't end well for you."

But then again, Dobbs thought, maybe the end had already come.

Twenty-Five

Even in the poor light just before dawn, Darius could tell how clean the alley was, the crumbling pavement looking as though it had just been swept. From the steel door at the far end, someone had hung a holly wreath. But it was only September; the perfect little berries had to be plastic.

Michael Boni knocked, and a few moments passed before Darius heard feet shuffling somewhere within. As the door swung open, the alley was bathed in music, playful notes dancing across a piano keyboard, accompanied by the resonant thumps of an upright bass. And then the trumpet entered, the player unmistakable. As Darius and Michael Boni passed through, Satchmo broke out scatting. For a moment, Darius felt as though he were stepping back in time. On the other side of the door, he half-expected to see a room full of closely shaven men gnawing on cigars as they stacked poker chips into miniature battlements.

But the room was almost entirely empty. The air smelled warm and yeasty. An elderly black woman stood with her hand on the knob. "Welcome," she said.

The place was a restaurant, but Darius couldn't begin to guess what kind. An assortment of mismatched booths lined the dining room, the walls decorated with landscapes from several different continents. Just inside the door, a marble-topped table that at one time must have belonged to a sidewalk café propped up a sign reading PLEASE WAIT TO BE SEATED.

Michael Boni nodded casually to the old woman. "How's business?"

"Suddenly picking up."

Constance led Darius and Michael Boni across the room to the farthest booth from the door. Leaning over the table, she tipped a lighter in the mason jar candle.

"We're not on a date," Michael Boni said, and the old woman frowned as he blew out the flame. Darius might have apologized for his rudeness, but by now Constance must have understood who she was dealing with.

As usual, Michael Boni hadn't bothered to explain their destination. It wasn't so much that he enjoyed surprises. It was just that—as best Darius could figure—Michael Boni preferred to be the only one who ever knew what was going on. But Darius had heard so much about Constance that this, whatever this was, hardly felt like a secret. He was just pleased to see the woman in person. But now that he was here, he realized she was nothing like he'd imagined, older and frailer. The way Michael Boni had talked about her, Darius had expected some sort of sage, not an elderly waitress who looked more than a little like his own grandmother.

"Well?" Constance said.

Michael Boni shrugged. "What do you have?"

"What do you think?"

"Stew?" Michael Boni didn't bother to hide his grimace. "Meat?"

"Not unless you brought one of your birds."

Michael Boni's eyes narrowed in on her, and she stared right straight back.

Darius wondered if Michael Boni had any relationships that weren't entirely antagonistic.

When she was gone, Michael Boni thumped his elbows onto the table. "What do you think?"

Darius paused to take another look around. He'd never seen anything like it: the ill-assorted furniture, the plastic plants, the crooked fixtures, the randomly assembled parts and pieces. "Did she do all this herself?"

"I helped." Michael Boni seemed so pleased with everything he saw, Darius couldn't help wondering if the restaurant was supposed to be like the lettuce, another of Michael Boni's symbols.

Constance returned with a tarnished silver tray, which she set down before them on the table. On the tray was a wooden cutting board, and on the board a bent and knobby baguette that looked like the branch of some ancient tree. The bread was ugly, but it smelled incredible. And there was a small pot of coffee and several cups. Constance may not have been a sage, but she could read Darius's mind.

"Would you do the honors?" She slid the board in front of him.

The teeth of the knife sawed in. Shards of crust, thick as bark, shot across the tabletop. And then, almost instantly, there was no more resistance. A puff of steam swirled out of the cut, and the flesh fell away from the knife as if it were no more than air.

"Try it," she said.

Darius put down the knife and picked up a slice. Together that golden shell and the fragile web in the middle melted into a cloud of warmth and nothingness.

The bread was one of the most delicious things he'd ever put in his mouth. Maybe Constance was a sage after all. Maybe, Darius thought, a second bite would answer the question once and for all. But just as he was reaching out for another piece, the door to the alley swung open.

McGee had arrived.

"I was beginning to wonder," Michael Boni shouted, as if over the clamor of a lunch-hour rush. And then something changed in his expression, a sour, unpleasant look of surprise.

McGee wasn't alone. Behind her, emerging cautiously from the alley, was a tall, pretty blonde.

"Who the fuck is this?" Michael Boni said.

McGee gestured for the girl to follow. "A friend."

McGee betrayed no reaction to the place, but the tall, pretty blonde was glancing around the dining room with her jaw set at an unpretty angle. Darius had seen her once before, through the glass of his guard booth. Just like on that night, she was following a step behind McGee, as if tethered by a string.

Michael Boni slid over to make room for McGee. Darius did the same for the pretty blonde. She gave him a faint, mechanical smile out of the side of her mouth.

"We haven't been introduced," Darius said, offering his hand.

"April."

He tried not to be offended that she shook so warily.

Constance had been watching silently, as if waiting for something to happen. Now, with everyone settled, she threw a kitchen towel over her shoulder and retreated to the back room.

Michael Boni was still looking cross. "Is there anyone else you two are planning to invite without telling me?"

"Relax," McGee said, slipping out of her coat.

April raised her hips and slid a phone from her back pocket, lowering her eyes to the screen. "Don't let me interrupt."

Michael Boni looked as though he was going to say something in response, but then he turned to McGee instead.

"It's fine," McGee said. "I'm listening. I'm here. Let's get started."

Michael Boni reached for the coffeepot, taking his time pouring a cup. Now everyone was waiting for him, which was how he seemed to prefer it.

His cup full, he slapped a notepad onto the table. "I drew a map."

McGee was quick to grab it. She spent a moment looking the drawing over. "There's another entrance here." She pointed to a spot. "More out of the way."

Then Michael Boni was staring at Darius, waiting for him to take a look. To say something, to have some sort of opinion. But from where Darius was sitting, the map was upside down. He tried turning his head. But even if everything had been right side up, he doubted he would've been able to make any sense of it. The place was too distracting. Plastic grapes dangled from the partition behind Michael Boni's head, making him look as though he were wearing giant purple earrings. Across the room, a small, duct-taped fish tank lined with pink and blue gravel sat beneath a sign that said SKATES SHARP-ENED WHILE YOU WAIT.

"Well?" Michael Boni said.

"It's fine."

"That's all you've got?"

Darius leaned forward, squinting into the far corner of the dining room, at something half hidden behind a pile of boxes. "Is that a barber chair?"

April glanced up from her phone and looked to where Darius was looking. "I think so."

"Can we focus on this?" Michael Boni said, tapping his finger on the map. "Can we leave the decorations for later?"

From the kitchen came the clanging of pots, the scent of onion and garlic sizzling in oil. Darius wondered how long it took to make a stew. A slow simmer, a low flame?

"What time is it?" he said.

Michael Boni frowned. "You have somewhere to be?"

Darius could think of a lot of other places he'd like to be. Unlike the rest of them, he'd been up all night working. Grabbing one of the mugs, he poured himself some coffee. Most of all, he would've liked to crawl into bed. That's where Sylvia was. Shawn and Nina, too. That was where all the sensible people were.

"How's the bread?" April asked quietly in Darius's direction, tucking her hair behind her ear.

"Delicious."

And Violet would be in bed, too. But that was an image Darius tried to wipe from his mind. He'd been trying to wipe it away for a long time now.

Michael Boni and McGee had drawn closer on their side of the table, elbows touching as they bent over the map. Darius hadn't been wrong about the two of them. They really were meant for each other.

April plunged the serrated edge of the knife into the crust, like a handsaw hacking through wood.

Michael Boni looked up, not bothering to hide his irritation.

April continued sawing until the bread tumbled free. "Oh," she said, "am I interrupting?"

"Yes," Michael Boni said.

"It's fine," McGee said. "That's why it's there."

The crust ground beneath April's straight white teeth. "So what's it going to be this time?"

McGee glanced up distractedly. "Hmm?"

"What are you demolishing this time?" April said, tearing off another hunk. "There was what—the shoe place, the supermarket, the . . ."

"Jazz club," Darius offered, and April thanked him with a tip of her crust.

"We can talk about it later," McGee said.

April leaned across the table, peering at the notebook page. "I want to talk about it now."

McGee tried to put on a patient smile. "You said before you didn't want to know."

"I changed my mind."

"If you want to help," McGee said, "great."

April looked from McGee to Michael Boni. "Help do what?"

"Isn't it obvious?" Michael Boni said.

April focused in on him. "Blow shit up?"

Michael Boni spent a moment sourly exploring the gaps and grooves of his teeth. "There's more to it than that."

April shrugged. "From the stories in the paper, I really couldn't tell."

Michael Boni turned to McGee. "Is she always like this?"

"No," April said before McGee had a chance to answer. "I'm trying something new."

"This has nothing to do with you," Michael Boni said.

McGee reached out and put her hand on April's slender arm. "I explained it to you."

"But *why*?" April said, pulling her arm back toward her lap. "That's what I want to know. This isn't you. You don't just destroy things."

"Have you been outside?" Michael Boni said. "Have you looked around?"

McGee nodded. "It's already destroyed."

"But this?" April glanced around the restaurant. "Is this what you want instead?"

"Why not?" Michael Boni said.

"It's still ruins." Darius said, the sound of his voice surprising even himself. "It's just ruins made into something else."

"What did you expect?" Michael Boni said. "Skyscrapers?"

Darius had never stopped to put it into words, but yes, he supposed he did. And why not? This place certainly wasn't what he wanted. Castoffs, scraps, leftover trash from businesses that had failed or fled or gone up in flames. How could McGee and Michael Boni not see how depressing this was?

"It's just nerves talking," McGee said. "Stress."

Darius took a slow sip of coffee. "It's been a long time since I felt this calm." He turned to April. "How about you?"

"I feel fine."

Darius turned to McGee and Michael Boni. "We feel fine."

346

In a whisper, April said, "Maybe it's the two of you feeling nerves."

Now Michael Boni was glaring at Darius. "You've known all along."

Had he? He was no longer sure. All he'd ever really wanted was to be a better sort of person, the sort of man who provided for the future, who fixed what was broken. Above all else, he'd wanted to stop being weak. But what would Sylvia say, he wondered, if she were to see him in this dump, surrounded by these characters? Would she see the new man he'd been trying to become?

They'd known each other more than thirty years. All the way back to elementary school. No one believed them when they told the story, how he and Sylvia had grown up on the same block, identical adjacent buildings, apartments on the very same floor, rooms in the very same corner. But they'd been kids; they'd thought everything worked that way. And how one day when they were eight years old, they'd smuggled rulers home from school, and in their separate bedrooms they'd measured the exact same spot on the exact same wall, and there they'd drawn a circle, and into that circle they'd pretended they could talk to each other. Into that circle they could say whatever they wanted, could share their every secret. This went on for years, until over time they gradually forgot, the circles eventually fading. But by then Darius and Sylvia were inseparable, no longer needed their imaginations.

The mistake Darius had made was assuming everything with Sylvia would always come that easily.

He'd tried to change, and he'd failed. Ever since the day he'd seen what was in Michael Boni's garage, Darius hadn't been able to go a single day without getting tangled in Violet's limbs. Nothing had worked out like he'd planned. He'd wanted to be a better person. Instead, he'd just made things worse.

In less than an hour, Sylvia would be waking up. If he wasn't there when it happened, he'd miss his chance to see her. Another day would pass in which he wouldn't get to curl up beside her, wouldn't feel the warmth at the back of her knees. And then Darius found his mind wandering up from Sylvia's knees to warmth at higher points on Violet, places less subtle but agonizingly unforgettable, no matter how hard he tried to forget them.

"Where are you going?" Michael Boni said as Darius rose from the table.

"Home."

April was sliding toward the end of the bench, making way.

"You can't leave," Michael Boni said.

But of course he could. It was just a matter of will, of following through. And Darius had been practicing. Not for this moment in particular, but it seemed to him now the skill was transferable. If he could just squeeze out of the booth and then allow his feet to carry him out of the restaurant, he thought, he'd be okay. He'd go home, wake Sylvia up, tell her what he'd done. She might forgive him; she might not. Either way, it would be over.

"You're a fucking coward," Michael Boni said as Darius reached the door. "I always knew it."

"I'm going, too," April said.

McGee's frown sharpened. "What do you mean?"

April shifted in her seat, slid the phone back into her pocket. "I'm going home."

"You just got here," McGee said. "You came all this way."

"Let her go," Michael Boni said. "We don't need them."

April rose, and McGee did, too.

April was so much taller, she had to bend low, scooping her friend in her arms, almost like a child. "I'm glad I came."

"I need your help." McGee's voice was muffled in April's shoulder.

"No, you don't. You never really have."

McGee said, "I told my parents you're coming."

"It's you they want to see, not me."

"I can't do it alone."

April shook her head, smiling sadly. "They're your parents."

"What do I say?"

"Tell them the truth."

McGee stepped back, laughing without a trace of humor.

"If you're so sure you're doing the right thing," April said, "tell them the truth."

McGee kept drifting backward, collapsing against the corner of the booth. "Everyone's gone."

Were those tears in her eyes?

"You can go, too," April said. "There's nothing stopping you."

"Everything we ever did was a failure."

"Go to Portland," April said softly. "Find Myles."

McGee looked almost disappointed. "Portland doesn't need me."

April looked as if she were about to say something more, but even from across the room, Darius could see it wouldn't do any good.

"Please be careful," April said, folding McGee one last time in her arms. And then she was coming toward him, and Darius stepped aside, holding open the door.

Twenty-Six

THEY ARE ASLEEP.

At this hour, as if they might be doing something else.

How little a tree changes, even over years.

Always one dog barks and then another.

Never alone.

And did I leave footprints across the lawn?

Mother, father.

And yet my tree, still.

Mom, Dad.

Otherwise, how incredibly silent.

Cold.

A winter carnival, a carny, and Myles picking his prize, a fluorescent green dog.

The random things one thinks of at the randomest times.

And what did I expect to find?

I should have brought another sweater.

Maybe to find the curtains drawn, something, anything, blocking the view.

Music, they say, for some reason being a trigger for memory.

Instead, an open window, the moon like a faint spotlight on their bed.

Familiar smells and tastes, too.

If I trust my memory.

As if I had anything else to trust.

The things one finds oneself wondering.

Knots and limbs, stabbing through the seat of my pants.

How something so large must have appeared to someone so small.

Thirty, forty feet tall to a girl two, three times shorter than the lowest branches.

Someone, as if I weren't thinking of myself.

And Myles grinning in the frigid air, as if that green dog were the answer.

To think I used to climb up here in shorts.

What was the question?

Nothing between me and them now but a window screen, a few branches and leaves.

Certain sensations you can never return to, never experience again.

Comfort, to a child, an insignificant thing.

If you're not careful up there, darling, you'll break your etc. etc. Quote unquote.

What did Myles think it meant, the dog's green fur, so bright it hurt to look?

The temptation to tweet and caw and wake them up.

The afternoon Mother brought home the mechanic, the song that was playing on her car stereo.

When you sit up in the tree staring, we wonder what you see. Quote unquote.

The ache in my back.

When we got back from Seattle, silently stuffing that green dog in the bottom of my duffel bag.

Like the world is a movie playing inside your head. Quote unquote.

And Myles never knowing I kept it.

In the driveway the mechanic raising the hood, and Mother leaving the engine running, the radio playing.

Before the tree itself, before I could climb, my fascination with the seedcases covering the ground.

And what was the name of that girl down the street who remembered events by the outfits she'd been wearing?

For me the place of memory always outdoors.

A summer day with the car stereo playing, and everything a little too bright, the sun, the blue and whites of the sky.

And in my head.

Propellers, were they called, the way they spun and twisted to the ground?

Wings?

No expectation of being able to see them at all.

The same duffel bag where I kept the poems Myles wrote, all those slanting, skidding rhymes.

Darling, what do you mean you don't want a tree house? Quote unquote.

Even after Mother and the mechanic went in the house together, the engine, the radio, still going.

A chorus repeating *baby, baby.*

Along with the CD mixes of songs Myles thought I'd like.

The girl down the street remembered what everyone else was wearing, too.

The mechanic Dad said he didn't trust.

Seedcases the first things I ever dissected.

A summer day, the engine running, and Mother walking into the bedroom and closing the blinds.

Our daughter the squirrel tamer. Quote unquote.

As if I would ever tame anything.

And it was the middle of the afternoon.

The brittle hulls, and inside the case the seed itself, slightly wet and bitter.

The yellow shorts the neighbor girl wore the day Dad ran over her dog.

His brown suit, her dead dog.

Dad rolls onto his other side, moonlit blanket rippling like a wave.

And where was I supposed to be that summer day?

A friend's?

A neighbor's?

When I was ten, I vowed I would never again cut my hair.

Was I supposed to be anywhere?

Along with the necklace Myles gave me for our first anniversary, a pendant of tarnished brass watch gears—which I told him I lost.

In her sleep, Mother scratches her cheek.

And for some reason they decided I should go to music camp.

Don't you think it'll be nice for you to make some friends, darling? Quote unquote.

Because mechanics are not to be trusted. Quote unquote.

Meaning what, precisely, by *not trust*?

Not to be trusted with one's car?

At seven? eight? nine? climbing the tree for the first time and discovering the seedcases in the tree were green and elastic, compared to the brown and brittle ones spread across the lawn.

Not to be trusted with one's wife?

You have a wonderful ear for music. Quote unquote.

This key, that key, whatever sounded nice.

And what sort of trust does that imply for one's wife?

From the tree, watching the blinds blow in, hearing them smack against the sill in the breeze.

A wonderful ear for music?

To this day I don't know what that means.

For a mechanic, I can admit a certain allure.

The blinds, which they've since replaced with curtains.

Or was that the squeaking of bedsprings, not the blinds at all?

There being a distinction between an ear for something and an actual skill.

An awe for anyone who can take something apart.

And my never having heard of such a thing as music camp.

And then put it back together, of course.

You'll love it; the cover of the brochure shows lots of trees. Quote unquote.

Sarcasm being amusing only coming from someone you don't loathe.

Did she know I was watching?

The curtains now, perfectly still.

Did she simply not care?

Her monogrammed suitcase I could have curled up in.

Stored everything I owned in.

Along with the black T-shirt Myles wore the night we played pool, which I stole from his floor the next morning.

As if there could be degrees of stillness, different degrees of not moving.

We simply wonder what you do up there all day. Quote unquote.

And I, for my part, wonder what you do in there.

Everything in their bedroom in shades of blue, the bedspread, the area rug, the lamp, etc. etc.

The suitcase is real leather and extremely valuable, so take care of it. Quote unquote.

Wondered then, wonder still.

The feeling of independence that comes from being able to do for yourself.

An enormous leather suitcase for a single pair of denim shorts, two red T-shirts, two pairs of socks, one pair of canvas sandals.

Blue pillowcases.

Blue molding.

Sitting on one of the upper branches the day they painted the bedroom walls.

Don't drop it, don't scratch it, don't let it get wet, don't etc. etc. Quote unquote.

The paint fumes in the leaves, as high as I could climb.

And then returning from camp a week later to find a tiny house in the crotch of my tree.

Not needing to depend on someone else to do for you.

Blue picture frames and a blue dust ruffle.

How could anyone live surrounded by only one color?

We wanted to surprise you. Quote unquote.

You always have a choice in colors. You might as well make them match. Quote unquote.

Along with the books Myles lent me that I never returned.

Even after I'd told them, insisted, I didn't want a tree house.

On the car stereo, a countdown of some sort—Top Twenty.

We thought a house would be more comfortable. Quote unquote.

Than a branch, arguably.

Along with a copy of the first flyer Myles ever made, Xeroxed until it looked like it was drawn with charcoal.

Children love tree houses, darling. Quote unquote.

The beginning pulses of a headache.

Probably the same children who play with dolls and laugh at clowns.

The dark, the strain on my eyes.

You could do whatever you wanted with it. Quote unquote.

Complete dependency.

My objections to playing piano.

Keys made of ivory?

A tree house with wood that was clean and new.

But a tree house is your own personal space. Quote unquote.

And me taking a stance against the poaching of elephants.

And yet there being no line waiting to get into the tree.

His chest rising, falling, rising.

Falling.

And in their bathroom, hand towels and washcloths, also blue.

Some of the wood weather-treated green.

And for weeks, me standing among the roots staring up at the tree.

And fourteen-year-olds with actual skill.

At the house in the tree.

Green wood!

Refusing to climb up.

And me not an exclamatory child.

I should have brought a thermos.

Coffee, black.

Blue bathmat.

The car stereo not loud, but loud enough the neighbors must have noticed.

And wondered.

You just have to give it a chance. Quote unquote.

An empty car, its hood raised, the engine running, the car stereo playing.

Along with the disk, Myles's video.

The Big Dipper pointing north.

To think, at one time, that meant something to someone.

Sailors, and sea captains, in any case.

Safe in the duffel bag with all the rest.

Stars, whose names I've forgotten.

Ornamental soap dish, also blue.

A greasy rag draped over the raised hood, slipping, slipping, as the engine idled and the hood vibrated.

A chill growing, a dew forming.

The yellow nightgown she was sleeping in the night her brother's joint set the den of her house on fire.

The pink nightgown I was supposed to have been wearing when they pulled back the sheets to put her into bed with me.

Further details of which I have forgotten.

A lake with cobwebbed canoes.

Infested with earwigs.

That video, the one thing Myles noticed missing.

And who ever heard of making a tree house from anything but scrap?

Leaves lightly brushing the outer walls in the breeze.

A man in your father's club drew up the plans. Quote unquote.

And of course, their self-satisfied smiles.

Blue toothbrush holder.

Around the trunk, the grass yellow and matted.

A blue blanket folded up at the end of the bed.

My tree, spoiled.

Even in their sleep, slight smiles lingering.

Myles tearing apart the apartment, looking everywhere for that disk.

Even in the moonlight being able to tell she still pretends her hair's not gray.

So stiff and uncomfortable.

Feeling myself grasping for something.

Making it all the way to the second most popular song in America.

Who ever heard of an architect planning a tree house?

Some number in the teens having been playing when Mother and the mechanic pulled up.

Myles searching and searching, and me silent, the duffel bag slumped in the corner.

A few dropped nails in the dirt, among the roots.

Nails that would grow fat with rust after months in snow.

Circling impressions of ladder legs.

The day at the camp, in the middle of the lake, I let both oars slip into the water.

Bark rubbed away below the crotch where the ladder leaned.

Long enough that the rag fell.

A few wedges cut into the arms from the stress of the frame.

The mechanic coming back out of the house looking mussed.

I can no longer remember if it was intentional.

Not mussed the way one would expect a mechanic to look.

Until finally I decided what to do.

Dad sleeps on his side, knees slightly bent, hands pressed together beneath his cheek, as if . . .

363

As if what?

Starting with the shingles on the little roof.

Then the mechanic closing the hood, getting into the passenger seat, and sitting, waiting, tapping the dashboard to the music.

Never, as far as I can remember, actually looking at the engine.

Camp must have been wonderful. Quote unquote.

Push the piano into the lake.

Which, of course, I considered.

An awe that what he might have seen in there would have made sense to him.

Why didn't Myles just burn another copy?

The moonlight, the darkness, the sheen of her nightgown, the shine on his forehead.

Mother had changed into a pair of blue shorts.

But the piano was wider than the doorway.

Dad at work, Mother inside, me sitting on the upper branches, prying shingles off with a stick.

Mother wearing dark sunglasses much too big for her head.

My head where the window used to be.

And yet.

My feet in the doorway.

Myles could've made a thousand new copies, as many as he wanted.

Even especially things we've grown attached to.

I just don't understand: it's as if the tree house is shedding shingles. Quote unquote.

Leaving the front door unlocked behind her, Mother getting behind the wheel and driving off with the mechanic singing.

I should have brought an extra layer.

The yellow shorts she didn't stop me from removing one summer afternoon when we were sixteen.

A different pair.

Maybe the mechanic was only listening?

For grinding, whining, knocking?

Recitals.

Sound, again, and its memories.

Sliding off the roof, twisting to the ground, some landing flatly, others on their corners, bending, snapping.

I nail them back in place, and then it happens all over again. Quote unquote.

And what does it all amount to?

A scorn for acquiescence.

Leaving the greasy rag on the driveway.

A test drive, merely?

Maybe it's the tree trying to tell you something, I said.

At which they frowned.

Why didn't Myles just burn another copy?

Strumming, drumming, cooing.

In my memory, only music and singing.

At the time all my reasons seemingly sound.

A final concert.

And every Saturday him climbing up the ladder and nailing the shingles back into place.

Up perplexedly and back down smiling, self-congratulatorily.

Leaving the greasy rag in the driveway, where Dad would find it several hours later.

A rag to wipe greasy fingerprints away.

All those years living with that bag, Myles never once asking what was inside.

While I watched from my tree.

Performing for the parents.

Even on the lake the awful noise.

Music, supposedly.

In thanks for footing the bill.

The blue sheets and blankets.

Grade-schoolers playing free jazz.

Sitting in the tree, watching Dad examine the mechanic's rag.

This side, that side, all of it greasy.

Teenagers shrieking off-key concertos.

The pianist playing this key, that key, all of them sour.

Until finally I buried his hammer in her flower bed.

By September, this time of year, half the tiles having disappeared.

Looking and looking for the disk, until Myles finally gave up.

Keeping the little window open rain and shine.

Especially rain.

Motivations never having thought to question.

Removal of screws from the hinges of the little door.

And me never letting on I'd watched his video once, let alone a hundred times.

Only a few a day, clandestinely, so as not to arouse their suspicions.

Inside the little door, a little straw mat the color and shape of a sunflower.

The barricade, the riot cop, and the girl, her turquoise shirt with the giant daisy.

New, never having been stepped on.

A need to believe in the attainment of ideals.

The riot cop and the girl, and their embrace.

Rain.

Rotted, having been rained on.

And then the cop's violent shove.

By the end of the month, the little shutters, loosened, blowing off.

All winter, from my bedroom, my childhood furniture, watching the little tree house fill up with snow.

The little curtains, white with daffodils, rotting.

In the spring, rain coming through the little windows.

Barefoot.

The embrace.

Dad and his ladder and an armful of shingles.

And a new hammer.

The shove.

Rotten particleboard crumbling.

Shingles sliding off by themselves.

Floorboards beginning to warp and rot.

The embrace.

Destruction being a form of dissection.

Inside, a little three-legged table with two little pale blue chairs.

The shove.

Now, all these years later, no trace the house was ever here.

Except for the nail holes, grown over, filled in.

The embrace.

A fluorescent green dog to guard my keepsakes.

And certain things I will continue to believe.

The shove.

Inside, the little walls all one color.

Blue.

Twenty-Seven

HE'D ALWAYS SAID her nose was her mother's. Her forehead too. Her mouth, her chin, her cheekbones, all her mother's. But Garland hadn't seen her in so long that he was surprised, after all this time, by her unexpected resemblance to himself. He couldn't have explained why, but it made him smile, such a superficial thing. And he couldn't pinpoint exactly where he saw the similarity. Not in specific features. Her eyes didn't come from him, but neither did they come from her mother, though perhaps he could see traces—the same walnut shade of brown, the same alertness. Nowhere in the family albums was there anything like them, so big, so round, like a pair of orbiting moons. Always one to take control of an uncomfortable situation, her mother had been the first to declare her a positively ugly baby, and with such insistence that she would challenge anyone—Garland included—who stubbornly insisted upon finding her cute. She had always been a bright girl, and he thought her moon eyes lent her a sort of omniscience.

Around the table they approached the meal from whatever direction best suited their disposition: Garland caught himself meeting every forkful with a contemplative tilt of his head; Muriel chewed slowly, glancing distractedly around the table, as if afraid of missing something important. She prodded skeptically at the food on her plate, although she had cooked most of it herself. As always, Garland had made the salad dressing, his own special recipe. In between bites, his daughter's eyes were surveillance cameras, sweeping every object in the room, every move of her parents', every stain in the carpet. Had she not been his daughter, Garland might have thought she was casing the place. He marveled that she seemed so relaxed, as if the years between them had simply been erased now that she no longer had a use for them.

His daughter wore a dress, of all things. Garland never would have guessed she owned one. Despite the season, it was a light summer dress—pretty in a way, but also disappointing. Not until she arrived had Garland realized he had been awaiting a girl in frayed jeans and sneakers with the soles worn low. An image born not of simple nostalgia, though, but from a profound sense that there was no other way for her to be.

In the days leading up to this dinner, Garland and Muriel hadn't been able to stop speculating about what it meant, this sudden, enigmatic reunion. Their daughter had offered no real explanation. Despite his wife's skepticism, Garland hadn't asked for one. She had said she was calling from a hotel, of all places. Nearby, in Detroit. She'd said she wanted to come for dinner. She was bringing a friend, a girl named April. In the end, the girl hadn't been able to make it, but their daughter had. And here she was.

Her hair didn't have her mother's waves or his—admittedly thinning—curls. She had dyed it. Blond. Every time he caught a glimpse of the color, he felt something seize in his heart.

Anyone observing them from a distance, Garland supposed, might think them strangers, stranded together by something as unspectacular as inclement weather. There was more truth to that, he thought, than in his daughter's apparent ease.

Rearranging the mushrooms on her chicken, Muriel lifted her eyes and with a voice gone dry said, "So how does he like the investment business?"

The words fell like raindrops in the desert, making Garland all the more aware of just how silent the house had been—not a noise, except for the baritone murmurs of the anchorman on the television he'd left on in the den.

From a stack kept warm under a folded cloth, his daughter selected a roll. As she split the bread in two, she happened to glance up, and she seemed surprised to find Muriel waiting for her to reply.

"Who?" their daughter said, butter knife still raised in the air. "How does *who* like the investment business?"

In the space of a moment, Garland watched his wife suddenly show her age, advancing ten years in as many seconds. Her eyes squinted as she tried to read her daughter's face, searching for an explanation, fissures appearing in the powder across her brow. It was as though she were trying to assure herself that this woman—whom she'd never really known as a woman—was, in fact, her own flesh and blood. Garland imagined her trying to fill in the years between the girl she remembered and the woman in her late twenties now sitting opposite her at the table. On the credenza there was a picture, a seven-by-ten, of his daughter at her high school graduation. His eyes were no longer what they'd once been, but Garland could make out the royal blue robe and the matching cap dangling by one corner from her fingertips. Her hair was streaked with orange, in her nose a silver ring. It was the last picture they had of her. Since then, her face had grown more stern, losing the last of its roundness. The grass at her feet in the photo was almost too green to be real. A day in late spring, and the sky at her back was perfectly clear, but she was unhappy. Garland didn't need to be able to make out her face to recall she'd been unhappy. She'd always disliked having her picture taken.

Perhaps that was it. She was simply expressing her objection. The picture was the closest thing Garland had to a tool for measuring the time that had passed, and it indicated only the physical changes, which he realized now were almost irrelevant. Who she had been in that picture he felt he would never know, any more than he could ever hope to know the person she'd become. Without either of those reference points, how could he possibly understand what had changed?

"Your fiancé," Muriel said at last. "Is it *Myles*?"

Garland regretted the way his wife said the name as though there were something dubious about it. But he could understand Muriel's impulse to draw her out, using what little information their daughter had provided over the phone. And he was glad, as well, that it was Muriel, not he himself, taking charge. He'd never excelled at these conversations, these silence fillers.

What they knew—what their daughter had allowed them to know—was that suddenly she was engaged. Suddenly she lived in Portland, a yoga instructor, her fiancé a financial analyst. To Garland and Muriel, everything could not help but seem sudden, coming as it did completely out of nowhere. But for all they knew, these facts had all been true for a long time now. It had been seven years since there'd been anything from his daughter other than terse e-mails assuring her worried father she was indeed still alive. The call that had come through two nights before was not the one he had long expected, not the one Garland had been spending these years preparing for. It didn't come from a jailhouse. It didn't come from the police. It didn't come from the FBI. She had not been arrested for dumping sugar into the gas tanks of bulldozers. She had not been attacking whaling ships or driving spikes into trees. She was not wanted for questioning. Most important of all, she was not dead, killed by a concussion grenade or by something similar of her own making. Even when she was a child, even from decades off, he had thought he could see these ends coming. And yet despite all the things he'd thought he understood about his little girl, here she was, not just alive but also well, healthy, a picture of inexplicable normalcy. How could Garland not feel baffled? How could he not wonder if, all this time, he had been the one who misunderstood?

When it came to this fiancé, this *Myles*, it was hard to know what to say. Never before had their daughter told them about a boyfriend. Never before had they met one. When they were all younger, Muriel had processed this slight in the only way she could, as evidence that their daughter had something to hide. And as for that secret, Muriel had assumed the worst thing she could imagine, an orientation of which she would never be able to speak in front of her friends. Far better that, Garland had always believed, than what he considered the far more likely truth, that it was *them* their daughter had wished to hide. From embarrassment or shame, who knew? She was their only daughter—their only child—and they'd had no practice with romantic things. Garland found it difficult to contemplate her love life now without wanting to start from the beginning, imagining the woman in front of him was not twenty-eight but twelve, and this Myles, whoever he was, merely a first fleeting crush.

But for Garland, such questions as these were idle curiosities at best. Who cared what the man did? Let him be a puppeteer, a traveling circus performer. What difference did it make? Why sit here and pretend that this absent man whom they had never met was more a stranger than the girl, the woman, sitting now before them, pretending all was well?

"Right," their daughter said. "Myles." And then she flashed an ambiguously crooked smile. "It must be the wine," she said, though she'd taken no more than one or two sips.

Muriel said, "Where did you two meet?"

His daughter stabbed for a potato and missed, scraping her fork against the plate. "A long time ago," she said. "Seattle."

"And"—Garland had to pause to clear his throat, startled to suddenly find himself speaking—"have you been together all this time?"

In his chest, Garland felt something simmer. He wasn't sure what it was. There was an element of relief, perhaps, a comfort to be found in knowing she hadn't been alone all these years, that she'd had someone to care for her, someone to love her, someone to protect her. Though as for the last, she would no doubt say she had no need.

But the relief, if that was what it was, played only a part. There was also something hotter, something sharper, something more painful. His fingers cramped around his fork. How could Garland not feel resentment?

His daughter wiped her mouth and laid her crumpled napkin on the table. "The food was delicious."

She reached out to pat Muriel's hand.

Garland was in the living room watching a movie a short time later when his daughter came out of the kitchen, where she'd been helping her mother with the dishes. She set her wineglass on the coffee table and lowered herself onto the couch, adjacent to Garland's chair.

"What are you watching?" she said, tucking her dress beneath her knees.

"I'm not sure," Garland said, taking a moment to gaze at the screen. "I was watching something else, and then that ended and the movie came on . . ."

"What were you watching before?"

"I don't remember exactly," Garland said. "I wasn't watching, really, just glancing at the set off and on. The TV was just noise to keep me company while I read."

"What are you reading?"

Garland glanced in his lap. "Oh, a book."

His daughter peered at the cheap paperback cover. "What's it about?"

"Oh, it's complicated," Garland said. "Something . . . it takes place in Russia."

"I've been hearing a lot about Russia," his daughter said. "Crime syndicates and all that. Is your book . . . ?"

"My book?" Garland said. "Well, it's complicated. Maybe it has something to do with that."

"Maybe it'll make more sense later," she said.

"No, well, I've read it before," Garland said, regretting the words even as they left his mouth.

"It must be very good if you're reading it again," his daughter said.

"Yes, I suppose," Garland admitted, "if you're into that sort of thing."

Garland picked up the remote and turned on the news.

"Have you been following the elections?" he asked.

She shook her head.

"The playoffs?"

Not that either.

"This thing with the Russians?"

"Someone must have told me about the Russians," she said.

It was just as well. Garland didn't know how he would've followed up, had she answered any of these things affirmatively. Every word of it was fluff. After all this time, would they really let the entire evening pass without saying a single thing that mattered?

Garland leaned back in his recliner, looking to see if Muriel was still in the other room. When he saw that she was, he lowered his head, and in a quiet voice, he said, "It's just that none of this is what I expected."

As he hoped she might, his daughter nodded. Not by way of response, but merely, it seemed, to indicate she understood. "I thought you'd be happy."

The remote nearly sprang from his hand. "Oh no," he said. "That's not what I meant." But he wasn't sure how to explain what he was trying to say, what words to use that wouldn't give offense. He had been waiting for this day for more than seven years, and yet now that it had arrived, he was afraid he understood less than ever.

377

"Do you live together, you and your fiancé?" Garland said, and then he waved off the need for a reply, turning embarrassedly to face the television.

"We do," she said, but Garland shook his head, wanting to insist it didn't matter. He wasn't trying to be the protective father. He said, "It's just, you were always so . . ."

"Independent?"

Garland raised his finger, an exclamation point. "Tell me," he said after a moment's pause. "Your house—what's it like?"

His daughter crossed her legs and straightened her dress across her knees. "It's sort of . . . a loft," she said. "Wide open, big windows. In the heart of the city."

Over the years, not a day had gone by in which he hadn't thought about his daughter and wondered what she was doing, what her life might be like. Left to his own imagination, he'd pictured her living in all sorts of places: an old farmhouse, a cabin in the woods, a rundown warehouse, everything she owned secondhand or homemade. Wherever it was, the home he saw in his mind was full of bohemians and radicals who came barefoot to the table and ate with their hands from mismatched plates. Not once had he considered, not once imagined, that she might rise each morning to an alarm clock, engaged to a banker, that the warehouse might be one of those fashionable galleries of polished granite and steel. The people on those dramas Muriel loved lived in such places. They had wine fridges and espresso makers. He never would have guessed his own daughter even owned a TV.

Garland could never admit such a thing to Muriel, but he had always admired his daughter for having had the strength of character, even as a child, to do what she wished, what she believed in. So to hear now that for so long he'd been so mistaken saddened Garland more deeply than he could ever have thought. If she hadn't left her parents to pursue a life she felt they couldn't understand, then why had she left? Was it that she hated them? He knew he'd failed her, but could she really hate him that much?

Having tried out the sentence internally in several different ways, neither of which fully satisfied him, Garland finally turned to his daughter and asked, "Are you happy?"

The slightest bounce came into her knees.

"That was—I'm sorry. I'm sure you are," Garland said. But he wasn't sorry.

Looking almost apologetic herself, his daughter glanced at her shoes, light summer pumps. "I don't know. Sometimes . . . I don't know."

"Of course," Garland added. "I only meant . . ."

"That's okay . . ."

In silence they watched a commercial for laundry detergent, pretending to be entranced by a kick line of leggy bubbles.

When it was over, Garland turned back toward his daughter. "You haven't said what brought you to town."

Now she was tapping her shoe against the base of his chair. "Business . . ." she began, and then she seemed to decide against saying anything more.

Yoga business? Fine. She could have whatever reason she wished. Garland was so close right now, he could touch her.

"It's too bad," he said, "that Myles couldn't come with you."

His daughter smiled. "I think you would've liked each other."

It was a mistake, he knew, to study each word so carefully, but they were all he had, and it disappointed him to hear her say *you would have*, as if they had already missed the only chance they would ever get. Surely there would be another, even if Garland had to wait another seven years. He didn't dare ask if he would be invited to the wedding. The answer, he feared, would be more than he could bear.

"You'll be flying back out tomorrow?" he said. "Back to Portland?"

His daughter lifted her eyes, and then she paused and raised her wineglass, seeming to study the streaks of red. She held the glass so long before her mouth that Garland gave up on a response, which he understood now would only make him feel even sadder. It made no sense to him that his daughter had left them and remained in silence for so many years, only to return with blond hair, wearing a sundress covered in flowers.

His daughter was still staring at her wineglass. Garland thought he could see some sort of dread in her eyes, perhaps of the questions still to come, the ones Garland was still struggling to formulate. He felt sorry for her. He hadn't meant for this to become an inquisition, but there was still so much he didn't understand. Garland had been gathering questions throughout his daughter's life, as if in anticipation of this very moment. Finally the moment had arrived, and Garland saw he had only two options, for there could be no middle ground: either he must ask every one of the questions, no matter how naïve, no matter how egregiously they might reveal his failings as a father—and then accept the answers. His other option was to ask none at all.

Twenty-Eight

a forty percent chance of rain and on Wednesday a high in the seventies and a low of sixty dollars a barreling through the finish line to the delight of delegates from around the world meeting to discuss decreases in production and then it's not what Jesus Christ can do for you but what you can do for a ninety-eight mile-per-hour fastball and a slider that's been absolutely phenomenal improvements in breast augmentation during the last half hour I've been talking with a representative of everything that's misguided about their tour bus was attacked by hysterical fans and

Round the voices went with the radio dial. After a while, McGee found, they all started to sound the same. Same inflection, same modulation—male and female, it didn't matter. She'd come to regret every second of attention she paid them. She was encouraging their incompetence, these mindless mouthpieces who did nothing but read. And yet still her ears followed each voice as it went by, clinging to some vague hope that it might manage to say something important, something that mattered, something to take her mind off the wait.

She'd been in the parking garage for four hours. But those four hours had begun to feel like something more, like days at the bottom of a mine shaft. All she could see of the sky was the rough trapezoid framed between the descending ramp and the concrete headers hanging above. That sliver of sky had been blue when she arrived. Now it was black.

It was nine o'clock. For the last forty-five minutes, not a single person had arrived. No one had left. The elevator and the stairwell doors remained mute before her. The half-dozen cars still parked here were all luxurious compared to hers.

The truck was Michael Boni's. That the radio functioned at all was nothing short of a miracle. She'd spent the first hour sitting in silence. It wasn't just the six levels of cement above her head that made her assume she'd get no signal. Nothing in Michael Boni's truck looked as if it could possibly work. There was duct tape holding together the dashboard and the mirrors were missing and the windshield looked like it had caught a brick. One of the window cranks lay on the floor mats, and the tape deck was vomiting ribbon. On the radio itself there wasn't a single knob. What had Michael Boni done with them? What had he done to the truck? She couldn't dream up explanations for anywhere near this much wreckage. He was temperamental; she was aware of that. But if she'd realized before what a gift he had for destruction, would she still be here now?

The antenna was about the only thing on the truck that remained intact. Higher up on the dial there was country and pop and Motown and pop and country and pop and Christian and pop. Then back down again to the bottom for the news.

At least Michael Boni kept a pair of pliers in the cup holder. With them it was possible to turn the tuner stem. Possible, but not easy, and the longer she spent waiting, the harder it got. Her body had grown tired of sitting still. A restless twitch was running up and down the backs of both knees. She needed two hands to steady the jaws of the pliers, making the orange band lurch slowly ahead.

minimizing the threat of an attack by rogue nations already developing weapons of mass mailing and other fund-raising strategies that appeal to a higher power, and if that happens there's little question from a caller, go ahead caller, yes you're on the air

Followed by sports scores and oil prices again and weather, weather, and even more weather. Why all this mania for weather? Did it really matter, sixty-four degrees or sixty-eight? Were there oddsmakers taking bets on the probability of rain? And traffic! She'd been sitting here so long she could've mapped the flow in and around the city. At rush hour, cars had been jammed heading out of downtown. She'd been just about the only one coming in.

In the next aisle over, a reserved spot beside the elevator doors, was the shiny black Cadillac, the one Darius—before he'd abandoned them—had told her about. The car hadn't moved in four hours. She'd had all the time in the world to study the lines on the trunk, the tread on the tires, the numbers on the license plate, the way the overhead fluorescent lights puddled on the finish. That the old woman drove a Cadillac was something Darius had mentioned in passing, not knowing how the information might come to be useful. McGee hadn't known either, but she'd made a point of remembering.

None of this was what she'd expected.

and rain increasing interest rates another quarter of an hour we'll be talking with the head of the American Way, a think-tank with close ties and two losses leading into the play-offs but the team doctors say

Oh, what do they say? she wondered with extravagant indifference.

She was reaching out again for the pliers, to turn them once more, when she happened to notice, out of the corner of her eye, the light above the elevator door. It was moving.

McGee reached for the ignition, but she turned the key the wrong way. Instead of silencing the radio, she nearly started the engine, catching herself just as the few working dashboard lights flashed on.

She slipped out of the truck as the elevator doors were parting.

After four hours of waiting, everything suddenly seemed to be happening all at once, before she was ready.

Out of the elevator stepped a gray-haired woman with her head in her purse, searching for her keys.

"Mrs. Freeman? Ruth Freeman?"

The old woman stopped, lifting her head from the mouth of her bag. She didn't answer, but she stopped. And as she watched McGee come toward her, she seemed to tense. If McGee had been a man, she wondered, would the old woman have kept moving, instead?

It was strange seeing Mrs. Freeman like this, in the flesh. McGee had been obsessed with her for so long that she'd come to feel as though she actually knew her, as if they'd met a lifetime ago. All the arguments McGee had had in her head, it was as if Mrs. Freeman had been there, too, taking part.

"What is it?" Mrs. Freeman said.

The good thing about the radio, the distraction, was that it had kept McGee from rehearsing this moment over and over, deadening it, turning it rote. The problem was, now the moment itself had arrived, and McGee found she didn't know what to say.

Mrs. Freeman shifted her weight, coming one cautious step closer to her car. "Who are you?"

"I need you to come with me," McGee said. She tried not to think about how she must sound, how all this must look. A parking garage, of all places.

The old woman hitched the purse higher up on her shoulder. "I don't suppose this can wait until tomorrow?"

"I'm afraid not."

Mrs. Freeman had her keys clenched in her fist. McGee wondered what the old woman might be prepared to do. The elevator doors had already shut behind her. The elevator itself was rising back up into the building. The Cadillac was still several yards away.

McGee had never thought to wonder, What if she didn't come? What if she refused? What if she resisted somehow? What in the world was McGee going to do then? In the old woman's place, what would McGee have done?

"Is this an abduction?" Mrs. Freeman said.

"No."

McGee could hear the edges of the metal keys grinding against one another in the old woman's palm.

"I'd like to know what your intentions are," Mrs. Freeman said. "Is this about a ransom?"

"I don't want your money."

"No," Mrs. Freeman said, "I didn't think you would."

McGee realized she'd forgotten all about stuffing her hands in her pockets, pretending she was armed.

What a joke this must seem to the old woman. McGee had managed to summon more rage toward the radio than she could right now. Fearing she was losing her nerve, she took another step forward, not certain what she intended to do.

Mrs. Freeman didn't budge. The only thing on her that moved was her eyes, darting over McGee's shoulder. McGee let her own eyes turn in the same direction, and she instantly saw what the old lady had seen: the elevator was moving again. And she noticed something else, too: the security camera tucked up among the girders, aiming straight at her.

How had she not thought of that before?

"Give me the keys."

Mrs. Freeman released the ring without a struggle. On the back of the remote opener was a red panic button, untouched.

McGee took the old woman's hand and helped her into the back-seat. Then she circled around to the driver's side and slid in behind the wheel.

The engine came alive the instant she turned the key. The dash-board lit up like a cockpit.

The car glided backward, and just as McGee was about to throw it into drive and race up the ramp, the elevator doors parted.

Darius was already running when he appeared, as if he'd somehow known exactly what was happening, precisely where they would be. And maybe he did. Maybe his partner was at the other end of the camera, directing his every move.

Darius was on them in seconds, slamming one hand onto the hood of the car, his other reaching around toward his holster.

Four months ago McGee and Darius had been sitting together on a loading dock, smoking and staring at a distant light and fretting over failures and half-baked plans. And now, somehow, they'd arrived at this.

"Stop." Through the glass it sounded more like a plea than a command.

She let her foot off the brake, and the car crept forward. Darius crept backward, keeping pace. She did it again, and so did he. It was as if they were dancing. Maybe they would do it this way, then. In ten minutes or so, a few inches at a time, they would reach the street. But by then, of course, the cops would already be here. Something told her they'd move more quickly for Mrs. Freeman than they bothered to for anyone else in the city.

"Just stop it already," the old woman yelled from the backseat.

The next thing McGee knew, the window behind her was rolling down. She reached for the buttons on the door panel, trying to figure out which one to press. But it was too late.

Mrs. Freeman poked her head out through the opening. "It's okay, Darius," she said. "There's no need for anyone to get hurt."

Hurt. There was another thing McGee had never considered. Raising her eyes from the window buttons to the windshield, she discovered Darius had pulled his gun.

And she was surprised, unpleasantly, by how steadily he held his aim.

"Let us go," Mrs. Freeman said. "Let us go."

When Darius looked at the old woman, his gun drifted slightly, shifting from McGee's heart to her shoulder.

"I can't—" he said. "I can't—"

"It's just business," Mrs. Freeman said. "I'll be fine."

All the while, McGee said nothing, clenching the steering wheel at ten and two. It was strange watching the two of them negotiate this without her, as if she were merely the chauffeur. Everything about this had turned ridiculous. Everything gone exactly wrong. And yet McGee could also see she was about to get out of here, and with Mrs. Freeman.

"Please," Mrs. Freeman said, "let us through."

Darius stepped aside slowly, reluctantly, standing there with his gun in his hand as the car jerked forward.

When they passed, McGee met his eyes. After all that, he didn't look angry. It was something else. An expression she felt familiar with, though she wasn't accustomed to seeing it on him: pity. He felt just as sorry for her as she did for him.

And there was something else she was aware of as they left Darius behind: he knew exactly where they were going. He'd seen Michael Boni's map. The question his eyes had refused to answer was, would he tell?

There was no traffic out on the street, almost no one on the sidewalks. But the lights were on at the stadiums. Along the curb, the sewers were blowing steam. It had grown chilly, just as every meteorologist within broadcast range had predicted.

They headed north.

"It was you, wasn't it?" Mrs. Freeman said from the backseat as her building shrank in the rearview mirror. "You're the one who broke in."

McGee curled her fingers around the wheel. The most important thing was to maintain control.

"They showed me your picture," the old woman said. "They showed me all of them."

"I've seen your picture, too."

When she looked back, Mrs. Freeman had disappeared from the mirror. McGee spun around, nearly pulling the car into the curb.

The old woman had ducked, searching for her belt buckle.

"Jesus Christ," McGee said, heart surging from her chest.

"Where did you think I went?"

They drove the next few blocks in silence, coming to a stop at a red light.

"What were you looking for?" Mrs. Freeman said. "Evidence of all my crimes? Lord knows it's not hard to find."

"You sure went to a lot of trouble to hide it."

Mrs. Freeman shrugged. "Maybe you were just looking in the wrong place."

"And where should we have looked?"

Mrs. Freeman turned toward the window. They'd left the business district behind, cruising now past blocks of empty storefronts, weedy lots.

"Anywhere," Mrs. Freeman said, gazing beyond the glass. "Everywhere."

"You take credit for all this?" McGee said. "You must think an awful lot of your little company."

Mrs. Freeman turned back toward the front. "Isn't that what *you* think?"

"I'm not that naïve."

"Anyway," Mrs. Freeman said, returning her attention to the view outside, "who said I was talking about the company?"

McGee once again felt a danger of the old woman slipping away from her. She had to stay focused, keep track of the timeline in her head.

The roads all around them were getting darker now, streetlights growing scarce.

"You think we're enemies," Mrs. Freeman said.

Michael Boni had suggested gagging her. Maybe the idea hadn't been so ridiculous after all.

★　★　★

It was ten minutes before ten. McGee had texted Michael Boni to let him know they'd arrived. She'd brought the car to a stop in a far, dark corner of the parking lot, concealed from the road. The building before them was just shapes and shadows, and high up above, as if floating in place, there was a small blinking red light.

"We're waiting," Mrs. Freeman said. "Why are we waiting?" Her voice was as calm and measured as it had been from the start.

McGee felt calm herself, particularly now that the car was still, the engine off, its various clickings and clackings having finally ceased. Even on the city's crumbling roads, the old woman's car had ridden as smooth as a speedboat. Now that they were here, the snug, silent interior made it easy to forget why.

"Could you turn on the radio?" Mrs. Freeman said. "I wouldn't mind some music."

McGee turned the key halfway. Anything would be better than talking. But when she tried to make sense of all the buttons and knobs, she discovered it was the most complicated console she'd ever seen. Unlike Michael Boni's, though, at least everything here was still in one piece.

"Upper left," Ruth Freeman said.

A moment later the old woman added, "Just push it in."

they care more about fish and turtles than they do about their country. More taxes, more regulations. I say, fine. Next time they need a job, let them ask the fishes

"Maybe we should listen to something else," the old woman said. And then after a brief silence, "Lower right."

McGee pressed a button, and on came the moans of a cello.

Mrs. Freeman's chest rose and fell, and a slim, relieved smile came into her face. "Do you like classical?"

It was Elgar. The concerto in E minor. McGee remembered a kid at camp, fourteen years old, who'd played it. Not well, but still. More than she could ever do. The music seemed fitting, here among the ruins of an abandoned parking lot, as if old man Elgar had had precisely this place in mind, a lament for this particular lost city.

"Not really." In the rearview mirror, McGee could see Mrs. Freeman squinting into the darkness, trying to make out where they were.

"We've never met before, have we?" the old woman said.

"We've never met," McGee said. "But I know you very well."

"Do you?" Mrs. Freeman took another slow, deep breath, and a fog spread across the window. "I suppose you do."

There was a pause, and McGee wondered if the old woman was busy contemplating the loss of all her secrets.

"In that case," Mrs. Freeman finally said, "I wonder if you might tell me something about yourself?"

"I don't think so."

The old woman sighed. "It would make this easier."

"What makes you think I want this to be easy?"

The old woman pursed her lips. "My husband will be annoyed," she said. "I was supposed to meet him for dinner after the symphony."

"Tragic."

"What you kids today call a 'first-world problem,'" Mrs. Freeman said. "Maybe a little disappointment will be good for him."

"Maybe it'll be good for you, too."

It was so overcast, there were barely even shadows outside. McGee couldn't remember ever seeing a darkness so thick and impenetrable.

"Are you married?" Mrs. Freeman said.

McGee didn't even bother glancing in the mirror.

"What about the others who were with you before?" Mrs. Freeman said. "Your friends?"

McGee turned to look out her side window.

"Where are they now?"

"Maybe they're out there," McGee said, waving her hand toward the darkness.

The old woman seemed to think about that for a moment. "I don't think so."

"What makes you think you have any idea?"

Mrs. Freeman leaned back. "You just seem like someone who's very much alone."

"I couldn't do this alone," McGee said, allowing herself a satisfied smirk at the car and her captive.

"There are different ways of being alone," Mrs. Freeman said.

"You want to analyze someone," McGee said, "analyze yourself. Maybe you should be thinking about what's wrong with you."

"If you were to ask my husband—"

"I'm not asking him," McGee said. "I'm asking you. What's your excuse for the things you do?"

"I suppose it's the same as yours. As everyone's."

"And what might that be?"

"Fear, first," Mrs. Freeman said. "And then, much later, regret."

"I'm not afraid," McGee said. The old woman was simply trying to weaken her, to make it seem like they were the same—two people sharing a sinking ship lost at sea. But really Mrs. Freeman was the captain, commandeering the only dinghy in order to save herself.

It was three minutes to ten. McGee searched among the posts sticking out of the steering column until she found the right one. With a twist, she turned on the headlights. And then the high beams. And for good measure, the fog lamps, too, illuminating the ugly hulk of a building in front of them. The lot was ringed with sodium lights, but they'd all been turned off. Every last loss had been cut. All except for the blinking red light, which marked the place like a hazardous shoal.

McGee pointed to the factory across the immense parking lot, the compressors and all the equipment now on its way to China. "Do you know where we are?"

"Of course," Ruth Freeman said. "It's ours."

"It was." McGee reached for her duffel bag. Inside were a few changes of clothes, her keepsakes, the little money she'd saved. She took out the cell phone Michael Boni had given her. Now she handed it to Mrs. Freeman.

"It's already dialed."

Mrs. Freeman looked at the phone and then at the building. "It doesn't matter," she said. "You know that, right? It's a write-off. An insurance claim."

"To you, maybe."

Mrs. Freeman set the phone down in her lap. "What if I refuse?"

McGee tucked her hair up under her hat. "You won't."

"And what about you?" Mrs. Freeman said. "Your life in exchange for a building?"

McGee shrugged.

Mrs. Freeman settled back into her seat. "I think it's a poor trade."

"I didn't ask."

"If it were up to me—"

"It's not."

"I'd leave it as it is," Mrs. Freeman said.

McGee offered a nod of exaggerated surprise. "I'm sure you would."

Mrs. Freeman gazed into the darkness still outside her window, at whatever else was out there. "This is what the world will look like after we're gone."

McGee shook her head. "That's one theory."

Mrs. Freeman had the look on her face of someone not accustomed to being contradicted. "Do you have another?"

"I don't believe in theories," McGee said. "Maybe I don't have your imagination."

"You're a doer," Mrs. Freeman said, "not a thinker?"

"When I was twelve," McGee said, "I destroyed the tree house my parents built."

Mrs. Freeman blinked at her uncertainly.

"I've never felt as much clarity as I did then."

The old woman raised her eyes, staring at the factory. "I tried to save it," she said. "I really did."

For the first time all evening, she looked as though she'd made a move without first plotting her defense.

"But I was too late," Mrs. Freeman said. "Years and years too late."

McGee realized a new piece had come on the radio, something she didn't recognize. "I told you something about myself," she said. "What about you?"

The old woman raised her hands, and for a long moment she studied them, the wrinkles and spots and burgundy old-lady nail polish. And then she lowered them again, folding her hands on top of the phone in her lap.

"I've never had a cigar."

McGee reached into her duffel bag and took out her cigarettes. She handed one into the backseat. "It's the best I can do."

Mrs. Freeman took the cigarette between her fingers. They were shaking more than they had before. "This must be important to you," she said. "I don't believe I'd have your courage."

McGee stretched out her arm and picked up the phone and placed it back in the old woman's palm. "Here's your chance."

Mrs. Freeman lifted her eyes, once again looking off across the parking lot. She put the cigarette between her lips. "How about a light?"

At first there was only one small explosion, a cloud of smoke and dust that enveloped the factory almost all the way up to the top of the smokestack.

McGee feared something had gone wrong.

But then the second explosion followed the first, and almost in slow motion, an enormous brick wall folded in on itself. Then came the third and the fourth and the fifth explosions, and even the red light on top of the chimney flickered out in the thick black haze. On the roof and on the hood and on the windshield of the car, bits of debris rained down like hail. Within moments, they could no longer see through the glass. In the backseat of the car, phone cradled in her hand, the old woman sat openmouthed, awestruck. The cigarette dangled between her lips, continuing to burn.

McGee opened the door and got out. Now fade away.

Twenty-Nine

THE DOG APPEARED one afternoon, uninvited, walking in the open front door and settling down beside the mattress. It didn't bark, didn't sniff, didn't explore. Went right ahead and made itself at home. It looked a bit like a corgi, squat with little legs. Dobbs couldn't imagine how such a ridiculous animal could have made it out there in the wild.

Inside the house, Dobbs had been making do with whatever Clementine brought him. Which on the day the dog arrived turned out to be a sack of broccoli and a couple of eggs.

"He's cute," Clementine said.

But he was also filthy.

Dobbs groaned himself into a sitting position. "Where'd the eggs come from?"

Clementine shrugged. "May-May's neighbor." She lifted the eggs out of the sack and set them up in a wobbly row on the table. "He went somewhere, I guess. Left a bunch of chickens."

She had a small knife in the bag, too. Through his swollen eyes, he watched her cut thick slices of cucumber. "Lean back," she said.

She arranged the cool cucumbers on his lids, not quite as gently as he would have liked.

"Feel better?"

"Better than nothing."

Clementine had been the one to find him after Mike and Tim left him here, bloodied, huddled up in a ball. Not for dead. Not yet. She'd risked another grounding, she'd pointed out, saving his life.

"I'm not sure it's worth the risk," he'd said.

That was two days ago. The cuts were no longer raw, but his ribs still hurt when he coughed.

He didn't blame Mike and Tim for what they'd done. He'd known it was coming. Everything had finally caught up with him.

"Give him an egg," Dobbs said, pointing blindly toward where he thought the dog might be.

"Do you have a bowl?"

"There's a pot," Dobbs said, waving his arm vaguely, "somewhere."

Clementine got up, and he could hear her feet dragging across the dirty floorboards. It wasn't a long search. The pot was probably the only object in what was left of the kitchen.

He heard the crack of the shell, and he peeled back the cucumbers on one eye. The yolk was like a bright orange sun. Three laps of the dog's tongue, and the egg was gone.

Clementine had gathered a small pile of sticks for him on one of her previous visits, complaining the whole time that he was crazy. "What are you going to do with these?"

"It's a surprise," he'd said.

He kept his knife and his finished pieces under the mattress. In addition to the pencil, he'd carved a tiny pool cue and an arrow.

After she left today and the cucumber slices lost their cool, Dobbs took out his knife. The dog lifted its head and snuffled back down again.

For the last day Dobbs had been working to duplicate his own index finger, one line and wrinkle at a time.

When Clementine returned a couple of hours later, Dobbs had his work stowed back away.

She'd brought another cucumber. "Ready for more?"

She was a good nurse, calm and dependable. He wished he had something more to leave her.

Dobbs dreamed he was on a cliff overlooking an ocean. Or maybe it was a lake. The horizon was far away. The sky was burning to the west. The trees were reverential, bowing out over the water. The rocky ledge looked as though it had just been cleansed with rain.

In each of his outstretched arms, Dobbs held an ankle, a man dangling over the ledge. Below the man's head washed the boulder-studded surf.

The man hovered there, still and peaceful, arms folded across his chest. His face was as smooth as polished granite. He was whistling quietly, a little tune that reminded Dobbs of carousels.

Dobbs felt no strain, despite the man's weight, despite the pull of gravity. Where did he get such strength? He could have held the man for hours. For days. Forever.

Instead, he let go.

It was dark when he awoke. The dog was curled up under the table on a pile of dirty clothes.

Over the last few days, the air had turned genuinely cold. They were into October now. Dobbs could sense the snow up there somewhere, preparing to fall. Wrapped up in his sleeping bag, he remembered his grandfather's wood-burning stove, squatting before the cast-iron door, feeding logs into the belly and then crawling into the bunk and waiting for the yellow roar.

And then he saw himself at dawn in a thick down coat, stepping out into the snow, the plume of breath as he raised his grandfather's ax and brought it back down, two perfect halves of split red oak tumbling off the stump.

Then, in Dobbs's dream, there was a sudden explosion, one so big, so loud, it rocked the house.

But he wasn't actually sleeping; the dog's claws cut Dobbs's cheek as it scampered away to safety.

That night's demolition, the fourth, was the biggest one of all. An old assembly plant, this time, shooting up like a fireworks display.

Or so the newspaper said. The next afternoon Constance sent Clementine over with a copy. The girl dropped the paper onto his chest and got down on her knees to play with the dog.

The story Dobbs read was like something out of his dreams. But here all the shadowy figures had faces. One of them belonged to McGee. There was a mug shot from the previous spring, her wide eyes cold and sleepy. This couldn't have been the effect the paper was going for, but she looked like a child, incapable of doing the things she was said to have done.

Dobbs had been unprepared to read the allegations they printed about her—the various crimes and conspiracies—but he had little trouble believing them. And even though he couldn't have said why, exactly, they even made him happy, as if the crazy things she was willing to do made his own pale in comparison.

McGee's wasn't the only picture in the newspaper. There was also one of a man, a Hispanic man, middle-aged. Dobbs vaguely thought he recognized him.

There was no mention of McGee's other friends. The only other person referred to by name was Ruth Freeman, a gray-haired lady who appeared in a portrait, far more distinguished than the other two. She was an executive, abducted from her parking garage. And she had been there, she said, to watch McGee make the call that turned the old assembly plant to dust. The building had belonged to the woman's company.

"It was harrowing," the executive was reported to have said. But she'd survived without a scratch.

It seemed McGee and Michael Boni had gotten away, but no one expected them to get far.

Asked to speculate about why they'd done what they'd done, Ruth Freeman said, "I can't imagine. I really can't."

But Dobbs could. All this time he'd had the sense he and McGee had been orbiting the same thing, but on different, intersecting paths.

It was quiet in the restaurant when Constance opened the door. There were none of the usual smells. No bread, no stew. Something about the place *looked* different, too. But what? Same battered furniture, same haphazard decor.

At the sight of his face, Constance winced. "I'll put on some coffee," she said, vanishing into the kitchen.

Dobbs took a seat in the knotty pine booth. The country grain made him think of crudely shaped mallards, of lakes far from the likes of Sergio.

Constance came out to join him, two cups and a pot on her tray. "They sure did a number on you."

She seemed to be in no hurry to pour, so Dobbs filled the cups himself. "It doesn't hurt any more when I breathe."

"What were you thinking?" she said. "This foolish business of yours . . ."

He shrugged. "I figured it was like swimming in cold water—you've just got to jump straight in."

"Stupid," she said.

"Maybe I should've just grown a garden."

"Where do they come from?" she said.

He realized now what it was that seemed different: the dining room was brighter. Constance had managed to get some of those light fixtures hung. Now he could see all the spots where the new paint didn't quite cover the old.

"Do you have any of that bread?"

"Where do they come from?" she said again.

"They're just trying to survive," he said, "like everyone else."

"What do they do once they're here?"

"Does it matter?"

"I live here," Constance said.

"You could bring a thousand people every day," Dobbs said. "The city would still be empty."

"I want to see them."

"They pay to come," he said. "They want to come."

"Now they're here," she said, "you're sleeping soundly?"

"Look at me," Dobbs said, framing his broken face for her.

"If you don't take me," Constance said, her gaze unwavering, "Clementine will."

The buses had stopped running hours before, but it was a mild night, and there was a bright haze in the sky. The moon was like a lamp with a thin paper shade.

Constance followed him with a vigilance he'd never seen on her before. As she walked, she seemed to study each passing house, each vacant building, as if all of it were newly suspicious, as if somehow he'd tainted everything.

Since they'd started out from the restaurant, he'd felt more awake than he had in a long time. Longer than he could remember.

The warehouse door was locked. Dobbs knocked, and in response there was only silence.

"It's me," he said. That brought a stirring, what sounded like chair legs sliding across concrete.

A thick arm wrapped in flames held open the door just wide enough for Dobbs to see through.

"What do you want?" Mike said.

Dobbs could make out the shape of Tim sitting at the card table. Neither of them was smoking, but Dobbs could smell their cigarettes. The water and sewerage van was parked in the garage next to Mike and Tim's gray pickup truck. Sergio was nowhere in sight.

Dobbs put his hand on the knob, but Mike held it in place.

Across the garage, Tim's cell phone screen flashed yellowish green and then went dark. A message sent to Sergio.

Dobbs turned back around, but Constance wouldn't meet his eye. She was looking past him, into the gap, trying to make out what lay beyond. The door started to close.

Dobbs felt his shoulder buckle on impact. But the door swung back open, and he stumbled in. Mike looked down on him in surprise as Dobbs slid to the floor, his shoulder a spiraling kaleidoscope of pain.

Both men were on him in an instant, but Mike was first, propping his boot on Dobbs's head, pinning it in place. As if Dobbs had some-where to go.

For good measure, they drew their guns, too, and they were so distracted, trying to decide whether to shoot him then and there or wait for Sergio, that they didn't notice Constance come inside. Not until she stood beside them did Tim finally catch her shadow out of the corner of his eye.

"Who the fuck is she?" he said, shaking his gun in Dobbs's face.

Though it felt like his ear was tearing against the cracked concrete, Dobbs tried to turn his head to see into the far room, where everyone—he hoped—was sleeping. But his eyes were going dim.

As she adjusted to the darkness, Constance noticed another room beyond the garage, a large space crammed with mattresses. There must have been a hundred, probably more. And here and there she saw movement, bodies large and small. Some of them appeared to be asleep. But it was hard to tell which lumps were people and which were bags and clothes. Along the far wall, in the faint moonlight, there was a silhouette resembling a woman with a baby at her breast.

Constance said, "I'm the one that's going to feed them."

Winter

Epilogue

THE VILLAGE WAS only two hundred miles from Mexico City, but to get there took eight hours on four different buses. With each transfer, the towns grew smaller. Each vehicle was worse than the last. The fourth and final bus was a metal skeleton stripped of anything soft—unpadded seats on unpaved roads. The windows were open to let in the breeze.

On that final stretch, all the other passengers were locals, peasants hefting cardboard suitcases secured with string. A few had even brought chickens, tough old birds, indifferent to the bumps. They were wiry and dusty and of no particular breed he could identify. Scavengers, able to survive anything.

Most of the time the bus seemed to be climbing uphill. But by the end of the trip, Michael Boni discovered he'd reached the coast after all.

Late in the afternoon, the bus dropped him off alone by the village square, a pale slab of cement sterilized by the sun. The place was empty; it looked as if it had always been empty. Adjacent to the square was the intersection where the town's two roads met. One of them was the road he'd come in on. Finding no one to ask for directions, Michael Boni picked up his bag and started up the other street, following the dense, heady smell of the ocean.

The road was wide and vacant, lined with brightly painted concrete walls. Over the top of the walls spilled the occasional spindly vine and the arm of a dusty tree. At regular intervals, the walls gave way to iron gates. Beyond the gates Michael Boni caught glimpses of private courtyards. A few potted plants, a leaning broom, a cracked, faded chair.

"A sleepy seaside town" was what the guidebook had called it. The book was ten years out of date, the entire entry only a paragraph long. But Michael Boni had liked the idea of a place that could be so easily summarized, containing only the barest essentials.

Up ahead the road rose slightly and then crested. At the top of the hill, a second-story balcony stood out against the blue sky. He saw something moving up there, somebody swinging almost imperceptibly in a hammock. The sign on the facade said HOTEL.

Michael Boni stopped in the shade of an open doorway and rested for a moment. He'd had no idea it could be so hot, especially in mid-December.

The guidebook had claimed there was only one hotel in town, a fact that didn't seem to have changed in the years since it was written. The town was too remote for foreign tourists, for anyone not looking to get away from everything.

The dining room was an open patio separated from the sidewalk by a low plastic fence. Even with the breeze pushing through, a sour perfume of fried fish hung in the air. Through the doorway into the kitchen, he saw a stooped old woman and a girl with long dark hair standing at a table, chopping tomatoes and onions. The older of the two saw Michael Boni and came out to greet him.

At first the old woman didn't seem to understand he spoke no

Spanish. The problem had been following him across the country-side. No one seemed to know what to make of a Mexican gringo.

But what he wanted now was easy enough to convey. The old woman pointed to a sign above the bar listing rates. There were two prices; the second floor, with its view of the ocean, was twice as much as the first. Michael Boni didn't need to count his pesos to know which one he could afford.

The woman called to the girl in the kitchen, Marisol. Marisol appeared at once, pausing only to brush a few loose strands of hair from her eyes. He thought he saw her smile, as if she recognized him.

"*Bienvenido.*"

The words, appearing out of nowhere, sounded like a name: Ben Venida, garbled in Texas drawl. Michael Boni turned to find the source striding toward him down the corridor. The man was dressed in khaki cargo shorts and a white linen shirt. Fit and tanned, with tousled, sandy blond hair. A shark's tooth dangled from a leather lace around his neck.

"*Me llamo* Shim," the man said. He took Michael Boni's hand as if he were bestowing a prize. "*Y usted?*"

"I don't speak Spanish," Michael Boni said.

"No kidding!" Shim looked delighted. "It's nice to see a fellow countryman." Shim motioned toward the empty street and the empty restaurant. "I was beginning to wonder if there's some sort of plague here no one told me about." His smile framed rows of bleached white teeth. "Well, people don't know what they're missing."

Michael Boni nodded, turning away.

"The *señora* will take good care of you," Shim said, aiming a grin at the old woman, who in turn regarded him with a complete absence of expression.

The girl leaned over one of the tables, wiping a circle on the plastic tablecloth.

Shim pointed to Michael Boni's lone bag. "Traveling solo?"

He nodded.

"Too bad," Shim said. "Such a romantic spot. The sunsets are beautiful."

Shim was constantly moving. In an instant, he was behind the bar. "You pour your own here." As Shim lifted a bottle from the shelf, the señora clenched the towel draped over her shoulder, narrowing her eyes.

Shim hoisted his glass. "Let me buy you a drink."

Michael Boni picked up his bag. "Maybe later." The señora was moving down the corridor, and he started after her, happy to have an excuse to get away.

When they reached his room, the señora opened the door with a bump of her hip. With a few waves of her hand, she revealed the room's amenities: a shower stall without a curtain, a bureau with one drawer, the switch for the ceiling fan. The only decoration was a ceramic crucifix nailed to the wall.

They were in the bathroom, the señora pantomiming how to use the electric shower, when footsteps paused outside his door. Michael Boni heard the slap of bare feet going up the concrete stairs.

Michael Boni unpacked and washed the dust from his face. When he passed through the restaurant on his way to the street a few minutes later, the dining room was once again empty. The street was empty, too.

A familiar voice called out from above. "Change your mind about that drink?" Propped up on the hammock, Shim once again raised his glass.

"Later," Michael Boni said.

Shim smiled and set the glass on his chest. "Don't think I'll stop asking."

The beach was a block from the hotel. There Michael Boni saw just how unvisited the village truly was. By the water's edge, two lone children were playing, forming and crushing mounds of wet sand. Beyond the tide line, their parents were shaking out their belongings and cramming them into a large knit bag.

The beach was at least a mile long, far larger than the village itself. At the top of the dune, a boardwalk stretched a few hundred feet in each direction. Directly in the middle lay a stack of folded wooden beach chairs and a concession stand. Inside, an old woman was closing the shutters. A boy approached carrying more chairs up from the beach. Down by the water, an old man in rolled pants secured the last of the umbrella canopies.

Michael Boni headed north, and when the boardwalk ended, he continued along the dune. Soon the entire village was behind him. He sat in the sand and watched the ocean for a while, hypnotized by the waves. A breeze crept inland. The air had quickly turned cool. He untied his boots. The stain and varnish on the leather assumed a new brilliance against the sand. He dug his feet in, feeling the day's heat buried like the coals of a dying fire.

The sun was setting into the ocean. Birds were singing in the trees along the shoreline, little black birds with streaks of yellow on their wings. Michael Boni thought of Priscilla, how happy she must be. Now she had the entire house to destroy, all by herself. And for the chicks, there was the garage and the yard and Clementine to watch them and all the garden scraps they could eat.

He wondered if any of them would even notice he was gone.

In the restaurant that night, the patrons were villagers, dressed in well-worn jeans and faded slacks. Shim had left his perch on the balcony. Michael Boni selected for himself an empty table by the side-walk. No one seemed to notice him.

A loud, boisterous group had gathered in the far corner. In the center sat a heavy-set man in a wide-brimmed straw hat, face and arms a ruddy brown. He looked as though he'd just come in from the fields. The others listened, occasionally laughing, as the man told a story. Michael Boni could make out only some of the words, not enough to follow along.

After a few minutes, Marisol came over and wiped off the tablecloth.

"How are you?" she said in halting English, smiling down at him.

"Okay."

"You are from the United States?" When Michael Boni didn't answer, she said, "I have a cousin in the United States."

Michael Boni nodded, reaching for his water glass.

"I want to go to the United States someday."

"Is this from a bottle?" he said.

Marisol took the glass and gazed at it a moment.

"I want to go to New York City," she said. "Or maybe Los Angeles. I want to make clothes." Still holding the glass, Marisol stepped back from the table and turned to the side. "You see?" she said. "I make this."

A plain blue dress with a sort of gold brocade sash at the waist.

"It's nice," Michael Boni said.

"Are you from New York City?" She extracted a laminated menu from under her arm.

"No."

"I return." And she and his water glass disappeared into the kitchen.

He knew enough to be able to make his way through the menu. The names were familiar, but there was no pozole. The specialty here seemed to be fish. He wondered if that was what these people were, these locals—fishermen.

In a minute, Marisol was back, the water glass she set down in front of him identical to the one she'd taken away.

"Yes?" she said.

Michael Boni pointed to the *taquitos,* the cheapest item on the menu.

"Oh, no, no, no," Marisol patted his arm and took his menu. "I bring you something better."

"That's okay," he said, trying to stop her before she walked away.

"Okay!" she said happily.

She came back fifteen minutes later with an enormous platter, an entire fish, a red snapper, head and all, buried in mounds of tomatoes and olives and capers and chiles.

"Better?" she said, grinning.

He stared at the melted, milky white eyes of the fish, feeling suddenly nostalgic for vegetable stew.

After a dinner he barely touched, Michael Boni returned to the beach.

From the top of the dune, he looked down to find that the tide had nearly reached the line of umbrellas in the sand. The canvas canopies rustled in the breeze, the moon lighting them from behind, outlining them in pale yellow flames.

Unspoiled. Untouched. No wonder his grandmother had been so miserable in Detroit. How could she be expected to forget what she'd traded in? How could anyone? He wondered what Marisol imagined when she pictured New York. Skyscrapers and window displays and theater marquees. The same fantasy world as Darius.

From a block away, he could make out the vague thump of some kind of music. All that was left after the breeze were the bass notes, thick and indistinct. They could have been coming from anywhere. But where else was there other than the hotel? And somehow he knew that Shim was responsible.

The moment he reached the patio, Michael Boni saw him, swaying among the tables with a plastic rose between his teeth. Mariachi burst from a small tape deck lying next to a bottle of tequila on the bar. Shim was performing as if the entire village were his audience, but he was alone. The dining room was empty.

"Hey!" Shim shouted, reaching for Michael Boni's arm.

In the kitchen, Marisol and the señora were pretending not to watch.

"Come on," Shim said. "You're on vacation. Dancing is good for you."

Michael Boni pulled away.

"Let me buy you a drink." Shim dipped his invisible partner. "You need a drink. You need to loosen up. I thought you came here to relax."

Michael Boni went over to the bar and snapped off the tape deck.

Shim threw up his hands in disgust. "No wonder nobody comes here."

Through the window, Michael Boni saw Marisol and the señora return to the dirty dishes.

"Don't forget that drink!" Shim shouted as Michael Boni hurried away.

The sky the next morning was an unimaginative shade of blue, as monochromatic and depthless as if sprayed by machine.

Coming down the hillside on the final bus the day before, Michael Boni had caught his first glimpses of the ocean—the first ocean he'd ever seen. Even then, from that distance, the water hadn't seemed quite real. People were always talking about the sight, but once he arrived, he realized how much more there was to it than that. There was the way the salt air gathered in his head and lingered there like alcohol. There was the ripe, living smell. He remembered once as a child going to the shore up near Port Huron with his family, but the sand there was gray and rocky, like standing on gravel. He'd never cared for the idea of things floating around down there that he couldn't see.

All that day, there was no sign of Shim at the hotel. Not once had Michael Boni seen him on the beach.

Was it too much to hope that Shim was already gone for good?

That night in the restaurant, Marisol was gone, too. She must have been given the day off. Michael Boni took the same table as on the night before. Eventually the señora came over and nodded wordlessly that it was time for him to order. When he pointed to the taquitos, she grunted and turned back toward the kitchen.

Michael Boni glanced around the restaurant. The heavy-set, sunburned man from the night before was back. It appeared he had a regular table, too. And much of the same crowd was once again surrounding him.

While he ate, Michael Boni observed the lighted doorways along the street, where shadows came and went. A couple of old men had set up folding chairs on the sidewalk. There was a café of sorts at the corner, where a half-dozen people sat in a circle, talking. When the breeze died down, he could faintly hear their voices.

He wished he had the language to ask the señora about the village. She reminded him a bit of his grandmother, the skeptical way she had of looking at him. He wished he could ask her what it was like to call a place like this home.

That night Michael Boni went for another walk along the beach. Perhaps a quarter-mile south of the boardwalk, he came across a pavilion set back in the trees beyond the dune. As he passed, he saw a band setting up inside. The dance floor was flooded with light, and perhaps two dozen teenagers sat at the tables along the walls. Outside in the shadows, several couples clung to one another on concrete benches. One of the young women sat facing him, her eyes closed as a young man in red pants pressed his mouth to hers. Michael Boni recognized Marisol's blue dress, the dark braid draped over one shoulder.

413

He was glad to see her in someone's arms, glad she might still have reason to stay.

§

Past the plaza where the bus had dropped him off, the road turned north. It was the morning of his third day, and this was the only direction, the only road, Michael Boni hadn't already explored.

He had only just begun down the road when the paving stones changed to gravel. He guessed he'd reached the edge of the village. But then he noticed the narrow street twisted a short distance farther, and up ahead he saw some sort of structure—he couldn't tell what it was—sitting atop a low hill.

Coming closer, Michael Boni saw several more such structures. A half-dozen concrete foundations filled with sand lined both sides of the unfinished road. It looked as if someone had planned some sort of development here and then changed his mind. Where the gravel ended, two hundred feet farther, there was a shell of what looked like a home. No doors or windows, just walls with holes where the doors and windows should have been.

On the edge of one of the foundations, in the shade of a large canopied tree, sat Shim, a camera and a notebook in his lap. At first Michael Boni thought he was drawing something, perhaps the grass growing upon the dune. But Shim wasn't looking at any one particular spot, and he quickly went through page after page in his notebook. Occasionally he would get up and snap a picture of something Michael Boni found not particularly interesting: a patch of ground, a tree. Several minutes passed before he noticed the surveyor's level Shim had set up on a tripod.

That evening, as Michael Boni lay on his bed, absorbing the faint breeze of his ceiling fan, there was a knock on the door.

"I'm buying you dinner," Shim said, smiling in the corridor.

Michael Boni found himself unprepared to think of a single excuse.

There was a crowd in the restaurant. The heavy-set, sunburned man and his circle of friends appeared to be celebrating. There were toasts and cheers. Michael Boni was grateful for the noise. Maybe now he and Shim could sit through a meal without having to talk.

Shim chose a table directly in the middle of the dining room. Before sitting down, he walked from table to table greeting the other diners. He seemed to know them all by name, and they seemed glad to see him.

After Shim was finally seated, Marisol approached with the menus.

"She's a beauty, isn't she?" Shim said as she walked away.

Michael Boni didn't like the way Shim looked at her. "She's a nice girl." Young enough to be Shim's daughter.

While they waited for their food, Shim took Michael Boni along on a guided tour of his Mexican escapades: the scuba diving in hidden reefs, the illegal deep-sea fishing, the most obscure tequila, the cleanest beaches, the most beautiful women. He'd catalogued it all. Every last cliché.

The nice thing about Shim was that once he started talking, he never stopped. Michael Boni could simply sit and let it wash over him. It didn't matter that he contributed nothing.

By the time Marisol brought their food, there was almost no one left in the restaurant.

Shim had ordered the snapper, and he eyed the plate in much the same way he'd eyed the girl.

"Do you know what it is?" he said, lifting his first forkful of rice.

Michael Boni turned away from the opaque, buttery eyes.

"The stuff you saw me photographing," Shim said. "Do you know what it is?"

Michael Boni took a bite of his taquito.

"They were supposed to be rentals." Shim leaned back in his chair. "But the company that built them didn't have the capital. They didn't take any of the necessary precautions. Not to mention they were careless about the people they hired. They ran out of money, they lost support. But where one man fails," he said cheerfully, "another succeeds. I mean, think of the possibilities: real hotels, real restaurants. A real resort. Pure. Pristine."

"Just what the world needs," Michael Boni said.

Shim shook the last drops of beer from the bottle. "I don't know about the world," he said, "but it's what *they* want." He nodded toward the window into the kitchen.

Michael Boni saw the heavy-set, sunburned man in there talking to the señora.

"Have you met the mayor?" Shim asked. "The hotel's his. The señora's his wife. He's the one that invited me here. I was skeptical at first, but he convinced me. The entire town wants it. This place is just wasting away."

"I like it the way it is," Michael Boni said.

"I think they might know a little more about it than you do."

Michael Boni set down his fork. "What do you know about me?"

"*Amigo*," Shim said, rising from the table, "it's time for that drink I promised you."

He went to the bar and came back with two glasses of tequila.

"To the village," he said. "To prosperity."

Shim drained his glass and went back to get the bottle. Michael Boni left his drink on the table, untouched. Then he heard music, the same music from two nights before, picking up precisely where it had left off.

Shim stood beside the tape deck wearing an immense smile.

Marisol came out of the kitchen and approached the table. Leaning against the bar, tapping his fingers against the side of his glass, Shim watched her clear away the plates and utensils, loading up her arms.

To get back to the kitchen, Marisol had to pass him again, and as she did so, Shim reached out and grabbed her.

"Dance with me," he said.

Marisol pulled her arm away, but Shim didn't let go. She pulled harder and broke free, but she lost her balance, and one of the plates fell and shattered.

"I don't understand why everyone is so uptight," Shim said as she hurried into the kitchen. "In a place like this. The ocean, the sun, peace and quiet, and no one will relax."

Michael Boni heard the señora yelling, and Marisol returned with a broom. He stooped down to help with some of the bigger pieces. She didn't seem to notice him. Then the song ended, and Michael Boni realized Shim had left.

Sitting alone at the table, Michael Boni tried to figure out what he should do. In planning his escape, he'd been thinking he'd need to go somewhere no one ever went—a town no one had ever heard of. But now he wasn't so sure. Maybe in a place like this he was too exposed. There'd be nowhere to hide if they ever came looking for him. And would they? It was impossible to say. He could trust McGee's silence. He wanted to believe the same of Darius, but he'd seen all too well how weak Darius could be.

A car was coming up the street from the square. Michael Boni could hear it from a long way off, the roar of the engine so loud it caused rings to form on the surface of his glass.

The car wasn't at all what Michael Boni had expected. Not a souped-up roadster but a weathered compact with anemic tires, window tint bubbled and curled around the edges. The car rolled to a stop, just as Marisol emerged from the kitchen. A boy got out of the driver's side, red jeans and shiny black shoes. The boy from the pavilion.

Marisol and her boyfriend got into the car and thundered off, leaving the dining room trembling in their wake.

A breeze traveled up the street from the water, stirring sand along the cobblestones and passing just as freely through the restaurant. And then the breeze moved on, carrying Michael Boni with it.

He wandered through the vacant village, to the square, then found himself following the road north. A few minutes later, he was at the spot where he'd found Shim earlier in the day. In the moonlight, the concrete shell of the bungalow beyond the gravel road looked like the tower of a sunken castle. The door and window holes had once been boarded over, but enough planks were missing that Michael Boni could climb through.

From inside, the place appeared relatively new, walls and foundation still solid. The windows offered a good view, the kind of view a person could spend the rest of his days and nights watching without feeling the passage of time. He wondered how long it would be before Shim would tear this place down, how long until the entire village would be demolished to make room for the resort?

Between a gap in the boards, Michael Boni watched the waves roll in and stretch along the shore. A bird swooped down, black against the setting sun, plucking something from the water. From somewhere in the distance, he heard a rumble. Like thunder, but when he poked his head back out through the hole, the sky was clear. Still, the rumbles continued, getting louder, coming closer, until at last Michael Boni recognized the familiar roar of Marisol's boyfriend's car.

Michael Boni arrived at the window overlooking the road in time to see the car come to a stop just a few yards away. Even at rest, the engine was deafening. Peeking through the window opening, he could see Marisol and the boy sitting side by side in the front seat, talking. How on earth could they hear each other?

Finally the boy reached for the ignition. The silence came so suddenly that to Michael Boni it was just as jarring as the engine itself. He stood there frozen.

From his vantage point, just slightly higher than the road, Michael Boni could see the boy's free hand gliding across Marisol's thigh—the blue of her handmade dress. The boy paused for a moment at her brocade hip, and then he kept going, past her hand and up her arm, stopping only once his fingers were cupped around the girl's small breast. His mouth left hers, traveling down her neck. The boy was almost entirely out of his seat, pressing against Marisol, nearly on top of her.

But she remained still. She hardly even seemed to be paying attention. What was she looking at? Not at the boy. But not at the ruins, either, or at the ebbing ripples and eddies of the sea. She seemed to be staring off in the other direction, toward the row of palm trees marking where the land ended and the beach began. The sky above the trees had grown dark. The birds were gone. The sun at her back was nothing more than a match head fading into ash. It was as if she weren't even here, as if she were dreaming of another place, of another life.

Michael Boni retreated slowly, silently from the window. He lifted his feet carefully out of the stray sand and dust. Clinging to the shadows along the wall, he worked his way back to the other side of the house. There was a big enough gap in the boards that he could climb out the other window. A short, easy drop to the sand below.

But just as he started to pull himself through the opening, Michael Boni spotted movement on the beach—a slim silhouette at the tide line, approaching from the south. The moment he saw the drape of the linen shirt and the bulky cargo pockets, Michael Boni knew who it was.

Shim didn't seem to have spotted him. The man was walking slowly, his feet gently lapped by the surf. When he was about even with the house, Shim stopped, still gazing out over the darkening water. Michael Boni was surprised to see him doing something so pensive. But maybe Shim was just sketching out more details of the future he planned to build here. Maybe out on the horizon, where the sun was almost gone, he was seeing the cruise ships that would dock here for daylong excursions; he could see the fortunes they would bring.

Acknowledgements

I wrote this book over the course of a number of years. Over that time, a lot about the landscape of Detroit changed. As a result, this novel is not a snapshot of any one fixed moment in time. Nor is it intended to be anything more than a work of the imagination.

Over the years it took for the novel to come together, a great many readers spent a great many hours reading a great many drafts. None more so (and more patiently) than Margaret Lazarus Dean and Bill Clegg. Their shares in the book number near to my own.

For guidance along the way, I also want to thank Charles Baxter, Genevieve Canceko Chan, Bryan Charles, Peter Ho Davies, Nicholas Delbanco, Scott Hutchins, Kristina Faust Kaminskas, Stefan Kiesbye, Michael Knight, Valerie Laken, Raymond McDaniel, Patrick O'Keeffe, Sharon Pomerantz, Gus Rose, and Fritz Swanson. Rachel Mannheimer steered the book insightfully through its final drafts.

John Kelleher was there with me during many of the misadventures that inspired this novel.

Acknowledgements

A travel grant from the University of Michigan provided vital research support for the portions of the book set in Mexico. I also received support in the form of a Hopwood Award from the University of Michigan for an earlier draft of the book. More recently, my position as Jack E. Reese Writer in Residence at the University of Tennessee Libraries, generously made possible by Dr. Marilyn Kallet and Dean Steven Smith, helped to ensure the completion of the book.

My title takes its inspiration from the poem "The Angels of Detroit," by Detroit native Philip Levine.

About the Author

Christopher Hebert is the author of the novel *The Boiling Season*, winner of the 2013 Friends of American Writers award. His short fiction and nonfiction have appeared in such publications as *FiveChapters, Cimarron Review, Narrative, Interview,* and the *Millions.* He is a graduate of the University of Michigan and is editor-at-large for the University of Michigan Press. Currently he lives in Knoxville, Tennessee, where he is assistant professor of English at the University of Tennessee.